Random Passage

Random Passage

Bernice Morgan

Breakwater
100 Water Street
P.O. Box 2188
St. John's, NF
A1C 6E6

*The Publisher gratefully acknowledges the financial assistance
of The Canada Council.*

German rights sold, 1996.
French rights sold 1999.

Cover photographer courtesy of Passage Films.
Photographer: Justin Hall

Canadian Cataloguing in Publication Data
Morgan, Bernice.
    Random passage
    ISBN 1-55081-051-0
I. Title.
PS8576.073R36 1991   C813'.54   C91-097712-7
PR9199.3.M67R36 1991

Printed in Canada.

Reprinted in 1992, 1994, 1995, 1996, 1997, 1998, 1999,
2000, 2001 and 2002

ACKNOWLEDGEMENTS

The author gratefully acknowledges the help of Canada Council; the good advice of Helen Porter, Joan Clark and Jennifer Lee Morgan, who read a much earlier, much longer version of this book; the encouragement of Newfoundland Writers' Guild; and of Jack McClelland; the work of Kyran Pittman who named the book; the Vincents—Aunt Sophie, Uncle Jack and Aunt Elsie, who showed me the Cape; and especially the support of George Morgan, cook, speller and computer expert during the writing of this book.

For my parents
Sadie Vincent of Cape Island
and
William Vardy of Random Island
and for their parents,
who thought hard work could make a safe place.

Prologue

It is spring and in the great pit at the centre of the sacred hill a fire burns as it has for a thousand springs. Old Ejew sits beside the fire, her hide-wrapped legs stretched towards the hot rocks. Between her knees the baby sleeps, its small round head resting pleasantly against the swell of Ejew's crotch. The old woman sings softly, a song about Ob-seeth the little bird who quarrelled with a blunt nosed fish, Mo-cu-thut, about ownership of a magic shell. It is a song Ejew knows well, she has heard it since childhood when her brothers teased her, calling her Ob-seeth, small quarrelsome bird. The song ends sadly. Ob-seeth pecks Mo-cu-thut's eyes out and the enraged fish leaps up, hooking its teeth around the bird's wing, dragging her beneath the water where the magic shell is lost forever in the sea. Despite its melancholy story the song has a cheerful tune and Ejew sings it over and over again.

Warm and completely dry for the first time since they began the painful trek to the coast, Ejew tells herself to rejoice: spring has come, her grandchild has been born healthy, the gods have again brought her family to this holy place. She should be thankful she still has three living sons who even now are on the beach waiting, willing the seals to come within range of their bone-tipped harpoons.

The thought of warm seal fat makes her mouth water and her belly cramp. To forget her hunger she concentrates on the soft sand supporting her back, on the warm baby between her legs and the glowing fire at her feet.

Gobidin's son Toma and the orphan girl Ubee come with more driftwood for the pile drying beside the fire. The children are thin as spirits with sunken cheeks and eyes made large by hunger. The boy shows his grandmother a long stick he has found and asks when they will eat.

"Mo she mell, mo she mell," Ejew tells him—very soon now, very soon.

The seal god will soon give them meat. Not just enough to fill their bellies today, enough to cut into strips, dry over the fire and eat for months to come. The family will stay on the seal cape a day or so, hunting on the beach and making tools beside the fire, replenishing their supply of scrapers and arrowheads from the flint that lies scattered all around the hill. By then, Ejew thinks, other families will have arrived and together they will move up the coast, to the salmon rivers, to the egg islands, hunting fox and ptarmigan, trapping seabirds, digging scallops. By the time the berry bushes turn red, their bags and baskets will be full of food. When they move inland to meet the caribou herds the children's cheeks will be round again and even under her old skin there will be a layer of soft fat. From time out of mind her people have come to the seal cape empty and left full, it will be the same this year. Ejew prays to the gods it will be the same forever.

This spring they were more hungry than usual. Her oldest son Gobidin had insisted that they take a circuitous route to the cape, coming not as they always have, down past the deep fiord where they might trap a blue whale, but trekking far inland, carrying their canoe across frozen bog and forest where there was nothing to eat. Where, when the caribou meat ran out, they had to rind twisted var trees and chew the inner bark for nourishment. Ejew could have objected to their not coming the usual way, as the oldest member of her family she had that right. But Gobidin had seen the Widdun, the men without souls, so she did not challenge his decision.

The Widdun had long been talked of around winter campfires. It was said they carried sickness, smelled of death and had no women or children of their own. Many of the people claimed to have seen them in the forest and one young man told of visiting a village where Widdun lived. He said they attached their houses to the earth and lived crowded together in the same place winter and summer.

Ejew herself had not believed such stories. The people were always seeing strange creatures, men or beasts or spirits. Then, last autumn on their way back to winter camp, Gobidin and his wife left the main party to hunt otter. On the second day the two had been paddling their canoe up one of the rivers feeding the fiord, when suddenly five Widdun appeared out of the woods, lifted up their sticks and blew fire through the air at the canoe. The fire hit Eeshoo and Gobidin, hit the small boat, spinning it around so that it rocked and began drifting backwards while the Widdun stood on the shore laughing and throwing more fire across the water.

When Gobidin came to himself the canoe had grounded on a sand bar, blood was running from a hole in his shoulder and Eeshoo lay dead in the boat beside him. He searched the shore and, seeing no Widdun, dragged the canoe deep inside a cave where they had sometimes slept. He buried his wife under the canoe in the cave and walked back across country to join the people.

Ejew's thoughts are interrupted by sounds from the beach, shouts from the two children and the laughter of one of her daughters-in-law. They must have killed a seal! She eases the sleeping baby off her belly, gets stiffly to her feet and, using padded leather mitts drops two hot rocks into the water pot. Struggling on her hands and knees she climbs up to the edge of the depression and peers down over the rim at the long beach. Up here there is no protection from the raw wind that whips grey hair across her eyes as she watches her sons carefully draw their harpoons in. They have a seal each.

She whispers thanks that they managed to spear all three seals at the same moment. The remaining animals have dived and will not surface until they are far out beyond the reach of the hunters.

It is customary for the women to take over once the seals are ashore. But this year there are only her two daughters-in-law, so the men help tie leather straps around the heavy carcasses and pull them up the beach. Once there would have been many women and girls to do this job, laughing and hurrying towards the place where Ejew stands, each one eager to be first to reach the holy fire with a seal. Men and boys would have been cheering them on and beside her, here on the rim of the hill, the old people would be cheering too—all the old ones, the chanters, the baby watchers, the tool makers, the basket weavers—the old ones from all the families that gather each spring on the seal cape to hunt, trade, sing, dance, matchmake and story talk.

Ejew remembers an old wise woman telling the children that even in ancient times strangers ("the others" she had called them) considered the cape holy. These others and the red ochre families had fought over the place for many years. Then, one spring, the others were not there. They never came back. Their time on earth had ended, the old one said, like the half-beasts they had vanished, leaving the people owners of all the world.

For a long time Ejew had forgotten the old woman's story about the others. Now she thinks of it often. Where did they go, those others? Do all creatures time on earth end—is that why, each year, there are fewer people on the cape? ...and, most horrifying question of all, one that has only recently occurred to her, is it possible that the others have come back disguised as Widdun to reclaim the world?

Ejew has been uneasy for a long, long time—so long that she cannot remember when the feeling started—before the Widdun killed Eeshoo, before Mattuis disappeared, before the coughing sickness came. Sometimes she thinks the oppressive feeling inside is all that keeps her from floating away into the spirit world.

That night when they have eaten as much meat as possible, when oil has been poured on their hands and into the fire to thank the seal god for his gifts, the child Toma brings his father the long stick he found on the beach. It is not made of stone, nor of wood, nor bone, nor any substance known to them.

"Is it a magic stick?" the boy asks.

Gobidin examines it carefully. It looks, he tells them, like part of a fire stick used by the Widdun, but it is harmless now, hollow and empty inside. They pass the stick from hand to hand, marvelling at its weight. They strike it off rocks and, when it refuses to break, throw it into the fire where it eventually glows bright red.

They wait on the cape for five days but, when no other families come and the seals do not return, they prepare to move on up the coast. While others pack, Ejew fills her shoulder pouch with ash from the holy fire and watches Toma dig beneath the charred wood for the long rod. Ejew tells him it will have burnt away but he pulls the thing, still whole, from the pit and rubs his hands happily over the smooth, smutty length of it. He holds it beside his body, measuring. The rod is twice as high as the boy, he squints down its empty inside at Ubee and Ejew and puts it to his lips, trying to make a sound as boys often do with hollow reeds. He is showing off, proud to have found such a unique thing. He explains gravely to the old woman and the girl how useful it will be. The strange stick will help them carry baskets, ford rivers and even dry meat over the fire.

Ejew holds out her hand for the stick. She has not touched it before and when the heavy, cold weight of it comes in contact with her skin she feels a shiver of distaste.

She returns the stick to the boy, "It's evil, throw it back into the sea."

Her grandson looks at her and knows she is serious. He is too polite to show surprise or to refuse the old one, but he does not move to obey, standing small and defiant with both hands around the rod.

"Be rid of it!" Ejew says sharply. Then to soften her command she murmurs a short prayer to the boy's spirit helper, reaches forward and touches his throat with holy ash, leaving the print of her thumb in the hollow.

Without a word Toma turns, runs down to the water, and as the girl and old woman watch, flings the unwholesome thing into the sea where it immediately sinks.

Part One

Lavinia Andrews

Chapter 1

Lavinia Andrews stops at the rock, the like of which she has never seen before, rising out of the sand, tall as a house, shining smooth and curved at the tip like a great, black finger pointing up to God. She circles the rock slowly until she finds a spot from which she can see neither the endless ocean nor the desolate huddle of people far back on the wharf. She slides down with her back tight against the black surface and discovers it to be slightly warm. Does this mean that sun sometimes shines in this grey, forsaken place?

Dropping her face onto her knees and wrapping her arms around her head, she weeps like a child. Eventually her crying gives way to small gulps, then stops. But she stays, hunched against the rock, face hidden in the tweed of her old skirt. The rough cloth, still smelling faintly of home, soothes her. She begins to relax, to examine what has happened, to think about where she is, what she might become.

She has never thought of herself this way before, as a person alone, separate from her mother and brothers, unrelated to the family standing back on the wharf surrounded by their boxes and barrels. She reflects, for the first time, on Lavinia Andrews ("A clean, decent girl who can read, count and scrub floors," Mrs. John had said.), a girl sitting on a sea-swept shore, husbandless, friendless, penniless, a sack containing all she owns lying beside her on the sand.

"I'd be better off if Ellsworth hung Ned like he threatened." The thought has been there, just below the surface for five weeks.

"I don't care, it's true—I'm here now and I'll never get back! How could I face it again? The empty, heaving sea—day in, day out, the slimy water, the dirt and stink. None of the women will get back—the men might, but not the women. We'll stay in this place 'til we perish."

The enormity of what Ned has done to them all, and her own heedless following, sets her weeping again. She tries to comfort herself. Maybe they will move away from the water. Inland there might be warm valleys, green fields.

"That's right, girl, tell yourself tales. You're as bad as Ned. Would people be living here on the rocks if there was a warm green place nearby? I'm seventeen, I could live fifty years yet. Fifty years! God, what will become of me?"

The question plays over and over in her mind, but there is no answer. She sits, face pressed into her skirt, sniffing, dozing a little, exhausted by crying and by nights and nights sitting awake beside Hazel.

Take a good look at her now. Lavinia Andrews, all alone on the long beach, hiding from both her own people and from the strangers, afraid of the cold ocean behind and the desolate land before. A cheerless November day it is. The only colour on all the sea-washed beach is in the green wool scarf the girl has wound around her head and the puffs of dirty orange hair that escape from beneath the scarf.

Five weeks ago, all in one night, Lavinia Andrews was uprooted from her own country, a soft, settled place compared to this. Five weeks ago she left a sure job with good prospects. Five weeks ago she left the handsome boy she'd seen selling puppets from a barrow—they had never spoken but would have. For five weeks she has sailed through two thousand miles of black, moving water, across the stormiest seas on earth. A rough passage in the hold of a merchant ship, a space built to transport pigs and sheep to French colonies in the New World.

For five weeks she has delayed both thinking and weeping. No time for vain regrets, not with children to wash and feed, to keep from drowning, to hold and comfort; with Hazel, who hadn't moved from her bed since the voyage started, to attend to. Picking lice from heads and blankets, scraping mould from bread and prying maggots out of meat, killing rats, scrubbing boards, lugging water down below and disposing of feces and vomit over the side had left her without energy to think about the life behind or the life waiting ahead.

Lavinia wakes with a start, feeling afraid, sure someone is nearby, sure someone has been watching her. But there is no one. Nothing but empty sand ending in deep shadows where sea and wind have gouged shallow caves into the overhanging banks. The sky is still grey and on the other side of the rock, the sea still pounds against the shore, slow and persistent as the heartbeat of a giant. An hour could have passed, or a lifetime, or minutes, or maybe she hasn't slept at all.

Since early morning, as *La Truite* came nearer and nearer to the empty coast, Lavinia had watched, wondering if people live in such places.

"Do not worry so much, Mademoiselle, I will set you down in a snug harbour," Captain Benoit said when he came upon her gazing forlornly at the dark coast.

"The hills are so black—like it's forever nighttime in there," she whispered.

The hills were not black but green, he told her. "Evergreen, you will have evergreen hills," he said and his broad, false smile frightened her even more.

When she asked where the town was, the place Ned had told them about, the place where they were going to open a store, the Captain made an awkward, uncomfortable sound. "Not here, not here." He held his fingers in a kind of triangle, "St. Jean de Terre Neuve there ... we are here."

Only then did she discover they were not going to that part of Newfound Land nearest England. *La Truite* was making for what the Captain called "the French Shore." His agreement with Ned was to put the Andrews family ashore in some English settlement along the way.

They are town people, how can they possibly make a living out of sea and rock? She reviews the possessions her family has brought: crockery, a few blackened and dented pots, a collection of old clothing and one or two coins, probably even now being bartered for a place to sleep. Not a cow nor a horse, not a seed nor tool among them all. How pitiful their belongings look piled on the wharf. How soft they look compared to the people who'd stood silently watching them come ashore.

Her mother had been the most brave. Jennie Andrews had walked right over to the woman, a short little body who wore so many layers of shaggy shawls draped around herself and her baby that she looked like a mouldy haystack with a tiny head on top.

"God's blessings on ye, Missis—I'm some glad to see a woman here." Her mother had bent forward to peer at the baby, just as she would have done on Monk Street. The round apple face atop the haystack had smiled, a wide, almost toothless, smile, and in a minute the two women were talking as if they had been neighbours all their lives.

Lavinia and Meg had hung back, hovering near Hazel, who had been carried ashore in Ned's arms and now lay on the wharf in a pile of bedding. Meg carried her own baby and held the hand of her nephew Isaac. The boy had gotten to be a real sook since his mother's illness and cried in fright as he was led down the narrow plank stretching between ship and wharf. The older youngsters, Isaac's sister Jane, and Ben and Meg's three girls, Lizzie, Patience and Emma, stood in line gazing solemnly at the children on the wharf, who, just as solemnly, gazed back.

Even the men had faltered, Ned hesitating beside Hazel's pallet before going forward, his hand outstretched. Ben, of course, had watched Ned, waiting to see what his brother would do before making any move himself.

Lavinia supposes that by rights the oldest son is responsible for all of them. But what could anyone expect of Ben? Ben, who since he was nine has spent every day sitting in the cart behind Old Bones, riding through the streets of Weymouth, bartering his motley collection of merchandise.

In Weymouth, Ben had no worries. His wife Meg and his brother Ned made all the decisions in his life, which suited him. He had no boss and that suited him too. Ned and Lavinia, and indeed almost everyone he knew around Monk Street, worked for the Ellsworth brothers. Ben, though not a churchgoer like his wife, thanked God daily that he did not have the Ellsworths lording it over him. This fact, however, was no help on the day Richard Ellsworth came to Monk Street pounding on the table and carrying a great book with Ned's mark in it.

Ned's mark in Richard Ellsworth's book landed them all in this dismal place.

Lavinia has always loved Ned most. Everyone has loved Ned. Her brother has been coddled, admired, surrounded with love—spoiled with love—since he first learned to speak. Lavinia and Ned look alike. Both have the same pale skin, the same bright curly hair, the same loose, disjointed bodies, the same ability to weave magic with words.

This attribute, which is to turn up again and again in the Andrews family, attracts great admiration. Stories can be told anywhere: deep in the holds of ships, in jail cells, down mine shafts, in rooms where people wait for birth or for death, in the mud of trenches, on ice floes and even, many generations later, beneath strobe lights and on the flickering screens of television sets. Ned uses this wonderful gift more than Lavinia, who is still in awkward transition between childhood and womanhood.

For seven years, Ned had sailed on Ellsworth ships. He returned from each voyage full of stories about terrible storms with waves taller than the masts, stories of ghost lights that hover above the water, of sea monsters with horns like unicorns, stories of beasts that live in the north country, creatures so wild and curious that they have no names.

When Ned told his stories, the kitchen on Monk Street would fill with neighbours. Every chair would be taken—people would even sit on the floor between chairs. Children would be shooed off to bed, not because anyone cared that they were missing sleep, but because they could not fit into the room. No one would leave until the end, which sometimes took half the night, because Ned loved watching faces change from dread to delight then back to dread again and could expand any story indefinitely.

Ned at least knows something about the sea. It is the only skill they have that might help them survive here. Does this mean they must all now depend upon Ned? For Lavinia, sitting on the edge of her cold new world, this is a bitter thought, one she does not want to dwell upon.

She pulls a book from the bag lying beside her on the sand. The words, "Ellsworth Brothers" and beneath, "Record of Shipping 1810 to ...." are written in gold on the cover. She begins to write. The first sentence comes quickly. She has been saying the words over and over to herself for five weeks. They bite into the heavy paper and she underlines them with a slash.

"It's Ned's wickedness that's brought us to this terrible place and I'll never forgive him."

She stops. In Sunday School she had copied out texts from the Bible, but this is the first sentence of her own she has ever written. The look of it, black and clean on the creamy paper, gives her a feeling of satisfaction, but she is unsure of how to continue.

Aside from Bible verses, Lavinia has written only lists, the interminable lists of Ellsworth household items. Even writing these had been a pleasure: "Ten petticoats, five white, two black, one purple, one rose, one blue. Twenty tea cups edged in gold with green leaves. Three nightshirts, two white... ."

Lavinia is the only member of her family who can write or read. She has read the Bible (or parts of the Bible approved of by The Church of England Society for the Improvement of the Poor), an Infants Primer (which, together with the *Bible*, the *Hymnal* and a *Book of Common Prayer* make up the Sunday School library), and *The Little Folks Book of Saints and Martyrs* (contributed by the minister's kindly wife to relieve the tedium of the primer).

Lavinia pulls her cold hands back into the sleeves of her jacket, folds them under her armpits and thinks. Where to begin? With Ned making a thief of himself? With the moment young Lizzie called to her down the coal chute? When that terrible ship pulled away from the docks in Weymouth? Or just now, coming ashore in this Newfound Land, stiff and pale, their poor things piled all around on that rickety wharf?

She tries to recall the first words of the three books she is familiar with. The Primer, she remembers, had a large 'A' on the first page with the words "A is for Adam the first man to fall." There had been a thick black picture of a sorrowful Adam, his head hunched forward, his hand holding a large leaf against his middle and at his back an angry angel. In one hand the angel carried a flaming sword, with the other he pointed beyond Adam to something unseen, unknown.

She cannot remember the first fearful words of the Saints and Martyrs but she knows how the Bible begins. She turns the book upside down and begins to write. She begins on the last page, writing toward the front of the book—toward a future she does not dare to imagine.

"In the beginning we all lived on Monk Street in Weymouth, in England, and we were all happy... ." she writes.

——— ——— ———

And so they were. In the four room flat over Mrs. Thorp's bread and pie shop, the lives of the Andrews family had a comforting order. In recent years, with Ned sailing regularly in Ellsworth ships and Lavinia earning three shillings a week up at Ellsworth House, Jennie Andrews had begun to feel she and her children were safe from starvation or the poor house. Jennie, a woman of great inventiveness, was inclined to attribute this not to her children's having grown and started to bring in money, but to the fact that old mad George, who had been king of England for all of her life had finally died.

Jennie had rented the flat on Monk Street the very day she and Will Andrews wed. They had not really wed, but had run away from home to live under a bridge on the outskirts of town, eating, and selling vegetables which they got from nearby farms—sometimes in exchange for work, sometimes by stealing. In the fall, the bridge could not protect them from the cold, and Jennie was pregnant, but they had saved enough for two weeks rent. Through the years, however, Jennie has told so many people about the wedding, about the straw hat she wore and the crooked old minister who refused to ring the church bells, that she quite believes the story. Will died before Lavinia, their third child, was born, but by then they owned the horse and cart. Jennie had managed somehow to pay the rent and to feed herself and the children until Ben was nine, old enough to take over the job of peddling used clothing, worn costumes of failed theatre groups and goods bought from burnt-out shops.

After the boys married and settled their wives in the flat, and after children began arriving almost yearly, the four rooms became crowded, but no one ever gave a thought to moving. Ben and Meg, their three girls and Willie, the baby, all slept in one room; Ned, Hazel and their two in another.

Jennie and Lavinia, who now spent only every second Sunday at home, shared the back room. They slept surrounded by crates, baskets and barrels stuffed to overflowing with unsold clothing, rolls of scorched cloth, silent clocks, chipped china ornaments, garish pictures in broken frames and a hundred other useless household items. This mixture of goods emitted a smell of age, of old fires, stale perfume, of cats long dead and meals long eaten. For Lavinia it was the smell of comfort, of sleep, of home. When, many years later, she read the word 'sandman' in a children's book, she immediately thought of the smell in the room she and her mother shared on Monk Street.

The kitchen in front was the room where the Andrews women knitted; made rag dolls, tea cosies and cushion covers from unsold garments; sorted and mended the old clothing; cooked, ate and cared for the children, all the time keeping a sharp lookout on the narrow, busy street below.

There were many advantages to living on Monk Street. Jacob Spriggett's blacksmith shop and livery stable was just around the corner, so Ben did not have far to walk on winter nights after he'd bedded Old Bones. They were near the docks where Ned could keep an eye on the comings and goings of vessels, watching for a good berth.

The Andrews family knew everyone on the street, and on all the streets around, and everyone knew them. Neighbour women came to the flat to look through new and rejected stock, to try things on, sometimes to buy. It was especially advantageous to live above a bread and pie shop. Mrs. Thorp let Ben's oldest girl, Lizzie, tend the store and was teaching her to bake. Sometimes she gave Lizzie burnt or squashed pies to bring home. Wonderful smells, and heat too, came up from the bread and pie shop, so that the Andrews' did not have to burn as much coal as their neighbours. On the two Sundays each month when Mrs. John Ellsworth let her come home, Lavinia was happy to get back to the crowded flat, to be surrounded by the barrels of clothing, the clutter of half-finished oddments, by her brothers' children and the neighbour children who came and went constantly.

It was all finished now—gone! Ended the morning Richard Ellsworth came riding down Monk Street in his best carriage with Jim Rice sitting up front like a young cock in his red breeks, yelling and cracking his whip over the heads of the beautiful Ellsworth horses.

Richard Ellsworth's annoyance could be measured not only by the fact that he had come himself, instead of sending his agent, but also by the speed with which he jumped down from the carriage, not waiting for Jim to open the little gate, barely waiting for the wheels to stop. The Andrews women, watching from the kitchen window, knew they were lost. Knew even before the man pushed aside poor Mrs. Thorp, who had rushed out of her shop, knew before he came thumping up the dark stairs two at a time, for all that he was a big man and must have touched the wall on both sides.

Richard Ellsworth burst into the Andrews kitchen waving a morocco cane and holding a leather-bound book.

"You," he jabbed at Ned's shoulder with the cane and tried to catch his breath at the same time, "you ... you great lumping rogue. It's you I've come to see!"

Hazel clutched Ned's arm, his mother and Meg moved to stand, one on either side, a small, horrified army facing they knew not what.

Except for Ned. Ned had known, Lavinia thought, for all his protestations of innocence, for all his telling them the fish he'd sold was his own. Ned must have known that Richard Ellsworth had caught him out, had been bound to catch him since Ellsworth Brothers controlled the salt fish trade in all of Weymouth.

Useless for Ned to say now, as he was to say many, many times in the future: "Bloody fish was me own, I worked for it, worked like a navvie diggin' up some old codger's potato garden when we was waitin' time in St. John's. I coulda been roustin' around grog shops with the rest of the lads—but no, I was bent on gettin' a few barrels of salted cod to sell—more fool me!"

Her brother started to explain this to Richard Ellsworth, but the man was having none of it. He poked Ned with his cane: "You signed articles with Ellsworths, didn't you? Well, didn't you?"

When Ned was slow to nod, Master Ellsworth flung the book he was carrying down on the kitchen table and flipped it open.

"See! See that! That means you were working for me, me, me!" With each 'me' there was a jab of the cane.

"By putting your mark there you signed a legal contract with Ellsworths—the two weeks you gave away were mine. Mine! So, you stole time from me. And how did you get that fish across the Atlantic, eh, how? In my vessel, that's how, that means you stole cargo space that could have carried my goods!"

This aspect of the affair had only just occurred to Richard Ellsworth. His face turned from red to purple and a little pulse began pounding at the side of his head. Ned, who had an eye for detail, was watching in fascination, unconsciously absorbing each twitch and gesture.

"You're a rogue, Ned Andrews, a rogue and a thief!"

Around Weymouth, Richard Ellsworth was reckoned to be a reasonable man and a fair master. Ellsworth profits, made from salt, rope and twine taken across the Atlantic and codfish brought back, were the same as those made by every fish merchant in ports around Devon and Dorset, where fortunes that would last for generations were being established. In fact, the firm may have made less than most, since many merchants charged their seamen keep if a voyage lasted longer that a set time, whereas Ellsworth Brothers paid hands the going rate per trip whether the voyage took two months or four.

Richard Ellsworth had come to Monk Street with the intention of giving the young whipper-snapper a good fright only. "I'll put the fear of God into Ned Andrews so he, nor none of his mates, will do the like again," he'd told his agent with more amusement than malice.

But something in Ned's face, some flick of insolence in the grey eyes, some shadow of bravado in the silly smile, had fanned the merchant's rage. The longer Richard Ellsworth considered it, the more grave Ned's deed seemed.

"Suppose every young Turk who sails on Ellsworth ships decided to imitate you and make money on the side? What then, eh, what then? Why, every man jack of 'em would really be working for himself. Ellsworth vessels would be sailing into Weymouth, their holds filled with other men's goods—why, we'd be made beggars of by our own people!" Fake anger had become real. He smashed his cane down on the table. One rickety leg gave way and the record book crashed to the floor.

Lavinia knew just how it had been—they had all taken turns telling her. Ned, of course, had played out the scene many times. Terrified children cowered in corners or clutched at the women's skirts. The three women, their eyes glued on the towering, red-faced man, ignored the children. Behind Richard Ellsworth, hovering in the open doorway, Mrs. Thorp had cried quietly into her white apron, and from behind her in the dark hall, a dozen dirty-faced neighbour children peered, ready to run the instant Master Ellsworth turned to go.

"A thief is all you are, nothing but a thief. No! Worse than any thief, setting out to ruin an employer who's trusted you. Stand up, fellow!"

This last order was caused by Ned, who, feeling his knees tremble and sure the tirade would go on for hours, had been slowly easing himself down into a chair behind which his mother stood, gripping the back as though she would fall if she let go. There was no longer any trace of smile on Ned's face, his freckles stood out like dark brown splotches.

Then, quite suddenly, the big man ran out of bluster. With a sweeping look of disgust at the wretched room, the pale women, at the snotty, tear-streaked faces of the children, and finally at Ned, Richard Ellsworth turned away. Once more pushing Mrs. Thorp aside, he flung the verdict over his shoulder.

"Be out of here tonight, you and your brats. Hear me—tonight! If you're in Weymouth tomorrow morning, by God, I'll have you arrested and hung."

With that, he'd pounded down the stairs, children scattering like pigeons in front of him. Young Jim Rice, who had been standing at the bottom, listening to every word, pulled the door open as his master stormed through, followed at a run, jumped into the carriage seat, flicked his long whip over the heads of the horses and took off at great speed down Monk Street accompanied by a few half-hearted boos and shouts from the bravest urchins.

Both Ben and Lavinia had missed this performance. Lavinia was counting pillow slips for Mrs. John, Richard Ellsworth's sister-in-law. Poor Ben, never dreaming this was the last time, was riding behind Old Bones, up and down the terraced streets across the bridge, just as he had done every Wednesday since he was nine.

The Ellsworth Brothers, Richard and John, each occupied half of a grey stone mansion known as Ellsworth House, built on a gentle rise overlooking the bay. The John Ellsworths had six servants: a cook-housekeeper, a kitchen boy, a gardener and three maids, one of whom was Lavinia Andrews. The brothers shared the services of Jim Rice, who did odd jobs and drove the two men back and forth to their business premises.

Because Mrs. John must always know the exact number of everything in her half of Ellsworth House and because Lavinia was the only maid who could count accurately and write, much of the girl's time was taken up following her mistress about, recording the numbers of such things as cups, candlesticks, handkerchiefs, lace collars, petticoats, pictures and pens. On that particular morning Mrs. John sat in the upper hall on a chair Lavinia had pulled from one of the bedrooms. Mrs. John wrote in a small book with a blue velvet cover as Lavinia counted sheets and replaced them in a huge chest.

Lavinia had enjoyed the morning's work. The smooth feel of silk and linen, the lovely colours, the scent of dried lavender and rose that had been sprinkled between the sheets, more than made up for having to work under the stern eye of her mistress.

The counting over, Lavinia had gone downstairs for her mid-day meal. As she entered the kitchen she could hear Jim Rice entertaining the cook and kitchen boy with an account of the morning's happenings, "...far as I can see every single one of them Andrews is to be hove out, right out of town by the sound of it. Mr. Richard, he.... "

The boy's voice died when he saw Lavinia standing in the doorway.

"Go on," she told him and listened in horror as he finished, somewhat less colourfully, the story of the morning visit to Monk Street.

"I have to go home—can I go home now?" Lavinia turned to the cook.

"I'm not mixin' into this. You'll have to go ask the missis." The woman rolled her eyes upward in the general direction of the front sunroom where Mrs. John took tea at this time of day.

"On no account are you to visit Monk Street," the mistress told Lavinia when she heard the story.

"You will be much better off to keep away from your family, Libby." Mrs. John thought Lavinia an ostentatious name for a servant and had never bothered to find out that most people called the girl Vinnie.

"Keep away from them all, in particular from that scoundrel of a brother. My husband and Mr. Richard are both fair men, I'll speak to them. They will see that you had no part in this affair and I am content to keep you in my employ."

"Oh but Mrs. John, Ma'rm, I just got to go down home and see how they are!"

Annoyed that she should have to repeat herself, Mrs. John did so only because she appreciated the girl's ability with the counting. "No Libby, you must not! I know this may seem hard now but it is for the best. You will disassociate yourself from your family, that way you can have a respectable life. You're a clean, decent girl who can read, count things and scrub floors. Why, someday you might even have cook's job. Wouldn't you like that?"

The woman waited, studying the tall thin creature in front of her, thinking how attractive Libby Andrews was, even with that outlandish coloured hair. The wretched girl didn't answer. She had a stubborn, sulky mouth, too wide for her face. Mrs. John told her briskly to be off down to the cellar and help Sally and Maud with the laundry.

Lavinia had taken orders from Mrs. John since she was twelve. She bobbed a curtsy, turned and went without a word to the cellar where the other maids were working over four large stone tubs. Although older than Lavinia, Sally and Maud (who were not Sally and Maud but had been assigned those names when they came into service) liked to have the younger girl work with them because she told stories, sang songs and made the time pass. Today, having already heard Jim's news, they understood her black silence and after a look of sympathy kept on working, moving from tub to tub, scrubbing, stirring and rinsing, stopping every so often to add hot water from big pots that hung over an open fire in one corner of the cellar.

Minutes later, the top of the coal chute opened and a handful of small stones rattled down into the coal bin. The coal chute came up at the back of the house, well away from the long curved carriageway. It was the accepted means by which families sent important messages to the servants at Ellsworth House.

The plain, pinched face of Ben's oldest girl, Lizzie, peered down the dirty hatch. "Is me Aunt Vinnie down there?"

"Nan says you're to come on home, fast as ever you can," Lizzie shouted when she saw Lavinia looking up through the gloom.

"Mrs. John says I'm to bide here!"

Lizzie, who still had to find her father, did not tarry to argue with her aunt. The lid slammed shut, depositing a fine film of coal dust over Lavinia's upturned face. She sat down on the floor and began to weep, tears making clean pathways through the dirt. Her friends tried to console her, saying things at Monk Street were probably not half as bad as Jim made them out to be. But her crying continued until they told her she should go on home: "After all's said and done, your family comes before her up there."

Lavinia considered their advice and, between sobs, declared that she couldn't go home anyway, not without her haversack.

"Aw go on, girl, 'tis only an old bag with yer nightshirt and everyday dress in it." Maud pulled her to her feet.

But Lavinia would not leave without the haversack, an ugly, mustard-coloured thing that hung on a nail in the top attic where the maids slept. It was her favourite, almost her only, possession: "Mamma made that bag from a cape Ben bought off a magic man. Took her ages to sew on all that black braid. I'd no more be parted from it than I would from... from me hair."

When it became clear that Lavinia would neither stop crying, go up and get her bag, or leave without it, Sally picked up one of the laundry baskets, went smartly upstairs and returned with the beloved sack safely hidden beneath crumpled sheets.

Her friends then wiped the worst of the coal dust from Lavinia's face and, with the help of the woodhorse, hoisted her up through the coal scuttle. This unnecessarily dramatic gesture (she could have left unnoticed by the delivery entrance) ruined the almost new dress of good brown stuff that Mrs. John had her servant girls wear. It did, however, have the effect of restoring Lavinia's spirits. Halfway up the chute she'd started to giggle and tumbled head first into the delivery path, laughing so hard that she had to sit against the house for several minutes before she hooked her bag around her neck and crawled through the hedge. As she galloped down the hill towards Monk Street she was feeling quite happy—Maud and Sally were probably right, Jim was makin' up half of what he'd told them.

When Lavinia arrived the flat was in chaos. Mrs. Thorp still stood in the hallway crying, partly out of fear that she might somehow be implicated in the stolen fish story, but, to her credit, mostly from sorrow that her old friend and confidante Jennie Andrews was being tossed out on the street because of Ned. "That limb of Satan," Mrs. Thorp, who had known him all his life, called Ned.

In the hall behind Mrs. Thorp the neighbour children had again taken up their place so as not to miss any of the excitement of this most memorable day.

Ben had returned home, been told of the disaster and dumped the contents of the wagon into the middle of the kitchen floor, where it lay in a glorious jumble of colour— bright tights, velvet vests, stained evening gowns, fur muffs, frayed lace curtains, beaded bags, good serge waistcoats, bonnets festooned with plumes, net petticoats, chipped porcelain, mateless gloves, rag dolls, sashes, fringed shawls, along with the unsold bric-a-brac that had been collecting at the bottoms of barrels for all of Jennie's married life: buttons and buckles, worn pencils and candle stubs, paste beads, combs, old socks all mixed together with yards and yards of slightly singed peach silk.

Ben's stock that day included several dozen of Mrs. Thorp's penny pies. These had been rescued from the floor by Jane, Isaac, Emma and Patience. Quite recovered from their fright, the children now sat, one in each corner of the kitchen, pushing the stale food into their mouths and smirking at the envious faces of their friends in the hallway.

Wooden barrels that usually occupied Jennie's and Lavinia's bedroom had been rolled into the kitchen. Jennie, Meg, Hazel and young Lizzie were all busy stowing things into the barrels, taking cups, plates, pans, spoons and pots from the shelves, and wrapping each item in pieces of clothing grabbed at random from the floor.

Lavinia stood in the doorway beside Mrs. Thorp, surveying the disorder for several minutes. No one noticed her until she spoke, "Mama—what's happenin'? What's this all about?"

Jennie Andrews did not even glance up. She slipped her favourite brown mixing bowl neatly into a fur hat and tucked it into the barrel.

"We're leaving, maid—leaving Weymouth—tonight if Ned can find a ship that's sailing." Her mother's voice sounded dead tired, detached.

Lavinia had believed Jim Rice's story but not his grim predictions. The worst she had expected was to find her mother and sisters-in-law crying, Ned temporarily chidden and without employment. It had not occurred to her that they would really be put on the street.

"We don't have to go—this isn't Richard Ellsworth's house!" Lavinia appealed to Mrs. Thorp to whom they had always paid the rent. The woman just shook her head.

Jennie looked up then and Lavinia saw that her mother's eyes were red. All her life Jennie Andrews had held with putting the best face on things. Lavinia had never before seen her cry and it frightened her.

"The house belongs to him, Vinnie, we only just found out. Seems like half the houses on the street belongs to the Ellsworths, along with the jobs."

"Someone could help us, something can be done..." Lavinia was frantic. "Maybe Reverend Warner could reason with him, maybe Ned can make amends."

"If you'd been here, girl, if you seen Richard Ellsworth, you'd know we got no hope. Ben's gone off to try and sell the horse and cart to Jacob." Jennie fought back tears. She loved the old horse. On a summer's evening she would often walk over to the livery stable with a treat for the animal. "Whatever Ben gets will be all the money we'll have."

"And what of Ned, where's Ned?"

"Down to the docks, lookin' for a vessel that's sailin'. Mr. Ellsworth says if we're still in Weymouth tomorrow he's havin' Ned arrested," glancing around at her grandchildren, Jennie continued in a whisper, "hung, he says and I think he will. He really will, Vinnie."

"What's to become of us all then? Where will we go?"

"Ned says we can make a good life in this new country he's just come back from... ."

"Mama! We're not goin' off across the sea on Ned's say so—you knows what he's like! Think about all the tales he told us about monsters and storms!"

"That was only Ned romancin'! He says it's a decent place and he can fish there and Ben can start a little shop. Ned says he been givin' thought to goin' there anyway and this only makes it sooner."

"Ned says—Ned says—when did Ned ever give thought to anything except foolishness? Sure, Ned can go if he wants, but what about the rest of us? We got no cause to run off—Meg, what do you say? How can you drag the girls, and little Willie, to some outlandish place you never heard tell of except in Ned's stories?"

But Meg, level-headed Meg, just shook her head. Lavinia could hardly believe that in a few hours her family had decided to abandon the only home she had ever known. If they must leave Weymouth surely there are places in England they can move to!

"This is all part of some scheme of Ned's—what do Ben say?"

"Well, girl, you know Ben." Jennie glanced at Ben's wife. "Excuse me, Meg, for all he's me own son I got to say it. Ben won't budge without Ned's say so, that's how 'tis been ever since they was boys. And what could we all do here, with one man gone and the other useless without him? I allow it's better we all goes together—and goes tonight before worse happens."

Lavinia took this to mean that Ned had decided and the rest had agreed. Still, she was not willing to give up. She pointed to Hazel, already seven months into pregnancy and sickly at the best of times.

"What about Hazel?" Lavinia always thought that her brothers had gotten the wrong wives. Sensible Meg would have settled Ned down, and timid, whining Hazel would have been the perfect match for Ben.

Hazel surprised her now, though: "Me and the two children are not stayin' here. If Ned goes, we goes, you knows that, Vinnie. Anyway, Master Richard said, 'take your wife and brats!'"

"Wife and brats—what do he think we are—slaves?" Lavinia was crying with shame and helpless spite. "He can tell us to leave this flat, but he can't tell us to leave the town. He's not a king—he don't own us!"

"As good as," Jennie returned to her packing, "even if he didn't have Ned arrested, who'd give him work, or have dealings with any of us if it meant bein' bad friends with the Ellsworths?"

Her mother was right. "We are slaves then—all of us," Lavinia said grimly. She looked from one to the other, waiting, hoping, to be contradicted. None of the women spoke or even raised their eyes from the joyless work.

Across her mind flickered the thought that she could leave right now. It seemed impossible, but up in the big house Maud and Sally would still be in the cellar scrubbing clothes. She could slip back in and no one would ever know she'd been away. "You can have a decent life," Mrs. John had said.

Instead she had walked into the room, picked up her mother's platter, wrapped it carefully in a pair of purple tights and laid it in a barrel.

Sitting now on the very edge of the Newfound Land, Lavinia records the kitchen scene in loving detail.

Until the day she dies she will be able to see them there, packing bits and pieces of their life into barrels. She will remember always how the late afternoon light fell through the narrow window. How, when her mother took down the old picture of a shepherd leading his sheep home, the unfaded spot underneath jumped at them, bright with deep pink roses and dark green leaves she had never before seen. She would remember Mrs. Thorp's low sniffling, the click of dishes and the familiar street sounds drifting up. Sounds of a town, of horses clopping over cobblestones, footsteps hurrying past, people's voices, children playing some street game, and far off the call of a vendor with autumn apples to sell.

Her account of the five-week trip across the Atlantic is less complete. It had been unusually stormy, even for November. The small ship had floundered through head winds that sent icy spray foaming across the deck. Women and children were trapped in the reeking hold where their belongings slid from one side to the other. Ben and Meg turned out to be bad sailors, which meant that Ned had to work twice as hard since part of their passage was to be worked off by the men. Poor Hazel went below and laid down before the ship had even cleared Portland Point lighthouse. Lavinia and her mother, with Lizzie's help, had to tend the sick and care for the children.

Ned, who had made this trip many times in Ellsworth vessels, although never this late in the year, was completely unaffected by the pitch and roll of the ship, the smells that oozed out of the hull, the half-cooked food, the foul drinking water, or the misery of his pregnant wife. As soon as the ropes tying them to Weymouth pier were pulled in, Ned became buoyant, as if the wind that filled the sails had puffed him up too, brought colour to his cheeks and sparkle to his eyes. His flat-footed gait that looked childish and awkward on shore fitted the roll of the ship. His face, very like Lavinia's, faintly freckled and surrounded by curly orange hair and beard, was always smiling. Even when the wind tore a sail in half and whipped the little ship around like a child's top, Ned seemed to be enjoying himself.

The only thing that cast even a small shadow on Ned's boyish happiness was that just two of the crew understood English. The one ship he could find crossing the Atlantic in November, *La Truite* was a French brig out of La Havre that had put into Weymouth for repairs to a broken mizzenmast. Sailing short-handed and with space in the hold, the Captain had agreed, for a price, to take the Andrews family aboard, a special arrangement between him and Ned that the ship's owner need never know about.

Still, the lack of an audience did not deter Ned. Lavinia recalled the day she had watched her brother give an imitation of Richard Ellsworth's tirade. Jumping onto a box, he assumed all the idiosyncrasies of his former master, puffed out his concave chest, turned red, yelled and pounded on the crate with a stick. Then he jumped down and became himself, cowering in front of the big man, knees trembling. Back and forth he went, spinning out the tale of his own downfall.

His sister looked on in disgust as the sailors, even those who could not understand the words, stopped their work to enjoy the show. The children, his own two and Ben's girls, who had been so frightened at the time, rolled on the deck with laughter.

"I don't see what's so funny, Ned Andrews, about being branded a thief and thrown out of your home along with your wife and children—and havin' all of us thrown out too." Lavinia spat the words at him when the play acting ended.

Ned just laughed. "Go on, Vinnie, it's good for young ones to get a bit of fun out of things that frighten 'em—good for me, too. Don't look so black, maid, wind might change and leave that sour look on your face forever—then that rich man who's waiting for you will go find another... ."

He burst into song, caught her around the waist and tried to dance her across the deck. Lavinia was having none of it. She pulled herself away, thinking how unjust things were. Although his foolish scheme to make a few shillings had left his family homeless, Ned was having the time of his life.

She wondered again if he'd known from the beginning what was likely to happen. The story about digging up the old man's garden when everyone else was carousing didn't sound like Ned. She wouldn't put it past him to have planned it all just to get them on this awful trip to God knows where.

During the day there was at least light, and work, no matter how unpleasant, to hold back despair. But when dark came and the little ship plowed into a wall of blackness, when they were all crowded into the hold, then they could hear everything, feel everything, imagine everything—rats gnawing at the food, timbers grinding against each other, waves smashing on the planks right next to where they lay. At night Lavinia wondered if they would ever see land again; imagined how it would be to drown in all that blackness.

The tossing of the ship, the vastness of the ocean and Hazel's illness frightened even Jennie, who became more religious than she had ever been on land. The older woman asked Meg, the only regular churchgoer in the family, to pray with her each night before sleep. The sight of her mother and Meg kneeling together only increased Lavinia's feeling of being lost in some great black void.

Through it all, Ned regaled them with stories of the new world. That was what he called it: "the new world." He liked the ring of the words. He would sit in a corner holding young Isaac and Ben's small son Willie, one on each knee, while Jane and his nieces squashed around as closely as possible.

"We're on our way to the outermost island of the sea!" Ned told the children. Larger than all of Dorset it was, a place where they could walk for a hundred miles on land no man owned, pick berries and fruit without anyone saying nay, hunt deer, catch in their own hands silver fish that swam right up onto beaches. This new world of his was filled with sunshine, misty rain and warm fogs that rolled in over the hills like a veil. He made up such wondrous yarns that the children were pop-eyed at their good fortune. Meg and Jennie would forget their prayers to listen and even Hazel could manage a smile while her husband talked.

The Andrews were town people. Their idea of country had been shaped by excursions taken once each year when dray men and their families travelled to the outskirts of Weymouth where a farmer lent them a newly cut field for the day. This glimpse of rolling meadows, separated by copses of low bushes, of neat pathways between ancient stone walls, of golden hay fields and the small brown birds that dive low over them, of blue butterflies rising in clusters from flowers, were pictures even the adults saw when Ned yarned. The children were sure life in the Newfound Land would be one long dray outing.

Only Lavinia refused to be drawn into Ned's fantasy. She remembered the great sea monsters he had described, and shivered when he spoke of the outermost island. She felt the wind grow colder each day and noted that the seamen looked with pity at the thin women and poorly dressed children who were their only passengers.

Then, three weeks out, in the middle of a tempest, with water and wind battering the ship from both sky and sea, Hazel went into early labour. Since Meg was still weak from her long bout of seasickness, Lavinia and Jennie had to do what they could for the woman. This was little enough. For days Hazel had been unable to keep food down and now seemed to be only half-conscious of what was happening. Ignoring their aching backs and knees, they knelt beside the poor woman hour after hour, keeping her clean, wiping her face and holding her hand, murmuring to her in low voices, aware of the children sleeping restlessly only feet away. A small lantern, hung from the planks above their heads, made huge swaying shadows on the bulkheads as the boat pitched into thirty-foot waves.

Suddenly the smell of warm blood was everywhere. In the middle of the blood lay a lifeless creature, tiny and surprisingly white, like a wax doll. Jennie looked at it carefully, then turned to beckon Ned, who was hovering just outside the ring of light.

"Come here," his mother said.

When it seemed he would not, she repeated in a hard voice Lavinia had never before heard, "Come here, Ned!"

Slowly, swallowing so you could hear, Ned came to stand by his mother. Jennie made him look down at the terrible mixture of blood, baby and afterbirth before she rolled it all together and pushed it, still warm, into his arms.

"Here, my son, 'tis yours, take it up and throw it into the ocean." Neither pity or sorrow showed on her face until he had turned away.

Kneeling beside Hazel, trying to stop the flow of blood, Lavinia was glad of what her mother had done to Ned. After that night, Ned never again told of how he had gotten into trouble with the Ellsworths. His stories became more and more far-fetched but now had nothing to do with the life they had left behind in Weymouth.

Of the last two weeks of their voyage, Lavinia writes nothing. There is a blank until the morning *La Truite* arrived on the Cape.

Despite the cold and a cutting wind, they had stayed on deck for hours, straining towards the spot where they would make land, the distant line of shore where a ruffle of white separated the dark sea from the darker hills. They came closer and saw sombre forest, cliffs that sliced down raw and grey into the sea, but not a sign of smoke, of houses, of people, roads, animals, or even open fields. Nothing but rock and wind-twisted trees. Sometimes the coastline disappeared completely, blocked out by squalls of fine snow.

Then Lizzie had shouted, "Look!" And up ahead was a line of white breakers, frothing around a place the Captain told them was Cape Random. The snug harbour he had promised is not a harbour at all but a point.

Ned rushed below to bring his wife, wrapped in blankets, above deck. Hazel's face had shrunken and yellowed, and she looked older than Jennie, but she smiled from her husband's arms, blinking at the white sky, happy to be up in the fresh air, happy to see that they were finally coming to land. Watching her, Lavinia knew that Hazel, who had suffered more than any of them, was not the spineless creature she had imagined.

—— —— ——

Cautiously, slowly, *La Truite* approaches the triangle of land, edging in between foam that hisses over sunken rocks. The Andrews family stand, holding onto the rail, watching. No one speaks. Lavinia can see that the place is like another, larger ship, jutting out into the sea—one side grey cliff, the other grey sand. A great, tilting, grey ship held only by a rope of sand to the dunes and dark hills behind. In the hollow between the sand and the cliffs there are rocks and low bushes.

A wharf, balanced precariously out over the water on wooden stilts, is joined to the land by a weatherbeaten grey shed. Attached to the wharf on either side are strange rickety platforms that look as flimsy as cobwebs. Flakes and wharf shudder as the vessel eases into place.

The only other building is a house, its raw wooden walls still cream-white, hanging with strips of bark where the logs have been roughly hacked into shape. Behind the shed and the house, behind rocks and bushes, past the connecting neck of sand, are the black hills. The tops of the hills are hidden by a sky that hangs like a drooping grey sheet over everything.

The wind, too, is unfamiliar, cold, persistent, an alien wind. Lavinia feels it breathe down her throat, down into her bones. She imagines her bones being coated with white rime from the wind. All around, to the sides and in front of the point of land, there is only sea.

There are people standing on the wharf.

After long consideration of sea, sky and hills, Lavinia makes herself look at the people. Her first feeling is relief—they are not the fur-covered pagans with painted faces and horned skulls she had half expected. Then she sees their faces, blank, unwelcoming, devoid of any human expression, and her relief quickly turns to dismay.

One of the men on the wharf is tall and darkly bearded, older than Ben. He alone comes forward to catch the ropes tossed down from *La Truite*. The others, a family Lavinia guesses, stand unmoving behind him, all short people and all, except the woman, thin—but not fragile. Light, wiry people, standing so still, looking up, alert as animals. Lavinia would not be surprised to see one of them climb the ropes and jump down onto the deck like a monkey she had once seen on a sailor's shoulder.

The father and children have mild blue eyes and fair hair. The father's hair is almost white and, with his wispy beard, blows around his narrow brown face in an eerie waving motion. The white hair and pale eyes make their faces seem dark as tanned leather. The woman might have darker hair and she seems stouter. It is impossible to know for sure because of the layers of shawl covering her and the baby she is holding. Besides the baby there are three children. A boy of about eight stands next to his father, one arm wrapped around the man's leg. There is a big girl near Lizzie's age and another boy who, as soon as the plank is down, comes clamouring aboard the ship, very like the monkey Lavinia has been thinking of. The first mate shouts in French at the boy but he pays not the slightest heed and proceeds to examine the ship from end to end as if looking for something he's lost.

The other people on the wharf do not stir. Their guileless blue eyes follow the Andrews family as they come ashore carrying baskets, barrels, their rolls of blankets—their poverty.

For long minutes the two groups study each other. It is terrible looking into the faces of strangers, but, Lavinia thinks, better, much better, than turning to look at the faces of her mother and sisters-in-law, or at the faces of the children as they see the reality behind Ned's stories.

Then Jennie jerks forward, hurrying to the woman with the baby, leaning over, saying something to the squat little creature.

Choking with embarrassment, Lavinia knows that any moment she will begin to wail. She searches for a place to hide, a place where she can be alone, and instinctively moves toward the ship. Suddenly it seems a safe place, a refuge. But Captain Benoit shakes his head, turns her about. He is in a hurry, anxious to get his vessel out with the tide.

Whatever is to be done will be done without her, Lavinia decides. She will not be part of the begging for a place to sleep. Far down the beach she can see a rock rising, shining smooth, out of the sand. She turns and walks silently, quickly, away from her family, towards the rock.

Chapter 2

Who would think that Hazel could stay alive so long? Maybe she won't be the first to go. We're hungry all the time. None of us want to get up in the morning...

Lavinia writes these words in late February sitting cross-legged on the floor near Hazel's pallet. Hazel's eyes are closed, as they are most of the time now. Her face is still and so white that she might already be a corpse. Bones and threadlike blue veins show through the transparent skin.

Inside the one-room shed, canvas sails have been tied to the ceiling beams, making a rough semicircle around the sick woman, hiding both her and Lavinia. The canvas is pulled open on the side towards the fireplace to catch what heat there is. Lizzie and the younger children sit on the floor directly in front of the fire. They play listlessly, moving chips of wood around a checker-board Ned has stained into the floorboards. Meg, holding Willie on her hip, has to step around the children each time she puts wood on the sulky fire or checks the pot of simmering turnip.

"You're a good maid to take care of Hazel," Sarah Vincent said yesterday when she saw Lavinia sitting near the sick woman's bed. Lavinia had felt shamed by the praise. She stays beside Hazel because inside the canvas enclosure she feels alone and safe.

Lavinia cannot understand this longing for solitude that has come upon her since they arrived on the Cape. It is something she never felt in the crowded flat on Monk Street or in the attic room she shared with Maud and Sally in Ellsworth House. The feeling worries her. It is strange, she thinks, to want to be alone in such a lonely place.

She remembers a man the children on Monk Street called Hod, who used to help Jacob Spriggett in the livery stable. One day Hod moved into a vacant field behind the stable, a place full of weeds, built himself a hut, and heaped junk all around the outside. Whenever the children went near he would scuttle inside, like a badger disappearing into the great pile of rubbish where you could not even see a doorway. Jennie said Hod was mad and warned the children to stay away from him. Lavinia wonders if she might come to be like Hod.

After the first awkward minutes on the wharf, the two families on the Cape seem to have melded together remarkably well. During the winter, little alliances have been formed, but none include Lavinia. Sarah Vincent, Jennie and Meg Andrews have become close and are called 'Aunt' by each other's children.

Meg and Jennie spend an hour or so every afternoon sitting in the Vincents' kitchen, talking and knitting. The two Andrews women have knitting needles, but, having quickly run out of wool, are now occupied picking apart and ravelling useless items such as tea cosies, cushion covers and fancy doilies they had packed around their dishes. The wild mixture of colour in garments knitted from wool produced this way makes the Andrews family identifiable from great distances.

The children, too, have discovered their own occupations and friends. Sarah's daughter Annie and Lizzie Andrews, almost the same age, are delighted to have found each other. They lay claim to the contents of the barrels, the exotic remnants of Ben's last day as a peddler. While wind baffles the shed, piling great white drifts against the door and window—a tiny square of glass not six inches wide—Annie and Lizzie direct the other children in something Annie calls concerts.

Donning net tights, plumed hats and lace gloves, and draping the peach satin over their heavy clothing, they act out long improvised plays that have no beginning and no end but continue from day to day. A world of kings and princesses, dragons and knights, characters taken from the stories Ned spins, along with bits of song from fading memories of Punch and Judy shows. The little girls, Jane, Patience and Emma, are made to sit in a row as audience or, sometimes under duress, are given small parts. Peter Vincent, who is nine, can be lured into the game and once in a while even Young Joe, the oldest Vincent boy, will play the part of king, sweetheart or knight—until one of the men comes into the store. Then Joe will stop in mid-gesture, fling away the offending cape and wooden sword, and, shamed at being caught in childish games, stalk away.

From her place near Hazel's pallet, Lavinia watches the ongoing drama and thinks of a hundred ways to improve the story, which tends to ramble on with much shouting, jumping about and weeping, but with little plot. Back on Monk Street she would have pulled a bit of net across her face, run over, declaimed a few lines and slipped easily into the fun. The effort now seems impossible. Through the long shadowy afternoons, she sits in a kind of half-sleep, watching demons and heroes shriek and dance between her and the firelight.

After such listless days Lavinia cannot sleep. At night she listens to the wind growl. She imagines the wind as a great white beast, humped just outside the Cape, holding them all between its terrible paws. Its breath shakes the shed.

"Someday," she thinks, "it will grow tired of playing and kill us." Even when she finally sleeps, the wind creature is there, a shrieking background to her dreams.

Bad as the nights are, Lavinia finds getting up each morning even worse: waking, hearing the wind, knowing where she is, feeling the creeping cold on her face and the gnaw of hunger that is always in her stomach.

The men cut evergreen trees, laboriously dragging them through miles of deep snow, then stacking them upright against the outside walls of the shed, hoping to block out some of the cold. Still, every morning, beds are covered with a powder of snow that has drifted in between cracks.

Each morning, one by one, they crawl out from under piles of clothing, blankets, mats, even brin bags. The adults get up first, driven by hunger and the need to relieve themselves in the bucket that is hidden from sight, but not from smell, behind stacks of drying firewood. The children, wanting only to spend the day in the nests they have warmed with body heat and sometimes with urine, have to be coaxed and pulled out of bed. Everyone moves stiffly, not only because of the cold but because of layers of clothing that cannot be taken off day or night. When someone must go outside, they take an overcoat from one of the beds, pulling it over everything else.

No longer able to get water from the small, now frozen, pond, they must bring buckets of snow into the shed each night. It takes several buckets of snow to make one bucket of water, and often in the morning the snow has not even melted. When they finally manage to heat a little water, Lavinia and Jennie wash Hazel and pat warm seal oil on the oozing sores where her bones have rubbed through her skin.

One morning Sarah Vincent came in while Jennie and Lavinia were changing the blood-soaked blankets. After watching for a minute she left. Returning with a bag of dry moss, she showed the Andrews women how to layer the soft stuff between sheets to absorb blood. After that there was less bedding to wash. Wet blankets take days to dry, hanging in rafters, adding the smell of wet wool to those of blood, urine, dirty bodies and boiled turnip that now permeates the store which, Lavinia wrote, had smelled pleasantly of rope, tar and oakum the day they arrived.

It is almost noon, but so dark that Lavinia can barely see the words she is writing. Outside, a winter sun shines faintly through great swirls of snow driven by a howling wind. The world is one blinding haze of white movement. Each time someone enters, a blast of wind and snow sweeps across the floor. The desultory checker game has ended, and children have crept back into their piles of bedding.

Despite the weather, Ned and Ben, along with Thomas Hutchings and Josh Vincent, are out in search of seabirds, checking the beach in hopes of finding a wild duck. Sarah Vincent says that the big grey birds are fat enough to give them all one or two good meals, but ducks are unlikely to be seen this late in the winter. Still, smaller birds are sometimes wounded and blown off course from the bird islands. They have had only salt fish and turnip to eat for four days now, and Lavinia's mouth waters as she thinks of roasted bird.

The disaster of coming to the Cape without a supply of food was brought home to Lavinia the morning after their arrival. She watched, mortified, as her mother, clutching the old black purse she has owned as long as Lavinia can remember, walked over to Thomas Hutchings to try and buy breakfast for the family.

Thomas Hutchings, trimming his beard at a tiny mirror propped on a shelf, did not notice Jennie standing behind him. Or maybe he only pretended not to notice, Lavinia thinks. She has come to dislike the man intensely.

"Ahem...." Jennie had cleared her throat and Lavinia, watching closely, fancied she could see a flicker of annoyance cross the man's face. He'd turned around but still did not speak.

"I'd be obliged if you could tell me how to buy some food," Jennie said.

Thomas Hutchings gave her mother one of the long expressionless looks Lavinia hates. "There is no food for you to buy, Mrs. Andrews."

Jennie had not understood. She'd opened the purse and pulled out her little store of coins, holding them out for him to see: "We can pay, we're no beggars, Mr. Hutchings."

The tall man's mouth tightened. This time Lavinia was sure it was impatience and dislike she saw.

"There is no food to sell. The only food here is my winter supplies—and they are not really mine. Everything here, including this store and, I'm told, the fish in the sea, belongs to Caleb Gosse, a merchant in St. John's. I am only his storekeeper. I work for him—in a way we all do."

"How can you be a storekeeper without stuff to sell?" Jennie Andrews, who had once bartered from door to door, is not easily squelched.

"I'm keeper of this store room—a caretaker—it's not a store for selling things. Next summer we will all catch fish, and make fish. When fall comes we'll settle up with Master Gosse. His ships will pick up the fish and send us our winter supplies, just as he sent mine out October past. This is a store room—not a shop—we don't have many shops. They don't use money much in this country."

As Thomas Hutchings spoke, Jennie Andrews took several steps backwards and collided with Meg, who had come to stand behind her mother-in-law.

"What will we do then, perish? What will we give the young ones to eat, what will we eat?" Something in her mother's voice—fear, panic, defiance—made Lavinia get up and go over to stand with Jennie and Meg, facing the man.

He sighed. "Here, I'll show you." He led them to the low end of the store. Here the roof came down to touch Thomas Hutchings' head and they could feel the sea pounding in below the floor.

"This is what we have. We'll share until it's gone: a barrel of flour, potatoes, a half sack of onions, a tub of pickled cabbage, three bags of turnip—I wondered why he sent me so many turnip but I now see it was providential—a sack of sugar and a puncheon of molasses. There's other stuff up in those tins." He nodded to a plank that had been nailed to the beams. "Some salt, tea, rolled oats, things like that. Outside by the door there's a barrel of partridgeberries and we've got a good supply of salt fish, thank God. That's it. Do you understand now?"

He spoke as though talking to children, backward children. Lavinia hated him.

"It'll be a good long winter, not another thing will come in here for five months, maybe six if the ice holds in to shore. I leave it up to you, Mrs. Andrews. Parcel it out, see how far you can make it go." He bent slightly forward, stared at her mother without smiling, made a sort of half bow and went back to trimming his beard.

Jennie, Lavinia and Meg were left staring at the food that would have to feed thirteen people for five or six months. Lavinia, however, was seeing not the food but Thomas Hutchings' scornful face, wishing she could have said something smart and nasty to him.

"He has this way of makin' you feel small and stupid. I don't like that man one bit," she said in a low voice.

"Like will have to be servant to must," her mother grimly voiced one of her favourite sayings before turning to Meg. "Well, girl, we got our work cut out for us. We're goin' to have to be awful mean to keep body and soul together 'til spring."

From then on Jennie, and sometimes Meg, doled out the day's food and cooked it. They calculated the least amount possible, giving the men the biggest share, feeding the children and often taking only pot liquor and a piece of bread for themselves.

Thomas Hutchings ate with the family and when he saw how the women were trying to make the food last he unbent a little. One suppertime he even complimented Meg on a roly-poly she'd made with partridgeberries.

With all their care, the potatoes were gone by late December. Then they came to the end of the cabbage. The barrel of partridgeberries lasted much longer than the sugar, but they were bitter even with a dab of molasses. Meg had built some kind of myth around the berries: they were bright and bitter and therefore must be full of nourishment. Each morning she made her own four children, along with Jane and Isaac, stand in line as she popped a large spoonful of the tart fruit into their mouths.

For almost six weeks now they have lived on salt fish, turnip, bread and tea sweetened with molasses. Some days the men get a few bull birds, tiny stragglers that have not gone south, tough and so small a man can hold two in the palm of his hand, but they take away the pains of hunger for an hour or so.

Five days ago, watching as Meg banged and scraped the last of the flour out of the barrel, Lavinia realized it is quite possible they will starve. As flesh falls away they feel the cold even more. Each morning when the men go out she can see that they move more and more slowly. Even Jennie, whom Ned used to call a plump pigeon, has become gaunt. Two-year-old Willie is refusing to walk about and insists on Meg carrying him all the time. The other children, who raced around like wild things when they came off the boat, creep back to bed and spend half the day sleeping.

Although her own supply of flour is getting low, Sarah Vincent sends a loaf of bread over each day. Hazel and the children each get a slice with a dribble of molasses as their midday meal. The women have a cup of the tea Sarah showed them how to make by boiling down spruce needles. The real tea they save for suppertime when the men are back.

Lavinia feels her own body shrinking. Sometimes she tastes blood in her mouth, imagines her teeth and hair falling out. Her dreams, and even her journal, are filled with thoughts of food, of warmth, and of death, particularly of Hazel's death. Despite the refusal of anyone to acknowledge it, Lavinia is quite sure that her sister-in-law is dying.

At night, before lying down beside his children, Ned comes over to kiss his wife and pat her hand. "You'll feel better when the winter's over," he says, or, "When we get into our own house you'll get well fast."

Lavinia turns her head away from the hope that skims across Hazel's pale face each night when she hears those empty words.

The coldest part of the store, the part that hangs over the water and where the few remaining supplies are kept, the men have claimed as their workroom. Lavinia can hear them talking, Josh Vincent telling Ned and Ben how to clean the two turrs they have brought back.

Josh has a piece of sailcloth spread across his lap. With the bird balanced breast-up, its head hanging down, he skilfully pulls feathers from the skin with a jerking movement. Thomas and Josh Vincent are continually baffled by the ignorance of the Andrews men, by the way they must be shown the same thing again and again.

"Where ya bin all yer lives, at all, at all," Josh says in his soft, slow voice, making the words a comment rather than a question, which would have broken the unspoken rule that a person's past must not be inquired into.

The talk turns quickly to more important things: the ice surrounding the Cape, the likelihood of getting a seal. Josh says seals should appear in the harbour any day now. In lower voices, they discuss the possibility of walking around the coast to a place called Inner Island to borrow flour.

Lavinia stops writing. The horrifying thought of men walking on ice over bottomless black water is banished by the quick hope that they might be saved after all. She strains to hear.

"We could take your sled and the gun—we might see a few birds or even seals," Thomas Hutchings is saying.

"How long would it take?" Ned asks and Lavinia thinks, "So, he does know she's dying."

"Oh, we wouldn't all go, only two of us. What do you say, Josh?"

"'Tis possible certainly. We'd have to wait for civil weather, work our way from reach to reach. Wind would slow you down, and snow squalls could blind you out there on the ice," Josh says.

"Yet, if we started early I expect we could make it before dark and come back the next day if the weather held." Thomas Hutchings' voice carries farther.

It is clearer, colder, more formal. Lifeless, Lavinia usually thinks, but something almost like excitement has crept into it as he speaks of walking across the ocean ice.

"I doubts it would be much use, Thomas. I knows what Father and the people up home had left this time last winter and I allow they're no better off this year. All along this coast there's people tryin' to scrape along 'til the seals come in or 'til supplies arrive, same as us," Josh says quietly.

"Yes, you're right," Thomas's voice is flat again, "the ice should break up any day now. If this cold snap passes we'll see some seals, and I expect Caleb Gosse to put flour and molasses on the first vessel he sends north."

Lavinia fancies she can hear reproach in the grim voice. "If it were not for us he'd have all the flour he needs, all the molasses and oil and firewood he needs—yes, and all the privacy, too." Her own new longing to be left alone has made Lavinia recognize the same twitching uneasiness in Thomas Hutchings. Watching him move away from them each night, she knows that their presence in the store irritates him.

Since the first day when he caught the ropes of the ship, she has been watching him, looking for signs of impatience, listening to his voice for the indications of rebuke she is sure are there. Whenever something happens, happy or sad, her eyes turn to Thomas Hutchings. Is he amused by Willie rolling across the floor like a ball? Is he angered by Ned's endless, ignorant questions? Made happy by a bowl of steaming stew or sad by a low moan from Hazel? Does his stomach cramp from hunger? Is he fearful of the battering of frozen sea under the shed?

She wonders what he would look like if he ever laughed. So far he hasn't. The knowledge that her family is so in debt to this man is hard to bear.

Only Hazel, drifting in the twilight world between life and death, has noted Lavinia's eyes: how they follow Thomas Hutchings, how her head is forever turned in his direction. The sick woman is thankful to have this little drama to watch, to keep her mind off the pain as she drifts in and out of the semi-sleep that is creeping up on her like fog.

At night Thomas Hutchings goes to sit by himself, lights a seal oil lamp and reads one of three books which by day are lined up between two small boxes on the shelf above his desk. He is an orderly man, maybe, sometimes, even a kind one. Lavinia has been astonished to see him take the broom to sweep up wood chips or feathers and she's heard Sarah speak of the day Charlie was born, how Thomas came over and cooked supper for all the family.

"Done good as a woman, better than some. Our Annie couldn't have done better, poor little maid, she was runnin' back and forth to me. And Josh—well, he's useless in the house, can't make himself a cuppa tea."

They have gotten to know the Vincents well. Each night after supper the family comes to the store to hear Ned's stories. Josh Vincent always brings an armful of dry wood which he deposits quietly beside the fire. Ned begins these sessions just as he used to on the boat, sitting on the floor with Willie and Isaac in his arms and the other children crowded around. But when the story gets going he cannot contain himself. He must set the boys down, jump up and act out each character.

After the night Ned dropped his still-born baby into the ocean, his stories changed. No longer the hero of all his tales, he now tells stories about pirates and buried gold, about beautiful Indian maidens, about villains who fight, swords clanging off rocks as they shout wild curses at each other. He tells of magical animals that roam the hills, animals that have vanished from every place on earth except the Cape, of ghosts that hover on the beach at night and lure ships to doom on the rocks, of women who float above snowdrifts wailing for lovers or lost children, of kingdoms drowned in the sea and princesses stolen by gypsies.

By bedtime, when the Vincents leave, only Young Joe will walk by himself. Annie and Peter cling to their parents, terrified lest they meet ghosts or spirits along the narrow path beaten between deep drifts of snow.

Over the years, Ned's stories will become part of life on the Cape. Hundreds of variations will be told around kitchen fires on winter nights by generation after generation. Details will be added, details changed, real events woven into the yarns. After a hundred years it will be impossible to know where the thread of truth intertwines with the warp of fable.

Hazel asks to be propped up so that she can see Ned, and, as the story unfolds, even Thomas leaves his book and comes over to the fire. He lights his only pipe for the day, and for a little while the smell of tobacco, pungent and spicy, covers the sour smell of the store and blends into the climax of Ned's wild story.

The night after Meg used the last flour, there was no bread for supper. The Andrews family sat on after the Vincents left, gazing into the fire, the smaller children dozing in the arms of the adults, no one wanting to leave the heat, to move to the hungry darkness of their beds. Then Thomas Hutchings had gone over to his shelf and taken down a large, round, tin. He opened the tin and took out a cake of hard tack.

"This is sailors' bread," he told the children. Giving the small rock-like roll a sharp knock against the stones of the chimney, he handed one egg-size lump to each of them.

"Take it to bed and chew on it, it will help you to sleep."

Every night after that, Thomas Hutchings passes hard tack around at the beginning of story-telling, and they can gnaw on it while Ned spins his extravagant fancies. It is strangely satisfying. Ned, who had eaten the hard bread on many voyages, calls it sea biscuit. He tells the children it is magic and will give them good dreams.

As Josh predicted, there is a break in the weather. On the last day in February, loud cracking sounds echo like gunshot off the rocks and hills. Patches of black water appear in the harbour ice, and soon there is more water than ice. The next week a wind from the north pushes arctic ice down the coast. Subtly different from the harbour ice in colour and texture, it drifts onto the

Cape in loose pans that grind together, rafting up on shore, sometimes tipping on edge like giant dinner plates.

One day near noon the store door is flung open and a blast of icy air proceeds Young Joe's bellowed announcement: "Swiles in! Swiles in!"

He vanishes without closing the door. The men are out in a minute, pulling on jackets, snatching up ropes and hooked gaffs they've had stacked against the wall for weeks. Peter Vincent, in the process of having a red sash knotted around his waist by Annie, pulls away and races after his father. Still wearing their dress-up finery, the other children follow. Meg manages to grab Jane and Emma to pull cuffs over their hands and jerk caps down around their heads.

She shoves Isaac towards Lavinia, "Here, you take him, I'll carry Willie. We might as well see them wonderful beasts. Come on Mam—keep ahold of him, Vinnie, or he'll be tryin' to catch a seal hisself!" And they are gone, calling over their shoulders to Hazel that they'll be back in a little while.

On the beach it looks as if some strange festival is taking place. Men edge back and forth, testing the floating ice with their long gaffs. Children streeling bits of coloured cloth squeal and shout as they clamour over the rafted ice pans, trying to find a perch from which they can see the seals.

The seals are about one hundred feet out, drifting on pans that are slowly moving closer to shore. Lavinia cannot see the animals until a cream-coloured shadow on one of the ice pans moves. She is disappointed: crawling awkwardly on ice, the seals look like dirty, legless sheep. Then one slithers into the water, swims in a graceful arc and disappears.

Thomas Hutchings turns to the noisy children, his face like a thundercloud: "Hush, for God's sake. Be still and quiet or you'll frighten them off!"

They obey instantly, crouching down behind great lumps of ice that have rafted up on the landwash, only their bright head gear and eager eyes visible.

Thomas has brought the only gun in the place, but they are short of powder and hope to gaff as many seals as possible. Josh has told them that his father and brothers catch seals in nets moored to the ice. Only the smaller seals come in near shore, he says. They have resolved that next spring they will have nets ready to set out.

Almost at once Josh Vincent finds an ice pan that will hold him. He leaps onto it and Thomas follows. The men wear several layers of clothing and heavy boots, but they jump with surprising ease from pan to pan, always landing in the spot calculated to hold their weight. Within minutes they are among the seals and Josh has gaffed one.

Young Joe, first taking a quick look to make sure his mother is not on the beach, leaps onto an ice pan. In an instant Ned Andrews follows. Ben makes a move as if to go, but Meg grabs at his arm.

It is all so casually, so quietly, done that Lavinia does not at first realize the danger. She cannot believe people would risk death with so little ceremony. Surely, at least, a flag should be raised, a prayer said. As this thought crosses her mind she sees Meg, still clinging to her husband's arm, close her eyes and bow her head.

Only then does Lavinia comprehend what peril the men are in, how deep the water beneath them, how fragile the floating ice pans, how unstable their balance. One change in wind, in tide, a rotten patch of ice, a foot landing two inches nearer the edge, and a pan will tip, sending them to their deaths. Lavinia, too, would like to pray but dares not take her eyes off the figures silhouetted against the whiteness. Ned, who scampers between pans of ice as though born to it, seems more at home than any of the others, more at home than the floundering seals.

Young Joe reaches the seal his father has killed, ties rope around the carcass and slowly drags it to shore, leaving a red path across the ice. The children creep soundlessly down to look, shocked at the stillness of the dead furry thing with its bashed skull. As soon as one seal is landed, Joe returns to the ice and begins hauling in another.

The men have dragged five seals ashore when Annie Vincent lets out a piercing shriek and pointing, runs to the water's edge. Every seal dives. The ice pans, spattered now with blood, are empty. They look toward where Annie is pointing and see Peter Vincent tottering on the edge of a large, tilting pan of ice. The pan tips slowly, showing its pale green underside and Peter lunges forward, falling, but managing to grab at a smaller pan where he clings with only his upper body out of the water.

Josh, Young Joe, Thomas and Ned all begin working their way towards the boy, moving with what now seems excruciating slowness—all except Ned, who is leaping from pan to pan with a kind of exuberance, almost as if he were flying. His curly red hair and beard rise and fall gracefully each time he jumps. His oversize boots seem to land on the ice before his feet, lifting off again just as the ice sinks beneath him. He seems euphoric, lets out a loud, happy yell when he reaches Peter and with a swoop hooks his gaff under the red sash that is just visible above the dark water.

By the time the other men reach them, Ned has the boy safely up on the ice. They bring him ashore and take him, face blue and teeth chattering, into his mother's kitchen. Sarah, crying at the sight of him, gives her son a good clout across the back of the head before stripping away his frozen garments. Bundling a blanket around him, she sits him down by the fire and delivers a long, loud lecture on what can befall boys who disobey their mothers.

The hours it takes to clean and cook the meat are an agony of expectation. The Vincents donate the last of their onions to a communal feast, and Lavinia writes that heaven must smell like seal and onions roasting. Everyone hovers near the fire, offering suggestions, asking when the meal will be ready, until even Meg looses patience, chases the men and boys outside and charges the small children to be seen and not heard.

Finally the meat is served, dark and crisp on the outside, dripping with fat, rich and gamy in flavour. They all eat and eat. They eat until they feel queasy and Lizzie gets quite sick.

That night they stay by the fire for hours, celebrating the seal killing with songs and stories. They now have meat, fur, fat and oil. They know now that it will soon be spring, soon ships will be sailing down the coast from Carbonear and St. John's. They have survived winter.

Long after the others sleep Lavinia stays awake, tormented by the pointless resentment she feels against the men who went out on the ice pans. Remembering how readily they leapt across the strips of open water, she tells herself she should only be thankful they had nerve for such work. Could she ever do such a thing?

Killing the seals was necessary, she thinks. God knows she's thankful to have a full stomach. Still, she resents the foolhardy bravado, the male pride that, mixed with necessity, makes the job more dangerous than it need be.

Men, Lavinia concludes, lack imagination. They see only ice and the seals, whereas women see the fathoms of black water below, visualize the frozen seaweed swirling and clutching.

"It's not a bad thing to be without husband or sons," she writes that night.

Chapter 3

Mary Bundle came ashore today—the nearest thing to a savage any Christian soul is likely to see. There's no telling her age but I allow she's older than Meg by a good bit."

So seventeen-year-old Lavinia Andrews, still thinking of herself as a girl, almost a child, wrote of seventeen-year-old Mary Bundle, who came to the Cape so furtively one day in April.

The boys have been watching the schooner since early morning, when Young Joe spotted her white sails shining out against the pewter grey sky. One by one the women and other children joined the boys down at the stagehead. The men were fetched from in back where they had been chopping firewood—poor stringy wet sticks that will smoke rather than burn. By noon every soul in the place, apart from Hazel, is standing on the wharf watching the first vessel they have seen since *La Truite* sailed away almost six months before.

Despite the seal meat that in recent weeks has supplemented their meals of turnip and fish, the adults know they are still dangerously close to starvation. They pray silently that the ship will turn towards the Cape, that she will have flour on board.

Although a freezing wind knifes in from the sea they all stand in a quiet huddle, except for Ned, who keeps warm by dancing each child in turn around the edge of the wharf. As he swings his daughter Jane, the little girl realizes what the sails might mean.

"It's Captain Benoit, isn't it Daddy, comin' to take us back home?" The child's thin face lights up at the idea.

Lavinia watches her brother go suddenly sober, stop dancing and pick Jane up in his arms.

"No my duck, it's not the Captain, he's not comin' back—this is home now, Janie."

The child starts to sniffle quietly. Ned pats her back and begins to sing one of her favourite songs:

> *I saw three ships come sailin' in,*
> *Come sailin' in, come sailin' in,*

I saw three ships come sailin' in,
With diamond rings for Janie... .

Lavinia has often heard Ned sing his daughter to sleep with the song, an endless list of promises. She has still not made peace with her brother and the song usually irritates her. But watching Jane's face, she feels sad that the world is not the joyful place Ned imagines it to be.

"I allow she's an English naval vessel. I minds Uncle Ki Barbour tellin' us how they used to come down this way burnin' every house that had a chimney. They once hung two men up in Pond Island, the navy did." Sarah Vincent made the grim announcement, then with a kind of cheerful satisfaction, added, "and you knows none of we crowd, except for Thomas, got any rights livin' in this place!"

News of a danger they have not heard of makes the children go still. Meg and Jennie ask urgent questions about house burnings and hangings.

But Josh shakes his head at his wife and, in a voice that holds no reproach, says, "Now Sarah, maid, you knows well as I there haven't been a thing like that done along this coast for twenty-five year or more. And even then them two what was hung by Naval Court was scoundrels run away from jail in St. John's."

"'Sides, there's only two chimneys in the place, Ma. Hardly worth comin' in for—and I do doubt anyone on that vessel, the way she's pitchin', even spotted them." Young Joe supports his father and without taking his eyes from the ship, adds: "Anyway Ma, she's too small to be a navy ship. I allow she's a fishin' schooner. What do you think, Mr. Hutchings?" The bravest of the children, Young Joe is the only one who ever speaks directly to Thomas.

The man nods absently, looking more dour than usual, Lavinia thinks, almost as if he is sorry to see the ship tack slowly around and heave in towards the Cape.

Thomas Hutchings is more than a little uneasy. He has guessed that the ship plowing towards them belongs to Caleb Gosse, the man who owns the wharf they are standing on, the building everyone calls "Thomas's store" and the exclusive right to collect all cod caught and cured along this strip of coast. A strange, florid-faced man Gosse is, a suspicious man who hired Thomas after a two-minute interview, told him that Red Indians were stealing him blind and directed him to shoot the first Indian who came near the Cape. But no Indians had come, and none will come, because they are only part of the mad old man's imaginings.

Such a man, Thomas Hutchings is thinking, will not be pleased to discover he has housed and fed a dozen strangers all winter.

As far as Thomas knows, Caleb Gosse has never set foot on the Cape, nor on any of the places over which he holds the power of life and death. Surely no merchant, even a mad one, would leave St. John's in the spring when his fleet has to be fitted out for the fishing season. Telling himself that his fears are groundless, Thomas makes a vow that tomorrow the Andrews men will begin building their own shelter, albeit he and Josh will have to do most of the labour. The Andrews family must be out of the store before the fish strike in.

"Looks like she's intendin' to go on north—still got her topsail and upper canvas struck," Ned says. He doesn't take note, as his sister does, of what surprise this comment brings to the faces of Josh and Thomas, who have written the Andrews brothers off as dullards.

The vessel is now near enough for Thomas to read her name painted in blue letters along the bow: *Tern*. A two-masted schooner, she is, a lovely sight as she comes towards the Cape, using the wind and waves to slip around the breakers.

"If I'm not mistaken that'll be Alex Brennan skipperin' her. Just watch how he follows the run, eases her in around the sunkers!" Josh's voice is full of admiration.

The *Tern* is indeed a Gosse ship. Alex Brennan waves to them from the deck as she drops anchor just short of the wharf and drifts gently in.

"Grand little breeze out there, old man, almost as bad as St. John's harbour on a fine day." The Captain's round red face beams with good humour but his eyes, shrewd and intelligent, miss nothing. Alex Brennan has sailed Gosse vessels along this coast for twenty years and can recognize the signs of starvation on the faces looking up at him.

Knowing all the questions before they are asked, the Captain announces at once what his cargo is: salt and small gear ordered from Gosse last fall. He tells them the price per quintal the merchant settled on for last summer's catch, what disasters have befallen St. John's in the winter months, and how the Gosse business is faring.

"He's doin' good, boy. Got two more schooners like this, the *Charlotte Gosse* and the *Seahorse*, on order from a yard down in Boston."

Alex nods pleasantly to the women and begins to tell Sarah that he's recently spoken to one of her brothers. He is about to deliver personal messages he's picked up along the coast, but Thomas Hutchings edges him away from the others and in a low voice asks what food supplies he has on board.

"I kinda' noticed your family increased during the winter." The skipper grins, then, seeing Thomas' impatience, adds quickly, "Yes, yes boy, I got some. Two barrels of flour and a keg of molasses you can have. The Old Man don't have to hear tell of it, we'll get them back into ship's stores when your supplies arrive."

Soon as the words are spoken Thomas turns to the women who stand nearby, straining to hear and tells them, "Bread tonight—and molasses, too!" He even smiles. Lavinia records the smile in her journal that night.

Alex Brennan orders two of his men to unload the food, directing them to take one barrel of flour to the Vincent house and one up to the store.

"We'll have hot bread for you before you leaves," Sarah calls over her shoulder as she trots home behind the men carrying her flour.

The men and big boys heave to, giving the crew a hand to unload salt, grapnels, twine and rope. Seamen are great gossips and the *Tern* has put into three harbours between St. John's and the Cape. They have news of births, deaths, marriages and sickness all along the coast. They know how fishing stages have fared during winter storms, what the old people say the coming summer will be like, which ships are going to the Front and which men along the coast have berths aboard them.

Alex Brennan stands listening to all this for only a few minutes before asking Thomas if they can talk privately.

"So there is bad news," Thomas thinks. He leads the Captain up to the store, gesturing him to a corner as far away as possible from where Hazel Andrews lies, seemingly asleep, although she will later be able to tell Lavinia almost every word the two men say to each other.

"I suppose Gosse has decided he doesn't need a man on the Cape—God knows it's true, I haven't seen a thief, red or white, and it's been almost two years," Thomas says, wondering what he will do if he leaves the Cape, surprised to notice that he is trying to contrive reasons why he should stay.

But when Alex Brennan turns around he is smiling, "What gave you that notion? No, I'd say now Caleb Gosse knows he got a good thing goin' here—he got better fish made here last year than he ever did before—more of it, too. No, 'tisn't that. Truth is, Thomas, I got something else for you on the *Tern*, another bundle." His smile is so broad that his little eyes have disappeared completely into the rolls of his cheeks.

"I got a bundle for ya on the *Tern*," he repeats, laughs out loud and slaps his knee, delighted at the look of mystification on Thomas's face.

"Ah, that's good, that is—another bundle, just what ya needs Thomas—a mysterious bundle ya might be sayin'."

"Alex, what in God's name are you talking about?" Thomas Hutchings leans forward to look into the face of the man who is now bent almost double, carried away by his own humour.

Seeing Thomas's concern, Alex straightens, wipes his eyes and tries to speak without laughing.

"Well, like I was sayin', we're on our way north for the summer, so we took on this woman, girl I s'pose, for cook. Signed her indirect like when the hand we had doin' the cookin' was took sick. A youngster—Tim Toop they calls him, 'tho the Lord knows what his real name is—runs messages for the Gosses. Anyway, Tim said he knew a good cook and fixed us up. She come aboard the day we sailed, looked small and a bit scrawny, but we paid her no mind, was busy loadin' and such. We got a decent supper, potatoes that weren't burnt and a good bit of fish, that's all we cared... ."

Thomas, realizing that this long-winded tale is not a message from his employer, is nodding in an absent-minded kind of way, his hands folded in front of him. It is an attitude Alex Brennan has noted before and it disquiets him. He skips quickly to the end of his story.

"Seems one of the bundles this cook brought aboard was a baby. Now she says the child is sick and she don't want to take it up the coast. She, her name's Mary, and all hands have started callin' her Mary Bundle, see? For a joke. She wants me ta drop her off here."

Suddenly Thomas Hutchings' attention is focused. "Good Lord, man, what will she do here? I've already got starving people without roofs over their heads, what do I want more for—and a sick child!"

"I told her she'd be better off stayin' on the *Tern* until she could get someone sailing back into St. John's. Comes to that I don't mind keepin' her aboard, there's not a squeak out of her or the baby—but I'm beginning to think there's reasons she don't want to go back—I wouldn't wonder either, nasty place for a woman by herself, St. John's is. I'm only guessin' about this, mind. She's close, hardly says a word to any of us. She's young, only sixteen or seventeen I'd say, but she works like a little dog."

Alex gives Thomas a poke in the shoulder. Another man would have received a hefty punch but something about Thomas Hutchings subdues the good-natured Irishman, makes him try to control his gestures and his laughter. Still, he cannot resist saying, "Maybe you do be needin' a woman yourself, Thomas?"

There is no responding smile. "That's unlikely. No, Alex, I can't see it. The Vincents certainly can't take on another mouth to feed, and I'm not going to accommodate anyone else in the store once I get shift of this lot."

"Fair enough. I'll tell her but that's about all I can do. She's comin' ashore anyway, she wants to ask the women about the baby. I expect she don't have too much experience herself, poor little sod."

Alex nods towards the pallet half hidden by the ramshackle arrangement of ropes and canvas: "Ye crowd got someone sick already by the looks of it."

"Hazel Andrews, the wife of Ned. He's the youngest brother. You saw him down on the wharf, the fellow with the fuzzy hair and beard and the big grin. Apart from the other daughter-in-law Meg, none of the Andrews crowd have much brains but Ned is worst of all, acts simple-minded sometimes. He fools around, dancing and singing like he's not got a care in the world and here his wife's been abed ever since they got off the boat. I'm starting to think she's never going to get up. Only a young woman and with two little children."

"Can't anything be done for her?"

"Sarah Vincent and the old woman Andrews, the brothers' mother, do the best they can. Yesterday they boiled down seaweed and tried to get her to take some—still—I don't know, I can't be worried about that."

Thomas changes the subject then, telling the Captain he'll not have to drop off landsmen on the Cape this summer. "I'm determined the Andrews lot will earn their keep, so we'll have enough hands on our own...." The men leave the shed, still talking in low voices.

The supplies are now ashore. The crew of the *Tern* stand chatting with Josh and the Andrews men.

"My sons, there's fortunes bein' made off we'um fishermen! Fortunes! Look at Caleb Gosse, him buying this vessel and two others in the same year," one hand was saying as Thomas and Alex came within earshot.

"Aye, and that's not the half of it." A seaman with a monkey face spits a great glob of tobacco juice over the edge of the wharf. "Not the half of it! Word's goin' 'round St. John's that Gosse do be buildin' a mansion in England—him what's got one of the best houses in town already, stone, it is, and he got premises down by the harbour, horses, a carriage and everything, accordin' to."

"The wife's cousin keeps Gosse's horses, he heard tell Gosse got a brother in government in England," another says and his mates nod sagely, agreeing there's money to be made out of fish.

"...so long's you're not a fisherman," monkey face says, and laughs.

Alex Brennan will not condone this kind of careless talk among his men. "Go on, Sam Billard, we all makes money outta fish—and if Caleb Gosse makes a bit more then it's only right. After all it's his vessels we're fishin' out of. What odds to ye what a gentleman makes? Now, get them supplies up to the fish store—and don't leave the jeezely door open, there's a sick woman in there."

The wind is moderating, and Alex calculates they will have no trouble getting off the Cape. "The hands haven't eaten—we might just as well have a hot meal ashore before castin' off," he says and looks around the wharf for Mary Bundle.

There is no sign of the woman and he guesses she is hoping to come ashore unnoticed. If so, it shows she knows nothing about these outports. He nods to Thomas and goes on board the *Tern* to find the cook.

The Captain goes below to the galley where Mary Bundle has been sleeping as well as working since they left St. John's. And there she is, sitting gypsy-like on the floor with everything she owns, including the baby, spread out in front of her. Startled by his arrival, she throws a grimy cloth over the strange collection. Then, as though thinking her impulsive action cowardly, the girl pulls the cloth away, sits back on her heels and watches as he stands at the foot of the ladder looking over her pile of belongings.

"A pitiful sight," Alex Brennan, a soft hearted man, tells his wife later. He cannot know that the pathetic waif before him has three stolen gold pieces sewed securely into her shift just between her small breasts.

"She had everything laid out like she was countin' it. The poor bawlin' baby, a pile of flannel rags, for the baby I s'pose, a dented kettle, a pair of boots, a flint box, a pretty little pin, two knives, a knitted scarf and an orange—I don't know where she got that—I haven't seen one in St. John's for nine month—oh yes, and two cakes of hard tack I daresay she lifted outta ship's stores. That was it, everything she owned in the world."

None of Alex Brennan's pity shows on his face. He scowls at Mary Bundle and nudges the kettle with the toe of his boot.

"Get this lot away, then, and stick the child somewhere. The men are half-starved. Come on, woman, let's get fed and off this Godforsaken sand-bar before daylight's gone. We'll take stuff ashore, you can cook us a hot meal in Thomas Hutchings' store."

Alex pulls a bag of vegetables from the shelf, picks up a hunk of pork and some salt fish and starts back up the ladder. The girl scrambles to her feet, knots the grizzly tablecloth around her belongings, rolls the still crying baby into a rough brown blanket, and snatches up the largest pot in sight before following him up the hatch and across the deck.

"...Thomas Hutchings tells me he don't want you here. Says there's no place for you to sleep and no way for a woman to get by on the Cape."

Alex does not look around as he says this, and so misses the quick backward tilt of Mary Bundle's head, a movement that brings her pointed chin jutting out. It is a gesture of defiance and determination, one that people on the Cape will come to recognize.

They all share the meal, a combination of vegetables, salt pork and fish boiled together in the big boat kettle. After eating, the seamen sit around. Having pulled off their boots and hung their heavy wool socks beside the hearth to dry, they look as if they might stay there forever, leaning back against the wall with their bare feet stretched across the floor towards the fire. Thomas Hutchings is there too, puffing on his pipe, enjoying the feeling of being full and the talk of politics, ships and fishing.

Josh Vincent, along with Ben and Ned Andrews, has returned to wood-cutting, and the women are down in Vincent's kitchen making bread, but the children stay, perched sparrow-like on top of barrels and boxes, eyes and ears open wide, not making a sound.

Lavinia is sitting in her usual place, listening to her sister-in-law, who seems to want to talk. Hazel has a fever, probably brought on by the noise and the unaccustomed smells. Lavinia holds a damp cloth to the sick woman's hot forehead but she is watching Mary Bundle.

Mary Bundle has not spoken a word. She packs leftover food and tin plates into the ship's pot, seeming intent on her job, never looking at the men, or even at her baby who is asleep on a pile of nets nearby. Lavinia wonders if the young woman is mute.

The fish store, with its one small window, is almost dark, pleasantly dim and hazy with the smell of tobacco. The voices of Thomas and Alex continue in a low drone. Occasionally one of the hands says something. The men would like to stay the night. The watching children are still. Hazel's disjointed words come more and more slowly, her eyes close and Lavinia sees that she is asleep.

Mary Bundle picks up the big kettle and pads towards the door. Nothing the woman does makes a sound. It is then, scrutinizing the dark, bony face in the shadows that the word 'savage' comes to Lavinia.

Eventually Alex heaves a long sigh, drains the last of his tea, and gets to his feet.

"That's it, lads! It's well past noon and I wants to be safe away from this Cape before dark. Come on, tea party's over, let's pull anchor." He clomps out, tipping his cap in Lavinia's direction as he passes the bed.

One by one, groaning, the men stand, haul on socks and boots, and follow. The children, as if released from a spell, hop down from their perches and trail behind. Lavinia sees that the baby is still sleeping in the corner, but she says nothing.

Down on the wharf there is a flurry of activity, the clamour that is part of the ritual of weighing anchor. It has turned into a beautiful day, cold and crisp. The water, so dark this morning, is now sparkling blue under a blue sky. The wind has changed and blown most of the ice offshore, the few remaining pans float like crystal plates on the smooth sea.

With the lines slipped and the sails ready for hoisting, the men call out last minute messages to each other. Sarah Vincent rushes down from her house holding a cloth bag of still-hot bread. She passes the bread up the side to Alex Brennan. in exchange he tosses down a pickled leg of pork.

"For yer suppers. Thanks for the loaf," he waves to the people on the wharf, and the *Tern* moves slowly away from the stagehead.

"See ye on the way back," Sarah calls, looking years younger than she had that morning. "That's a wonderful man. A real Christian for all he's one of them papists," she tells Meg and Jennie.

They watch the sails snap out, cream coloured now in the afternoon sun. Up on the hill the sounds of chopping stop as the men, too, watch the *Tern* come around, catch the breeze and move majestically out past the rocks. It is almost an hour before she disappears between blue sky and blue sea.

Another hour passes before Mary Bundle comes, silent as a cat, into the store and picks up her baby from the pile of nets. She goes over to Lavinia and holds out an orange. She does not speak and there is no smile on the sharp little face. She just stands there, small and so unmoving that, despite her thinness, she seems sturdy. The bright fruit glows in the gloom of the shed.

It is the first orange Lavinia has seen since leaving Weymouth. She would like to have it just to look at but already saliva is running down her chin. She takes the orange, peels it very carefully, dropping the rind into her pocket to grind up with tea or to rub on her hands. She sections the fruit, takes one small piece for herself, gives a piece to Mary Bundle who has been watching, and slowly feeds the rest to Hazel.

Another hour passes. It is almost dark when Sarah discovers Young Joe is missing. No one has seen him since the *Tern* left. After a search of the places he might hide they conclude he has stowed away aboard the *Tern*.

His mother, she who had made not a sound during childbirth, wails aloud: "...he'll drown, never be heard of again! Half them youngsters goin' down on the Labrador drown or get stolen by Eskimos!"

Jennie and Meg hover. Meg reminds her that Joe is, after all thirteen and a sensible lad who will not go near the water. Jennie asks what Eskimos would want stealing white people's children, don't they know how to make their own?

Sarah is finally pacified by Thomas: "If Young Joe had to go to sea he couldn't have picked a better skipper than Alex Brennan—like you said this evening, he's a good, decent man."

Josh agrees, "The boy will be back in a few months and all the better for it. He'll know how hard life is on the sea and stop hankering after every ship that passes."

Sarah sensibly dries her eyes, allows they are probably right and tells Mary Bundle she can sleep up aloft in Young Joe's bed until the boy comes home. No one else, except Lavinia, seems to have taken any notice of the young woman, who had been standing back, quietly waiting for Thomas to say what was to be done about her.

That night even Sarah seems replete and tranquil. Ned brings Hazel over to the fire. There is a faint tinge of pink in her cheeks and she reaches out to touch the faces of Jane and Isaac before the children go to their beds. Thomas Hutchings has withdrawn to his desk where he sits writing. One by one the others leave the fire but Ned sits on, holding the blanket-wrapped woman in his arms like a child.

Nearby Lavinia lies awake, brooding on the things Hazel had heard Thomas Hutchings tell Alex about the Andrews family and listening to the wind which tonight seems faint and far off.

Then, below the sounds of sleeping children, below the scratch of Thomas Hutchings' pen, Lavinia hears Hazel whisper, "I'm so sorry, Ned—sorry to be so much trouble to you—to everyone...."

Then the sharp intake of her brother's breath, "Hazel, you're no trouble. Hazel—love—don't leave us...."

Lavinia cannot believe the voice is Ned's. It is the voice of a man who has seen a knife go into his chest and knows he must die.

She rolls into her blankets, holds her hands over her ears to shut out the private words. She says a prayer for Hazel, then one for Young Joe. Trying to sleep, she lists the names of every soul on the Cape. One gone and two added makes twenty-one people. She finds herself again thinking about Mary Bundle, wondering if they might be friends.

Then she sleeps, and there is silence except for the soft fingers of wind feeling their way around the walls of the fishing room and, far out in the Cape, the low grinding of ice as the pans nudge each other landwards. Everyone sleeps, even the man and woman in front of the dying fire.

In the morning, Hazel is dead. Ned takes the weeping children down to the Vincent kitchen. Thomas and Ben go to make a grave. Jennie, Meg and Lavinia are left to wash Hazel and dress her in the red tartan she had been married in.

It is the first time Lavinia has touched a dead body. She marvels at the difference death makes to human flesh. She remembers Hazel well and happy, how she used to watch for Ned from the window on Monk Street, her face bright with expectation as he kicked the door open, flung his canvas bag onto the floor and rushed towards her.

Lavinia tries to hold this picture in her mind as they wash Hazel's poor body, tie a strip of cloth under her chin and pat oil on the sores for the last time. The red dress is now far too big and Meg must sew it into place at the back.

When Hazel is dressed and laid out, the women seat themselves stiffly in a circle around the body. Sarah Vincent and Mary Bundle come, both holding babies under their shawls, and sit beside the Andrews women. Lizzie is there, too, but she keeps to one side, almost behind Meg. After a few minutes Annie Vincent slips in the door and comes to sit by Lizzie. Despite the fact that they are seated on woodhorses, boxes and puncheons, there is a strange formality to the gathering. Each woman in turn recalls a kindly memory of Hazel: her love of babies and small children, her patience in the face of pain, how she could sew such small neat stitches, how she loved Ned and his stories. Only Mary Bundle, having barely glimpsed the dead woman, has no contribution.

Afterwards the children come in, and the men, who wrap Hazel in canvas and tie the body onto a plank. They carry her up to the point, to a hole the men have taken all morning to dig in the frozen ground.

Lavinia wonders, as in later years others will wonder, why the graveyard (for that is what it will become) has been placed out on this finger of the Cape most exposed to sea and sky. She will come to know that on this coast all things— houses, faces and graves—look out to the sea.

The wind cuts in, whipping clothing and drowning the few words Thomas Hutchings reads from one of his books. Meg asks that they sing one hymn and leads out. One by one the others join in:

> Unto the hills around do I lift up my longing eyes,
> From whence for me shall my salvation come,
> From whence arise.

The words, faint and thin as smoke, are pulled away by the wind.

Isaac and Jane begin to wail as their mother's body is lowered into the ground. The women pull the children back and down the side of the point, across the beach and up to the Vincent's kitchen before the men begin to shovel lumps of frozen gravel onto the pitiful shape.

Lavinia turns away then. She goes down to the empty fish store, rolls up the last blood-stained blanket, the moss and the boughs that made the bed where Hazel has lain dying all these months. Stuffing blanket and boughs into the fireplace she stands watching for a few minutes as they burn. She hauls the canvas from the rafters and with a brush scrubs at the large dark stain in the wooden floor. She cannot remove the rust-coloured mark and finally pulls the big splitting table they eat from over the place where Hazel's bed has been.

When Lavinia is finished there is no sign of the dead woman. From this day Hazel's name will rarely be mentioned. Her children will forget her. After a year or so the words, which Ned will cut tomorrow on a wooden marker, will disappear, the marker will crack, fall over and blow out to sea. But by then there will be other graves on the point.

Chapter 4

Will spring ever come to this God-forsaken place? Week after week ice mountains float past. Sometimes one stops and sits for days watching us before moving on.

During April and May, people disappear from Lavinia's journal. She forgets to write about her own family, about the Vincents or Mary Bundle, even about Thomas Hutchings. She becomes so occupied with the barrens, the beach, the sea—always the sea—that it seems she is living alone on the desolate coast.

That year hundreds of icebergs drift down from the Arctic Ocean. Day and night they glide slowly, silently past the Cape like ghosts of lost cathedrals. In their perpendicular walls great fissures appear, jagged windows through which an eerie blue-green light glows. Sometimes, as Lavinia has written, one is grounded, hovering against the sky until some convolution of wind, wave or whale loosens it. Then it moves majestically on, disappearing at the rim of the world.

The bay fills with flannel fog that comes creeping up onto the Cape, curling down into hollows, covering rocks, hills, house, fish room, covering everything in a moving, drifting shroud. Outside, one must feel one's way about, voices rise hollow and disembodied out of the muffling stillness.

It freezes one day, rains the next. But the knife sharp cold of February is gone and Lavinia abandons the store, leaving the cooking, the cleaning, all the griefs of women, to her mother and Meg.

Sometime during the bleak winter months Lavinia noted that her menstruation period had stopped. She had been glad—less blood, less chance of embarrassment in the terrible intimacy of the store. Now as she shuts winter away, along with her preoccupation with death, starvation and freezing, her body and mind, in complete accord, appear to reverse the aging process and make her once more a child.

She joins Ben's and Meg's daughters, Lizzie, Emma and Patience, who together with Ned's Jane are still playing dress-up with the moth-eaten garments brought in barrels from Weymouth. On decent mornings Lavinia and her nieces leave the store, troop down to the Vincent house where they are joined by Annie and Peter. Then, with Lavinia in the lead, they trail off along the long beach. A strange procession the Andrews girls make, in their multi-coloured garments tied around with bits of fraying cord. Beside them the Vincent children in decent sheep's wool sweaters, caps and cuffs, look like sparrows that have joined an exotic flock.

Each morning the children search the beach for driftwood, feathers, shells, smooth stones, star fish, and the bleached bones of small creatures washed up by the sea. This occupation, which can take hours, sometimes brings strange rewards. Once the sea cast up a round stone with the face of a woman cut into its surface. Another time they discovered the sea-washed jaw bone and teeth of some huge animal the children agreed must have been larger than a horse. Once they found a square, oilcloth-wrapped and tightly tied package, which, when opened, revealed a pristine set of playing cards. They took the cards to Meg Andrews. She had instantly and ceremoniously tossed them into the fire with the chant:

> Cards and dice are the devil's device
> God's desire is to put 'em in the fire.

After that dismaying experience the children agreed they would show nothing else to grown-ups but keep their finds hidden in the dunes above the beach.

One day when playing in the small grove of scrawny trees they called the woods, the children come out by chance on a ridge, a black outcropping of rock that rises sharply behind the Cape, and find themselves looking directly down on the tiny community where they live. Seeing it from above, realizing how precariously it hangs on the edge of rocks and sand, all laughter and talking stop. It is near noon, a grey day filled with mist and little swirls of fog left behind by the pillar of cloud hovering now just outside the Cape. Below is the fish store, the wharf, the Vincents' house and the faint web of pathways woven between. All now strangely unfamiliar, all completely empty.

Into the mind of each child the same thought creeps: "The grown-ups have gone." They have been left behind, alone.

Patience begins to whimper, "Where's Mam, where's mam...." She tugs at the garish scarf tied around Lavinia's waist but her aunt, caught in the same nightmare, whispers, "Hush!" and they were all still again.

Down the curve of beach stretching away to their left, breakers roll sluggishly in and out. Footprints made this morning have already vanished as though they had never been. Directly below, the flimsy buildings are as insubstantial as mist and seem to move slightly each time the sea breathes beneath them.

Something is down there, crouched below the flakes or flattened against the far side of the big rock. Whatever it is knows they are up here looking down. The creature is not afraid, it hides only to work out some terrible secret plan. Where are the adults?

The children stand for long minutes, still, silent, watching, waiting. Each holds a delicious rock of fear, a feeling almost sexual, that only children know.

Lizzie breaks the spell. She snatches Patience up, turns and with a loud whoop races for the safety of the trees. The others follow, making as much noise as possible but sure that if they turn or look back they will see the dreadful thing watching them. In the enclosed dimness of the woods, the thin trees protective around them, they fall on the moss in a heap and lie laughing foolishly.

Only Patience still shivers and weeps, "That was a bogey man, a big bogey man."

The others laugh and Peter calls her a sook. But they all know she's right.

Late in April, the children find that one of the sandy hills above the beach is really a hollow bowl containing the remains of old fires. Scattered around are bits of charred bone, half-burned driftwood, a thousand shards of shiny black flint, some clearly shaped into arrowheads. Rose bushes, now brown and brittle, grow in a wild tangle around the rim so that a person might pass within feet of the depression and not see the hideaway or even dream of its existence. Down in the hollow, hidden, sheltered from wind and sea, the children feel safe.

They call this protected spot "the place" and scoop shallow shelves along the sides to hold things found on the beach. They eat there, sharing the contents of their pockets—slices of turnip, hunks of dry bread or hard tack, scraps of roasted fish, lumps of frankum gouged from the trees, rose hips and winter shrivelled berries. Later they will roast caplin here, chew the tasteless orange-red cracker berries, eat early spring fern, and sorrel which they call Sally Suckers. The children will eat anything, even sea rocket, which grows on the beach and is pepper hot.

On days when the sun has warmed the sand they lie like the spokes of a wheel, feet together, backs along the sides of the depression, half-dozing while Lavinia spins out a story about a race of giants who one time danced around this very fire, carved arrowheads and cooked huge animals that have now vanished from the Cape.

They grow more confident and begin to light fires inside the circle of black stones. Sometimes they roast fish and toast bread. One day Peter Vincent brings a scrap of torn sail to the hideaway and on one side rigs a kind of awning that gives shelter to crowd beneath on wet days.

Of the adults only Thomas Hutchings, who had discovered the ancient fire during his first lonely months on the Cape, knows of the hollow and is aware that the children have claimed it as their own. He makes this discovery one warm day in early spring when he goes there to brood, away from the clamour of the store.

Pushing aside the bushes he is suddenly, coldly afraid. Someone has been here. He stares down. Something red as blood is spilled across the circle of blackened stones. For a terrible instant Thomas thinks he has come upon the remains of a primitive sacrifice. Then he blinks, sees that he is looking at the old velvet cape the Andrews girls play with, notices the piles of shells, the feathers and driftwood and realizes that the children have taken over his retreat.

Thomas never mentions the hollow hill to anyone but when he sees the place again, many years later, he will remember the cold terror of that long ago morning and wonder if he had been forewarned.

Each day, from the door of the Vincents' house, Mary Bundle watches the children race across the beach, sees them disappear over the crest of the hill and longs to go with them. She cannot understand Annie Vincent who is only twelve but often as not tells Lavinia, "I can't come out today, girl, Mam needs me to mind the baby."

Gladly would Mary have tied her tiny daughter to her back and run after the others. But she knows that what is acceptable behaviour for Lavinia Andrews will not do for her. In Mary's eyes Lavinia, with brothers to provide for her and a mother to pamper her, is safe and secure. Whereas she, without friends or family, must be inconspicuous and useful. In the Vincent household she turns her hand to whatever job needs doing to earn her keep and Fanny's until they have to move on. She is sure it will only be a matter of months until, through some turn of fate, she will leave the Cape just as she has left so many places in her short life.

Mary has a simple creed: "The thing is, I got to leave a place better off than I come—or no worse off anyway." She mutters it to herself each day and keeps a sharp lookout for a chance to add to her collection of belongings.

She sleeps with the Vincent children in the back half of the loft, on Young Joe's bed which is a kind of shelf built against the sloping roof. Although her back is usually cold at night, although there is no safe place there to count her hidden possessions, she likes sleeping in the loft. She cuddles Fanny's little body into hers and the roof slopes protectively down over their heads. She hopes Young Joe will never come back from the Labrador.

Mary wonders at first why Sarah Vincent makes her uneasy. Sarah is kind, cheerful too, despite her prophecies of doom, and Mary is not timid. Dozens of small cloth bags containing dried kelp, seeds, crumbled petals and rose hips, hang around the Vincent fire. Bunches of wild flowers, wintergreen and savory, baskets of moss and bits of twisted root hang from beams. Mary wonders if Sarah is a witch. She has some knowledge of witches; her own mother, she believes, had been one. "Much good it did her," Mary thinks, keeping a sharp look-out for unnatural qualities in Sarah.

One day Sarah even said, "I'm a witch, you know, all the Loveys women are witches, me mother was a witch before me—and Nan, too." Sarah was mixing paste for toothache at the time. She chuckled, but Mary knew she meant it. She goes to great pains to keep on the good side of Sarah, always avoiding looking her in the eye.

Mary is greatly attracted to Josh Vincent, for all he is, by her estimation, old. She likes his soft hesitant voice, and how, when he cannot avoid speaking to her, his mild blue eyes slide off her face and gaze absently past her shoulder.

Most of all she admires the way Josh gathers things. He never comes through the door without an armload of splits, a bucket of water, a bit of driftwood, a fish or seabird. Josh Vincent is the first man Mary has ever seen caring for his family and it wakes in her a longing to be cared for that is stronger than any desire she has ever felt.

"Josh is the kind of man I'd like to have," Mary thinks and looks quickly at Sarah, fearful that she's been caught coveting the witch's husband.

But Sarah, hoisting a kettle of water onto the hob, is talking, as she does by the hour, about Young Joe, predicting that he'll come home half-frozen, maimed, starved or married to one of those heathen Eskimo women, who are, according to Sarah, no better than they should be with men who fish off the Labrador during the summer.

Sarah talks most of the time, never seeming to mind when there is no response. Mary reckons this is because living with Josh has taught her not to expect conversation.

Despite believing she is a witch, Mary likes Sarah and, in a strange way, trusts her. Sarah, for her part, treats Mary as another daughter, very like Annie but quieter and even more biddable.

Imperceptibly the days lengthen, and frost begins to leave the ground. Although there are no leaves yet, there are buds and a smell of new green in the woods. The men now work outdoors from dawn to dark. They cruise good wood, cut during the winter miles back from the Cape, down the coast and begin to stud up a house for the Andrews family.

Thomas Hutchings has ordained that the house must be closed in before the fish come. A garden must be cleared too, more wood cut, repairs made to the wharf, boats caulked, and nets mended and barked. There are not enough hands to go around and any child venturing within shouting distance of an adult will immediately be given a job. Even a small child can fill a brin bag with wood chips, hold a tool, pass nails, gather grils from the beach, watch the fire or keep an eye on one of the babies.

During this time two more vessels arrive. Josh's brother, Ezra Vincent, brings three goats down from Pond Island in his skiff. The *Molly Rose* from Carbonear puts in out of a storm and the schooner *Drake* from St. John's drops anchor in the lee of the Cape. The *Drake* is a big vessel, and must heave-to offshore, but the Captain and several hands come ashore in a dory.

The ships bring news of the world outside. England has had the worst winter in living memory. There is talk of another treaty with the French. A dissident preacher is working his way down the coast, and Ezra says the crowd in Pond Island are not going to let him ashore. In St. John's the government's bankrupting itself, bringing stone-masons out from England to build a big place for the new governor. They have a price fixed on the head of Red Indians now, they'll give five pounds to any man who can bring one in alive. These things are subjects for conversation and endless speculation long after the vessels have gone.

When the *Charlotte Gosse* arrives carrying the remainder of their summer gear and provisions, including more salt, Lavinia overhears Thomas Hutchings tell the Captain to bring a load of fish back to the Cape to be made. Later she asks Sarah Vincent what this means.

"Makin' fish, maid, is—well, it's makin' fish." Sarah shakes her head, at a loss to describe something that even the smallest child along the coast knows.

"'Tis splittin' it, guttin' it, saltin' it—makin' fish is what we does when the men is out fishin'. Now, last summer Gosse had two hands here helpin' make fish—but this year with all ye crowd we can make our own and more. That's why Thomas is tryin' to get extra fish for us—if we can make more fish we'll have more credit with Gosse for gear and winter supplies."

In the short time before the fish are expected to strike in, the women begin to clear a place to grow potatoes. Meg and Jennie Andrews, along with Sarah and Annie Vincent and Mary Bundle, spend the best part of each day working in the spot where Josh cut last year's firewood. It is a narrow, fairly flat strip of rocky soil between the wooded area and the outcropping—the place from which the children had looked down at the empty Cape and been so afraid. Not a promising location for a garden, but almost the only one possible in a land newly emerged from eons beneath glaciers.

The women have established a routine from which they seldom vary. Each morning, when the most necessary household chores are done, the babies fed, the day's water hauled from the pond, the pot of salt fish set to simmer over the banked fire, they pack Sarah's wooden chest.

This container, half the size of a coffin, a seaman's trunk for generations of Gill men, was taken by Sarah as a blanket box when she left Pinchards Island to marry Josh. Into the bottom of this chest the women fold a thick quilt, on top of which they put an iron pot filled with hot coals, a kettle, food, extra clothing and whatever else they can fit in.

They have scrounged an unlikely collection of tools, things the men can spare from more important work: a blunt axe, a pick, the long iron rod Josh found tangled in his net last summer, a shovel, a length of rope and several brin bags. Meg carries as many tools as she can, Jennie and Mary carry the chest between them by its rope handles, and Annie trails behind with a baby in each arm. Meg's two-year-old Willie usually runs ahead of the women, who make slow progress up the twisting path to the clearing.

Upon reaching what they already call the garden—although it is nothing but rocks and tree stumps—they start a fire with the hot coals, piling on blasty boughs until it crackles and sends a shimmer of heat up into the cool morning air. They wrap Mary's baby Fanny and Charlie Vincent in warmed quilts and lay them toe to toe inside the now empty sea chest. The women take great satisfaction in this efficient arrangement, which was worked out by Mary Bundle.

"For all Mary's quiet, she's not stunned. She got some good head for figurin' things out," Mary heard Sarah tell Meg Andrews one day. The description pleases Mary, who takes pride in her ability to figure things out—a skill she has noticed most people lack.

Work in the garden is back-breaking. Hour after hour the women pry rocks up out of the hard earth and carry them to a loose stone wall they are building between the garden and the cliff edge. Sarah, the only one with any experience at growing things, says that the coldest winds come in from the sea, that if they lay their garden crosswise between the line of trees and the rock wall it will be protected. The women often have to tie a rope around the larger boulders and, using the iron rod as a lever, push and pull until they come loose. Then they roll and drag the big rocks over to the pile they hope will become a wall. Sometimes it takes most of a day to move just one rock. Two rocks withstand their best efforts and finally, after days of sweat and strain, they conclude that these are the tip of the cliff that must lie just below the shallow soil.

The women pile roots and underbrush onto the fire that grows as the day progresses. Their faces become ingrained with smoke and soot, their fingernails tear and split, blisters rise, break and bleed until their hands grow as hard and calloused as the men's. During the first weeks arms and shoulders pain constantly. Jennie has to sit sometimes, resting her head on her knees, waiting for the pounding behind her eyes to pass.

When the sun sinks to the tops of the spruce trees, they stop work. Gathering up tools and children, they trudge home to get supper before the men return. The women are bone weary. The sea chest, heavy as lead, bumps against their legs. Willie cries to be carried and they move stiffly back through the last light, walking on their own long shadows that proceed them down the steep path.

For all that, the women love working on the garden. It is exhilarating to be outside, to smell the earth, to feel the air on your face and the warmth of sun between your shoulder blades. At midday they always take a spell, sit on the ground eating bread with cups of black tea and the salt fish that has been roasting all morning on flat stones near the fire. Taking time to look around at what they have done, they talk quietly, become female again, tidying their hair, rubbing aching limbs. Mary and Sarah nurse their babies.

Sitting by the fire with the smell of burning boughs, tea and roasted fish filling the air, with the babies fed and quiet, with Willie curled in his grandmother's lap, with winter over and gone and their garden coming to shape around them, they talk, get to know each other, begin to love each other.

Jennie speaks of the flat on Monk Street, of Mrs. Thorp's bread and pie shop, of the cart and of old Bones, the horse. She says nothing of why they left these things to come to the Cape.

Sarah tells about her grandmother Loveys, who was the first woman along the coast.

"Borned three children, Nan did, without another woman to help her. Saw two of them die, one soon as it was born and one scalded to death when it was three. Mother were the oldest and she said Nan was never the same after. Had it hard, poor mortals. Sometimes no one even knew they was here—and sometimes they didn't want anyone to know—they was that scared of being caught and dragged back to England for something they done. Me own grandfather jumped ship from an English man o' war. He'd been pressed, so the first time they come ashore to take on water he ran off. The boys was half-starved and beat for the least thing. He had no use for the navy, or for the English come to that."

Sarah shakes her head. "'Tis only the last few year it's been fit to live along this coast. We got things easy now compared to them times."

During these exchanges Mary Bundle sits rocking Fanny and says not a word but she feels the contentment. There by the fire they all feel happy, satisfied that they are doing something worthwhile, something unlike cooking and cleaning: something that will last.

When they go back to the work, standing stiffly because their muscles hurt, Jennie Andrews often grumbles that Lavinia should be helping, "instead of gallivantin' with the young ones."

"Still and all, she takes the youngsters off our hands so's we only got Willie to keep an eye on," Meg always says. How would they talk, discuss women's problems, with young maids around? Having them there would spoil the lovely peace, the feeling of completeness.

Spring has separated the people on the Cape into three distinct groups. At night, bone tired, they come together only to eat supper and fall into bed. The long nights of story-telling have stopped for the present.

Only Ned's young son Isaac crosses from group to group. After seeing his mother buried on the Cape, the child had cried for hours, a terrifying wail that had subsided into hacking sobs. Neither his grandmother nor Meg, who had cared for him during Hazel's illness, could pacify the four-year-old. Very late that night Isaac fell asleep in his father's arms. Ned sat all night holding his son, just as he had held his wife the night before, rocking the boy gently each time he began to weep.

The next morning when Ned left the store Isaac screeched and held his breath until he turned blue. In desperation, Meg bundled him up and went after the men. Since then, Isaac has not let his father out of his sight. Now the boy dresses himself, eats breakfast with the men and goes wherever Ned goes. A small red-headed shadow of his father, he walks with his hands in his pockets and adopts Ned's rolling gait.

"The young one'll take up the pipe before he's five," Ned says proudly.

It never occurs to the men that they have to mind the boy. They send him to fetch water, carry tools and do other small jobs. Only at night when Ned is in the room will Isaac go to his aunt or grandmother or play with another child.

Isaac's becoming helper to the men is deeply resented by nine-year-old Peter Vincent. A puny, sour looking child, Peter, in Young Joe's absence, has become the oldest boy in the place.

Lavinia, whose journal has quickly lost its Biblical overtones, writes of Peter: "The child's a pure imp through and through—carries trouble with him so's there's always someone bawling when he's about."

Then, out of the mist, caplin come rolling up onto the beach. Great living waves of silver that leave a spongy carpet of eggs on the sand. At first the youngsters are beside themselves with excitement. Screaming, they scravel to catch the cold, wriggling bodies in their hands, flinging the tiny fish at each other, tossing them into baskets and pots, pulling them out of their boots. Lavinia, barefooted with her skirt hitched up around her waist, is like a child.

Dancing into and out of the icy water, snatching the darting creatures that swim in their hundreds around her feet, she is happy for the first time since leaving Weymouth.

"So," she thinks, "one thing, at least, Ned told us was true!"

Soon, though, they grow very tired of caplin. Caplin are everywhere, frying in pans, hanging on lines to dry, smoking around the fire, spread on rocks, on flakes, salted down in barrels, packed in bait boxes, and, most hateful, hauled in slimy buckets up to the garden and left to rot into the thin soil. The very air smells of caplin, their skin and hair reeks of caplin, and everything they eat tastes like caplin.

The walls of the new house are up. A rough chimney, cobbled together of stone and clay, is just finished when the cod come. The men pull canvas over the unfinished roof and nail it to the rafters. It takes just one or two trips, everyone carrying armloads of clothing, bedding, pots, a picture or a dish, for the Andrews families to move in. Their only furniture is a table and two long benches made by the men during the winter. By dark they are in their new home: one room, without inside walls, without windows, without a sleeping loft, but the women are delighted to be under their own roof, even one made of canvas.

Ned swings up onto a rafter and announces grandly that the place will be called 'Andrews House.' In a long, flowery and Lavinia thinks, embarrassing speech, he thanks Thomas Hutchings and the Vincents for their hospitality to "us poor homeless strays washed up by fate on the Cape."

Meg passes around tea and raisin buns. The men eye the walls with satisfaction, hit their hands against the roughly sawn planks to show how solid the house is, and talk of what still needs finishing. Before winter they will chinse the cracks, board up inside walls and fill the space between with dry grils, maybe put up inside partitions and build a few shelves—they are full of confidence. The women smile at each other, and the children, their faces flushed with excitement, play hide and seek between the boxes and barrels. The warm and moonlit night comes softly through the open door, smelling of earth and woods and summer. Down on the shore the sea laps gently on the sand and the encompassing blackness seems safe, even protective.

Meg asks Thomas Hutchings to say a prayer for the house. Lavinia, having forgotten it was Meg who used to coax Jennie into attending church, is surprised at this request. So, she notes, is Thomas Hutchings. Nevertheless he agrees and with good grace pronounces some strange, holy words over the house before they separate to sleep.

The next morning before light the men are on their way out to the fishing grounds. There are only two boats on the Cape. Josh Vincent owns a good-sized punt, a sweet boat built by him and his brothers, and Thomas a dory which was stowed under the fish store when he arrived. The dory is cranky, as Josh says, "whoever built her done a poor job of it. By rights she should be scuttled."

The previous summer, Josh had Young Joe fishing beside him in the punt. This year he suggests that Ned and Ben go shares: which means Isaac too must be accommodated in the small boat. The child takes up space that should be used for nets or bait, but good-natured Josh shows him how to keep out of the men's way by curling up aft.

Isaac turns out to be a better sailor than his Uncle Ben, who never fails to get sick during the first hour on the water. Ben's condition is made even worse when, on his first trip out, he discovers that, loaded with cod, the punt has only three inches of freeboard. Grim necessity and a need, very like Isaac's, to be near Ned, keeps the poor man clinging to the side of the heaving boat, trying to follow Josh's shouted orders without looking at either the dipping sky or rolling sea. The alternative, of focusing his eyes on the boatload of squirming, slippery fish, is only slightly more acceptable. Ben spends much of his time at sea gazing longingly towards his roofless house, wishing with all his heart he could be up there, shaping out a log or nailing down planks. To the surprise of everyone except his wife, Ben Andrews has turned into a skilful carpenter.

Thomas fishes alone from the dory. He is not a good fisherman and prefers it this way. Some days, though, he takes pity on Peter Vincent, who stands each morning, stiff and stubborn with hurt, watching as his father and the Andrews men, with Isaac in the boat, cast off. Thomas tells the boy to climb aboard, warning him sternly that he will have to keep the hooks baited.

In the garden, now a half-cleared triangle, the hastily planted potatoes are abandoned to their fate. Each day the men make three or four trips to the fishing ground along the shoals offshore and the women must spend every waking minute down on the flakes gutting and splitting fish. When the *Charlotte Gosse* comes in, there is even more work. Fish landed from the schooner has been just lightly salted. The women must finish curing it: spread it on the flakes each day, turn it, stack it, put it inside if it looks like rain or cover it with bark on clear nights to protect it from damp.

Jennie Andrews smiles now to think of herself asking to buy food from Thomas Hutchings. As she works, she thinks of what she has learned in the past eight months: how to clear rocks from ground, how to slide a knife through a cod, flicking its guts into the barrel at the end of the table, how much salt to spread on fish, when to turn them. She has learned that the food they will have next winter will depend upon these things, upon the credit they can build with Caleb Gosse, upon how much fish the men catch and how much the women make. It is a formula she now understands completely.

At fifty-two, Jennie is the oldest person on the Cape and although every bone in her body pains, although her hands crack and bleed and her legs swell so that she can no longer lace her boots, she works as hard as any of the women. Not only must the Andrews family earn food for the next winter, they must settle up for the food they ate last winter, for the gear Ned and Ben are using, for the salt. Even, God forbid, should Thomas Hutchings request it, pay for the use of the store and the flakes.

Lavinia, Lizzie and Annie, "the young maidens", Sarah calls them, take turns away from the flakes to haul water and cook for the men who have mug-ups between trips. They bring endless kettles of tea to the women, who drink it still half bent over the drying cod; by then it is painful to stand straight. They all work like beasts. Even the small girls, Jane, Patience and Emma, fetch and carry, tend babies, shoo goats away from the flakes, or stand with boughs waving at the hordes of flies that would make the precious fish maggoty with eggs. Day after day, the men heave fish up onto the wharf until every inch of flake is covered and the remaining cod must be spread out on rocks.

Not even in the long days of midsummer is there time to do everything. Thomas makes lighted torches soaked in cod oil, fixing them to the ends of the flake and they work on, far into the night, cutting, scooping, scraping, until they can no longer lift their arms. Some nights none of the adults go to bed, but drop, still wearing the gut-spattered, salt-encrusted clothing, wherever sleep overtakes them, waking a few hours later to begin again.

July and August blur into a haze of weariness. The women, who had become so close while clearing the garden, are silent, and when they do speak, are gruff, as if salt has laid a crust on their throats. There is no laughter, no easy talk. Words require energy they cannot spare. With their slow, deliberate movements, their red rimmed eyes, their hair caked with dirt, they look like trolls newly come into the light from some underground cave.

Days pass without husbands and wives exchanging a word, and mothers barely notice the existence of their children. One night Meg wakes, staring into the dark, her heart pounding. She cannot remember seeing Willie all day. She sits up and feels around. The child is not lying in his usual place beside her and Ben. Suddenly she is sure her son is drowned. She thinks how easily he could have slipped off the edge of the wharf or fallen between the cracks—disappeared. Who would notice? The sound of the sea would not change, the gulls would go on screeching, his mother would continue to spread fish as the little body was swept into the undertow and carried out to sea.

Meg's hands shake and she has to swallow the bile that rises in her mouth. She crawls about, finds one of the torches, lights it and looks around at her family, sleeping, just as they had in the fishing store, on boughs and quilts. She steps carefully between them, bending to hold the light near each face.

She finds her son, dirty-faced and smiling like a cherub. He is sound asleep, squashed between his sister Lizzie and his Aunt Lavinia. Meg straightens, tears of tiredness and relief spilling down her face.

Holding the flickering light higher, she studies her family, strewn like dead people about the floor. She notes the look of grey exhaustion on Jennie's face, the tight lines that never relax, even in sleep, around the mouths of the men. She remembers Hazel and wonders who will be next to die. Then she shakes herself. Pushing away the black despair, she lies down for the hour or so left until dawn. Before sleep overtakes her she whispers a prayer to the God who lived in the grey stone church in Weymouth—the God she hopes has kept track of them and still knows where they are.

The next day Meg knots a length of rope to the straps of Willie's overalls and ties the other end around her own waist. It is an awkward arrangement that annoys both the mother and child, but it gives Meg some peace of mind and it continues until summer is over.

One day late in August the *Tern* heaves into view. Josh Vincent, out in the skiff, sees her first but keeps on pulling his nets, only nodding when Ned and

Ben point to the vessel. By the time they get to the stagehead with their load she has dropped anchor.

Josh climbs up onto the wharf in time to see Sarah standing ramrod straight in the middle of the sea of split fish. She holds one hand over her mouth as Alex Brennan walks, with unusual slowness, across the flake towards her. There is no sign of Young Joe. Foreknowledge of what the skipper is about to say drops down on Josh.

Facing Sarah, Alex shifts his weight from foot to foot and studies his hands with grave thoughtfulness as if he has never seen them before.

Josh slides his arm around his wife and says stiffly, "Well man, out with it, whatever it is."

Alex shakes his head, "The boy's lost," he says quickly, knowing there is no easy way.

"It was a fortnight ago Tuesday. Your Joe and the other youngster we had aboard, Ted Fifield from up the shore, went out in the punt haulin' lines—well, the fog come down all of a sudden."

He stops, looks in despair from Josh to Sarah, to the others standing in a silent circle. No one speaks and he plunges on, finishing with one gulp of air, "...that's how 'twas. We never saw a sign of them after, kept our whistle blowing and a light fore and aft all night. The fog never lifted 'til morning, it were clear as a bell then but there wasn't no sight of the lads, or of the punt. We come 'round and brought the *Tern* into land, a place called Fox Harbour. I even sent the bait boat ashore and the men searched but 'twarn't a sign."

When he stops speaking there is no sound. Just the swish of water that lies all around, soft as butter in the morning sun. From behind the swollen knuckles Sarah holds pressed against her mouth, there comes a noise like someone choking. It seems to the people standing there that the sound goes on forever before Jennie puts her arm around her friend and leads her up to the house. Josh watches them go, then he turns to Alex, opens his mouth as though to ask something but no words come.

"I'm sorry b'y, some sorry. He were a good lad, hard working. The men and meself thought the world of him. When we squares up we'll put him in for whatever share he would ha' got." Alex reaches toward Josh, but doesn't quite touch him. The Captain is desperate to have this over with and relief floods across his face when Josh shakes his head, turns and follows the women.

Spreading his hands, palms upward, Alex says, "There was nothing I coulda done. Not one God-damn thing!"

Then, remembering something, he reaches inside his shirt and pulls out a handful of black fur. He looks at the biggest boy, "You Joe's brother?"

Peter nods and the man puts the squirming animal into the boy's hands, "Here, Young Joe brought this aboard from the Eskimos we met in Fox Harbour. I guess he's yours. They're good dogs, people up there set great store by them, use them for all kinds of work."

Alex turns to Thomas. "There wasn't a thing we coulda done," he says again.

"I know. We all know that." After an awkward pause Thomas asks, "How was the summer?"

"Pretty good. We'll know better when we sees what price fish is gettin'—I got a full load aboard now so we'll make another trip down pickin' up what's been made ashore," Alex says, and the two men turn toward the store, deep in conversation.

Seeing their Captain finished with the unpleasant business, the hands come ashore, standing around to chat with Ned and Ben, who unload the morning's catch from the skiff.

The children, seeming to have already forgotten Joe, clamour for a chance to hold the tiny Labrador dog. Meg hesitates, looks towards the Vincent house, but decides to leave the job of comforting to Jennie. She joins Mary, Lavinia and Lizzie, who have already started to gut the fish being tossed up on the wharf.

Chapter 5

The days are beginning to draw in again, the ground is hard and on cold mornings water in the pond is caught over. Our second winter in this place is almost here and I still long for home. Mamma and Meg never speak of Weymouth any more—I think they've forgotten all about it.

As Lavinia writes, separated from her family by the large barrels that she has arranged to hide her sleeping place, she is surrounded by the raw smells of the Cape: of sea and fish, of sap drying in new walls, of oakum stuffed into cracks, the tang of partridgeberry jam Jennie has made that day, of boiled vegetables, the rancid odour of fat that the men rub into their boots each night, and the smells of sweat and dirt.

None of these are as real as the smells she remembers. The closed-in smell of Weymouth's dirty streets, a mixture of ale and food combined with hundreds of years of horse droppings and coal smoke. The wonderful smells of Ellsworth House: the butter and egg smell of the pantry, the smell of ironed linen, of waxed wood. The smell in the little attic room she'd shared with Maud and Sally, of rose soap the girls used, and the aroma, almost like baking bread, that seeped up on warm days from paste under the flowered wallpaper.

She lies in bed, longing for what has been left behind—a world of peopled streets, of papered walls, of friends. A world where she'd had a job, earned money.

Lavinia forgets that in Weymouth most of her wages went to her mother; remembers only that she'd been able to buy bits of ribbon, sweets, lace gloves, the length of moss green velvet she still has tucked away in her bag, sometimes presents for the children.

Here she has no money—none of them do. Nor ever will as far as she can see. Lavinia only discovered this at the end of the fishing season when they all gathered in Thomas Hutchings' store to square their accounts.

All summer Thomas kept a record of fish the men landed, of fish dropped off by Gosse vessels and of the fish they made. A few days before the *Tern* was to pick up the last load of cured fish, he asked everyone to come to the store while he did the tally.

Thomas Hutchings placed a sheet of ledger paper on the floor and carefully set his inkpot beside it. Then he knelt down and wrote the names Josh Vincent, Ben Andrews, Ned Andrews, and Thomas Hutchings across the top of the paper. Slowly turning the pages of a small notebook he began to list numbers, explaining each number as he wrote it in beneath one of the names.

It was clear to Lavinia that Thomas Hutchings was sure none of the people gathered around him could read. She had watched her labour being tallied into Ned's account, her mother's into Ben's. As she opened her mouth to protest, she heard Thomas say: "Sarah's, Annie's and Mary's work, we'll tally into Josh Vincent's account."

It was then Lavinia had seen the look of the black anger on Mary Bundle's face.

Thomas saw it too. Very deliberately he returned the pen to the ink and looking directly at Mary, said. "If any of you have questions about what I'm doing just ask—as you can see I'm crediting each household with the work of the women and children it will feed this winter." He'd paused as if waiting for comments.

"I daresay now he'd be some put out if one of us wants it done a different way," Lavinia had thought.

Mary lowered her eyes, but not before Lavinia caught the look of quick realization and something else (what, Lavinia wonders) that had flashed across the small, intelligent face.

In that instant Mary Bundle resolved she would marry Thomas Hutchings. If Mary could add nothing to her possessions without a man—then a man she would have. And since Thomas Hutchings seemed to control the distribution of credit, if not of money, she would have Thomas Hutchings.

Mary studied the man as he wrote out their order. Ben, Ned and Josh have faces like old leather but Thomas Hutchings' face is darker even than theirs. His black hair is starting to turn grey just over his ears but it is thick and clean looking. His nose is too long, too narrow and he is inclined to look down it as if sighting along the barrel of a gun. He has a stern, unbending look—but that might be all to the good, Mary thought, adjusting desire to reality.

He is almost as old as Josh Vincent, she concluded. More substantial though—Josh looks as if a strong wind would blow him away. "Sawed off and hammered down, but tough as nails," Sarah describes Josh, and the same could be said for most of the men along the coast, all of whom have a brittleness about their bodies that comes from generations of overwork and malnutrition. Thomas is taller, taller and broader than any of them.

In the weeks after Alex brought news of Young Joe's drowning, Mary had watched Josh Vincent even more closely than before. In daylight he hardly exchanged a word with his wife and they never touched. They appear to go about their daily lives without communication, yet Mary discovered that this was not so.

Night after night, across the half-wall that separates the loft, Mary could hear Sarah weeping, insisting that she would know if her son were dead. Night after night, she caught the low murmur as Josh soothed his wife. The soft sound of the man's voice would go on until Sarah sleeps.

What secret creatures men are after all, Mary thought. "Why, they're more sly, more hidden, than women—anyone with eyes can know what women feel but who'd ever see Josh Vincent cares about Sarah like that?"

She had abandoned her half-formed idea of owning (for that is how she'd thought of it) Josh. After assessing Ben, Ned and Thomas she concluded they'd all be more trouble than they were worth.

"I'd do better by meself," she decided and set out to earn her own way on the Cape.

Next spring she had planned to build herself and Fanny a house. She knew she would need help but, Mary reasons, "Josh and Thomas helped the Andrews brothers build their house. Why shouldn't they help me?"

She'd have her own walls around her, look out of her own windows, bring home her own wood and eat food she herself had earned. Having, after days and days of silent thought, come to this decision, she stopped paying any attention to the men in the place.

When lightly cured fish was unloaded from the *Charlotte Gosse* she had been gleeful. "So there is a way of making money here, even for a woman." She immediately began to calculate, painfully, for she was uncertain about addition and ignorant of subtraction, how many coins she might have in her small hoard by spring, when her house could be started.

With this idea in her mind Mary drove herself all summer, determined to work harder than any other woman in the place. From Sarah she learned how to snap the head off a fish with the side of her hand, how to slit it from throat to tail, gut and spread it, learned when the day was too mausy or too hot for good drying, and a hundred other things about curing fish. Mary had been the first person on the flakes each morning, forcing herself, in the sick half-light before dawn, to begin carting fish down from the shed, spreading it out before the others arrived. It was she who had worked out a way of stacking the fish top to bottom so that air would get between the layers, she was the one who had gotten Ben to nail slats together so that two women could carry a quintal of fish at a time up to the shed. All this, thinking she would add to her collection of coins when the accounts were settled.

Watching Thomas Hutchings tally up their work, she saw how foolish the idea of owning her own house had been. Her work was all for nothing. No credit would be written on the paper for her, no coins pressed into her outstretched hand. People live and die along this coast without ever seeing money—why had she not realized this?

Even the men got no money, just little marks scratched in after their names, marks that show how much flour, sugar, potatoes (for only a sad few have been harvested from the acidic soil of the new garden) how much molasses, kerosene, cloth, needles, tea and salt, how many pairs of boots, and how much fishing gear they will get from Caleb Gosse in exchange for their work.

The realization chilled Mary to the core. But, unlike Lavinia, she had no soft memories of the past and shed no tears for it. The instant she knew there would be no money, and that Thomas Hutchings has almost complete power in the matter of credit ("For," she reasoned, "how do we people know what he's writin' down on that bit of paper?"), Mary determined she would have Thomas.

As soon as the Andrews family moved into their own house, Thomas Hutchings went back to eating supper with the Vincents. Mary now takes advantage of this to attract his attention. Since her nature is neither outgoing nor flirtatious this is an altogether awkward effort consisting of piling extra food on his plate, rolling her hair up more neatly than before and contriving to bump into him in doorways and along paths as he comes and goes.

She continues these small strategies for months with no noticeable results. Thomas becomes convinced that the young woman has some disability. She continually seems to be knocking into things and stares at him so strangely that he cannot decide if she is simple-minded or just near-sighted. He avoids her whenever he can.

Months go by and Mary becomes desperate. She gives no thought to abandoning her plan but knows that some action is called for. She considers leaving her bunk under the eaves of the Vincent house, walking in the dark up to the fishing rooms and crawling into Thomas Hutchings' bed. Some long solitary night she might have done just that had not instinct warned her that such a blatant act would repulse Thomas who, she has observed, is more fastidious about his person, his food and his surroundings than anyone else on the Cape.

The habit of coming together after supper to hear Ned's stories has resumed in the long nights of midwinter. Sometimes they sit by the Andrews fireplace, but the chimney has never worked properly and, despite having been torn down and rebuilt, still sends billows of smoke into the room in certain winds. Because of this, the nightly entertainments usually take place in Thomas' store, just as they had the previous winter.

They do not light lamps but sit comfortably near the firelight, darkness shut out. As Ned talks the women knit and Ben whittles tole-pins, a chair leg, or a doll's head for one of the girls. Mary finds it encouraging that Thomas no longer spends these evenings sitting alone at the little desk.

One moonlit night, as they crunch over packed snow on their way back to the Vincent house, Mary and Sarah, each carrying a baby, drop behind the others.

"'Tisn't one bit of use your settin' your cap for Thomas Hutchings—that man is pure blind when it comes to women." Sarah speaks quietly without turning her head to look at Mary, who is walking at her heels along the narrow path.

It has not occurred to Mary Bundle that anyone might notice her silent attempts to attract Thomas Hutchings. She never thinks that others might be observing her as closely as she does them. She is embarrassed, glad that Sarah has her back towards her.

Yet she sees no point in denying what the older woman knows. "What can I do then? I wants me own roof over me head, a place for me and Fannie. I can't live forever with you and Josh."

Preoccupied with her own problem, Mary almost collides with Sarah, who has stopped to yell at one of her sons. "Peter Vincent! Don't you dare go down to the landwash this time of night—get home and into bed or I'll have the hide off ya!" Sarah shakes her fist at the boy before turning to face Mary. "I'm thinkin' you should set your cap for Ned Andrews," she says calmly.

Mary is insulted. Had the path been wider she would have brushed around Sarah, gone in and to bed without a word. But Sarah stands like a big sack of potatoes touching the snow banks on either side.

"Ned Andrews! Him what's always up to tomfoolery, laughin' his stunned head off at some joke! How can you think I'd marry the likes of that?" She is angry and hurt that Sarah should have so little regard for her. "I wants better than Ned Andrews can do—I wants to be as well off as you are with Josh."

In truth, Mary was thinking that when she gets to Sarah's age she doesn't want to be still sleeping on a rope bed in an open attic, eating fish and potatoes seven days a week and never setting eyes on a bit of real money from one year to the next. She sees Sarah smile and remembers, too late, that the woman can read her thoughts.

"Go on with ya, Mary Bundle—you and Thomas would be like pallbearers together. You needs someone with a bit of fun in him. Someone like Ned Andrews."

"'Tis Thomas Hutchings I got a mind for and 'tis Thomas Hutchings I'll have!" Mary's voice is hard, her chin, as Sarah later tells Josh, "stuck out like a jib."

"Suit yourself girl, but Thomas is a deep one. There'll be more to catchin' him than pullin' a connor over the wharf." Sarah studies the younger woman for a minute, squinting at her in the moonlight. "More than pullin' the tail of your dress over your head, too."

They continue towards the house without another word, and for several days there is a coolness between the two women.

February gales sweep down on the Cape. Winds slice into the unprotected headland, lashing the sea into waves that freeze layer upon layer on the wharf and along the beach. During a week of such storms, none of them move from their own fires. To venture out in the great swirl of whiteness would put one in danger of going blind, losing one's way and suffocating in the snow.

Evening gatherings in the store stop. To save wood and keep from freezing, everyone goes to bed early. The women heat beach rocks in the fire, wrapping them in rags to make one small spot of warmth in the icy beds. No one sleeps alone. Peter huddles with the dog, Annie squeezes in with Mary to make a warm nest between them for Fanny and Charlie. On such nights Mary lies, holding her back away from the cold wall, thinking about Thomas Hutchings all by himself in the fish store with the sea pounding in underneath.

Then in late February, they wake one morning to a strange, unnatural calm. Even before their eyes are open they can hear the silence, feel the difference: air that does not catch in your throat each time you inhale.

Women drag bedding outside, open doors to air musty rooms. Men and boys cleave more firewood and check boats that have been buried for months. Mary, helping Sarah wrestle wet blankets onto a line, can see Lavinia and the children skimming rocks down on the landwash. "Some life that one got, silly as her brother, gormless lump of a woman actin' like a youngster!" she mutters.

Sarah surveys the dripping world. Rivers of melting snow have already turned paths to mud, "We'll pay for this, mark my words. It'll be worse than ever by tomorrow or the day after... ." Then she stiffens, drops the blanket, screams and begins to run towards the water, slipping on the ice and mud, crying out, "It's Joe! It's Joe! It's Joe!"

And sure enough, Mary can see a small boat making in towards shore. Not even Mary's sharp eyes can make out the figures in the boat but she does not doubt for a minute that Sarah is right. She turns to call the others before taking off towards the wharf herself.

Within five minutes everyone in the place is down there gazing at the strange spectacle of a boat arriving in February. As she comes alongside, they all recognize Ezra Vincent's skiff with its rust-coloured sail. Sarah is beside herself. She would walk out on the water if Josh did not hold her back, shaking his head and saying quietly, "Now girl, have a thought, how can young Joe be on Ezra's boat?"

But he is. To the others, the lanky young man who climbs onto the wharf bears little resemblance to the boy who disappeared on board the *Tern* a year before but Sarah flings her arms around his neck. "I knowed it was you—I knowed it," she sobs.

Grinning at one another, touching Joe as if to make sure he is real, everyone asking questions at the same time, they move in a covey towards the store. Once inside the questions dribble out, and they stand around staring at the strange young man. The youngsters especially are astonished by the change in Joe, who is now several inches taller than any of his family. His hair is almost white and sticks out like broom straw. His face is dark, long and narrow and, Lavinia thinks, has the same mixture of good humour and stubbornness as the faces of Sarah's goats.

The only familiar thing about Young Joe is his clothing. The ragged melton breeks that come just to his knees, the heavy jacket that used to belong to his father, also much too short of sleeve, are the things he was wearing the day he disappeared. Awkward in his new body, Joe shuffles about, fumbling with the rope belt that holds his breeks in place.

When he realizes they are waiting for him to explain his long absence, he takes his time working out what to say. Still, when he speaks his voice is confident, with none of his father's hesitation.

"Well—well, how it come about, me and Ted Fifield were out in boat haulin' a few lines after supper when the fog come down—I s'pose Skipper

Brennan told you," the boy paused as if trying to recall something that happened years ago.

"We couldn't see a thing. For a spell we could hear the *Tern*'s whistle but couldn't tell in the fog which way it was comin' from. Then we got right foolish, goin' off in all directions at once 'til we lost an oar. There was a good sea runnin' but I often been out in worse, and 'twasn't too cold, so we decided the best thing was to lie down in the bottom of her and hold on 'til morning.

"By the time morning come, the fog was gone but we'd drifted well down around Fox Harbour and into Indian Harbour. Course we didn't know that then. We only knowed there were no sign of the *Tern*. We was pushed in with the tide and grounded in a little cove as neat as if we'd sculled her in ourselves—we was some lucky, plenty of places we coulda' smashed up on the rocks."

The boys had stayed on the beach for days, tying a shirt to the remaining oar in the hope the *Tern* would come by and sight them. It was warm fall weather, and with a brook running into the sea, there was drinking water. They had three cod in the boat but no means of cooking them. On the second day they began eating the fish raw.

After five or six days, they decided to make their way along the shore, walking inland when it was necessary but always keeping the sea in sight. They were not too worried, figuring that sooner or later they would come upon some livyers or a fishing schooner up from Newfound Land.

"We walked for three days, gettin' more and more discouraged and hungry. The flies were something fierce, tormented us half to death. We kept alive on the few berries that were ripe and tried to jig fish but didn't get a thing. We saw all kinds of birds and some wild animals Ted said was fox and marten. We even tried to fix up a snare with the line but never did get the rights of it. I tell you we were about reconciled to starvin'—with all that food around us too—when we come upon this family of Eskimo. They was just breakin' camp to move back up country."

Ned, frustrated by the boy's matter-of-fact recitation, kept interrupting, asking Young Joe for more details. Lavinia knew her brother was already imagining himself telling the story, thinking of embellishments he could add to such an adventure.

"I s'pose them Eskimos was some surprised to see you two—what do them people look like? I hear tell they dresses like animals, that right?"

Young Joe grinned and pointed to his unusual footwear. "No sir, they's the smartest people you ever saw for makin' stuff—look at them boots!" He began to show Ned how the seal skin had been cut and stitched with fur inside on the foot part and outside on the leggings.

Ezra Vincent told his nephew to leave all that for later. "Just tell 'em the bones of the tale, lad, or we'll be here all week!"

The boys had travelled with the Eskimo family for almost four months, moving leisurely along the flatlands below a long range of mountains, living well off fish and game until, some time in November, the group met up with five trappers. The men were walking towards a coastal station where, they said, a vessel from Fogo was supposed to drop their winter's supplies.

"We hardly knew what to do. Ted didn't trust the trappers, but they got along all right with the Eskimos—that was good enough for me so we travelled back down to Fox Harbour with them, and we were only waitin' there three days when the brig *Little Ephraim* came in. Her captain was Hezekiah Guy and he agreed to take us back to Fogo. Then it was weeks before we got as far as Pond Island, and I been there ever since, staying with Nan Vincent, waitin' for a chance to get home."

The winter's day is already darkening by the time Joe finishes, and his uncle, who has been quietly sitting at the splitting table with the other men, gets to his feet.

"That's all very well and good, and I'm glad ye got the boy home but that warn't why I took the chance on comin' down this coast in February month," Ezra Vincent begins.

No one heeds him. All around the store little conversations have broken out. The men want to know who owns the *Little Ephraim*. If Captain Guy is the same man who fished out of Cat Harbour last year? What do Eskimos hunt with? And the women, leaning against the walls, turn to one another, say, "Lord be praised!" and marvel at Young Joe's luck. The children, their first shyness over, want to know if he's seen a snow house or polar bear or brought another dog home.

Ezra reaches behind him for the iron rod and bangs it on a barrel. "Look a'here, I got serious business with ye lot. Listen to what I got ta tell ye!"

They hush, the mood of jubilation changed in an instant by the urgency of his voice.

"Like I said, I didn't come down this coast in winter just so's ye crowd could hear a good yarn or even to bring Joe home. He could as well got back next month, or the month after comes to that. No, I come 'cause something's happened we figured ye crowd should hear tell of."

Ezra tells them that a week ago, in the middle of the bad storm, eleven people, two of them women and three children— one only a baby— stumbled into Davisport, the tiny settlement just across from Pond Island. Starving and half dead from exhaustion, the people had been walking for three days and spent two nights in the woods. They were frostbitten, and it looked like the youngest woman, Ida Norris, might have to have her foot taken off. It was a miracle any of them were alive, Ezra says.

There are no questions now, only shocked silence. "They was from Shamblers Cove. They'd been burnt out on a Sunday night by the crew of a light brigantine. English or American, one of the men said she was. Anyhow, they come ashore like Turks, pillaged all the supplies, loaded everything: flour, sugar, even all the fish they'd kept, onto the ship—about fifteen men all told, with guns and long sticks. Then, you'd hardly credit it, they pushed the Shamblers Cove people out into the snow, set fire to the three houses and made off."

The people had survived only because the oldest man, Lem Parsons, was an expert hunter and had a gun stored in a tilt he owned back in the woods. They had managed to shoot a fox and two birds. Lem kept them moving by day, built shelters of boughs and made fires at night. "'Tis a jeezely wonder any of 'em come out of it alive!" Ezra says.

"We thinks was American privateers done it. Heard tell last winter there was two lots of 'em raiding fish and furs wherever they could along the coast," he concludes.

Well satisfied now with their attention, he looks around the circle of faces, folds his arms and adds, "I doubt that they're full yet, so when the Davisport crowd got word to us in Pond Island we started makin' our plans."

"What'll ye do if they come ashore?" Sarah asks.

"Well, the Davisport people got everything packed and they're comin' out to Pond Island today, along with the poor souls from Shamblers Cove. There's six men there, and we'll have a good few sealing guns and gaffs. We got twenty-one able-bodied men ourselves, and I expects we'd got a few women who'd fight too if it comes to that. I allow we'd make a good show of it if they tried to come ashore." Ezra's voice is as mild and emotionless as his brother's, but Lavinia has no doubt that he and twenty like him could hold off any number of privateers.

"Now ye crowd here, what have ye got? Josh, Thomas, Ned and Ben—and now Young Joe, I s'pose. Say five men and a bunch of women and youngsters," Ezra shakes his head. "And one old gun. Ye wouldn't have the chance of a snowball in hell."

No one contradicts him. They have lain awake at night worrying about ice and wind, about savages, about animals in the forest, but never for a moment has anyone given thought to the idea that people like themselves might come ashore to steal what little they have.

No one except Sarah who reminds them of her warnings: "I told you, told you a thousand times we shoulda built in back of the woods, not out here where every Frenchman passin' can see us plain as day."

Useless to say that no one has ever heard Sarah give such advice. Useless to point out that it had not been the French who raided Shamblers Cove. As she says, "What difference when you're froze in a snowbank who put you there, English or American, French or Turk, brigantines or pirates, fishing admirals or the British Navy, you're still froze, innit ya?"

Ezra cuts into his sister-in-law's discourse: "Why I come is this—we figured that in this calm spell ye could pack up and coast back up to Pond Island same as the Davisport people are doin'. With my boat and Josh's we can take a good bit of yer provisions and ye can come back here in six weeks or so. There'll be more vessels along the coast then and them bastards'll go back wherever they come from."

Ezra Vincent has been standing, but now he sits down and looks slowly around the circle of people: at his brother and Sarah, at their children, at all their blank, guarded faces. The winter faces of the children turn up to the adults, women look at the men and the men avoid each other's eyes, each hoping one of the others will speak. Not even Thomas is willing to take the lead in this decision.

The silence draws out. Ezra begins again to describe the desperate state of the refugees from Shamblers Cove, that even their boats were burnt, how sick the young ones were, that the woman with frozen feet might die. Getting no response, he appeals directly to Josh: "Will and Mudder both said you's to come. Mudder said she can't abide the thought of Sarah and them children bein' out here on the Cape with Turks plunderin' the coast." Ezra gives his brother a hard look, willing him to speak. But there is only silence.

"Bugger'em!"

The voice, quick, clear and defiant, comes from the circle of women. Everyone turns to look at Mary Bundle. She stands, mouth agape, as astonished as the rest at the words she's uttered.

Then Ned Andrews starts to laugh, his high insane laughter. He begins to dance around the table slapping his knee.

> Bugger'em all, bugger'em all,
> Bugger the British,
> Bugger the French,
> Bugger the Yankees
> and bugger the rest!

Ned sings and dances around and around. The children break into smiles and dance around behind him.

Lavinia, Annie and Lizzie join them, weaving between gear, provisions and people, chanting the little ditty at the top of their voices, dancing in and out among the shocked adults.

It takes a minute for Meg to regain her composure. One by one she grabs her three daughters, pulling them out of the ring, calling to the other children, "Stop this! Ye hear me, stop! Ye should be on yer knees praying instead of cavortin' like a bunch of heathen savages."

She gives each passing child a flick. They collapse onto a pile of nets and rope, where they lie giggling. Ned and Lavinia, who have been in the lead, jig around one more time before they, too, drop breathless to the floor and sit smiling at each other for the first time in months.

Ezra Vincent has watched this display of bravado in silence. When it is over he turns to Josh: "Well, old man, that's about what I figured, 'tho I never expected a song to be made of it. I good as told Mudder ye crowd wouldn't budge. But she would have me try." He grinned at his sister-in-law, "Don't people down here eat? Thought I smelled fish cookin' when we passed your door."

Sarah is aghast—she hasn't fed her family since early morning! The women go to rescue food that had been intended for dinner, Thomas lights a small oil lamp and soon they are eating bread and fish.

The novelty of idleness gives the day a dream-like quality, and an air of detached gaiety comes over everyone. They sit, taking their time, eating and talking. The Labrador pup wiggles out of Young Joe's arms to run happily back and forth between him and Peter, being fed bits of fish by both brothers. The scene inside the store seems unreal, as insubstantial as happiness, as precarious as the false spring outside.

Knowing it is useless to coax them to leave, Ezra relaxes, gives them all the news from Pond Island, comments on how much Charlie has grown, asks after the goats he brought Sarah the summer before and tells about a big dog that came with the Shamblers Cove people.

"Like this one, only the size of a small pony. He belongs to the old hunter I was tellin' ye about. Accordin' to him the dog tore the arse right out of the pants of one of them pirates. They took a shot at the beast and he made off into the woods. Lem thought the dog was gone for good. Then, that night when they'd stopped for a spell, he come tearin' out of the woods, frightened the poor mortals half to death, them thinkin' it was a wolf or something. Both the dog and Lem bin' stayin' at our place this last spell and I daresay the great brute will be sleepin' on my bed this night."

Ezra drains the last drop from his third cup of tea and stands up. "Well, Sarah maid, got a place for me to lie down? Soon as ever 'tis light I'll start home—who can tell when this civil spell will end, and I'd be stuck here with ye crazy people for the rest of the winter."

Next morning they come down to see him off, watching as the little craft, hugging the shoreline, disappears into the mist. The weather is still mild. They spend the day making preparations to defend themselves, all the time keeping watch on the ocean and the sky.

The muzzle loader is brought out, cleaned, oiled and propped, ready for use, behind the door of the store. The women pack the old wooden chest again. This time they put in a piece of canvas, brin bags, flint, salt cod, bread, quilts, a kettle. They carry the box, just as they had in the spring, up back to the garden at the edge of the woods. If worse comes to worst they will have to cross the neck, walk up the coast, skirting deep chasms where the sea cuts in, make their way through black hills, wade over frozen bog and barrens. At least in the sea chest they will have food and the means of making a fire.

As they pile rocks around the sides and on top of the box to keep animals off, Sarah shakes her head. "I doubt we'd be able to even find this if, Lord forbid, we needs it—especially if it snows tonight."

"Oh, you'll find it, Sarah. You'll know just where it is. Just like you knowed it was Young Joe in that boat yesterday, just like you always knowed he warn't drowned." Mary doesn't look up. She keeps busily rubbing mud from her hands, half afraid of what she's said.

Sarah seems bewildered. "Whatever are you talkin' about maid? I allow me eyesight is 'bout the same as yours."

Mary looks around. In the growing darkness she can barely see Meg and Jennie halfway down the path and well out of earshot. It might be a long time, before she has another chance to talk to Sarah alone.

She leans forward and grabs the older woman's sleeve, "You can help me, you got to help me." She pauses, takes a deep breath. "Put a charm on Thomas Hutchings for me, Sarah—a charm to make him want me."

"A charm! Girl, you foolish or somethin'? Me put a charm on Thomas—I never heard tell of such nonsense!"

"You can, you can! I knows you can!" Mary whispers fiercely. "Look—I don't want you ta do it for nothin'—I knows witches never do anything for nothin'."

"Witches!" Sarah is incredulous, not sure whether to laugh or be angry.

Mary digs inside the front of her old jacket and pulls something out. "Look, look what I got, you can have this. If you helps me you can have it." She squats beside Sarah, who is still half-kneeling by the wooden box.

"Look, just look, isn't it pure marvellous? Isn't it beautiful?"

It is both marvellous and beautiful. The two women, threadbare and grey in the dying light, lean forward to gaze at the small circle of purple and blue stones that twinkle up from Mary's dirty hand.

"It is, that it is," Sarah says softly, touching the brooch reverently with one finger, "I never seen nothin' like it in this world."

Lost in admiration, she has forgotten about being called a witch, forgotten what Mary has asked her to do. Very quietly, Mary says, "You can have it for yourself—or for Annie if you likes—just put a charm on Thomas Hutchings."

Sarah snaps out of her reverie. Shakes her head, "I can't. I don't know how. I tell ya I'm not a witch. I don't know how to make charms... ."

"Yes you can! I knows you can, I been watchin' and I knows," and Mary (just as she had seen someone do long ago) bends forward and pins the brooch to the inside of Sarah's coat.

"There now, it's yours, just for you to see, just for you to know you got." Mary pats the spot under which the brooch is hidden. "When we gets back to the house you make a charm, a good charm on Thomas so's he wants me." She stands and without another word starts down the path.

After a minute Sarah follows.

The sound of Annie's voice, shouting, comes to them as they near the house. They find the place filled with smoke, the girl sloshing water onto the fire and yelling instructions to Peter, who seems rooted to the floor behind her.

"Go get Mudder—Go on! Get Mudder and Mary too, quick!"

Seeing her mother, Annie drops the bucket on the floor. She begins to cry and hit Peter at the same time. When the girl has calmed down, she tells them that Joe thinks he's seen a sail far out off the Cape; that everyone had gone down to the stagehead, but Thomas Hutchings sent her and Peter back to dout the Vincent fire.

"Well, you done that anyway, child," Sarah pulls her daughter towards her and wipes soot from the girl's face with the corner of her apron, "'tho I don't think Thomas will be much pleased with the cloud of smoke you're sendin' up the chimney."

When they get down to the wharf, it is so dark they cannot tell if there is a ship out there or not. Ned, who can identify the outlines of dozens of vessels, is sure he's seen the brigantine Ezra described.

"I got a good look when she first hove into sight, and she's got the same riggin'. She's big, bigger than anything I seen come in here."

"Maybe she won't get in, someone not used to the Cape would have to be wonderful careful gettin' past the sunkers with a vessel that size," Josh reassures his wife, shaking his head at Joe when the boy points out, almost hopefully, that the ship might have longboats to put ashore.

Thomas Hutchings turns away from the sea. "We're doing no good standing here speculating. It'll be hours before she can get in to us, so let's try and be ready. You two," he points to Joe and Peter, "bring food and bedding, as much as you can, up to my place. All hands will sleep in the store tonight. The women can bring water and buckets and extra jackets and such—there'll be no fires or lamps for them to steer by."

As he speaks he glances towards the houses and, for the first time, sees the cloud of white smoke hanging over the Vincents' chimney.

"Sweet Jesus, what's that, a signal?" It is the first and only time anyone on the Cape will hear him use profanity. It is recorded gleefully in Lavinia's journal.

"Ben and Ned, you two finish the shelter we started down here so we can take turns watching all night. Josh, you and I will bring stuff down, the gun, gaffs—and the torches we had left over last summer. If she comes in, at least we can have a warning and be down here ready for them. Like Ezra told us, the only chance we'll have is to stop them when they come up out of the boats."

It is a grim prospect, but one they have no time to dwell upon during the next hour of frantic activity. Thomas shouts instructions and everyone hurries back and forth, stumbling over one another in the dark.

It is only later, lying in the store, trying to sleep, that Lavinia realizes that maybe not all the running about, fetching and carrying, was necessary. Perhaps Thomas Hutchings had done it just to make them tired, to keep them from thinking about what might happen this night.

Without light, without heat, without even the boughs that usually cushion their bones, they huddle under piles of bedding on the floor of the fish store. Their ears strain for a signal that will tell them they must rush down to the wharf prepared to shoot, burn or push strangers back into the sea. Lavinia cries herself to sleep.

Eventually everyone except Mary Bundle falls into a fitful sleep. Mary starts up each time she hears the door open or close as the men change shifts during the night. She can see nothing. The shed, dim even on sunny days, is pitch black.

Then—sometime in the middle of the terrible blackness—Mary feels a man's hand pull back the edge of her quilt, a man's hand slide along her side and a long body easing itself down under her bedding. She gasps, but a finger touches her lips, a hand slides around to cup the back of her head and she relaxes.

"It's worked! Sarah Vincent's charm on Thomas has worked!" she thinks triumphantly.

She presses towards him, responding with passion that has more to do with fear, and need, and cold, than with the sensible plan she had worked out in the Vincent loft. She rolls over onto the man and locks her mouth down on his.

It is all over very quickly. Too quickly, Mary thinks. Promising herself it will be better next time she lies beneath him and licks a drop of sweat from the hollow of his neck.

He brings his face down, kisses her again and, in what seems to be one movement, peels away from her, out of the quilts, and is gone.

Mary smiles and curls her warmed body around little Fanny. It was well worth parting with the brooch. She falls asleep planning the house she and Thomas Hutchings will build next spring. She has already picked out the spot.

In the morning, just as Sarah had prophesied, winter is back. Driving snow pounds against the shed. Outside, everything is white, and drifts have filled in the pathways, covering yesterday's mud.

The men coming up from the wharf smile, stamp snow off themselves, pluck ice from their hair and beards.

"We're safe as houses," Ned says, forgetting already how unsafe houses are. "Any vessel tryin' to come ashore in this gale'll be pounded apart on the rocks." He looks flushed and happy, as if they have won some great victory.

"Let's get this fire going and something hot inside of us before we freeze to death." Only Thomas is still glum. Mary peers at him expectantly but he neither smiles nor looks at her.

She is dismayed—didn't last night mean anything?

Then her glance falls on Ned Andrews. He is sitting cross-legged on a barrel, leaning forward like some oversized gargoyle, his curly hair and beard ablaze like blasty boughs around a face that beams on her with overflowing love and good humour.

Mary picks Fanny up and walks across the shed to stand demurely beside him.

Chapter 6

A few hours after I went to sleep there was a terrible racket—I woke up thinking the pirates had come ashore after all, that we were about to be murdered in our beds. I daresay Thomas Hutchings heard all about it by now and thinks we Andrews are a rowdy crowd along with everything else.

Dead tired after a night in the freezing store and a day of carting belongings back to the houses through knee-deep snow, they eat supper as soon as it is dark and go directly to bed. In her corner Lavinia finds young Jane, who often shares her bed on cold nights, already sound asleep under the great pile of blankets and clothing.

Because of the barrier she has constructed around her bed, the first noises do not wake Lavinia. The sound of a birch junk hitting the barrels, followed by a string of terrible oaths in an unrecognizable female screech, jerks her awake and half out of the quilts, her heart thumping in fear.

She extracts herself from the heavy coverings, crawls over her still sleeping niece to peer across the top of a barrel, certain she will see her family being slaughtered. What she sees is her brother Ned chasing his small son around and around the room. Ned is bellowing at the child, and Isaac responds with blood-curdling screams.

Jennie, and Meg, who holds a candle, are standing on the sidelines calling Isaac's name and making ineffectual grabs at the youngster. He evades them easily, whirling around the room like a scalded cat, leaping over the bodies of his relatives. Each time he passes the woodpile, he snatches a junk and flings it in the general direction of Mary Bundle. Mary grips the handle of a dipper of sloshing snow water and swears loudly as wood crashes around her.

On the floor, Ben, along with his three daughters and Willie, rest on their elbows and watch the spectacle in silent wonderment, ducking misdirected junks of firewood.

Mary Bundle and Ned Andrews are both stark, staring naked.

Lavinia rises from behind the barrel in time to see Mary step quickly towards the oncoming ball of fury, brace her feet and let swing with the icy contents of the dipper full into Isaac's small, red face. Unfortunately, much of the snow water sloshes over the private parts of the man who is in pursuit of his son.

Ned and Isaac stop dead. There is a unified sound of indrawn breath, then silence. Absolute.

With admirable presence of mind, Lizzie takes a quilt from her sleeping place, goes quickly over, wraps it around her dripping and exhausted cousin, and brings him back to Lavinia's corner. Out of sight of his enemy, Lizzie tucks the boy's face under her chin and begins to coo him to sleep.

Ned and Mary dive into a pile of bedding and cover themselves. Jennie, shaking her head helplessly, seeming at a loss as to what action might be appropriate, begins to gather up the wood in an absent-minded way. Then, weariness overcoming her, she abandons the job, goes over and crawls back into her bed, pulling quilts over her tousled grey head.

Only Meg is left. She stands like some old goddess, tall and pregnant in her long flannel nightgown, surveying the battlefield. For a minute or two she seems to hesitate, and Lavinia, watching from her hiding place, expects her to blow out the candle and settle down beside Ben.

Instead, red-faced but determined, Meg marches over to stand above the two lovers (of whom Lavinia can see only the top of Ned's curls) and proceeds, in her clear voice, to give them a piece of her equally clear mind.

"Never! Not in all me born days did I see such a display—no better than two cats. I vow I'm ashamed of me life that such a thing could happen in this house! Do you think then, just because we're livin' in the back of beyond, that you can act like heathen? Do ye think the Good Lord can't see us? He can! And what about them innocent children—Ben's and mine—yes and yours too, Ned Andrews, poor motherless creatures! I make no wonder Isaac, poor little mortal, is half scared out of his wits! Wakin' up and findin' a stranger and his father goin' right to it—and neither of ye with a stitch on! You'll never learn to think, Ned Andrews—cares about nothin', do ya? No odds to you makin' a holy show of us all!"

Meg continues in this vein for some time, glowing with righteous wrath. In the end, she turns her attention to Mary, cowering with Ned: "And you, Mary Bundle—hark to me! I'll not have you lyin' in sin in the same room as them children! Now get up, get dressed and get back down to the Vincents' right this minute—fast as ever your legs can take ya!"

Ned makes as though to rise from his prone position, protesting this turfing of his beloved from warm bed to cold snow.

But Meg will have none of it, "Not one word out of you, Ned Andrews! I'm that vexed I got a mind to chase you both out like you is—you'll be married in the eyes of God and man afore you shares this bed again! And another thing, Mary Bundle, if I ever again hears such words as come out of you this night, I swear I'll wash yer mouth out with lye soap!"

There is not a sound from either Ned or Mary. Meg stands above them tall and white, and Lavinia, remembering again the angel expelling sinners from the garden, falls back onto her crowded sleeping place stuffing the corner of a quilt between her teeth so no one will hear her laughing.

When she wakes, Lavinia wonders if she could have dreamt the chaotic scene. There is no sign of Mary Bundle, of spilled water, scattered firewood, or of the angel with the fiery sword. There is only Meg, her brown hair coiled neatly around her head, a very ordinary Meg wearing her old black sweater, sitting at the table with Ben, Ned and Jennie. Quite everyday, all of them, eating porridge and talking softly so as not to disturb the still sleeping children.

"Be reasonable, woman, where will we find a minister to marry us in this out of the way place?" Ned is asking quietly as Lavinia walks towards the table.

"Thomas Hutchings will marry you—he's a minister," Meg's answer takes them all aback and causes Lavinia to splash hot tea over her hand.

"And you'll just have to leave off work on the boat for a spell, Ben, I wants partitions up inside this house before the wedding."

Neither Thomas Hutchings' protestations that he is not a member of the clergy, Mary Bundle's angry assertion that she "...wants none of them church people sayin' words over me and Ned" nor Ben's objections to being pulled away from his boat-building, will sway Meg.

The previous fall, after just one season on the water, Ben Andrews had gone to Pond Island for three weeks to learn carpentry from Will and Ezra Vincent. Ben had come back to the Cape and immediately laid the keel for the boat he and Ned wanted—a duplicate of the little skiff the Vincent brothers fish from. Once the seams of the house had been chinsed, the chimney again patched and the roof made tight, Thomas Hutchings, Josh and Ned had joined him in the rough lean-to to work on the boat.

In Weymouth, Ben had done no more carpentry than driving a nail or two for the women to hang pots on. Only since coming to the Cape has this unsuspected talent been revealed. Ben, who cannot hold his head up in a boat, will in time become the most respected boatbuilder in all Bonavist'.

A painstaking craftsman, he spends hours walking the woods around the Cape, studying each tree, looking for those with the long, graceful lines of a ship. Sometimes he searches for a week without seeing such a tree, then he often finds several together. A whole family of twisted trunks. He comes to believe that in such places the ground contains something that attracts sea wind, drawing it down into roots, shaping trees to fit the sea. He shyly tells Lavinia this idea when she comes upon him one day standing in front of a gnarled tree trunk looking as though he is having a conversation.

"If a person took enough care they'd find every rib and plank needed for a boat in the same place, trees that would just fit together into a vessel 'specially grown for this Cape—I allow tho', that would take more skill than I got."

It is the only fanciful thing she has ever heard Ben say, and it makes her think of him differently. Lavinia begins to watch him work, noticing how he will run his hand along a piece of wood, feeling the grain. She sees that his drawknife, peeling away the long creamy shavings, is really uncovering the shape Ben knows is in the wood.

New confidence comes to Ben with his growing skill and, to their amazement, Josh and Thomas find themselves under the supervision of their former pupil.

During the fall and winter, only jobs the women and boys cannot do—mending nets or hunting seabirds and geese—distract the men from boatbuilding. Everything seems to take priority over constructing inside walls or building beds and shelves—frivolous concerns of women—and the Andrews family has continued to sleep on the floor of the big room where they live, eat and cook during the daytime.

Yet Meg persists in her determination to have partitions up before the wedding, and eventually the men give in; leave off planking the skiff and begin dividing the Andrews house into rooms. Still Meg is not satisfied. Bent on making a memorable ceremony of Ned and Mary's wedding she asks Jennie to bake a cake using what molasses is left and even cajoles Sarah into slaughtering her last goat, the little nanny she's been treating like a pet since the other perished.

Near the end of a long winter, with food supplies low, all spirits, excepting those of the bride, lighten at the prospect of a wedding celebration. The children make pink candles with bits of wax and partridgeberry juice, and the young maidens iron lace, ribbons and other scraps of adornment, managing to concoct a surprisingly presentable bridal veil with the remnants. Even Thomas Hutchings seems to recognize that Meg is a force no one can stand against. He falls in with her plans, consenting to learn the words she and Sarah deem necessary for a Christian wedding.

Only Mary Bundle takes no part in these preparations.

When Meg forced her out of the Andrews house, Mary had returned to the Vincent loft in the middle of the night. Next morning she was tending the fire, cooking, cleaning and minding babies just as before. Except that Young Joe had reclaimed his bed under the eaves and Mary had to sleep on the loft floor beside Annie and Peter, life continued as it had been all winter.

In the flurry of activity before the wedding, only Sarah notices that something is wrong. Mary is even more quiet than usual, and Ned, who turns up daily at the Vincent's door with gifts weird and wonderful—purple shells threaded onto fish line, a basket of baby fern dug from under snow, a comb carved from bone—gets no smiles or loving looks from his prospective bride. Sarah decides to have a word with Mary.

"Should be dancin' on air you should, gettin' a man like Ned Andrews! Not many men'd come courtin' a woman with a youngster," Sarah said one morning after Ned had left without even a word of thanks for his gift. Then, studying Mary's downcast face, another reason for the young woman's gloom occurs to her: "I s'pose you're not already married, is you?"

Aghast at her own boldness, Sarah is neither surprised nor offended when Mary turns away muttering about people minding their own business.

The cause of Mary Bundle's distracted air and long silences is something the young woman can hardly put a name to, much less talk about. Good sense tells her that Sarah is right, she is lucky. Of the two marriageable men on the Cape she has gotten one. Not, albeit, the one she paid for. (She considers demanding her brooch back from Sarah but upon reflection decides it is better to have a witch in her debt—and, after all, she knows where the brooch is.) She hasn't got Thomas Hutchings, who can write, who has a job and who, Mary is sure, would have understood the bargain she was willing to strike. She has Ned Andrews, who says he would walk barefoot over hot coals for her. Ned, who every morning stands at the door with promises, songs and presents. When she sees him there, his hands held towards her, a smile on his foolish, freckled face, Mary feels a rush of tenderness and is afraid.

A docile bride, Mary sits in the Vincents' kitchen on her wedding day still wondering if she should go through with the ceremony. She submits to the ministrations of Lizzie and Annie, who are set on piling her wiry black hair into a smooth arrangement of combs and ribbons. Sarah stirs a huge pot containing the odd bits of goat not already roasting over Thomas Hutchings' fireplace. The room is filled with the chatter of Lizzie and Annie, the smell of stew and Sarah's muttered complaints about her two oldest sons, who can be heard outside, bickering as they chop wood for the fire.

Brotherly spats between Peter and Young Joe have changed to warfare in the weeks since the older boy came home. During the year when they thought Joe dead, Peter had relished the role of eldest son. He loved working with his father, took pride in his growing competence on the water and in his acceptance by the men working on the boat. He had almost forgotten the short rivalry between himself and Isaac Andrews which ended as soon as he'd seen that the men thought of Ned's son as a motherless baby to be pacified. All winter Peter has helped the Andrews men build their boat, revelling in the thought that he will be his father's shareman this summer.

Then Joe turned up. Not drowned on the Labrador but tall and tough as a whip, being embraced and cried over by his mother and Annie. Joe, confident with new easy laughter and sly looks for silly Lizzie Andrews, Joe receiving the thoughtful attention of his father and the other men when he talks about how Eskimos hunt, how seal boots are made, what Fogo is like, or how his uncles in Pond Island do things.

Seeing Peter's resentment, Sarah tells her son he should be glad his brother is alive. But it is no use. All Peter knows is that he was happy and is now miserable.

The brothers' hatred of each other is focused on their quarrel over the dog. Peter's disappointment at not being next to fish with his father may in time have been forgotten, had the boys not immediately begun to argue over ownership of the Labrador dog Peter had named Skipper.

Joe insisted that Skipper had been his dog first—was still his dog, since he'd given his belt buckle to an old Eskimo woman in exchange for the puppy. The dog's name, Joe said, was not Skipper but Unayok, which was what the Eskimos had called him.

The puppy, a cross between a husky and a Newfound Land dog, had already grown huge and resembled a shaggy black and white bear more than a dog. The animal had spend half a year sleeping with Peter, being fed by the boy and following him everywhere. The only dog on the Cape, Skipper has already learned to pull a sled piled with wood. Peter knows the dog has helped him make a place for himself in the men's world, and he has no intention of letting Joe take the animal away from him.

The poor beast has been thrown into a state of total confusion by Joe's return. Something in the deep recesses of his dog brain recognizes the boy who tucked him inside his coat, carried him onto the ship and held him warm against his chest during the first miserable nights away from the furry body of his mother. But Peter has fed him, it is Peter's voice he has learned to respond to and it is Peter he plays with for hours, sniffing the boy's footprints and finding him wherever he hides.

Sarah is constantly having to mediate between her sons. "For sweet mercy sake, let the poor child keep the shaggy beast—what do you want a dog for?" She tries to divert Joe by teasing, "Sure it's a wife you'll need soon."

But Joe will not be cajoled out of his determination to own the dog. He gives his mother the tight-lipped stare she remembers from the day he stowed away aboard the *Tern*.

"I never did see anybody so set on gettin' his own way," she tells Jennie. "Contrary as Johnny Garrett, that youngster is once he got his mind set on something."

On the day of Mary and Ned's wedding, the bickering has been going on since early morning. The boys are at the chopping block, supposedly cutting splits for their mother, when Joe abandons the job, calls the dog and starts towards the fish store where the men are yarning and keeping an eye on the roasting goat. Seeing Skipper run out from under the house to follow Joe, Peter calls and the dog comes bounding back. This keeps up for several minutes, the frantic animal running back and forth between its two masters.

Then Joe turns around, walks back to his brother, grabs Peter's jacket and shakes the smaller boy so hard that his feet are lifted clear off the ground.

"Leave the poor brute be, you little nuisance, he's mine and he's goin' up to the weddin' with me!" Joe gives his brother a final shake and sets him down.

"You—you—I hates you!" Snot, tears and fury spill over as Peter waves the axe under his brother's chin. "I could kill you, I could."

"Go on Petie, you're just a sook, momma's little sookie baby," Joe taunts with deadly knowledge of his brother's vulnerable spot. "Go on, sook, you couldn't hurt a fly. Look—look, I dare you, go on, I dare you... ."

Joe lays his trigger finger down on the chopping block, "There sookie Peter, I double dare you!"

The axe goes up and comes down. Blood shoots from Joe's hand into the horrified faces of both boys. The severed finger lies on the block like an ugly swollen grub. Joe's terrible scream and a vicious snarl from Skipper, who in that instant has chosen his master and is leaping at Peter, brings Sarah rushing from the house followed by the others.

Sarah hauls the savage dog away from Peter's face and pushes her son towards the kitchen. Turning to Joe, who is bent over, holding his mutilated hand and moaning, she shrills: "Serves you right ya stubborn great fool—you'll loose yer hand and maybe yer' arm with blood poisoning from this, see if ye don't! 'Twill be your own doin'!"

Sarah is crying, her voice croaking in fury and fright. Already she can see the hand becoming poisoned, festering, turning green. She has seen smaller wounds than this cause death and is frantically trying to think of something to prevent such a thing happening to Joe.

Annie and Lizzie run out into the muddy yard. They are followed by Mary Bundle, hair falling to her waist, ribbons and bows dangling around her shoulders, she stands next to the chopping block and gazes around as if waking up. Then, as Mary tells them afterwards, she hears her mother saying "...and I patched him up with frankum... ." Just those words, nothing else, but clear as clear.

Mary picks up the gruesome finger, runs into the house and comes out with a spoon. She goes over to newly cut balsam firs that are stacked upright against the house and scoops a glob of frankum from one tree. Dragging Joe behind her into the kitchen, she smears gum first on the severed finger, then on the bleeding stump and carefully fits the pieces together, "like Ben joining an arm onto Emmie's doll," Lavinia will write.

Sarah, seeing what Mary is about, gets needle and thread and directs Lavinia to tear up and scorch strips of white cloth for bandages. She holds the hand of her half-fainting son still, and Mary, calmly as if she were darning a sock, proceeds to sew the finger on with coarse white stitches.

"I hopes to God I got it right," Mary says when the finger is bandaged. Then, feeling a good deal more cheerful, she washes as much blood as possible from her person, planks herself down on the stool she'd occupied earlier and tells the pale girls, "Get on with fixin' me up or Ned'll be down lookin' for me."

The wedding ceremony is over before Sarah remembers Peter's bleeding face and goes in search of him.

The incident seems to have no serious effects upon Young Joe. He remains as stubborn as ever, and his finger grows cleanly together, stiff and crooked so that he will never be as good a shot as his father—or as Peter. Otherwise he is unaffected. The bad blood between the brothers remains.

Other participants in the event are not so untouched. The most immediate consequences are felt by poor Skipper, who in a thrice is demoted from pet to working dog, ejected from his place by the fire and forced to crawl up under the house for shelter on cold nights.

On Mary Bundle's life the event also has a lasting effect. In addition to delaying her marriage by an hour or so, the rejoining of Joe Vincent's severed finger establishes her as the medicine woman of the Cape. Sarah, with her knowledge of herbs, with the powder she scrapes from bark, the roasted roots, the boiled seaweed, has held the position of healer. However, Sarah, together with her moss and herbs, brings heavy sighs and prophecies of doom to sickbeds. Mary will treat each person with the same cool detachment, showing no more emotion at the dozens of births and deaths she will eventually preside over than she has when sewing her untidy stitches through Young Joe's finger. In time Mary learns all of Sarah's remedies and adds dozens of her own.

But of all creatures, two- and four-legged, who have a part in the chopping off and rejoining of Joe's finger, it is Peter Vincent whose life will be most changed, although this will not be apparent for some time.

For now, Peter is surly and silent. The boy pushes his mother away when she tries to wash the cheek that will forever carry the red circle of Skipper's tooth prints, takes no part in the eating, in the singing and storytelling that continues until midnight. He sits, black and accusing, outside the circle of firelight, hating them all, vowing he will show them someday.

Chapter 7

Mam's proud as punch over the house. She got all her do-dads unpacked at last—the painted shell Ned bought from a sailor who'd been to the south sea, the old clock she had from her own Mam and the funny looking plaster birds she used to get off gypsies on market days—they makes a bit of colour—all the same I wish we had the boots and jackets she traded for them birds. Mam gave me the shepherd picture I always liked so much.

Lavinia hangs the picture on the wall near her bed, but seeing it there against the rough planks seems to seal her doom. After a few days she puts the picture away in her bag, and stops forever writing of Weymouth and Monk Street.

Clothing and footwear brought from England have worn out and cannot be replaced, needles have snapped, knives become blunt, are sharpened and wear thin. There is no waste on the Cape. Nails are straightened, slivers of soap and candle stubs saved, scraps of fat and ash from the fire collected, thread, pins, buttons are hoarded like gold. Tools are oiled and mended, worn boots taken apart, used to repair those less worn and, when beyond saving, made into straps for snowshoes or makeshift hinges on gates and shed doors. Garments are patched, repatched, turned, cut down, brailed together, the sleeves of one item fitted into the body of another. Despite all, things break, crumble, rust, disintegrate, fade, lose their shine, until it seems to Lavinia that life itself has turned grey. She longs to see colour, to smell green, to taste green, is in a rage of impatience for spring.

Winds blow from the north, from the west, then from the north again, ice advances and retreats, the seals come and a sulky, damp spring follows.

By then Mary Bundle, for so she will always be called, has slipped unobtrusively into the life of the Andrews family, moving around the crowded house so efficiently, so silently, that Lavinia sometimes forgets her existence.

That year, as soon as ice moves offshore, Frank Norris arrives. Frank, his wife Ida and their young daughter were among the people burnt out of Shamblers Cove. During the terrible trek the woman's feet froze and the family spent the winter with Frank's people in Pond Island.

"Accordin' to him, she's better now but never wants to see Shamblers Cove again—and I can't say I blames her," Sarah, who has become Frank Norris' confidante, tells the other women.

Frank and his helper, a cousin named Angus Hounsell, sleep at the Vincents. They begin at once laying out stone foundations for a house that Sarah says is to be two stories high with proper bedrooms. The cousins are a civil pair, friendly but quiet, handsome, stocky men, capable of working eighteen hours a day.

The Andrews boat is still not finished, and this summer Young Joe will be fishing with Josh. This leaves Ned and Ben at a loss to know how they will get out on the water. The problem is solved when Frank Norris suggests the Andrews men use his dory in exchange for whatever help they can give him evening times.

Soon all the men and boys are congregating each evening to work for an hour or so on the Norris house. The walls are already up by June when a two-masted skiff ties up at the wharf and unloads not just finished lumber, but a wondrous variety of household goods: felt, glass, wallpaper, furniture, oilcloth, sheeting, even pictures, lamps and cutlery. So stunned are the Cape people by this abundance that they shy away from Frank Norris. That evening only Thomas Hutchings turns up to help with the house.

The next morning Frank's cousin, Angus, without any apparent purpose, wanders down to the stagehead, where he stands making desultory conversation as the women gut fish. Unable to abide such idleness, Mary passes him a knife, "Don't just stand there gawkin', if you got nothin' else to do—work!"

He takes the knife and for the next hour, helps slit throats and gut, all the while carrying on a low conversation with Sarah Vincent, who works steadily beside him. When Ben and Ned tie up with another load, Angus moves over to help them heave cod up on the wharf.

"Sick or something, old man?" he leans forward to stare into Ben's pale face.

Ben shakes his head and continues to fork fish out of the boat. But Ned, happy to break the uncomfortable silence, explains that his brother has a delicate stomach, "Like a young maid, he is b'y, fair upset at the sight of all poor, dead little fish—gets the green heaves ever' single time we goes out."

Shaking his head gravely, Angus studies Ben, whose face has turned beet red during Ned's explanation: "Nothin' worse than seasickness. Sure, why don't we two change places? You go up and help Frank and I'll fish with Ned here—I'd rather be on the salt water any day than drivin' nails, and I noticed you're better'n me with the nails."

They change places immediately. Angus and Ned pull off for the fishing grounds. Ben goes eagerly towards the hammering, never again to set foot in a boat.

When the men leave there is a short silence until Jennie says, "Well Sarah, aren't you goin' to tell us what you and Angus was jawin' about?"

Sarah cracks the head of a huge fish against the edge of the splitting table. "I allow, maid, we misjudged Frank Norris. Angus's and Frank's mothers are sisters and accordin' to Angus all them lot is poor as church mice. 'Tis Ida, Frank's wife, whose people are well off. Ida was a Talbot from Bonavista. I heard tell of them all me life, merchants, a hoity-toity bunch." She flicks cod livers into the blubber barrel.

"Sent the daughter to school down Boston way, accordin' to Angus, and never been reconciled to it that she come back and married a fisherman—were so put out they had nothin' to do with her ever since. Still, they musta' heard about the trouble this winter past. Took pity on 'em I s'pose, after all, blood is thicker'n water. Angus says Frank didn't even know all that stuff was comin'."

"I allow we should all go up after supper and give him a hand," Meg says, and the other women nod.

Except for Mary Bundle, who makes a small, dismissive sound and asks Sarah how people like the Talbots get to be merchants.

"By buying stores and vessels," the older woman snaps and quickly turns the conversation to the interesting subject of marriages—those families have agreed with, and ones that have resulted in parents never speaking to their offspring again.

"Only cause I can see for that is if a youngster married a crook or lunatic—or someone outside the church," Meg says. In a whisper she asks Sarah if Ida Norris' family could be Catholic.

"Oh, I doubts that! None of them people along the Cape Shore is. Far as I knowed the only Papist I ever seen is Skipper Brennan and you'd never think it with him, would you now?"

That night everyone returns to helping with the Norris house, which progresses at an amazing speed. Angus continues to fish with Ned. He also spends more and more time with the women. Mary complains she cannot turn around without tripping over the young man.

For almost two years, Lavinia has not considered herself part of the adult world. When possible, she roams the countryside behind the Cape or works at jobs usually assigned to children, helping Annie and Lizzie care for the babies, bringing water from the pond, weeding or keeping flies away from the drying fish.

When Meg says, "I s'pose you knows young Angus Hounsell got his eye on ye?" Lavinia is shocked and frightened. But after watching Angus for a day, she is forced to acknowledge that her sister-in-law is right.

The idea dismays her and she takes elaborate care to stay out of his presence. The precautions work until one evening, just at dusk, returning from the garden she finds the young man standing in her way—waiting. She stops a few feet off. The two eye each other without speaking for some time. It becomes apparent that whatever words Angus had planned to say have vanished from his mind. Still he stands, smiling and hopeful, confident that Lavinia will read his mind and respond to his unasked question.

His assurance infuriates Lavinia. Unready and unwilling to discard the protection of childhood, she has no patience for this silent declaration.

"I gave him a good hard shove so's he landed arse over kettle in the bushes, his mouth gaping open like a fish. Then I turned on my heel and came home," she records that night.

The incident takes the wind out of the man's sails. He stops hanging around the flakes, avoids the Andrews house and carefully ignores Lavinia for the remainder of the summer. In July, when the Norris house is finished and Frank goes to Pond Island to fetch his wife and daughter, Angus leaves the Cape without bidding anyone but Ned goodbye.

Jennie and Meg, who have watched the hapless wooing with great interest, chide Lavinia for letting so good a catch get away, and "lovesick as Angus Hounsell" becomes a saying that will endure on the Cape long after both Lavinia and Angus are dead and gone.

The Cape people have a proprietary pride in the Norris house. They have all helped with the work and wander in and out inspecting each stage of construction. Although no one puts the feeling into words they all think it a good omen that such a fine dwelling should be built in the place. Its permanence gives the men confidence, makes the women feel happy and hopeful.

Late in the fall, Ben begins to talk of building another room onto the Andrews' overcrowded house. Even Josh Vincent is caught up in the dream, "In ten or twelve year I don't doubt this place will be bigger than Pond Island," he says.

Ned, of course, agrees: "Them waters are swarmin' with fish, enough to keep a hundred families for a hundred lifetimes—makes sense to live out here where all hands can get back and forth to the fishin' grounds three or four times a day and come in loaded to the gunn'ls each time—I 'lows, old man, we picked a good spot!" He slaps Ben on the back, "Go ahead boy, build a room, build two or three rooms!" He assures Mary she'll have a house as good as Norris's in a year or so.

On the day they expect Frank Norris to bring his wife and daughter to the Cape, Sarah, Jennie and Meg make an unprecedented decision. They will take a few hours away from the flake, have a little party to welcome Ida Norris to her new home. Mary is not consulted and if she had been, would have pointed out that no one welcomed her to the Cape. However, she too is taken with the idea of sitting around in the middle of the day drinking tea like a lady.

It is mid-afternoon when the four women meet in the Norris kitchen. They spread Jennie's lace cloth on the table and spend a pleasant half hour arranging and rearranging plates of sweet loaf, sliced bread and a dish of partridgeberry jam around a jar of purple sea peas. When the holes in the cloth are covered they stand back to admire the effect. Then, setting the kettle to boil, they take a tour of the house, "Just to make sure everything is to rights."

Moving slowly from room to room the women make small sounds of admiration, they touch the smooth surfaces of polished furniture, test the great billowing feather bed, run their rough fingers over the curlicues incised into lampshades. They stand, dreamcaught in doorways tracing the patterns of roses, forget-me-nots and other small flowers that climb the walls, marvel at rug-covered floors and whitewashed ceilings. The house has no less than six glass windows.

"Think of a man doin' such a thing," Meg says, touching the lace Frank Norris has hung at each window.

Replete with wonder they come downstairs, not a cobbled-up ladder, but real stairs with a curved bannister and painted steps, and settle in the sunny kitchen to await the arrival of their hostess. Knitting lies untouched in each woman's lap. They sit in silence thinking of the dark, damp interiors of their own houses, of how raw and unfinished the rooms will seem tonight. Sarah, Jennie and Meg feel sad; wonder if it might have been better, after all, had they not seen a house like this. But Mary could weep with spite, scream at the contrariness of fortune that bestows so much on some women, so little on others.

Almost as if she's heard such thoughts, Meg says, "The ways of the Almighty are strange, and it's not our place to question them."

"I'll question them, then! I don't care if I'm struck dead for it!" Mary says quietly. Refusing to raise her head or look at their shocked faces she picks up her knitting, a lumpy grey garment she has been working on all winter.

And the others, ignoring her blasphemy, fall to talking of what Frank's wife will be like.

"I been thinkin' maybe, with her education, she could teach the youngsters to read," Meg announces.

This novel idea fairly takes Sarah's breath away. They discuss it for some time before turning to the condition of Ida Norris' health.

"Angus told me the poor soul cried and moaned some lot after her feet thawed. Out of her mind with pain she was. Then one of them festered and turned black as tar. He said there was even talk of cuttin' it off—a man up the coast a ways cut the frozen feet off his little girl and she lived."

"But who'd have the nerve to do a thing like that?" Jennie shuddered and murmured something to the effect that they shouldn't be talking of such things in front of Meg. She nods modestly in the direction of her daughter-in-law, who is pregnant.

But Sarah is not to be deflected. For an hour she recounts other, less successful, operations she'd heard of being done in desperate circumstances, ending with the opinion that it was just as well they didn't take Ida Norris' foot off, for, according to what Angus Hounsell said, "after a good long spell she got better, the skin knit over and the infection dried up. Angus said she's able to get around on her own now."

"I s'pose when you comes right down to it, she deserves a bit of comfort after all she been through," Jennie says. Meg and Sarah agree. Mary is silent.

"It don't bear thinkin' about what things people have to go through," Sarah sighs. But they do think about it, giving long and detailed consideration to the ills human flesh is heir to.

Meg puts an end to the gruesome conversation by suggesting they say a little prayer for the house and the family, especially for Ida Norris, asking that she enjoy her new home in good health. The women bow their heads as Meg lays this request before the Almighty.

Minutes later Ida Norris walks into the kitchen on the arm of her husband. They know at once that their prayer is not likely to be answered. The young woman's eyes, bright and blue as marbles in her pretty doll face, gaze vacantly past the faces turned towards her.

"Fair gave me the shivers," Jennie tells Lavinia that night. "Like we wasn't there at all—like she was lookin' out through the walls at something we couldn't see."

After standing in front of them a minute, Ida speaks. In the clear, stilted voice of a child reciting lines, she says, "It has been a long journey and I will to bed."

She turns away from the gaping women and goes slowly, slowly up the stairs, one small gloved hand gripping Frank's arm, the other clinging to the rail. Her injured foot, covered by what seemed to be a leather sack, drags behind her like a knotted tree stump.

In the days and weeks that follow, they seldom see Ida Norris. She apparently spends most of her time in bed, never crossing her own door. When the women visit, as they do at first, they have to follow the sound of Ida's voice echoing through the empty house. They usually find her sitting in the rocking chair beside her bed, declaiming lines of poetry about towers, knights, ladies and lords. The visits stop, and eventually months and even years go by without anyone on the Cape setting eyes on the deranged woman.

Three-year-old Rose Norris is well able to manage without the attention of either parent. She turns up at the Vincent or Andrews table for meals and is, according to Sarah, "Saucy as a black, wild as a goat and altogether spoiled through bein' made a pet of by Frank's people."

The small girl attaches herself to the untidy group who still traipse over hill and dale behind Lavinia Andrews.

Frank never speaks of his wife, nor of their life together before coming to the Cape. Close about personal affairs, he treats Ida's strangeness as a temporary aberration, an inconvenience which will soon pass, and counters any inquiries with, "Oh, Ida just needs a bit more rest."

On subjects he does not consider private, Frank Norris is an agreeable, easy going man. He continues the arrangement Angus made with the Andrews brothers, fishing with Ned himself now, at the tail end of the season. Ben returns to work on the Andrews' boat, forgetting for the time-being his resolve to build an addition onto their house.

There is an abundance of fish this year, even late in August the sea is boiling with them. It's a crime, the men say, to have to sleep. One load is barely split and gutted before another is being heaved onto the wharf. It is unusually hot. The women take off as much clothing as they decently can. Still, beneath the oiled aprons, their petticoats and long skirts stick to their bodies. After an hour on the flakes they are drenched in sweat.

Children work just as hard as adults; even the small ones, Isaac, Willie and Charlie Vincent, who has just started to walk, learn to turn the fish and cover it when the sun gets too hot. Still they fall behind and the men have to stop fishing in order to help the women. This makes everyone short-tempered, for, as Sarah says, "Who knows but this is the last day they'll be out there—you can never guess the mind of a cod."

"We wouldn't be so hard put if her ladyship'd come down and give us a hand!" Mary hisses one day, jerking her head towards the Norris house. She doesn't even lower her voice, although Frank is standing right alongside her at the splitting table. The work continues without pause but there is a kind of hush as they wait for Frank's reaction.

"Mary is right, for once," Lavinia thinks. "It's not fair, her up there in bed and all us down here workin' like dogs." Still, she knows Mary would not have said any such thing if Ned was within earshot. Ned never keeps score of what is owed him, nor of what he owes. None of the men appear to. Lavinia reflects on this as she scrapes grey slime off her hands with the back of a knife. She wonders if men are more generous than women or if they have some kind of male reckoning she is not aware of.

Frank takes his time answering, running his blade neatly up the white belly of the cod before looking straight into Mary's face. "Well, maid, I 'low it'll be a good long spell before you'll see Ida able to do this kind of work."

Unrepentant, Mary stares back at him, waiting for something more.

"Yes—yes, I s'pose you're right," Frank says, then, "I tell you what, I wouldn't give your Ned just a shareman's part of our catch—we'll split even. How do that sound to ya?"

Mary nods, satisfied with this arrangement. It seems not to have occurred to her, Lavinia notes, that all of them are doing part of Ida's work.

Two days later, in the middle of the hottest day of the year, a day when the sea seems to have cast a glitter over the land and especially over the rows of salted fish, so that everything shimmers and floats in the hot air, Meg Andrews suddenly doubles up and starts to retch.

Later, she will tell Jennie that she'd been feeling labour pains since early morning, but could not bring herself to lie down when everyone was working so hard. They barely have time to get her, half-dragged, half-carried, up to Thomas Hutchings' store before she gives birth to a boy.

"Well girl, you finally done it, got a brother for young Willie—I knows now he won't have his nose broke!" Jennie chuckles, patting her daughter-in-law's cheek as she tucks the tiny baby into the curve of Meg's arm.

In much less than an hour, leaving Lizzie to sit beside her mother, the women are back on the flakes.

That night Meg becomes delirious. Mary and Sarah, knowing that a fever must burn itself out, take turns sitting in the airless store. They keep a fire going, change wet sheets, replace the quilts Meg constantly pushes away, sponge her burning face and try to spoon wintergreen tea between her cracked lips. But the fever doesn't break and by dawn Meg is raving, calling out bits of hymns, asking again and again for Ben, although he is right there bending over her.

Jennie is beside herself with worry. She sits with the sick woman every minute she can take away from the fish. On the second morning she pulls Sarah and Mary aside. "I'm afraid she's dyin', we're goin' to lose her just like we done Hazel. There must be something we can do?"

Sarah shakes her head, "I'm worn out tryin' to remember something. 'Tis childbed fever she got, I seen more than one die of it—me own cousin Mena Lush from Pinchards Island... ."

Jennie cuts her off. "When I was a girl I recollect someone comin' in to bleed me mother... ." She doesn't dare suggest they try bleeding Meg. When neither Mary nor Sarah responds, the older woman returns to her daughter-in-law's bed and sits crying quietly.

Meg moans and tosses. Her usually serene face is distorted, her hair all undone and sticking to her damp skin. The room is humid, reeking with a sickly sweet smell—the smell of death, Mary thinks.

"I don't see no sense in takin' more blood outta somebody who already lost as much as Meg," she says. Mary is surprised to see that both Jennie and Sarah have turned to her—as if expecting to be told what to do. "I wishes we still had the goats so's we could at least feed the baby."

The fever has dried up Meg's milk and the infant cannot keep down the mixture of grated hard tack and water they boil and strain through a piece of cloth. Mary resolves to have a goat or two on the Cape before her own baby is born.

Although there is nothing they can do, the three women stay with Meg all night. Towards morning, Sarah and Mary go to their houses for an hour or so, leaving Jennie standing beside the sick woman. When Mary returns to the fish store, Jennie is still there, looking as if she has not moved. Tears are streaming down her face, but she is smiling.

"She's better, the fever's broke. She opened her eyes and knew me, but she's asleep now," Jennie is dizzy with relief and exhaustion. Although she has not slept for three nights and is still wearing the stiffened cod-spattered dress she donned the day of the birth, Jennie refuses to go back to her house for a rest. The old woman spends the next hour trying to force a few spoonfuls of water between the baby's blue lips.

The baby dies before sunset but no one can cry, or even feel much sorrow, so great is their relief at Meg's recovery. When she wakes and discovers the infant has died, Meg becomes hysterical with weeping and insists that Thomas Hutchings must baptize the poor little creature and give it a name.

Under her mother's direction, Lizzie sets the flowered bowl filled with pond water on a white cloth she has spread across Thomas's desk. With Meg watching from the bed, Thomas holds the tiny body, dips his fingertips into the bowl, touches the paste-like forehead with drops of water and in the name of

God the Father, God the Son and God the Holy Ghost declares the child to be John Benjamin Andrews, a member of the community of saints.

Meg is satisfied: "I don't know what we'd ever do without you, Thomas, you been such a comfort to us all."

She lets them take the baby away to be buried, and falls asleep again. Jennie touches her daughter-in-law's cheek. "I allow she'll be all right now, I'll go have a bit of a wash and a lie-down before I gets back to the fish."

Despite the baby's death and Meg's illness, despite the presence of a crazy woman, a feeling of satisfaction permeates the Cape that fall.

Four barrels of good cod oil, ten puncheons of pickled herring and eighteen tubs of partridgeberries wait to be picked up by Alex Brennan, in addition to the huge stacks of salted cod. Thomas reckons they will be able to pay off all of last year's debts if Caleb Gosse can get any kind of price for this year's catch.

They have a good supply of fish laid by for themselves too. Two dozen big salmon are salted down, potatoes are ready to be harvested, and any day now grey geese will fly over and thousands of smaller birds will alight on the pond each evening. They again have goats in the shed behind the Vincent house and the barrens are red with berries.

"Like I always said, we'll all be rich one day," Ned tells them. He urges Ben to build onto the Andrews house, "So's we'll have two houses side-by-side. You know, all one but with two front doors—like Ellsworth house. How'd you like that, Mama?" Ned nudges his mother and grins, "We'll call it 'Andrews house'." He gets Lavinia to trace "Andrews House" on a piece of good wood and begins to burn out the letters.

Ned is his old, exuberant self these days, joking, singing, telling extravagant stories about his accomplishments, confident of the future. "Sure look at us, we already owns a house and a boat, and 'tis only early days yet."

He cannot pass his wife without dancing her around or smacking a large, loud kiss on her serious mouth. Although Mary makes disapproving noises at these displays, Lavinia catches her smiling at Ned when she thinks no one is looking. As her belly grows, Mary's face gets rounder, the sharp lines soften, she talks more. That fall Mary Bundle has many reasons for happiness. One is a secret that no one else knows.

On her way home from berrypicking one day Mary had noticed the crescent of moist dark earth just behind the pond where they get water. She must have walked past the spot a hundred times without seeing it, but on this particular day some slant of autumn light made her realize that what she had thought to be bog is really dark black soil. She set the blueberries down and walked slowly around the perimeter of the rock-free spot, pacing it, trying to calculate how much work it would take to plant out.

Mary has a dim recollection of seeing her mother bent for hours over a garden. She herself has no idea of what growing things need but good sense tells her that this dark earth contains something missing from the coarse grey clay in the garden they have cleared up by the woods.

She holds the secret all winter, saying not a word to anyone. The next spring, taking half a bag of cut potatoes, she secretly plants them in one corner of what she has decided will be her garden. All summer long she keeps checking on the potatoes, finds that they need little weeding and are growing much faster than those planted in the upper garden.

For the first time in her life Mary feels content enough to plan a future. Her first child by Ned, a boy they have named Henry, was born during the winter and is thriving. Fanny has at last climbed down from her mother's arms and joined the other children. Isaac, although he still tags along as Ned's shadow in the daytime, at least leaves them alone at night, and one of the goats, which she and Sarah coddled like babies through the winter, has added two kids to the herd.

In early August, unable to contain herself, Mary pulls up some of her potatoes and is gratified to find they are clean, round and of good size. She calculates that the next spring she will plant out all of this garden. If they can trade vegetables she and Ned might get ahead enough for Ben to begin building the addition he is always talking about onto the house.

Mary is tired of living so close to her husband's relatives. Although she does not bicker with Meg or Jennie, there is no warmth between her and the other women. This does not bother Mary, indeed she is hardly aware of the closeness between Meg and her mother-in-law. She is again pregnant, concentrating on the question of how to make room and food for the children she and Ned seem likely to have each year, how to ensure they will never know want, never be beholden to the whims of a master.

Mary yearns over the little crescent of land. She loves it. Instincts passed down from countless generations of peasants tell her that here is something even more valuable than coins. Every chance possible, she goes to the pond to dote over the scrap of soil. Then, afraid someone will notice how often she fetches water, she limits herself to one visit each week.

The piece of land is larger than she had at first thought, and her plants occupy only a small part of it. She longs to fence it in, to make it hers, but knows she cannot without attracting attention. She lies awake beside Ned mulling over the problem, and finally manages surreptitiously to pull four spindly tree trunks down from the Andrew's wood lot. She drives one into the soft earth at each corner of her land.

Not even to Ned does Mary speak of the land. It is the height of the fishing season again, and once more they are numb with work, dropping into bed too spent for speech, much less passion.

It has been accepted now that Ben Andrews will stay ashore. As Ned says, "Ben's never had nerve for the water and what sense makin' a poor fisherman out of a good carpenter."

This year Ned is fishing out of their own skiff and has taken Peter Vincent with him. Peter, still surly, skinny and quick, is given to inflicting sly punches on Isaac, who accompanies them in the skiff. For all that, the Vincent boy is good as a man on the water and proud to be shareman to Ned, with whom he gets along better than he does with his own family.

During the summer, Ben is occupied building a salt room onto Thomas's store and finishing off the Vincents' loft. Thomas, Josh and Ned have all agreed to credit part of their catch to Ben's name. Mary, who keeps close watch on the increasingly complicated financial arrangements of the Cape, reasons that if she can grow enough potatoes, and maybe other vegetables, they will not have to bring so many in from St. John's and she too will get fish credited to her name.

Summer days climb to the frenzy of activity that, as always, drops off when Alex Brennan picks up the last load of salt cod. Although the men will keep fishing into October, catches are now small and the women have time to pick berries, pickle fish and harvest the potatoes and cabbage growing in the upper garden.

The day they begin digging potatoes, the other women discover Mary's duplicity. Instead of going with them to the garden on the hill, she turns off towards the pond carrying her shovel and brin bag. Mystified, Sarah, Jennie and Meg stop to watch as Mary walks to the far side of the pond. For the first time they notice the dark green plants—a good six inches taller than those they are about to dig—and the thin sticks marking each corner of the plot. They watch in silence as Mary bends and, turning over the potato plants, begins to fill her bag.

Sarah Vincent, seeing from Meg's and Jennie's faces that they are as surprised as she by what Mary is doing, walks over to the new garden, goes to each corner, and using all her strength pushes the posts over one by one. Then, without a word, she turns and walks alone up the steep path to the garden they cleared together.

Jennie Andrews takes a long look at her new daughter-in-law and shakes her head before following Sarah. When she gets to the potato plot Sarah is already bent over, turning the plants. Although her face is half-hidden under the shadow of her faded cotton bonnet, Jennie can see that Sarah is crying and knows that her friend feels betrayed. She takes a step towards the other woman but Sarah pulls away and continues working.

Jennie sighs. Wondering what she can say to comfort Sarah, she walks over to the great pile of rock they have pried out of the earth. The thought occurs to Jennie, as it often has lately, that something inside her has run down, that each year she has grown softer, more pliable, until now hardly anything of what she once was remains.

From here she can see all around the point where the sea shimmers in a great, blue semicircle beneath a clear sky. Behind her, dark evergreen is splashed with the yellow of birch and dogberry. On the other side of the small woods is the bog where the grass and bushes are now golden brown, where red marshberries grow close to the ground and round circles of shallow water reflect the sky. Jennie cannot see the bog, the barrens or the neck from the outcropping, nor can she see the hills beyond the neck where she has never been, where the men go in winter to cut wood. Once they worried her, those black hills, but now she likes to think of them there, all those dark, crowded trees between her and the world.

All this at her back, and in front the sea and sky, and the little pond reflecting the red and gold bushes, reflecting Mary, who digs in the brown earth as if unaware of Meg standing nearby watching her.

From the outcropping of rock above them, Jennie Andrews can see the two women beside the pond, and more. Down beyond the pond, near the houses, she can see Ben plane a door to be fitted on the goat shed, sees young Annie Vincent spreading quilts out to dry. Down the beach she can see her son Ned who, with Thomas Hutchings, is scraping the bottom of Thomas's boat. She cannot see Josh Vincent and his oldest son, Joe, but knows they are hand-jigging along the shoals, knows that on the other side of the neck Peter Vincent and Frank Norris are hauling wood down to the shore. The children are somewhere around with Vinnie. Jennie thinks she can catch the echo of their voices from the trees behind her; from the trees also she can hear the bleating of a goat they will have to find before dark.

All this Jennie Andrews knows, thinks, imagines and sees as she stands looking down, smelling the sea and the woods, hearing the sounds of children, of animals and birds. She is overtaken by a great rush of happiness.

"But I must have been happy before now!" Surely when she was young she had been happy, when she and Will Andrews lived under the bridge, when the children were little, when she was a child herself—she must have felt happiness.

Yet she cannot remember being happy—being happy and knowing it like she does at this moment, so that the feeling occupies her, makes her forget the ache in her legs, the gnawing pain in her chest, makes her want to give thanks to a God she's always secretly doubted. She wishes Richard Ellsworth could see her, wishes he could know what a favour he did, turning them out of Weymouth.

"How glad I am," Jennie thinks, "that Ned brought us to this place." She resolves to tell him so this very night.

Then she sees Sarah, remembers why she is standing here like this, and her joy is swept away by anger. Without thinking, maybe with some memory of Richard Ellsworth's cane in her mind, Jennie snatches up a long branch and with great purpose marches down the rocky path much faster than she came up, faster than anyone has seen her move for many years.

"You—you—Mary Bundle, you—get right over here this minute—I got a thing or two to say to you, my maid!" Jennie is talking even before she reaches the spot where Meg still stands, watching in astonishment as her mother-in-law sweeps towards her, waving the switch above her head and clomping each foot down as though they have never given her a moment's pain.

Jennie passes Meg by without a glance and marches on towards Mary, who straightens up. If the dog Skipper had suddenly appeared and begun to give commands, her daughters-in-law could not have been more amazed. Jennie sometimes grumbles, but never does she give an order, shout, or make a decision.

"Come here you!" Jennie comes to a halt and kicks one of the posts Sarah had pushed over.

Mary Bundle walks sullenly to the edge of her garden, and stands, chin out, bracing herself as if ready to do hand-to-hand combat with her mother-in-law.

"I'll not have it—you hear me! I'll not have it!" the old woman screeches. "You understand this, Mary Bundle—understand this, that woman up there...," Jennie gestures towards Sarah, who is still bent over the plants in the upper garden, not even looking their way, "we would ha' starved or froze a dozen times over without her help! Shared everything she had with us, Sarah did, now you goes behind her back and fences a garden!"

Launched into the first tirade of her life, Jennie Andrews discovers the pleasure of shouting out words that follow free, loud and fast upon the angry thought. She continues on for a good ten minutes, throwing out sounds that ring over the pond and bounce off the rocks.

She is still shouting, head back, feet planted apart, the stick waving about as if she were some mad conductor directing seagulls, when, in a split second, all movement stops. All sound stops. Jennie Andrews crumples to the ground still as a rock.

She is dead before Meg and Mary get to her.

Before the winter comes, but not without argument, the garden will be divided into five sections. Mary and Ned will get the piece where the crescent is deepest, a concession to Mary's insistence that no one else would ever have thought to plant anything in the bog. Meg's and Ben's section will be to one side of Mary's. The Vincents will have a plot on the other side with one of the triangular-shaped ends going to Frank Norris and the other to Thomas Hutchings, who will never farm it.

But all this, the dividing of the fertile land, the fencing of it, the building of cellars to store the vegetables that will grow there, is still in the future, unthought of as they ease the suddenly small body of Jennie Andrews onto the door and carry her back to the house she has been so proud of. They are stunned into silence at the suddenness of this death, the first for which they all feel grief.

Chapter 8

We were in the clearing picking up chips when Ned and them came. First the dogs started barking, they smelled the men. We smelled them ourselves before we could see them—a wonderful stink of dried blood and seal oil.

The men have been expected home all week. Mild weather and an offshore wind has driven the ice out, making open water between the reaches, so they will have to walk down from Pond Island through bog and woods.

Not recognizing the figures that come slowly and stiffly through the woods, the children become still, sniffing the air like wild things ready to run. Each face, even those of the older boys, holds the look of suspicion, awe and controlled fear that Lavinia has noticed is their first reaction to anything strange.

The men walking towards them wear the same jackets and pants they left in several weeks before, covered now with layers of grey slime that have hardened so the clothing seems made of dull metal that crackles with each awkward step. Their faces, too, are grey and their hair, which is crusted in dirt, spikes out from under their knitted caps. Lavinia can understand the children's apprehension. The creatures coming through the woods do not seem like flesh and blood, but rocks roughly hacked into the shapes of men.

All are grim faced except for Ned, who musters a smile that shows his lips are cracked and bleeding. Ned and Young Joe hold Josh up between them, pulling the older man along. Frank Norris trails behind carrying the long gun, gaffs, hauling ropes and four canvas sacks that had contained wool socks, cuffs, clean underwear and food when the men left home.

The dogs know who the men are, and they dance around barking and jumping with joy, licking hands, making little darts at the slow moving feet. Suddenly Isaac lets out a shout, races forward and flings himself at Ned, almost knocking him and the two Vincent men over.

"'Tis Da—'tis Da home from swilin', ye dummies!" Isaac, who is now thirteen, seems much younger as he runs back and forth between his half-brothers and Ned.

One by one the children, still shy, go up to the men. Each takes a sack or gaff to carry. Only Charlie, Josh and Sarah's youngest, stays beside Lavinia, his near-sighted blue eyes fixed on his father, limp and sagging between Joe and Ned. The boy looks as if he is about to weep.

"What's the matter, young Char?" Lavinia puts her arm across his shoulders. The boy has just recovered from the cough and sore throat he gets every winter, under her hand his bones are delicate as a bird's and she can feel his breathing. A sudden sense of the boy's fragility, of human fragility, frightens her. She gives Charlie a push: "Run on down and tell your mudder your Da and brother are home—just as scurfy as the last time—and lousy too, I expect."

It is the eighth year men from the Cape have gone to the ice. By now everyone knows that the rest of the day will be spent hauling water, scouring bodies, scrubbing clothing and delousing hair. The wooden wash tubs, cut down from puncheons, will be dragged in from back porches and the women, in a rage to be rid of all that dirt, will scrub the men down. Clothing so worn and filthy that it cannot be washed will be burned on a bonfire the big boys build outdoors. A pungent mixture of turpentine, vinegar and liniment, warmed in cracked saucers, will be rubbed into the men's scalps and their heads will be tied around with rags. Only when every louse and nit is guaranteed to have expired will the rags be unwound and burned and the hair scrubbed with soap made from lye ashes and blubber. This treatment, Ned maintains, is why so many men along the coast have heads as hairless as eggs. He, however, has kept his own fuzz of red curls. Each year Mary threatens to shave his head before he leaves for the ice.

Scrubbed and dressed in clean clothing, the men will finally be permitted to sit and eat until they fall asleep, their heads dropping onto the tables. The women and boys will carry them to their beds where they will sleep for hours. After sunset, though, they will have recovered sufficiently to turn up for a recounting of this year's trip. But looking at Josh Vincent's closed eyes and haggard face, Lavinia thinks it will take more than a good meal and a few hours sleep to restore him.

They are halfway down the path when Lizzie, now Young Joe's wife, comes hurrying towards them with the baby on her hip. Right behind her is Sarah.

"I told you this, didn't I tell you this, Josh Vincent, goin' to the ice at your time of life! Pure foolishness! It'll be the death of you, that it will... ." Sarah arrives, harping, and continues to harp as she eases her shoulder under her husband's arm, freeing Young Joe to go off towards his own house with Lizzie. There is no sign of recognition from Josh and, across his inert body, Ned asks Sarah where Peter is.

"Only the good Lord could tell ya where that one's got to. Might be out on the Funks for all I knows—and me his mother! Took off for Muddy Hole, or so he said, not three days after ye left. In a real state he was, over his father's makin' him 'bide here. Had his mind set on goin' to the Wadhams for the summer—didn't even wait till I had the dory hove over. Thomas and Charlie, God love him, tho' he's not been well, been helpin' scrape her down. I tell you it been a hard spring... ." Sarah chatters on as they move in slow procession towards the houses.

The familiar sound of his wife's carping rouses Josh. He does not open his eyes, but a shadow of a smile plays across his mouth and his drooping head nods and nods as though he is in a happy dream.

At the Vincent house, they ease the half-conscious man down onto the kitchen couch. Meg is already heating water and has dispatched Emma and Patience to the pond for more.

Ned and Frank Norris, Rose clinging to his hand, children and dogs following behind, go on towards the Norris house where Annie Vincent has been sleeping, keeping an eye on Ida and Rose since Frank left. As the procession comes near, they see Annie standing in the door. She walks down the path and takes one of the sacks from Frank. Something about the gesture is so instinctive, so wife-like, that Lavinia glances up to the windows above, but the grimy curtains do not move. There is no sign of Ida Norris, although Lavinia is sure the mad woman is watching her husband's homecoming. Ida sees everything on the Cape. They sometimes catch glimpses of her face as she moves from window to window, following the day's activities. Children whisper to each other about Rose's mother and scurry past Norris' house.

With Isaac on one side and Meg's Willie on the other, Ned continues on toward the Andrews house. His younger sons, Henry, Alfred and George ("the Three Kings," Ned calls them) and Rose (a canny child who never goes into her own house except to sleep), prance around, pushing and joshing each other in a happy parade. Lavinia and Fanny trail behind, not quite part of the rejoicing herd that moves up the path to the double house with two identical front doors.

Ben stands in his own doorway smiling at his brother's triumphant return. Ned's oldest child, Jane, grown now to a pretty young woman with a round face and pouting mouth, is in the other door holding Moses, her newest step-brother.

There is no sign of Mary Bundle, and for a moment Ned looks worried. He calls "Mary!" Then, past Jane's shoulder, he sees her pouring water into a tub and a smile of pure happiness flashes across his face.

Since her marriage to Ned, Mary Bundle has had two miscarriages and has given birth to four sons, but to Lavinia she seems not a hairsbreadth changed from the day she came down from the *Tern* carrying Fanny in one arm and her earthly belongings in the other. The jaw and chin are sharp as ever and, although she softens briefly during each pregnancy, the fullness of cheek and breast disappears as each child is born. There is no extra fat, no drooping, no relaxing of the urgency that gives Mary's simplest movements such purpose. She is still silent except for her rare outbursts, which have become legendary, still quick and hard as a lightning rod, charged with energy that is never used up although she works continuously.

Steam is rising around her, her black hair has slipped down from an untidy bun, her dark dress is rumpled and her apron askew. She kneels forward and puts her elbow into the water, testing its temperature, as intent on the action as if she were brewing a mixture to breed dragons or cure death. She doesn't even glance up as they surge through the door. Ned pushes forward, grabs her around the waist and pulls her up, lifting her clear off the floor.

Standing, irresolute, just inside the door, Lavinia sees Mary's unguarded face tilted back as Ned brings his bleeding lips down on hers. The room around them is aswirl with steam, heat, shouting children, barking dogs and Ned's loud, exuberant laughter.

Lavinia is unaccountably vexed by the scene. For years she has lived apart, separated from the other women by an invisible wall of her own indifference. The joy in Mary's upturned face touches and disconcerts her—and for the second time today. The same feeling, a sense of loss, faint as perfume wafting across from another world, had come over her when she watched Annie Vincent take the sack from Frank's shoulder.

Lavinia snatches up two empty buckets and rushes out of the house.

It is quiet by the pond. She watches clear water swirl into the buckets and tries to calm herself. She wonders where Thomas Hutchings is. Thomas is the only person, aside from Ida, of course, who has not shown up to greet the men. During the winter he often comes to the Andrews house to talk to Ned but each spring when the men leave for the ice he withdraws from the lives of the women and children. They have been here for almost twelve years but Lavinia still takes the man's aloofness as an insult, a deliberate, silent objection to the presence of so many people on his Cape.

Deep in thought, and half hypnotised by the swirling water, Lavinia is startled by a small sound—someone is standing right beside her.

"Fanny! For pity sakes girl, you scared the wits half outta me!"

Lavinia is sorry as soon as the words are spoken. She is sure Fanny gets pleasure from creeping about, materializing like a wraith from behind a bush or rock, and she tries always to disguise her astonishment at the girl's appearance. Fanny moves as silently as her mother, but whereas in Mary the silence makes you forget she is there, it seems to draw attention to Fanny. The girl is small and dark like her mother but loves brighter colours. Fanny has gathered the relics of Lavinia's former life, taken everything left in the old dress-up barrel to be her private wardrobe.

Today the girl is wearing a cut down dress that dangles around her ankles. Over the dress she has draped a piece of net that might once have been white but has turned fousty green with age and mould. The net flutters about her thin shoulders like broken moths' wings, twining with a reddish cord twisted around her hair and ravelling down her back.

Sarah Vincent maintains that Fanny's been led astray, like a girl she knew on Pinchards Island, taken by the fairies and changed. Lavinia thinks Sarah might be right. Certainly the little creature who now stands smiling beside her looks more like a fairy's child than a daughter of brisk, down-to-earth Mary Bundle.

Fanny's silence, her smug smile, irritates Lavinia. "Cat got your tongue?" she asks.

Fanny shakes her head. She moves to sit on a rock and pats the spot next to her, never taking her eyes from Lavinia who, despite herself, sits down and leans forward towards the girl.

"What is it?"

"You know when we was up gettin' wood, just afore the men come this morning?"

"Yes, yes," Lavinia nods. They are both whispering.

"I seen someone watchin' me, I thinks it was the king of the gypsies!"

"What did he look like?" Lavinia croaks, then, shaking herself, snaps, "Oh, for Lord sakes, Fanny, the king of the gypsies lives in England! That's Ned's old prate you're goin' on with, the only people on the Cape is us!"

"This warn't a people, Vinnie—not like anyone I ever, ever seen," the dark little face is scrunched up in earnestness, "but he looked nice, like he wanted me to come into the woods with him."

Can the girl be serious? Lavinia wants to warn her about something—but what?

"Come on, Fanny, pick up one of them buckets. Your mother will be havin' a fit if she runs out of water while two of us is lollygaggin' down here."

The child doesn't move. "If he asks me, will I go away with him, Vinnie?"

"Yes girl, never say no to a king. Now, come on!" Lavinia sets the two buckets upright and flicks a handful of water over the girl's head. Bright drops spatter into the net like small jewels.

"Maybe she is a princess of the gypsies and her father is looking for her," Lavinia thinks. "She is beautiful." Annoyed with herself for such romancing, she grabs the girl's hand. "Come on, Fanny, up to the house, Ned'll be turned to a prune waitin' for clean water."

But the girl pulls her hand away and Lavinia leaves her there looking like some exotic mussel that has grown onto the rock.

Up at the house a show is going on. As a token gesture to decency, Mary has draped quilts over chair backs to make a shaky screen around the tub before proceeding to strip her husband. She tosses salvagable items of clothing into the iron pot of water that is boiling on the fire and passes the most dirt-stiffened garments on a long stick over the heads of assembled children to the boys, who are tending a fire in the front yard.

As each item is pulled from Ned's body, Mary comments on the condition of the garment or of her husband. He stands meekly in front of her, grinning across the quilts at the children ranged along the wall.

"That's the end of that good wool vest yer poor mother knit... ." An unidentifiable object, its once bright colours dirty grey, is consigned to the fire.

"Ribs like a spavin' cow!" A torn and filthy shirt is flung into the iron pot.

"Look at you, Ned Andrews—happy as if you had the best of sense and them good pants in rags." Mary throws the stinking trousers though the door.

"Aw go on, love, them was an old pair of breeks Tom Toe dropped on Ben's cart a hundred year ago." Ned smiles down at the top of his wife's head. "Watch out now for the next layer, don't want to ruin the family jewels, do we?"

Mary gives him a hard slap on the bare backside as she hauls off the grey underwear and throws it into the bubbling cauldron.

By now every child in the place is standing around the circle, relishing the spectacle of lanky Ned Andrews being stripped down to his pale freckled skin. He is enjoying it too, making faces at them as he does a little jig, one foot in the wash tub and one on the floor.

Lavinia marvels at her brother. How can he push off the terrible weariness she'd seen on his face earlier? She laughs along with the children at the sight of Mary chasing him around the tub, flicking a wet cloth at him and, finally, pushing him down into the water. He pops up like a jack-in-the-box, makes a horrible face across the quilts, and Mary, her patience at an end, chases them all out, slamming and bolting the door behind them.

Lavinia, who has long accepted being treated as one of the children, stands watching the fire for a few minutes, then drifts into Meg's and Ben's house. Although the houses look identical from the front, Ben's side of the house is larger since he built two extra rooms, one above and one below, onto the back. Since Lizzie married Joe Vincent, Lavinia has shared the lower back room with Emma and Patience.

Ben is alone in the kitchen, poking the fire beneath two pots, one containing fish stew and the other an eider duck. He tells her that Meg and the girls have gone to help Sarah.

"Some racket next door—I allowed for a spell the wall was comin' in," he grins at Lavinia.

Lavinia looks around thinking to give Ben a hand, but she can see nothing to do. The room is spotless; the long shelf above the fire and the wooden benches on each side glow with the oil Meg rubs into them. On the white scrubbed floor are hooked mats, and on every chair and bench patchwork cushions are set just so. Even the knitted shawl is folded neatly across the back of a sofa Ben has built against the wall. For the first time Lavinia sees how comfortable the room is. Because of Ben's carpentry and Meg's housekeeping they have the nicest house on the Cape.

"You can peel a few potatoes if ya got a mind to," Ben points the poker towards the table and Lavinia brings the brin bag and a knife over to the fireplace.

It is not often that she is alone with her older brother and it comes to her that she would like to talk to him. She wonders who Ben is like, maybe their father, who died before she was born.

"Ben, do you believe in fairies?"

Ben is a cautious man. His greying hair and carpentry skill has given him an air of dignity he lacked when young. He stirs the stew, gravely considering his sister's question, the first she has ever asked him.

"I don't know, Vinnie, girl. I hears Ned tellin' them stories of his, and I wonders about such things. He believes in 'em, you know, or at least when he's talkin' about 'em he believes. Now Sarah, I allow she believes in 'em all the time—I seen her scatterin' crumbs in the woods for fairies. I don't know, meself.

Afore I come to this place I didn't believe in nothin'. Back home when Mama and Meg used to go to that little church over Handley's Lane I never said nothin'—but I never went. Still and all, since we come here I'm not so flick to say things are not there just 'cause you can't see 'em."

Ben pauses, considering what he is about to say. "You know, lots of times I'm the only person in the place. When other men are out in boat, the women in the gardens and you off with the youngsters somewhere, I'm up on one of the roofs or around back workin' on an outhouse or somethin' and... " he stops again as though embarrassed, "you know I gets this queer feelin' come over me, like there's something about—fairies, or angels, or whatever it is that Ned and Meg believes in—and you know, Vinnie, it's not a bad feelin'. Whatever it is, 'tis good, I can feel it."

Lavinia, who had expected a quick dismissal of her question, is speechless. She thoughtfully peels the potatoes, cutting out rotten bits, saving them with the peel for the goats. They are both silent until Ben eases the pot containing the baked duck away from the ashes. Wrapping an old mitt around the hot handle, he leaves, explaining that Meg has instructed him to take the bird to the Vincents for their supper.

Lavinia sits on in front of the fire. It is mid-afternoon, a kind of holy stillness has settled over the place. By now the four men are asleep, the children have been shooed off to play away from the houses and the women, Mary, Sarah and Lizzie each in her own house, and Annie down at the Norris house, Lavinia supposes, will be quietly putting the kitchens to right. The fire in the Andrews' yard has burned low but the smell of seal fat still hangs thick and oily in the air.

When it gets dark, the youngsters begin making the rounds of the houses. This is a new custom, started only last year when the men returned from sealing, but the children have no intention of forgetting it. The men have not forgotten either. At each house they are waiting, even Josh Vincent, who will be unable to walk for months, is propped up on the sofa, ready with a bag of candy.

Lavinia doesn't ask which of the men, in the alien, crowded streets of St. John's, had thought of the children back on the Cape. Who had ventured first into a store? She guesses it might have been Ned, can imagine him urging the others to face down a haughty store clerk, to spend some of their hard-earned coins on sweets for the youngsters.

Again this year, tucked away in a corner of each man's sack, is the same brown paper bag of identical hard candy the children call freelies and will remember all their lives as the most wonderful taste in the world.

Sixty years later, Charles Vincent, a distinguished missionary returning from service in India, when asked by a Boston reporter to recall memorable events of his life, will tell first of freelies.

"I can see them now," he said, "my father and the other men, how they would reach into the grease-stained bag and hold out three candies to each child. I can see the hand, calloused and cut with twine, sometimes with blisters and spots of frostbite, the thick knotted stumpy fingers cupped, holding three sweets, always three, always the same. White they were, with pale red, green and yellow stripes like pen lines. They smelled of seal oil that had soaked into the brown paper. Nothing since has matched the mouth-watering expectation I used to feel, reaching out for those candies."

By the time the children get to Ned's house, the adults have already congregated there. The talk is all of seals, sealing vessels, sealing captains and sealing disasters. Every boy in the room is determined that one day he too will go swilin', will somehow get in to St. John's, sign on under one of the great sealing captains, will sail north to walk over ice floes among herds thick as sand on the beach, will come home with real money in his pocket, with candy for other children.

"I'm nigh on twelve year old—Uncle Ned says boys no older'n me goes swilin'—next year I'm goin'," Willie, who has remained an only son and youngest child, announces to his mother.

Meg turns her mouth down at this but wisely says nothing. Rose Norris, however, gives the boy a hard kick, "Deed you won't, Willie Andrews, not unless I goes too." Rose wears Willie's cast off overalls and with her short stubby hair that Frank hacks off around the edge of a bowl, looks like a boy.

Isaac, who is three years Rose's senior, tells her that girls don't go sealing. She jumps on him and proceeds to pound him with her fists until her father pulls her away.

Ned, dandling Moses on his knee, is delighted with Rose. "Maybe by the time you're old enough, girl, women'll go sealin'. Maybe you'll be as good a swiler as yer father. We Cape Random men is the best ones you can have on ice, even the Barbours and Blackwoods says that."

Ignoring black looks from Meg, Ned is off, telling Rose her father can track seals down across the miles of ice, leap over black cracks, clamour up great ice mountains, smelling the seals out.

Frank himself says nothing. Lavinia notes that he has his head wrapped in rags, is as well-scrubbed as the other men, and wonders if Annie washed him down. She looks quickly across to Annie, who is sitting next to Josh, holding her father's swollen feet on her lap. As long as Lavinia has known her, Annie has been doing for someone. Quiet and biddable, she waits on her three brothers, her father, and now it seems, on Frank Norris.

When Ned's story ends, the children stare round-eyed at Frank. And Charlie Vincent, who has been quiet all day, says he will go next year too. "If we can get berths, me and Peter and Isaac and Willie—the lot of us'll go—Uncle Ezra'll see we gets places. He knows all them sealin' captains."

"No, me son, that you will not!" Josh Vincent shakes his head with unusual firmness.

"Me and mine will never go to the ice again—no, not s'pose we starves. 'Tis all very well for Ned there to tell fine stories, but truth is 'tis not fit for a human creature to live days and days on nothin' but molasses tea and hard tack. Some years the ice is that thick we got to cut a lead—get out with saws and cut a lead—then haul the vessel along with ropes. Cut 'n haul, cut 'n haul 'til ya reaches open water—dangerous, brutal work!" Josh's pale face is flushed.

Near tears, Annie pats his hand, repeating, "Pappa, Pappa, Pappa," over and over.

But he doesn't even hear her. "Then ya gets inta the fat and you're goin' over the side. Famished, with a blizzard blowin', your feet and face frozen and you half-blind jumpin' across open water. I seen times we put our hands inside the seal carcass just to thaw out, yes, and to get a bit of heart or liver—eatin' it raw, we're that hungry. Then comin' back to the ship dead tired and sleepin' on top of great piles of stinkin' pelts. And in the end you gets fifteen pounds or so. No me son, 'tis like a lot of stuff—sounds better in stories than 'tis for them doin' it. Neither you nor Peter will go. Not long as I has anything to say about it."

They are shocked into silence. Josh, who rarely speaks more than two words together, has said all this—things none of the men have ever spoken of—in his wonderfully soft, slow voice. The silence is finally broken when Ned starts to hum.

Young Joe pulls from his pocket a jews-harp he got from another sealer in exchange for a pair of cuffs. After the children have examined the strange object, Joe puts it between his lips, strumming along to the old song.

Ned immediately stands up and planks Moses into Meg's lap. He snatches up the red calico brought from St. John's and, draping it around Mary Bundle's head and shoulders, begins dancing his wife around the crowded room. With the pillow ticking tied turban-like around his head to trap lice, Ned's face, browned from weeks of wind, sun and ice, is, dark as Mary's. Clinging to each other, they whirl about in the firelight.

Watching her brother and his wife dance, Lavinia thinks they look like gypsies, like the people Fanny spoke of, and again she feels the dull longing for something that has passed her by.

Then Fanny jumps up, pulls at Ned's arm, snatches the red mantilla from her mother's head and dances off with her stepfather. The spell is broken. Mary shrugs, grabs Lavinia's hand, pulls her to her feet and, as the others clap, they too dance about between the chairs and people.

That night Lavinia cannot sleep. In the room she shares with her nieces she lies wide awake, wondering why the day's events have so disturbed her: Young Joe going off so happily with the baby and Lizzie (Lizzie, whom she has always thought of as a child, now a wife); Annie waiting at the end of the path for Frank Norris; Mary's face suddenly beautiful as Ned bent to kiss her.

Maybe she is lonely—but she's known that for a long time—chosen it, in fact. Telling herself to concentrate on other things, she tries to count the noises she can hear—an old trick that usually makes her sleepy. Tonight there is no howl of wind or hiss of snow, only the gentle breathing of Patience and Emma and, outside, the soft click of dories on collar, the swish of sea and the gurgle of small stones that roll back underwater. That is all.

Still, she cannot sleep. There is an aching hollowness down through her, almost a pain. She gets up and goes to sit on the front step. Not a thing is stirring, and the only light in the place is in Thomas Hutchings' fish room. But by the moonlight Lavinia can see everything clear as day—the furry heaps of two dogs curled down beside the fence, a mat left on the line, even the pale ash of the fire the boys made today. Up against the cliff face, pine studs of the house Peter started, then abruptly abandoned, stand out shining white against the sky. Why would Peter Vincent build a house?

It is a warm night for this time of year, but not warm enough to sit outside in bare feet. Coming out of her meditation, suddenly aware that she has forgotten to pull on the seal skin boots she has been wearing since last fall, Lavinia goes back inside, thinking to return to bed. Instead, she pulls the old bag containing her belongings down from the nail above her bed. Then she pads, still barefoot, back out to the big room.

Settling on the floor by the fire, she rummages in the sack and pulls out her leather boots, the boots she had worn from Weymouth. She's made them last by going barefoot in the warmest weather and by wearing the sealskin boots Meg and Sarah make in wintertime. The seal boots are warm and dry when it's very cold, but Lavinia thinks them awkward and they never keep the damp out. From now on, though, she may have to wear them, for her good boots have fallen apart during the winter.

She fingers the bits of worn black leather and begins to cry. She cries on and on, trying to be as quiet as possible. It is the first time she has cried in years. It feels foolish to be dripping tears onto a pair of mouldy soles, ragged laces and uppers, still she cannot stop. The thought comes to her that she cannot remember having cried since her mother died. She cries on and on as if making up for all the years without weeping.

It is all so hopeless—all worn and hopeless like the boots. There is no way to replace them, no way to replace anything. Her labour on the flakes is credited to Ben. Which, after all, is only right since she lives in his house and eats at his table. Ben and Meg are probably the best-off people in the place, but even they have no money.

And Ned, with his crowd of children, certainly can't help. She saw what he brought home today, a paper of pins and five yards of red cloth for Mary, a pair of caulked leather boots for himself and the candy. When Mary chided him for buying the calico, he'd answered cheerfully that he still had seven pounds to credit towards his bill with Caleb Gosse. Mary had run her hand over the bright cloth and said quietly, "We'll go to our graves paupers."

"I'll just have to go barefoot like the youngsters," Lavinia thinks as she drops pieces of boot into the ashes.

The fire flares up and she sits, watching the boots redden, curl up and crumble.

An hour later, when Meg's bare feet, followed by her flannel covered rump, descends the ladder from the loft room where she and Ben sleep, Lavinia is writing in the journal. It is the first entry she has made in ten years.

"I told Ben I heard something down here, I allowed one of the dogs sneaked in." Meg crosses the floor, sits on a corner of the quilt Lavinia has wrapped herself in, and stretches her toes towards the heat.

She sees the charred outline in the red cinders and asks, "What you been doin', burnin' boots?"

"They're gone, maid, rotted right apart durin' the winter. I was trying to figure out what I'd wear on me feet from now on," Lavinia closes her book and slides it back into the bag.

"You're good at writin' aren't ya, Vinnie? I sees you down on the sand, sometimes teachin' the youngsters their letters."

Lavinia nods and waits. Meg seldom talks aimlessly. When Lizzie had married Joe, it was Meg who suggested that Lavinia move in with her girls. Still, she has never been close to Ben's wife, always feels like a small child in Meg's presence.

"I've not had a friend since Ned—not in all the years we been on the Cape," Lavinia thinks, sadness rolling back in like fog. There is really no one for her, she might always be alone. She examines this idea, wondering if she can stand a lifetime of loneliness.

"...and that Reverend McDowell—the Church of England clergyman come down the coast two summers ago." Meg looks up and realizes that Lavinia has not been listening. "Oh Vinnie, you knows who I'm talkin' about, the preacher baptised Ned's boys and married our Lizzie to Joe Vincent."

Lavinia remembers a tall man with a terrible cough.

"A real scholar that man were—you'd never know his father were a miner in England. Think of that, his father a miner and him a minister!"

Meg is glowing with this marvellous bit of information but Lavinia doesn't know what to make of it. She wonders how Meg could have discovered such a thing from the dignified clergyman who had stayed on the Cape barely long enough to administer the sacraments.

Sitting back on her heels and smiling expectantly, Meg waits. Although she has thickened at the hips and waist, Ben's wife is still a handsome woman, with high cheek bones and skin that stays smooth even when she works on the flakes.

There is a faint blush on her cheeks as she prompts Lavinia. "Don't you think that's a good idea, Vinnie? You think our Willie could be a scholar?"

Lavinia is stopped from laughing by the earnestness of her sister-in-law's face. Willie is the apple of Meg's eye. She dotes on the boy and expects his three sisters to do the same. Most of the time they do, and the attention of so many women has, in Lavinia's view, turned Willie into a sook. Only the frequent trouncings applied by Rose Norris, smaller than Willie but tougher, has saved the boy from being completely spoiled.

"I s'pose Willie could learn if he put his mind to it," she says, thinking that Meg's son is not quarter as smart as Charlie Vincent, who can already read any word she writes in the sand.

"Oh, he'll learn quick enough once you get started! We'll let him be for the summer, but when fall comes I'll see to it that he settles down to it."

Whatever Meg is getting at is not something she's just thought of, for she has it all worked out. "Tell me again, Meg, just what it is you got planned."

"School, girl, school! For Willie, for the rest of 'em, too if they minds to. You'll be teacher, and soon as ever he can, Ben'll set to work on a big room out to one side. A school room with an outside door so's the youngsters can come and go without streelin' through the house. We'll build it on out that way. We'll need a chimney, too, won't we?"

The problem of a chimney seems to be one that Meg has not solved but it occupies her for only a second. "Ben'll work that out—and I'll get Thomas to order a book, maybe two books. Ben and me talked it over and we'll figure out some way of payin' for 'em. Ben thinks Thomas might want a twine loft built above the store."

Lavinia is aghast at the idea of teaching, "Meg, you seen me down on the sand teachin' the young ones their letters, but they only minds me long as they thinks it's a game. They'd never abide for me to be a real teacher! Anyway, I don't know anything to teach. Sure I can barely read meself—I only got two winters of Sunday school."

"Oh go on, Vinnie, if you can read you can teach—after all 'tis all in books. You only got to keep ahead of the youngsters. I'd do it meself if I could read," Meg dismisses her objections.

"And Vinnie, for the ones goes on, like our Willie, why when you learned him all you knows then maybe Thomas could take him over. Thomas writes right good and you know what, one day I heard him say some foreign words! Oh Vinnie, wouldn't your poor Ma be proud to know her grandson come to be a preacher!"

So! This is Meg's dream—her son a preacher! The highest calling she can imagine for her darling. Lavinia watches her sister-in-law rock back and forth, hugging the idea, aglow with pride at the thought of Willie a man of the cloth.

"You'll help me, won't you, Vinnie?"

"I s'pose I can try," the answer seems ungracious in the face of such joy, so Lavinia adds, "I'll do the best I can, girl."

Quite unexpectedly, Meg kisses her and Lavinia remembers another emotional night scene, the morning after which Meg had returned to being Meg. Maybe, she reflects, every nine years or so Ben's wife goes through some turmoil that lasts just one night. Maybe in the morning she will have forgotten this school business, will never mention it again, just as she has never referred to the morals of Ned and Mary after her midnight harangue.

What an unusual person Ben's wife is underneath! Studying the woman beside her, Lavinia wonders if Meg is ever lonely. Suddenly solicitous, she pats her sister-in-law's knee, "I'll do what I can."

Meg jumps up and goes over to the boxes Ben has built as seats on each side of the fireplace. The large bench facing them is always filled with splits, but Meg lifts the lid of the smaller one, which is her private storage space.

She takes out several balls of wool, an armload of quilt scraps, a half-finished mat and then a small china jug made in the shape of a cow, with large blue eyes and a ribboned tail. The cow jug, once one of Jennie's most cherished possessions, makes Lavinia smile.

"I'm savin' for Willie," Meg shakes the cow before returning it to the bench. "Here, here's something for you—no sense sittin' there cryin' about worn out boots when there's a good pair right under your nose," she says and passes a cloth sack to Lavinia.

Inside the sack is a pair of nearly new women's boots, still shiny, with buttons down the side rather than laces. Lavinia runs her fingertip reverently around the toe, "Where ever did they come from?"

Meg looks into the dead fire. "They belonged to poor Hazel," she says, "No sense in buryin' good boots—I was savin' 'em for one of the girls."

"By rights Jane should have them." Jane will need boots, Lavinia thinks. She wonders if Meg knows that her daughter Emma and Ned's Jane have been talking for years about leaving the Cape; that last fall they even asked Alex Brennan if he would help them find work in St. John's.

"Jane got feet the size of flounders. She wouldn't go near them boots," Meg says.

"I don't want to be walkin' about in poor Hazel's boots," Lavinia says, but without conviction. She does not really care that the boots had belonged to Hazel, long dead and with the words already worn away from her wooden headstone; doesn't even care that the boots should rightfully go to Jane. It flashes across her mind that maybe everyone is as greedy as Mary, only Mary doesn't bother to hide it.

"Let Jane earn her own boots and I'll earn these," she thinks. She pulls on the boots and buttons them up—knowing full well that she is sealing some kind of pact.

"You'll have to tell young Willie to mind me—if I'm goin' to teach him, he'll have to stop larkin' around with Rose and Isaac all day," Lavinia says, wondering why Meg gives her a wry smile.

"Never you mind, I'll bring our Willie to his porridge—give him a good talkin' to once the fish are in. And I'll get them books ordered too when Alex Brennan comes!" Well satisfied with her night's work, Meg turns away and climbs the ladder to bed.

The fire has gone out, the sky begins to lighten but Lavinia sits on, wondering if she will live to regret the bargain she has just made.

Chapter 9

We completely overlooked Reverend Eldridge when he first come. Looking back on it now I can hardly credit such a thing. I suppose we were so taken with the Gill boat and with Sarah's brothers we never noticed the good old man, left him sitting in the cold without so much as a word or a nod.

Meg and Sarah especially are shamed by this lack of hospitality. They try so successfully to make up for it on future visits that the old clergyman will come to think of the Cape as a second home. "A place of refuge, a sure and certain help in time of storm," Reverend Eldridge describes Cape Random in a notebook that will eventually find its way into the London archives of the Methodist Church.

The Gill vessel, a neat little bully with one sail, is enough to lift your heart. The morning she arrives, Thomas Hutchings, along with the women and children, is down at the landwash with a fire lit under the tar pot. Still crippled from his trip to the ice, Josh Vincent sits on an upturned puncheon splicing new rope for a swing. In front of him, Rose and Willie squat, watching his hands magically weave one piece of rope into another. The spring morning is warmed only a little by pale sunshine and the pungent smell of hot tar Thomas is using to repair his boat.

Sarah recognizes her brothers' vessel from a mile away. "That'll be Calvin and Clyde goin' up toward Black Tickle—belike they cut wood up that way last winter—they'll cruise it back before dark."

Her voice is wistful. Her brothers have stopped in at the Cape only once since she and Josh moved down from Pond Island.

"'Tis hard not hearin' from mama or me sisters from one year to the next. Still, you can't expect men to understand that," she says now as she has many times before.

"That's one sweet little boat," Josh says. He has great respect for his wife's brothers.

The Gills, who live on Pinchards Island, are a smart lot. People along the shore say that from May to October Calvin and Clyde Gill never sleep. Josh doesn't doubt it, certainly they're the most successful fishermen this side of

Bonavista Bay. He can't fault them. Still, he wishes they would come by more often to relieve Sarah's mind about her family. He is thinking this when the bully begins to tack around.

"Seems to me she's comin' in," he says.

A look of dread comes over his wife's face, "Something's happened up home then—something's happened to Mother."

Sarah knows that Mary, and sometimes even Meg, make fun of her dour forecasts but she cannot help herself. "'Tis Mama, I allow Mama's dead, Josh," she says with grim finality and begins to cry.

"Do men always expect to see bawling women when they bring their boats in to shore?" Lavinia wonders. "What else can they expect? No one makes a special trip with good news and since women go nowhere, bad news must come to them." Lavinia does not consider herself part of the group she identifies as women.

Before moving to the Cape, Sarah used to see her brothers each summer when they came to Pond Island for gear. Lavinia remembers her saying they would always have a package from Pinchards Island.

"Some little thing Mama made—a pair of leggings for Young Joe when he was tiny, bags of herb tea or the salve she stops bleeding with. She sent me that hooked mat I still got, the one with kittens and roses, and 'twas her gave me them lilac bushes. Mamma got lilacs set out all alongside the fence up home. And one time, when I were in the family way with Peter, she sent a jar of cooked caribou meat."

At Jennie's graveside, Sarah had kissed Lavinia. "'Tis hard girl, with yer mother gone. I knows, I been among strangers all me married life," she had said.

Now she laments aloud that she never made Josh take her up to Pinchards Island. "We could'a gone—'tis not far by water—not far by water... ." She repeats the phrase over and over.

Josh nods absently, watching Clyde and Calvin bring the bully smoothly around the shoals. Working in perfect unison they haul the canvas in, bring the vessel alongside and make her fast.

It is just as well that Sarah prepared herself. Her brothers do little to soften the news. Each man makes a sort of bob towards his sister, a jerky gesture that looks like the beginning of a kiss but is still-born six inches from Sarah's wet face. The men are twins, sandy-haired, spare, and, like most along this coast, twice as strong as they look.

"Sorry, maid—'appened just before Christmastide."

Knowledge that her mother has been dead for months makes Sarah weep even louder.

"Now maid, don't carry on—she had a good life and she were well along in years," one brother makes a weak attempt at comfort.

"She were fifty-six, Calvin Gill—fifteen year older than me!" Sarah says with bitterness that Josh tries to cover up by asking if his mother-in-law had been sick for long.

"She's not been herself since last fall, but not what you call sick, not till the end," one of the men— Lavinia cannot tell one from the other— says.

"Mrs. Lush come in to sleep when she was took bad, and of course Bride and Greta was there."

Sarah's brothers take turns speaking. Each can manage only a few words at a time. Their voices are very like Josh's: soft, without emphasis, as if they have never had to shout in all their lives.

Although they are Sarah's relatives, their faces too seem to Lavinia to resemble Josh, not in the bones or colouring but in the open, innocent quality. They have the same guileless look.

Helpless before the woman's sobs, the men fall silent. Then, remembering that they have another errand, they brighten a little. "We got something for you from Mama, something she wanted you to have."

They go back to the boat and uncover a huge sideboard, which, with the help of Thomas, Willie and Charlie, and in the end Annie, Patience and Lavinia, they hoist out of the boat. The thing is shiny black and so bedecked with fretwork, scrolls and curlicues that it looks more like a church altar than something to hold dishes. The wharf seems to sag beneath its weight, and Josh expresses doubts it will fit into their house.

"'Tis only old stuff Mama got from Grandmother Loveys," Clyde, or Calvin, says apologetically, as if to assure his sister's husband that the gift is no reflection on his ability as a provider.

"'Tis always been passed down to the oldest girl, ya understand," the other brother adds.

"Mother took to broodin' at the end—worried about everyone, she were."

"Kept us runnin' for weeks, guv away all her do-dads, divided her crockery up between the girls."

"...one day it'd be a pile of quilts to take over to Aunt Edwina Hounsell, another time she made Clyde take a yaffle of rounders across to old Mrs. Pike."

"You remembers Mrs. Pike, she lived alongside us for years. When her husband drowned she went to bide with Lem and them."

Sarah has stopped crying, she reaches forward to touch each of her brothers. "You was good sons to her, I knows that. And I'm obliged for the sideboard. How's Greta and Bride—and young Sarah—and your own crowd, how are they?"

Absolved, the brothers relax, take turns reciting news of courtings, births, deaths and marriages on Pinchards Island.

"...and half the place's been saved... ." This last item brings their joint monologue to an abrupt end. Looks of shock, guilt, then sheepish amusement cross both faces in quick succession.

"We forgot all about the old codger," Calvin slaps his knee and is silenced by a jab in the ribs by his brother, who, with a loud artificial cough, announces: "We got the Reverend Ninian Eldridge aboard. He's one of them Wesleyan preachers."

The announcement is met with silence. The Gill men begin edging towards the boat, then pause, seeming to feel it necessary to prepare the people on the wharf. "This preacher's a queer duck," Clyde explains in a half-whisper.

"Your brother Ezra walked him over from Pond Island, Josh. That were weeks ago when the ice was still in. He been on Pinchards Island ever since—holdin' what he calls revival meetings."

"Yes, boy, we all been revived—all Wesleyans now, the whole lot of her, all gone over, 'cept me and Calvin here."

"So, if ye crowd are not fixed to have yer souls saved within the fortnight ye better not let the Reverend ashore."

"Since I never had me soul wasted I can hardly have it saved. What's 'saved' anyhow, and what's all this about Wesleyans? Them the ones called ranters I once heard tell of?" Sarah scowls at her brothers, "We'um Pinchards Island people always been Church of England."

"Not now they i'nit. Greta and Bride, and Mary Jane too, all our crowd turned over... ."

"...along with the Parsons and Sainsbury's, and Aunt Elsie Hounsell and her crew."

"What would poor Mama say? And her hardly cold in her grave!" Sarah is shaken to hear that her relatives have so quickly abandoned the established church. "I can't think what's got into ye at all, followin' after some foolish feller when we been Church of England time out of mind."

Clyde winks at his brother. "Well, Calvin old man, we'd best hoist sail and take the Reverend on up to Cat Harbour or some other godless place."

"Makes no odds to him I s'pose, one place is good as 'nother for savin' souls."

Nodding soberly, the two make as though to return to the bully.

But Meg Andrews is already in the boat. Everyone watches as she makes her way towards the stern where the minister must be sitting, quiet as a mouse and hidden from the people above by the half-reefed sail. They see Meg bend forward, say something, then hold out her hand as the man stands. He comes up to Meg's shoulder. She takes his arm and leads him, as if he were one of the ancient blind prophets, carefully up from the bully.

He is very old, bent and shrivelled, wearing a black suit that has not fitted him for a long, long time.

Alfred whispers, "Is that God?" in a frightened croak. Mary silences the boy with a sharp crack on the ear and the old man looks towards them. Maybe he smiles, maybe not. It is impossible to tell, but his face seems to compress into even more wrinkles.

Lavinia will write later, "He looks like a roasted caplin far as I could see, though we didn't get to study him long, account of Meg marching him right by us and up to the house."

That night they assemble in the fish store for Reverend Eldridge's first meeting.

Meg has been busy. With Annie's and Lizzie's help she has pushed everything against the walls, scrubbed the floor, pulled the splitting table to the front and covered it with her white cloth. She has set Jennie's brass candle holders, one on either side, to make an improvised altar.

The old man stands, his claw-like hands splayed out on the cloth as if to support himself. He blinks and looks slowly around. It is not yet dark. Enough light seeps through the single window for him to see his audience, sitting in two untidy rows on the floor. Leaning forward he takes time to scrutinize each face. The silence grows long. A fly buzzes around his head and swoops to pitch on the back of his hand. Fanny begins to giggle uncomfortably but stops abruptly when he fixes his eyes on her.

After he has made a careful assessment of each face, he removes his hands from the table, straightens, and begins to speak. Then everything changes. Before their astonished eyes he grows taller and younger. His hands become knives slashing into the air, pulling down familiar phrases to crash around their heads, billowing the old, mystical, moving story of a Christ oppressed with their sins, sacrificed for their shortcomings, taking their guilt upon him and rising triumphant. A Christ unwilling that any should perish but that all, all, every one of them—the voice rises, he looks into each face—every one should be brought to the glory of his mercy.

Words ring out in rolling cadence and are caught in the minister's hands, twirled and flung out again into the circle of white faces. The room becomes dark, but no one moves to light the candles. No one moves. He talks for an hour, filling the whole Cape with the sound and the fury, the love and the mercy of his God.

At last, he falls exhausted into the chair and becomes once more the shriveled old man they had watched come up from Gills' boat.

There is a communal sigh, an expelling of breath. Moses whimpers. Without speaking to each other or to the man who sits behind the table, his eyes closed, looking for all the world like a crumpled brin bag, they shuffle out.

The fishing season having not yet begun, meetings are held each night for a week. When he is not behind the pulpit, the Reverend Eldridge hardly speaks a word, spends his days reading the Bible or hunkered down watching someone at work. The old man can stay in this squatting position for hours, never taking his eyes from some mundane task: net making, carding, whittling, sawing wood. It doesn't matter if it's women's, or even children's work—all work fascinates him. Work, he tells them one night, is a kind of prayer.

The Reverend Ninian Eldridge, born in China of Quaker parents, has been a world traveller and his theology is a wonderful distillation of Hinduism, Buddhism and Christianity, only accidentally related to the teachings of John

Wesley. Despite the fact that his congregation understands only half of what he preaches, they are all caught in his spell. By the third meeting most of them have come forward to be saved.

Sarah has been completely won over by the old man's sermons. She rejoices when Josh and Charlie, Young Joe and Lizzie are saved, gives Annie no peace until she joins them and prays day and night for Peter, wishing he were home.

"My wayward boy would benefit some lot from your words, Reverend," she tells the holy man, extracting the promise that he will watch out for Peter as he travels on up the coast.

Aside from Ida Norris, whom no one counts, only three people do not go to the revival meetings—Ned and Mary and Thomas Hutchings.

From the first, Mary made it clear that she would not go. "I got nothin' to do with preachers, I wouldn't trust one with me shimmy, much less with me soul—s'posin' I got such a thing."

Despite this, she is willing for her children to attend the nightly meetings. "Go on for Lord sake," she says, "I'm glad ta get ye out from underfoot for a spell—and take Moses with ya. Jane or Vinnie can bring him home if he gets cranky." She even tells Ned to go, "If ye'r weak minded enough."

Ned would like to go. He has a great curiosity about religion, about all the bright framework of ritual men weave to keep their darkest fears at bay. When Ned is listening he believes, for not only is he the perfect storyteller, he is also the perfect audience for stories. Voices calling from mountaintops, fire from heaven, monstrous beasts with heads like men and thunderbolts that rip apart the sky. Ned, hearing, seeing, held captive by all of these, recognizes in Ninian Eldridge a soul mate.

Reluctantly he decides that his obligation is to sit with Thomas Hutchings, who, having been turfed out of the fish room without even a by-your-leave, takes refuge each night in Ned's and Mary's house.

The absence of Ned and Mary from the meetings does not concern Meg greatly, but she feels remorse that Thomas doesn't see fit to attend. "Mary Bundle will always do the contrary thing, and Ned is like a lump of taffy in her hands—but Thomas, why Vinnie, he buried your mother and poor Hazel too, and he married Ned and Mary," Meg tells Lavinia.

Even now Meg cannot bring herself to speak of the tiny son Thomas baptised and buried. But she remembers, and is shaken by Thomas' antipathy to Reverend Eldridge and his message. In Weymouth, Meg, along with Lavinia and Jennie, had gone to Methodist Chapel. While the other two considered the services little more than a weekly entertainment, for Meg, each sermon had been a revelation and in the end she alone had been converted. She is convinced that her prayers have brought the minister to Cape Random and is mystified by what seems to be Thomas's disapproval.

"I s'pose he's one of them strict Church of England people, thinks 'tis a sin to have anything to do with dissenters," Sarah concludes after much discussion, and looking a bit shamefaced, adds, "You knows, girl, I felt the same meself when Clyde and Calvin first told us about him, but my, you can see the Holy Spirit shinin' right outta that man!"

The meetings have been going on a week when the *Tern* arrives with the spring load of salt. Reverend Eldridge decides he should continue on up the coast with the vessel the following day.

Skipper Brennan, a devout Catholic, agrees, with some reluctance, to drop the man of God off in another community, "Though never you fear 'twill be a C of E place," he tells Thomas that night as they sit in Ned's and Mary's kitchen drinking black tea, to which he has added a splash of rum from the flask in his jacket pocket.

It is pleasant in the kitchen. They have let the fire die and opened the door. The glow of sunset seeps in, along with a small breeze that cleans out the sour smell of winter. They are all at ease, very comfortable as they sit there only half hearing Alex's talk of politics, of people in far-off St. John's trying to form a government.

"How can they talk of forming a government for the island when people like us are tucked away in places they've never heard of?" Thomas asks only to be polite. Even for him such events seem unreal, unrelated to anything that happens on the Cape.

Mary doesn't hear a word the men are saying. She sits a little way off, drinking her rum-laced tea and cutting up half-rotted potatoes for seed. She is trying to think of some way to keep potatoes from rotting. The problem occupies her mind every spring. She has a dim recollection of seeing sliced apples strung on lines to dry before a fire and is wondering if this would work with potatoes. Or maybe she could try pickling them like cabbage? She ponders the problem as she enjoys warm rum and the absence of her rowdy sons.

Ned has edged his stool near the door where he can hear music drifting up from the fish store. He is trying to catch the words, wishing he was down there listening to the minister's message. He is tantalized by the bits of sermons he's heard Meg and Sarah discussing.

Along with the Cape people, several crewmen off the *Tern* are in the fish store, almost thirty people seated on the floor in front of Reverend Eldridge. The room has become over-warm, and dazed flies buzz above the barrels stacked around walls where motes of dust flicker in the fading light.

The man has been preaching for two hours, interrupted by one hymn—

Waft, waft, ye winds his story
and you, ye waters roll
till like a sea of glory,
it spreads from pole to pole.

Still they sit in breathless wonder, not an eye moving from the preacher who towers above them. The buzzing flies, Meg's soft "amens" and a faint wheezing that comes from Mattie, who has fallen asleep in her grandmother's arms; these and the whoosh of sea beneath the floor are the only sounds in the room. Even Lavinia, who for the first hour had stood by the door thinking she might slip out and join the unbelievers in Ned's kitchen, has slid silently to the floor and sits hunched forward as the sermon reaches its crescendo.

The impossibly long, black arm is raised higher and higher, the claw-like fingers stretch out as though they would snatch the Lord from off his heavenly throne and bring him down to the fish room to face them. The strong voice, so youthful, so deep, so vibrant, so at variance with the man's appearance, rises and falls. Then the voice stops, everything stops. Lavinia could swear that even the sea beneath them is silent.

Then the arms sweep down: "Repent and be saved every one of you—be saved for your own souls' sake. For the wrath of the Lord is great and will not be denied, yea it reacheth unto caves and deep places, into the outermost parts of the earth, even unto the falling of the sun it reacheth, unto the freezing of the sea, unto the moons being turned to blood!" His voice drops to a whisper, "But His mercy, ah His mercy my friends, is everlasting. Everlasting, all-forgiving, all embracing."

The hands return to the splitting table, but softly this time. There is a whoosh of sound, the sea crashes in under the fish store, the flies begin buzzing and Jeremiah is once again a dried-up old man.

The instant the Reverend's voice stops, Young Joe brings the jews harp to his lips and begins, in plaintive monotone, a cry for mercy that is picked up by Meg's clear voice. One by one the others join in.

> Were the whole realm of nature mine,
> That were a tribute far too small;
> Love so amazing, so divine,
> Demands my soul, my life my all.

The hymn expresses perfectly the longing they all feel. Each time it is about to end, the preacher, with an almost imperceptible nod, signals to Joe to begin once more.

Tears stream down the old man's parchment cheeks. This is his last night with them, and he is determined to wrestle their souls from the devil.

Fanny is first to go up. Sobbing, she stumbles to the front, flings herself down before the improvised altar and wipes her eyes in the corner of Meg's best table cloth. Lavinia, who is trying to stay outside the weaving miasma, watches the small, dark child and thinks that now Fanny will have new fancies to add to her old ones. Soon almost everyone in the room has gone forward, even the Three Kings. Ned's sons look strangely pale and chidden. Lavinia is left sitting beside five uncomfortable seamen from the *Tern*.

The singing goes on and on. Lavinia longs to believe, but many doubts—and yes, cowardice at the thought of Ned's joshing—hold her in place. She keeps her gaze fixed on her hands which are carefully folded in her lap, is aware that the men around her have gotten to their feet and are quietly going through the door. Dismayed to see tears falling onto her lap, she jumps up and starts for the door herself. But Meg, still singing, hands outstretched, face radiant as a bride, comes towards her. Lavinia is undone, she takes Meg's hands and is led to the front. She is aware, as she kneels, that another voice, louder, stronger, more confident than all the others, has joined in the singing.

"Love so amazing, so divine, demands my soul, my life, my all!" Ned bellows as he strides through the door, across the floor and straight to the front where he falls on his knees. Flinging his arm around his sister's shoulders he shouts, "Lord be praised!"

No one is left seated. The song ends, Reverend Eldridge bends over the converts, touching each bowed head. He prays over them and in one fell swoop accepts them all into the Methodist church. Before they leave the fish store he writes each of their names, twenty-one in all, in his book—the first official acknowledgement that anyone except Thomas Hutchings lives on Cape Random.

There is hardly a dry eye in the place the next day as they bid good-by to the old man. He promises to come back, charging Meg and Sarah with the responsibility of holding Sabbath services. As he makes his shaky way up the gangplank it seems impossible that he has been on the Cape only eight days, even more impossible that such a man should have sat unnoticed in the Gill brothers' bully for an hour.

After the preacher's visit, Lavinia finds herself living in a world of signs and wonders, a world perversely out of joint with her own shucking off of bemusement. A dizzy feeling, not unlike seasickness, comes over her. It will last all through that summer and into the autumn.

Yet it is a spring like any other. Caplin come in and cod follow as they do every year. Curing fish is the same as it is any summer: the cutting, gutting, washing, salting, turning, packing, drying; the great, all-consuming race to gather in food, to pickle and boil, roast and smoke, to store it in barrels and jars, in root cellars and lofts against the winter.

Long, long days, and short nights, mercifully short, for Lavinia's nights are full of dreams. Quite different from the waking terror of cold and hunger that haunted her during the first winters on the Cape, these are nightmares that drop like a shroud down upon her as soon as she is asleep. She dreams of fields covered with rocks that she alone must carry, must lay, one atop the other, making stone walls that are torn apart by some laughing unseen force each time she turns to gather more rocks. This dream, if it is a dream, is repeated night after night. She wakes sobbing, drenched in sweat, feeling a terrible guilt she doesn't understand.

Sarah Vincent says it's the Old Hag and steeps wild camomile for Lavinia to drink before bedtime. But the nightmares persist until she is afraid to sleep and often sits exhausted, scribbling disjointed sentences into her journal until dawn.

Nor is Lavinia the only one with dreams. Sarah reports that Annie spends her nights tossing and crying out and young Rose Norris has dreamt three times that the entire Cape had vanished, swept out to sea by one giant wave.

"'Tis because we been saved. Like Reverend Eldridge said, Lucifer is among us seeking whom he may devour," Meg, who has a retentive memory and can already quote parts of the Bible, chapter and verse, tells them.

She decides that the building of a schoolroom can wait. If the men have any time at all they must, for their souls sake, Meg says, begin work on a church. Without money or experience such a prospect is daunting, but Meg knows with God's help and under her husband's direction it can be done.

"I wouldn't even know where to start, Meg. You needs special stuff, tools and material for such a thing," Ben protests, but Meg says the Lord will provide a way.

The men, themselves affected by the strange atmosphere, agree they will begin on a church soon as the season ends. They too have seen things. Frank has a fearsome encounter with some great sea monster that wrapped its tentacles around his boat. He escaped by chopping at the thing and returned to shore shaking with fear, one of the monster's dreadful suckers floating, grey and spongy, in the bilge water. Only days later, around midday, Young Joe comes ashore with only half a load, telling them that such an unearthly quiet, such a strange green light had come suddenly down on the water that he'd expected the end of the world.

"I pulled in lines and headed for shore. If 'tis the Second Coming I wants to be with me own when I faces it," he explained as he climbed up onto the wharf, surprised to find the women spreading fish as usual.

Meg and Sarah had a word of prayer right then and there, got themselves a cup of tea and waited. When nothing happened they returned to the fish, and Jo, rather sheepishly, but insisting he'd felt the stillness and seen the unearthly light, got back into his boat and fished within sight of land for the rest of the day.

The children, of course, are worst of all. During the summer after their conversion, they seem to bring daily stories of bizarre happenings: they have seen elves, pirates, Indians, rings around the sun, daytime moons, two headed dogs and strangers—always strangers. The stranger is their most persistent fear.

Every child on the Cape has seen the stranger and can describe him in great detail. Fanny and Rose still talk of the day when, with Lavinia, they had all looked down on the empty houses of the Cape, insisting now they had seen the stranger that day. His face is long and dark, they say, with pointed horns sticking out of his animal head. The stranger wears a long black cape.

The children persist in their habit of confiding in Lavinia although now they are often rebuffed. She, who since they were toddlers has spent her days exchanging stories, playing games and huddling with them in the hollow hiding place, now tells them crossly to stop their prate about monsters and ghosts, be done with this talk of strangers. First the youngest ones, then the older children withdraw from her. By the end of summer she is adrift in limbo, neither child nor adult, stranded in a byway she should long ago have passed.

Fanny is the last youngster to abandon Lavinia. Now thirteen, Fanny should herself be graduating into the adult world. She is a strange child and has been at odds with her mother since the day she was pushed from Mary's lap when Henry, her first stepbrother, arrived.

Fanny usually roams alone around the Cape but this summer she too feels afraid and begins to tag after Rose, Willie, Charlie and Isaac who are all near her age. They do not want her. Her endless whispered secrets, her intense manner and her earnest little elf's face annoy them—really they are a little afraid of Fanny. They chase her away, hide from her, sometimes, when they are feeling brave, try to frighten her. When this happens the girl seeks out Lavinia but she, too, grows impatient with the child.

Fanny's only refuge that summer is with Jane and Emma. The young women have grand plans and are always ready to have their fortunes told. But even this amusement is sometimes denied Fanny, for Meg and Sarah are dead against fortunetelling. "Conversing with the devil," they call it and scatter the three girls with awful warnings.

As the fishing season progresses, both adults and children are too tired to be afraid, reports of mysterious happenings stop and Fanny goes back to roaming the woods by herself.

Lavinia, the Old Hag no longer sitting on her chest at night, is interested only in what she can feel and touch: the gritty crystal surface of the dry cod, soft slimy guts that float in the water below the wharf, the rough silver grey splinters of the wharf itself, the multi-coloured specks of sand—crushed bodies of a million sea creatures. All the minute details of everyday life suddenly leap into focus for Lavinia. For the first time she begins to hear the quiet conversations women have—talk of a child's fever, what their mothers had said about this or that, how to prevent miscarrying, what they pray for, the pain in their backs, the timing of their periods, how the berries are coming, ruminations about the question of sin, what is cooking over their fires. She catches glimpses of lives as varied as the grains of sand.

Were it possible, if they would leave her alone, if there was not always another pile of fish waiting to be split and gutted, Lavinia would like to stop, sit down, let her feet dangle over the edge of the stage. She longs to stare at something—at anything, the back of her own hand, at a leaf, a drop of water, the scale of a fish—to stare for hours and let soft woman talk fall around her like mist. Although nothing appears to be happening, although it seems to be a summer like any other, she feels too much is happening. Lavinia wants time to stop, to hold still until she can study it, understand its design.

One day in late summer, when the run of fish has slackened, Meg suggests that Jane, Emma, Patience and Lavinia take the youngsters to the barrens behind the Cape for a day of berrypicking. Although berries are a necessary addition to the winter diet and the only fruit they ever taste, berrypicking is considered a holiday, not really work. Children, and sometimes women, spend whole days with buckets and pails, counting themselves lucky to be on the barrens or in the autumn woods, away from the fish flakes for a day.

That morning when they get to the berry grounds, Lavinia, as always, wanders a little way off from the others. She likes to pick by herself, enjoying the low sounds from the nearby woods, the distant voices of children calling out to each other, the feeling of sun on her shoulders and neck. Eventually the sounds blend, then fade. She falls into a kind of trance, aware only of the warmth, the dull plop of berries falling into her bucket, the rhythm of her hand as it moves back and forth, back and forth, time marked only by the slowly rising level of berries.

Around noon, Patience begins banging on her bucket, a signal to come together for a mug-up of goat's milk and molasses bread. After eating they separate again. When Lavinia returns to her corner of the marshy clearing, Fanny follows. The girl keeps close to Lavinia not saying a word as they move from bush to bush.

Then, "I saw the stranger again." Fanny's voice is serious, matter-of-fact. "He was over there watching us."

"Go on with you, Fanny, you're all the time seein' something." Lavinia doesn't take her eyes from the wine-coloured berries, flicking them expertly into her cupped hand.

Although Sarah maintains they are foolish to let the youngsters go about the woods alone, Lavinia has always felt safe inland, away from the sea. True, the woods are dark and full of shadows, and even on the brightest day only needles of sunlight filter down the spindly trunks that grow so close together; true there are fox and lynx, wildcats and, according to Sarah, bears in the woods. Yet Lavinia and the children have explored for miles around the Cape without seeing any large animal, without falling into hidden holes, dropping off cliffs, or being taken by fairies—all the things Sarah warns them of.

"Tempting providence, it'll happen sooner or later, mark my words."

Lavinia is smiling to herself, remembering, when Fanny says softly, "There he is, Vinnie, over there in the woods watching us now."

A cloud passes over the sun, and Lavinia shivers with foreboding, knowing, in the instant before she raises her head, that she will see something.

She does. From the deep secret shadows at the edge of the woods a disembodied face, unblinking eyes, stare at her. Slowly Lavinia stands up, forcing herself not to scream. With her eyes on the sinister face, she fumbles for Fanny's hand and when it slips into hers hisses, "Run!" and pulls the child around, away from the circle of trees.

The stranger in the shadow of the woods does not move. Lavinia can feel him watching as they run. Berries spilling on the ground, buckets banging painfully against their legs, they race towards the group on the other side of the bog.

"Don't dare tell them what we saw!" Lavinia jerks Fanny's arm for emphasis just before they reach Jane and Emma. Snatching up coats, the remains of food, the buckets, she calls to the others to come on: "It's clouding over, it'll be pelting in five minutes."

Patience and the young ones follow meekly, silenced by something in her voice, but Jane and Emma turn sookie, protesting that their buckets are only half-filled. "'Tis not either going to rain, Vinnie Andrews! Thinks you knows everything, you do."

"Not another word out of you two. Get across there and down the hill this minute or I vow I'll skin ye both!" Lavinia says in a voice no one has ever heard before. Without another word they obey.

Halfway down the steep hill above the Cape, Lavinia notices Fanny whispering to a bug-eyed group of children of whom only one is skeptical. "You'm all the time tellin' lies, Fanny Bundle," says Rose, giving the other girl a push.

"Is it true Aunt Vinnie—did ye see a black stranger in the woods?" Isaac asks.

Fanny is delighted for once to be the centre of attention. She smiles at Lavinia, cocky and sure that she has a witness to her tale.

"Don't pay that one no heed, she's forever romancing," Lavinia glares at the girl, who begins to wail at this unexpected betrayal.

The louder Fanny cries, the more Rose and Willie make fun of her. Charlie and Isaac take pity on the girl and begin punching her tormentors. The procession becomes more and more disorderly as they near home. Lavinia is hardly aware of it. She is deep in thought trying to remember just what that still face looked like.

She does not speak of the stranger in the woods to anyone; tries to convince herself she had imagined the dark face. Might it have been some trick of light falling on a scarred tree trunk? Yet that night she writes in her journal, "The children are right, there is a stranger in the woods, and I don't think it's the devil."

Chapter 10

Since the weather turned cold we been having lessons every day. Meg makes Willie sit down at the table with me. Rose Norris comes to keep him company but they do not learn much. Ned's crowd streel in and out whenever they feel like. Charlie and Patience are the only ones who have any interest. Meg found a book Captain Brennan left behind, called Ten Decisive Battles in the History of the Empire. *Not even Charlie Vincent will read it. I'm some sick of having people tell me what to do.*

The last sentence is underlined with a dark slash. Hardly a day passes without one of the adults coming to Lavinia with some new idea of what should be taught to their children: Ben thinks the boys should to be able to measure board and draw out plans on paper, Sarah says all that's needful is to learn the Bible by heart, Mary wants her sons to be able to tally fish and count money. Meg, since school is held in her kitchen, makes constant suggestions.

It is Ned, however, that Lavinia finds most irritating. Every morning her brother interrupts the lesson. Planking himself down beside the students, he waits impatiently for a chance to ask some foolish question: How are stars set out in the sky at different times of the year? Where do names like Andrews and Vincent come from? How could a person go about figuring the amount of water a barrel would hold? Where do caplin go in wintertime and do the same ones come back to the Cape year after year?

After setting the conundrum Ned waits, bright, expectant, seemingly innocent, for her answer. Useless to tell him she doesn't know, he only shakes his head, looks sad, leaves and next day is back with another question. Although Lavinia puts on a brave front for the children, she can feel her confidence draining away as the winter progresses.

The day Ned comes into the kitchen full of smiles asking that she name all the oceans in the world, Lavinia abandons decorum. Slamming *Ten Decisive Battles* down on the kitchen table she stalks up to her brother. "How would I know such a thing, Ned Andrews? You're cracked, b'y! Sweet Lord, you been sailin' on oceans for twenty year—you know their names?" she screeches and has the satisfaction of seeing Ned temporarily speechless.

He rallies immediately, reams off a list of words that may or may not be the names of oceans, winks at the delighted students and swaggers through the door.

Lavinia chases the youngsters out and turns in childish rage to Meg. "I fair hates that Ned! 'Tain't right, him tarmentin' the life outta' me like that—and I can't abide teachin'!"

Meg gives her an amused look, "You gets too stirred up, Vinnie. Ned's only makin' a bit of fun—all you Andrews pays too much heed to talk."

"I don't know what to be doin'—they all wants something different. I'm too stund! How can I be teachin' stuff I don't know?"

"I'll put an end to Ned's idleness, never you mind. Between us we'll teach them youngsters to read and write—and not concern ourselves with what the rest wants."

Seeing her words have mollified Lavinia somewhat, Meg adds, "But Vinnie, you must never again take the Lord's name in vain. Don't fret girl, once you gets the knack of teachin' you'll find it comes natural."

"Me and Rose is goin' run away to Labrador if ye crowd keeps on with school stuff," a voice from the doorway says matter-of-factly.

Meg dives for her son, grabs his ear and hauls him into the room. "No, medoubts you'll go to Labrador, Willie Andrews! Not while I got breath in me body, you won't!" She glares at Rose who stands hesitantly on the doorstep with the other children ranged behind her. "Let that one go if she got a mind to, I s'pect she's the one put you up to this. Now get back to yer places or I'll chastise every last one of ye!"

By spring Lavinia's journal has taken on a more cheerful tone: "Josh Vincent's feet are almost better, Lizzie and Joe got twin boys this time. Spring is here, today Fanny brought home a clump of the little white flowers Sarah calls 'fallen stars'."

Then, a few days after Easter Sunday, she writes, "I thought I'd learned better sense this winter but after what happened today on Turr Island I'm not sure. I allow I shouldn't say a word against Fanny when I get such queer fancies myself."

Turr Island is little more than a cliff that breaks the sea about two miles off the Cape. The custom of egging on the island was introduced by Sarah Vincent the year after the Andrews arrived. Since then the women and children have gone there each year on the first warm day.

Sarah's grandfather was a great egger who used to take her and her brothers with him to the offshore islands. Cape Random men, however, do not consider egging a fit occupation for males. They hunt seabirds around the cliffs of Turr Island and sometimes fish off its sheltered side, but turn up their noses at egging.

"Nasty work, stealin' eggs off poor little birds—I don't know how Christian women got nerve for it—pure barbarous the lot of you," Ned teases as he helps shove off the two boats.

"No mistake, you'll help eat them though when we gets back!" Sarah says. She and Meg, together with Willie, Emma and Patience are in the dory rowed by Annie and Isaac. Lavinia and Charlie row the larger boat carrying Mary Bundle, Fanny, Jane, Henry and Rose Norris.

The morning is still and sunny with not a breath of wind. So clear they can even see the green place atop Turr Island. The women and children are in a marvellously happy mood. As the dories pull away, they call and wave towards the beach where Alfred, George and Moses stand in a scowling line beside the men. Lizzie, who has also stayed behind, cannot wave, for she is holding her twin sons Elias and William, one in each arm, and has young Mattie clinging to her skirt. Mattie is teething and the hand not holding onto her mother is stuffed into her drooling mouth.

"Poor Lizzie'll have her work cut out for her this day," Meg says.

The women in the boats nod. They feel great pity for the young mother, but no one volunteers to stay behind.

"'Tis hard havin' them so close—I hopes she don't get in the family way again for a spell. Twins runs in our family, there's Calvin and Clyde and mother had another lot who died, they was tiny and all blue...."

Sarah's account of the tragic birth is interrupted by Mary Bundle, who suddenly stands up and shrieks, "Ned, Ned, look to that little bugger—grab him quick before he drowns!" She points to young Moses, already up to his knees in freezing water but still splashing his determined way towards his mother.

"Go back ye little devil—I swear that child got no nerves," Mary is shaking her fist at the small boy but he pays her no heed.

Thomas Hutchings wades out, snatches Moses by the slack of his pants and, to everyone's surprise, keeps on walking. He scrambles over the side of the nearest boat.

"Here, take him before he sets out for England," he passes the dripping child over Lavinia's head to Mary, then, sitting down, pulls off his own boots and empties them over the side. Charlie asks if he wants to be taken back.

"No, no boy, I think I'll take a little holiday—anyway if we go back you'll end up taking Ned's other two imps," and with a bemused smile Thomas settles in the stern.

Lavinia, sitting directly in front of him on the rowing seat with Charlie, thinks Thomas Hutchings looks well pleased with himself, happier than she has ever seen him.

Later she writes, "It was strange altogether, him jumping into the boat like that, then sitting there grinning to himself like the cat that ate the cream. He just left his boots off, turned up his pants and sat with his long legs stuck under our seat."

She has dropped her eyes from his face and is studying his feet. They are thin and brown even this early, little hairs catching the drops of salt water drying on his skin. Suddenly looking at his feet seems more embarrassing than staring him in the face. Lavinia wonders if he is watching her. She raises her eyes and stares past him at the Cape, which seems to be sinking into the sea.

The Cape must be the edge of a great mountain jutting out of the ocean, Lavinia thinks, imagining underwater paths, bushes, rocks. If you could hold your breath long enough you could walk along those paths from the Cape to Turr Island.

The sky above and around the island is alive with sea birds. A dozen species of murrs, turrs, puffins and gulls scream and wheel like demons. They dive at the boats as if they would crash into the upturned faces, then, at the last instant, lift and spiral back up, their wings transparent against the sun.

The birds circle, hover, line up the boats and dive, repeating the pattern over and over again. The youngsters yell, pointing imaginary guns, shouting "Bang, bang!" The perpendicular cliffs are streaked with white. Occasionally droppings plop onto the boats and the people, adding to the merriment of the children.

Turr Island is tiny with steep sides topped by a small green plateau where there is a shallow pond and three stunted var trees. There is only one place to come ashore on Turr Island, a blanket-size cove barely big enough to beach two boats.

As they climb ledge by ledge to the green crown of the island, Sarah reams off advice: "For mercy sake Anne, tie up them apron strings 'stead of havin' them streel behind like that.... All hands stay together now, lights been seen on Turr Island.... Remember them rocks is slippery, mind how Rose had like to break her neck last spring!"

This is almost true. Rose had, in fact, broken her wrist the year before. The girl had not mentioned the pain until the following day when her hand and arm had swollen to the size of a molasses puncheon.

"Josh says he saw a bear out here one time when he was passin' in boat. Sitting on a ledge it were, eatin' eggs cute as a Christian. Mind now, put bread in yer pockets to keep off the fairies."

Sarah never stops, warning them of dangers, real and imagined, until Mary says, "Aw girl, leave off harpin'—there's no more fairies than there is witches." She gives the older woman a hard look which Sarah doesn't even notice.

At the top of the island, they pile food, bread, salt fish and bottles of tea, along with extra clothing brought in case the wind veers, in one big heap, spread a piece of canvas over everything and weigh it down with rocks. On their first trip to Turr Island they had returned to the green place to discover that birds had torn food out of baskets, ripped open bundles and devoured every scrap of bread and fish while they had been egging.

Once the food is made safe, everyone is counted off into groups of three or four. At least one adult goes with each cluster of children. Meg then gives her set speech about obedience, about watching out for each other, not going too near the edge and leaving one egg in each nest. She demonstrates for them how a blast from the goat's horn hung around her neck sounds.

"When you hears that, scravel back here fast as ye can—unless 'tis rainin', then you goes on down by the boat."

The piece of canvas, the goat's horn, the counting off, Meg's speech, are the same each year. On the Cape, anything done once and found useful becomes a ritual.

Mulling over the way women have of threading small ceremonies onto each season, Lavinia absent-mindedly follows Thomas, Fanny and Rose down the short drop to a ledge where Fanny has already spotted a nest. Rose is cranky at being counted off with so tame a crowd, having expected to be paired with her cohorts, Willie and Isaac.

"For pity sake, Rose, hush. If you're smart about it maybe we'll get more eggs than the boys," Lavinia says.

The words are hardly out of her mouth before Rose wiggles onto a needle of rock that seems to hang in space. Lavinia grabs the girl's ankles and holds on as Rose scoops four eggs from a large nest, deftly passing them one by one back over her shoulder. Wearing Willie's outgrown pants gives Rose a wonderful advantage over the other females. "It's a shame all the women can't cast off their skirts and petticoats when they come to Turr Island," Lavinia thinks, watching the girl squirm backwards on her stomach.

In two hours, baskets and pockets full of eggs, Fanny, Rose, Thomas and Lavinia have worked their way back down to where the boats are pulled up. They pack the eggs in a bait box between layers of wet sand. Rose insists that Lavinia, then Thomas, count the eggs and is well pleased to find that the four of them have gathered thirty-seven. Whooping with glee, she drags Fanny back up the path to get more.

"By the time we started back towards the top, Thomas Hutchings' spell of good humour (about as cheerful as Ned would be a day when everything had gone wrong) was past. He hardly spoke one word all morning. I couldn't make out why he'd come, it was like dragging a fog bank around. Mary Bundle is always asking him if it's a crime in his church to crack a smile. I had a good mind to ask the same—but didn't have nerve for it," Lavinia later wrote.

Because Thomas and her husband are friends, Mary has acquired a kind of brazen sauciness that no one else dares with Thomas. In the past, Lavinia has guessed that Mary's half-joking manner covers dislike for Ned's friend.

Lavinia has often watched Ned and Thomas talking late at night by Ned's fire. Dour Thomas rations words and smiles like a miser, never telling anything about himself, while Ned flings lies and truth helter skelter, smiling and singing, loving everyone, telling anyone anything. Sometimes, when it gets late, Mary will give Thomas a push, "Go on home, boy—me and Ned wants to make babies."

The first time she had heard Mary say such a thing Lavinia thought she would die of mortification. Thomas Hutchings had flushed beet red, glanced at her, jumped up and stalked out the door. But Ned had caught up with him and, still talking, walked him all the way down to the fish room.

Since then Lavinia has heard her sister-in-law say the same words a dozen times—a dozen times she's watched the two men leave the house and walk slowly through the night in deep conversation. When they are alone Thomas seems to do as much talking as Ned.

Climbing the narrow path behind Thomas Hutchings, Lavinia speculates on what the men find to talk about year after year.

"Meg tells me you're becoming a real schoolmarm."

Later, Lavinia will try to estimate how much time passed before she realized he had spoken—a minute? Two minutes? Three? She has lived within yards of this man since she was seventeen. For one winter they slept in the same room, ate at the same table, and his face is as familiar to her as the faces of her brothers. Yet this is the first time he has ever addressed a remark directly to her. When she does finally realize he has spoken, that she has not imagined his question, it takes more seconds for her to think the words over, searching for some hidden sneer.

He has not looked back, but keeps walking on with Lavinia directly behind, edging around a narrow jib in the path. From above Rose calls: "Hurry up, there's thousands and thousands of eggs up here by the cave."

Over their heads her voice echoes and repeats: "thousands of eggs, thousands of eggs, by the cave, by the cave."

He stops and turns. Suddenly they are only inches apart, facing each other. Her eyes focus directly ahead—on his mouth. She looks down at the pocket of his shirt, concentrating on the pocket. It contains a scratched tobacco tin and his pipe. The shirt is faded blue, one corner of the pocket has been mended. Lavinia studies the stitches, counting them. Fifteen stitches, neater than she could have made but in black thread so that the patch shows clearly.

The sound of sea slamming against the cliffs far below, the screeching birds circling around, the excited voices of Rose and Fanny above, all blend, all sound far off, unreal. Only the faded cloth inches from her face is real. She will not look up.

Does he touch her? Lay his fingers for an instant on her cheek? She thinks so—is almost sure. But later she is not sure. Lavinia knows what tricks her imagination can play.

The pocket disappears. He turns away and begins to climb towards the voices.

She feels sick and so dizzy she might fall tumbling into the sea. She leans her head against the wet cliff and closes her eyes, glad for the solid rock, for the cool dampness. After a minute she follows, climbing slowly.

"What a dunce he must think I am, not able to speak for meself. Some school marm! I could have said something, asked him about books for the youngsters."

She stumbles along, thinking now of a dozen intelligent things she could have said, of questions long wondered about she could have asked. Her misery is interrupted by the sound of rocks sliding, by the thump of his feet as he jumps down to the depression in front of the dry cave, by the sound of Rose's voice risen to such a screech that every bird on the island takes off in a great flurry of wings.

As Lavinia pulls herself up towards the ridge she hears Thomas Hutchings say "No!" in a voice that comes only in the face of death. She immediately thinks that some terrible accident has befallen Fanny.

But when she drops into the triangle of slimy grass and bushes at the cave mouth, Fanny and Rose are quite safe. They stand with their backs towards her, just inside the shadow of the cave's overhanging lip. Lavinia looks past their shoulders into the dark mouth of the cave and sees what they are staring at.

A man has toppled over on his side from a sitting position. A man who has been dead for a long time. The man in the woods? Unthinkingly she leans a little forward, looks at the face. At where the face should be, the birds have been. Lavinia turns quickly to the sun, stumbles away, retching into the bushes.

"I should have called out to warn you," Thomas Hutchings is standing beside her. His voice is cool, formal. He has the grace to look away as she straightens up, wiping her mouth with the hem of her skirt.

"I think there might be another one—back farther—or a pile of rags. There's something back inside there." He looks towards the cave, sees Rose and Fanny edging towards the dead man and shouts at them to get back: "Don't dare go in there! That man might have died of plague for all we know!"

The girls pull away but have no qualms about filling their basket from nests scattered among the crevices around the cave. Thomas returns to kneel beside the body.

Lavinia sits well back from the gaping cave mouth and waits. The scene before her—the man kneeling in sunlight by the dark cave, the girls scavenging among the nests, Rose in overalls and bare feet, Fannie in her gaudy rags, the enraged birds that dive and scream—seems strangely familiar.

She cannot stay near the cave. Hardly aware of what she is doing, she turns and climbs quickly to the plateau where she sits on the grass with her head resting on her knees. She has never been seriously ill in her life, but the trembling and cold sweat on her forehead frighten her.

"I am dying," she says aloud, then, knowing she is dramatizing, she shuts her eyes, concentrates on controlling the shivering, on not thinking of the things that have happened in the short time since they packed the warm eggs into layers of cool sand. She thinks about sand, about the beach around the Cape and how the sea sweeps it clean each day. After a time she begins to feel better.

When she looks up, Thomas Hutchings is standing nearby, watching her. He reaches under the canvas, pours out a cup of strong, cold tea and passes it to her.

"I don't wonder you're sick." Not taking his eyes from her face, he gestures behind him, down the cliff from where the girls can be heard but not seen.

"Don't let what I said about the plague worry you—that was only to keep those two vultures from going into the cave. They're off in search of the boys—can't wait to tell everyone there's a dead man on the island."

He sits down several feet away from Lavinia. Both of them are facing the sea which is all around, vast and shimmering in the sunlight. The scattering of islands look like tiny chips of chalk. Landward, towards the Cape, great white sea horses race along the shoals outlining their own beach.

"Once men thought that gods lived in places like this," Thomas says. They sit in silence, caught between sea and sky, watching birds swoop and soar in graceful arcs above and below them.

In a while, they hear Sarah's talking as she climbs the cliff with Mary and several children. Lavinia fancies the women give her and Thomas an odd look but they say nothing. Thomas does not mention the dead man. Mary blows a great blast on the horn and soon others are scrambling up the path.

The children, agog with the gruesome discovery, cannot be distracted even to compare the number of eggs each has gathered. Moses falls instantly asleep in Annie's arms, and is rolled in one of the jackets and left to lie on the moss as they sit around and eat, still talking about the man in the cave.

"Ya think he might be a pirate come ashore to bury his gold?" Patience asks Lavinia seriously.

"...or maybe a Red Indian, ye knows all them arrows we found in... ." Willie is about to speak of the children's secret place but Rose Norris jabs him in the side. "Go on ya dummy, sure how would an Indian get out here?"

Willie maintains that his father told him Indians build their own kind of boats from scooped-out trees. "Not so!" Rose says and the two begin pounding each other, rolling over and over in moss.

Meg reaches out, separates them and cuffs them both gently on the head. She does this two or three times each day. The action is automatic and it does not interrupt the conversation she is having with Sarah. "I allow it's some poor fisherman got driven off in dirty weather and wrecked up here."

"That old fire we seen signs of down on the beach was probably them burnin' their boat, hopin' someone would see it—I told you there was lights on this island!"

"I s'pose we woulda heard if anyone along this coast was missin'?" Annie asks. But they cannot be sure, sometimes it takes months for a piece of news to travel just a few miles.

The thought that the dead man might be a fisherman silences the women. They finish eating as the youngsters tally up the number of eggs gathered.

Thomas picks up the piece of canvas and goes back down to the cave. Half an hour later he returns, telling them that there are two men down in the cave.

"The other is well back in the dark, from what I can tell he probably died earlier. It looks like someone tried to pile rocks around the body in a kind of cairn. There's a line and jigger and a dip bucket on a ledge just inside the cave—nothing to tell where they came from, but I'd say they were white men."

"One of the men from the *Tern* told us betimes servants run away, rove around the woods in gangs. Maybe that's what they was," Charlie suggests.

Meg pauses from gathering up their belongings, "We're not goin' to leave them here without a Christian burial?" She looks at Thomas.

"I'll talk to the men, likely we'll come over tomorrow—bury them here or back on the Cape. I doubt you could dig a grave on this rock." He stands. "We'd best be getting back, it'll be dark in no time."

They climb down, skirting around to the north of the dry cave. Even the boys are sick of the subject of dead men. Only Rose and Fanny, eager to milk every bit of glory from their discovery, are still talking of it as they get into the boats.

"For pity's sake, will you two give it a rest! Count your eggs, look at the sea, go to sleep, or if you must talk, then let it be of something else!" Thomas, who rarely speaks to the children, is sharp and impatient. There is not a word from either girl for the remainder of the trip.

Lavinia lets Isaac take her place at the oars. She leans into the prow of the dory with her back to the others, watching the water, half-hypnotized by ripples that spread out from the boat as it glides through the salmon-pink sea. In the other dory, Meg begins to sing and the rest join in. It is a plaintive song with a dozen verses, each one ending: "My love is gone and will not come, tho' the tide rolls on for a thousand miles."

The words of the song drift across the smooth water. The Cape comes closer, its houses, squat, with cottage roofs and lean-to porches, look safe and snug. Lavinia can make out the narrow paths, even see goats up on the ridge where they will soon plant potatoes. She can see the men waiting in front of the fish store which is bleached silver but like everything else—the fences, the goats, the outhouses—the men themselves, is now bathed in the peach-grey light of evening. It is a perfect moment and Lavinia, half-asleep in the prow of the dory, forgets for an instant the cold and hunger and begins to make peace with the place.

She is the first out of the boat. Not waiting to hear the others tell of the day's events, she walks quickly away past the fish store, up the path, past the Vincents' house and into the empty Andrews house. She goes directly to bed and, pulling the quilt over her head, is asleep in five minutes. Hours later she wakes, takes her journal and leaves the house quietly.

Down on the beach in the white moonlight she sits, her back against the big rock, and writes a confused account of the day.

Chapter 11

Well, Emma and Jane are gone. I doubt we'll lay eyes on either one of them again. For all their talk about going to St. John's to get jobs and make money, the plain truth is they're off to look for husbands. But I'm content to bide here.

Lavinia is more than content this summer. She is marvellously, unreasonably, happy, but having controlled her natural flamboyance for so many years, she cannot commit such extravagance to paper.

It has been a radiant summer—a series of windless, sun-filled days in which rains fall softly at dusk or just before glistening dawns. A generous season of plentiful catches, bountiful gardens, bushes heavy with berries and goats' milk of a creaminess that must be commented upon with each sip. A summer so splendid it will be remembered as the golden mean by which all summers to come must be measured.

It is a sensuous season in which women touch their faces, their arms, feel their own skin for the first time since they were young; a season when men long married have wanton thoughts; a season when Lavinia grows beautiful, more beautiful than she will ever be again. Long days of sunshine give her skin a glow and turn her orange hair to copper. She pins it up in a roll, but it will not be contained and slips continually from the restraining pins to curl around her ears and neck.

That summer, the older children, grown tall, do adult work on flakes and in boats; are suddenly aware of their bodies—and of other bodies—of hips, thighs, breasts, of smells, of smiles, of glances. The sea is warm enough to bathe in and, unbeknownst to others, two brave souls do, dancing on the beach, white as sea spirits in the moonlight.

It is a summer when all things seem possible. When Ned's ship, so long overdue, must surely come in; when Josh Vincent's feet, crippled these two years, heal; when Lizzie's twins, undecided since birth whether to live or die, grow round, brown and loud; when Peter Vincent kills two hundred beach birds with one shot. A summer when potato vines push, green and lush, straight out of rocks, fish leap into boats, and huge trees fall with one stroke of the axe.

The men are able for anything that summer. They close in a school room alongside Meg's kitchen, cruise heavy timbers down the shore from Indian Bay, prop up the wharf and even, after Reverend Eldridge pays his second visit (bringing Ned, who has backslid, to the seat of mercy again), talk of laying foundations for a church before the ground freezes.

One summer's evening, Meg cajoles the others to go with her to look at the spot she's chosen for the church.

When they reach the place, well back toward the neck, Ben points to a huge granite rock, almost flat and flecked with pink and grey: "The front of her will lodge along there so we'll have a good foundation."

Sarah protests that the church will be too long a walk from the houses in wintertime, and Mary, who has come on this expedition reluctantly, says she can't see what they need a church for anyway. "Foolish as loons, the lot of us, traipsin' out here to talk about puttin' hard work into such a thing."

Ignoring all objections, Meg describes the church she has in mind: small and white, a wooden copy of the stone chapel she and Jennie had attended in Weymouth.

"And ships passin' will be able to see it from either side of the Cape, see the spire for miles and miles out," Ben tells them.

"You mean we could light a signal up there if someone got caught on the water in a storm?" a practical use for the church mollifies Mary a little.

They stand, heads back, squinting up at the imaginary white spire, delighted with the idea of passing vessels watching for the tip of their church to appear out of the sea.

Meg takes her husband's arm. "Only two things I longs for in this world," she says softly, "to see a church in this place and to have our Willie doin' the Lord's work." Then, seeing that Mary has overheard, she adds, "Of course that be in the Lord's hands—let's have a word of prayer before we goes back."

Lavinia, who had also heard Meg reveal her heart's desire, smiles at her sister-in-law's neatly combed, bowed head. Meg has changed remarkably since coming to the Cape, no longer the malleable woman who had been satisfied to spend her lifetime as a peddler's wife.

During the summer, Lavinia, watching with new awareness, has seen Meg look up from some household task to gaze happily around at tables and chairs she's polished to a gleaming smoothness; at shelves lined with jars of jam, bags of soap, candles, oil, bread; at the solid walls of the house her husband has built. After such an inspection Meg invariably says: "The Lord's been good to us!" The words are protection—a charm against the sin of pride, against the sin of avarice, against satisfaction with the knowledge that she and Ben are the most prosperous people on the Cape.

With the church site chosen, the men begin spending a day each week cutting timber. It is a long walk, across the neck and back to the hills where big trees grow. Leaving the felled trees to be dragged home over the snow next winter, they mark out the church and lay sills according to a plan Ben has scratched into a piece of lumber.

No one but Mary asks how they can afford the church, how to pay for nails, paint and putty, for roof felt and tar. These, along with the final adornments of glass and copper, will have to be brought from St. John's, bit by bit, year by year, as their credit with Caleb Gosse permits—a process that seems possible in the wonderful confidence of that summer.

As Lavinia abandons her prolonged childhood, her desire to sort, catalogue and organize returns. She fills page after page of her journal with lists: people, places, the names of dogs, boats, flowers, leaves, birds, kinds of shells. When she doesn't know a name she makes one up. She seems to be creating a world, pinning it down, making it permanent.

She would like to write down the names of all the places round about, longs to see a map of the Cape, of the Newfound Land, a map showing just where she is in the world. A map with names of every cove and bay. But there are no maps of the Cape, nor is there, in Lavinia's mind's eye, any picture of the world. She has no concept of continents, oceans, no image of the Americas with a triangular shaped island, almost as big as Ireland, broken off from its upper edge. She knows only that she once lived in Weymouth, England and now lives on the other side of the world—imagines herself clinging to the rim of a dark unknown hinterland facing an unending sea.

Lavinia fancies that seeing it all on a map would make her feel safe. She knows there are such things, remembers vaguely having dusted framed maps in the Ellsworth House. She tries to recall them but can only conjure up images of sea monsters and fish-tailed cherubs that adorned the corners. She quizzes Ned and, finding him no help, wonders if Thomas Hutchings could make a map for her. She thinks about asking him but has not gotten up the courage.

Although there are no paper or oilcloth maps on the Cape, Lavinia begins to see that other, invisible maps, exist. Meg and Sarah have maps: Reverend Eldridge's word pictures of Paradise, learned by heart, showing the exact dimensions of a city walled in jasper, sapphire and emeralds; it is the women's sure and steadfast destination, one to which they are determined to go and to take their husbands and children. Mary Bundle has other destinations in mind, more earthly but no less well-defined for all that.

The men's maps, Lavinia imagines, are of dark submerged continents where wrecked ships and drowned seamen lie. Precise diagrams of every contour, cliff, channel, every undertow, shoal and ledge for miles around the Cape. Throughout the year, men hold behind their eyes: (Lavinia has seen the reflections) pictures of wet pathways where millions of codfish, rising and falling between drifts of seaweed, swim through currents of warm and cold water.

The children's maps, she has always been aware of—they consist of paths that criss-cross the Cape, over bog, around marsh and pond, paths through sand dunes, across barrens. Paths goats make up the sides of hills, paths to the men's tilts back in the woods, hidden paths to secret places and the strange unearthly paths no one ever walks but which are always there—worn by what?

Then there are the other, most intriguing paths of all, those bridging the worlds of children and adults. Paths unseen and unseeable until, in the fullness of time, knowledge of them is bestowed on the child.

Lavinia has seen this happen, seen how, one day, a girl will raise her head to listen, as if for the first time, to the crying of a child, to the sound of an oar being hauled in, to a man's voice, to the screech of a saw pulling through wood, to some comment one of the women might make. Within a week, the girl will be able to tell, at any minute of the day or night, precisely where every soul in the place is. Then—or so Lavinia imagines, for it has never happened to her— one morning before light, before the girl has awakened, a map, new and totally different, will be imprinted behind her closed eyelids.

The gift will come, the girl will wake and hear the morning sounds—of goats' hoofs clattering down the rocks, the bell-like sound of boats on collar, the lap of water—and the map of her day, her life, will be there all spread out. That day the girl will not come out with the children, will never again skip rope, play house, collect shells and bits of broken china. Mysteriously she has become a woman, a possessor of secret charts that foretell phases of the moon, the ebb and flow of tides and blood.

It has already happened to Lizzie and to Annie, and this summer, watching carefully, Lavinia sees and records the process in her nieces Jane and Emma. She waits through the golden summer and fall wondering when such revelations will come to her.

Only Mary is surprised when, near the end of that summer, Meg's and Ben's daughter Emma, and Ned's Jane announce that they are going to St. John's when the *Charlotte Gosse* comes. The cousins have talked of nothing else for years but Mary, deep in her own preoccupations, has neither heard nor heeded.

If she feels any regret at the idea of Emma's leaving, Meg hides it. She begins immediately to rip Ben's heavy coat apart for turning and recutting so that her daughter will not appear in St. John's looking like a streel. One day she even suggests to Patience that she should go with her sister and cousin.

"You're steady Patience, you could keep an eye on them two, you knows what Emma is like—and I don't put much faith in Ned's Jane."

Meg has always felt a gnawing sense of unease with her oldest daughter. Emma has inherited Lavinia's tallness and orange hair along with the narrow hawk-like face of some unknown ancestor. As she confides in Sarah, "Patience and Lizzie are home bodies like meself, their hearts are inclined to the Lord, but I got to say I'm not sure about our Em. She's more like Vinnie, not made for this world."

In Sarah's opinion, Emma, whom she has observed making eyes at Peter, will do fine in the world.

"She's a sly one and got the sauciest tongue I ever heard in the head of a young maid—I'm not sorry she's going," Sarah tells Josh. But to Meg she only nods, "I knows, girl, I lies awake more nights worrying about our Annie than I done about all three boys put together." Her sigh conveys the helpless love and hopeless bafflement of mothers for daughters.

Since Patience doesn't want to leave the Cape, Meg must be content with extracting a promise from Emma that she will ask to get time off to attend church.

"Church is the best place for them young maids, they might find a decent husband in church. Besides, if Emma gets settled down in St. John's then 'twould be easier for Willie when the time comes for him to go. To get more education—you know—when you gets all the learnin' you can inside his head," Meg explains to Lavinia.

Lavinia cannot resist asking how they will know when Willie's head is full, "'Tisn't like a bucket, you know Meg, we can't see it splash over."

"Don't smile like that, Vinnie, next thing you'll be a scoffer, bad as Ned. If the good Lord give them old Israelites a sign, then I don't doubt he'll give me one. He's watchin' out for this place and for Willie too. Emma and Jane goin' into St. John's is all part of his plan, mark my words—and he's watchin' over you, too, Vinnie."

Before such faith Lavinia is silent. "If the Lord got a plan for me I do wish he'd hurry and let me know," she writes in her book that night.

The good fishery extends into the fall. The men are still hauling in boat loads of fish when the *Charlotte Gosse* comes to pick up what has already been cured. Since fish are plentiful all along the coast, Alex Brennan expects to be back again before winter. The young women, however, cannot be persuaded to take a chance on his returning and insist they will go with him now.

The night before the *Charlotte Gosse* is due to sail they have a get together in the schoolroom Ben has just closed in. Added to his side of the Andrews house, it is a low-ceilinged lean-to, containing a built-in bunk bed for Lavinia, a long shelf, a bench and one box-like desk at the front. So far there is no fireplace and no window, but the room has two doors, one leading outside and one connecting with Meg's kitchen.

The new room cannot contain everyone, but the night is warm and they spill out, standing on the grassy patch beside the house to watch the men, who have built a bonfire and are roasting fish and new potatoes. The blue wood smoke, pungent with the smell of roasting fish, drifts into the schoolroom where the women have spread food out on the desk. Beside a big pot of fish and brewis are platters of trout and salmon, baked sea bird stuffed with breadcrumbs and savory, bowls of mashed potatoes, turnip and new cabbage, plain and sweet loaf, jam tarts, jugs of goat's milk and pots of tea.

After the women have arranged each dish precisely, they stand back, hands folded over their aprons, to admire what they have created. The laden table gives Meg and Sarah such a feeling of security they could look at it forever. Inexplicably they want to weep. Instead they call everyone in, make them stand around while Meg gives a homily on thankfulness before asking Thomas to say grace.

After they have eaten, an air of celebration takes over. Ned, becoming very merry, organizes everyone he can round up into two rings, one inside the other, around the fire. He shows them how to circle, the rings moving in opposite directions, clapping hands, winding in and out and singing.

> Green gravels, green gravels,
> The grass is so green,
> And all the fair maidens
> Are shamed to be seen... .

The song, alive with wistfulness and expectation, drifts with the smoke back into the shadowed hills and down the silver moon path to the sea.

Meg and Sarah, each holding one of Lizzie's twins, sit on the doorstep watching the dance, tapping their feet to the old rhyme. They are both thinking of Jennie Andrews, wishing she were here. How Jennie would have marvelled at all the food, how she would love to hear the singing, to hold the sleeping babies who are her great-grandchildren. One by one, Josh, Ben and Alex Brennan leave the ring and come to sit beside the women.

Sarah finishes recounting for Alex the wonders of the summer just past and Meg says: "'Tis the first blessed time since we come I don't live in dread of winter."

Ben slides his arm around his wife, "The worst is over girl, 'tis goanna be a great place now we got good boats and gardens." Sounding almost as confident as Ned, he tries to estimate what their catch for the summer will be.

"There's talk in St. John's the Spanish want great amounts of fish this winter—and the Spanish got gold. This might be the year the price will be good and fish plentiful the same time," Alex says.

"Took four quintals of fish to get one barrel of flour last year—'twould be nice if Spanish gold could change that," Sarah remarks dourly.

"Picture," Josh's voice is wistful, "picture how it'd be to get all squared away."

They try to guess how much fish it would take to pay off all they owe, or even, wonderful thought, to get enough so they could pay for next year's provisions ahead of time.

Regretting having mentioned Spanish gold, Alex tries to deflate their expectations. "A lot goes into calculatin' the price of fish, boy—the cost of stuff like salt and gear that got to be brought over from the old country, storms delayin' ships, vessels lost at sea—a lot of things we people don't see. I doubt Caleb Gosse himself could tell you what we'll get for this year's catch."

Lavinia has not joined in the ring game. She sits nearby on the grass, listening, watching as the silhouettes, hands joined, prance around the fire. Ned, Mary, Frank Norris and yes, even Thomas Hutchings, are still dancing with the youngsters. She wonders if Alex Brennan could have passed around his little bottle. There is no sign of it but the men seem unusually childlike.

The talk turns to the girls' trip into town. Alex promises Meg that his wife is on the lookout for them and will see that they get good places in service. Just then, as if hearing their names, Jane and Emma arrive, flinging themselves on the grass beside Lavinia.

"Why don't you come to St. John's with us, Vinnie?" Jane props her chin on Lavinia's knees and repeats the question, "Sure you was maid in a big house before you come here—you'd have no trouble to find a place."

The thought of going with them has not occurred to Lavinia. She wonders why.

"Go on, Jane, you knows Vinnie got her eye on someone." Emma gives Lavinia one of her sly, unsmiling looks. "We might as well ask Annie Vincent to come with us." She nudges Jane and they laugh.

This is not the first time Lavinia has heard Jane and Emma speculate about the relationship between Annie Vincent and Frank Norris. No one else on the Cape has ever mentioned it aloud, but these two talk of it constantly. She wonders if they talk about her in the same way.

"Ye'r foolish as odd socks, both of ye. Maybe Annie and me'll go off ourselves. Only we'll go farther than St. John's, I 'low." She hopes the idea of herself and Annie setting off to seek their fortunes will divert the two girls.

"Go on, Vinnie, you should come with us—sure there's no one here to set your cap for—except Thomas Hutchings, of course." Emma pauses significantly. She leans forward to peer into Lavinia's face. "Didn't he kiss you that day on Turr Island? Sarah Vincent told the Ma the two of you looked some queer when she come up to you that day."

Lavinia is glad the people on the step are still talking among themselves, glad that darkness covers her confusion. She would like to slap the malevolent face inches from her own.

"I hardly spoke two words to Thomas Hutchings in me life," she says sharply, "and I haven't seen but the back of his head all summer. Ye two better watch out for yer tongues if ye gets work in a big house. I tell ye, mistresses of them places don't want servant girls passin' gossip about."

"Lizzie says the three of ye, Annie, Pash and you, will all be old maids," Emma said with great satisfaction.

Jane is kinder. With the leave-taking near she is afraid and would dearly love for her aunt to come with them to St. John's. "We'll get new dresses, Vinnie—and shoes, and hats—and Captain Brennan says there's a playhouse in St. John's—imagine Vinnie, a playhouse!"

"Don't let Meg hear you talkin' of playhouses, young lady, and you saved!" Lavinia is astonished at herself. A year ago she would have been incapable of uttering such words. "Perhaps Lizzie's right. I am turning into an old maid aunt."

A wave of depression rolls over her, followed immediately by a desire to show her nieces, to give them something to talk about on their trip into St. John's. Suddenly brave, Lavinia jumps up, bouncing Jane's head off her lap, runs over and breaks into the ring, slipping between Thomas Hutchings and Frank Norris.

Thomas gives her a quick smile before turning to say something to Fanny, who is on his other side. Lavinia is very aware of Thomas' hand holding hers, of his arm with the shirt sleeve rolled back to the elbow, of his shoulder that sometimes touches her hair as they circle around.

Then, with pleasant amazement, she notes that her other hand, the one being held by Frank Norris, feels tingly too. Frank is slightly shorter than Lavinia, stocky but handsome with a broad open face and wiry black hair that curls around his ears and neck. Better looking than Thomas, Frank is, really, Lavinia thinks. She feels wanton and happy.

On the other side of the fire blurred faces sweep by: Annie, Isaac, Lizzie and Jo, Charlie, Willie, Rose and Patience. The singing picks up tempo, the circle moves faster and faster. Lavinia flings back her head and watches stars whirl like pieces of mirror in the black sky. Her hair is flying around her face, her skirt billowing out, her feet barely touch the moving earth. She is dizzy with motion and with some fever she's never felt before. Only the firm grip of Thomas and Frank hold her down, keep her from spinning up like a spark from the fire, like Elijah in his chariot, twirling into the sky before the astonished eyes of Jane and Emma.

Someone is laughing and laughing. It is Lavinia Andrews.

That night, lying in the bunk built against the schoolroom wall, sleeping alone for the first time, she longs for someone to come, fancies she can hear the door ease open, hear footsteps crossing the empty floor towards her bed. She waits, aching for someone, for Thomas or Frank, for anyone—but no one comes.

Next morning on the wharf, waiting for the *Charlotte Gosse* to cast off, she hears Alex Brennan call her name. She steps forward, foolishly expecting him to invite her aboard, tell her to hurry, get her things, come along with Jane and Emma who lean now against the rail, gazing down, smiling cool smiles, already detached from the people they are leaving behind.

"Sorry maid, I altogether forgot I had this—it got your name on it," Alex drops a parcel down to Lavinia. It is wrapped in oiled cloth and tied with thick string and has her name written on a card attached to the string—Miss Lavinia Andrews. How wonderful, she thinks, that someone in a city she has never seen dipped a pen in ink and inscribed her name so carefully. She runs her finger over the loops and swirls. The parcel contains books. She can feel the stiff ridges of the covers through the wrapping. Hugging the package she steps back from the edge of the wharf and waves as the lines are pulled in and the *Charlotte Gosse* moves out into the Cape.

"I'll say many goodbyes from here." The thought, so like one of Sarah's prophecies, makes her shiver.

"What's the matter, Vinnie, a goose walk over your grave?" Meg, who has not cried over her daughter's leaving, reaches for the package and lifts it, testing its weight as if gauging how much education it contains.

"Well girl, you're a teacher now and no mistake. Ben'll have to drive a good few nails to pay for this lot."

Lavinia expects Meg to take the books, but her sister-in-law passes the parcel back unopened. "They're for you—how long do you allow it will take for Willie to get through them?"

"A lifetime—two lifetimes," Lavinia thinks, but she shrugs and says, "I don't know, Meg, a year or so I s'pose, it depends if he pays attention." She feels exceedingly cold, already tired.

That night when Lavinia is alone, she unwraps the books: a big English Bible, the same Primer she remembers from Weymouth Sunday School and a thick, much-battered copy of the works of William Shakespeare, of whom she has not heard. She wonders who chose the books. Could Thomas have given Alex Brennan a list—or did some shopkeeper pick them out, or Alex Brennan's wife, the unseen woman they have come to depend upon for countless favours.

Sitting on her bunk, Lavinia begins to leaf through the unfamiliar book, but finds the print too small to read by candlelight. She places all three books on the shelf Ben has built right above her bed. The bindings reflect the candlelight, giving the room a finished look.

She fishes around in her old bag and pulls out several objects, a picture that once hung in the Monk Street kitchen, a purple and white sea shell and three rocks. She arranges the shell, picked from the beach her first day on the Cape, and the rocks—an arrow-like sliver of shiny black flint from the secret hollow and two egg shaped stones flecked with orange from Turr Island—on either side of the picture. The plaster frame is badly chipped, but the picture itself is unchanged: rusty sheep and smocked shepherd still walk home along a grassy lane edged with flowers and overhung with stately trees. The soft English countryside seems unreal, unlike the England Lavinia remembers. She studies the picture carefully, wondering why it once made her weep.

The objects on the shelf make the room hers: she arranges and rearranges them several times before she is satisfied. Then, feeling cheered, she blows out the candle. Before falling asleep she thinks: "I've already gotten a pair of boots, three books and a room of my own out of teaching. Maybe I haven't made such a bad choice after all, not leaving with the girls."

When the weather shows no sign of changing, Meg insists that classes must begin despite sunshine. Although Lavinia is the teacher, Meg considers herself in charge of the school. On the first morning, she gives the resentful scholars a lecture on the evils of sloth.

"Ye'll come in here first thing each morning, except for Sabbaths of course, and ye'll stay here 'til Ben comes home for dinner. Mind, if there's any trouble I'll be on the other side of that door!" Displaying a special switch made from small twigs bound with a piece of leather, she instructs Lavinia on how to use it should any child disobey.

Meg includes all the children in her warnings but never takes her eyes from her beloved son. Willie, sitting next to Rose Norris, looks as downcast as possible for one of his hopeful nature. Meg waves the switch at them, hangs it on a nail near the door and with a parting caution disappears into her kitchen, leaving teacher and students in a state of deep, silent despondency.

The children and Lavinia sit in a circle on the floor. The room is cool and quite empty except for a square desk, a backless bench and the bed, which is covered by a quilt of bright diamonds that Jennie pieced together on Monk Street. The quilt makes a splash of colour in the darkness. Lavinia takes a deep breath and looks around at her students. There are eight of them, nine if you count Moses, who is really too young to learn.

Lavinia opens her mouth and realizes that she has no idea what to say: no concept of what a teacher must do, no plan. This is very different from marking letters in wet sand, even different from reading around Meg's kitchen table. To cover her confusion she walks over and flings the outside door open.

The room is immediately filled with light and warm sunshine. "We will all begin by marking out this letter," she holds up the primer, "A is for Adam...."

Only Willie has a conventional slate to mark on. He even has sticks of brittle grey chalk, a rag and a small bottle of water. Lavinia wonders, as she has in the past and will in the future, how it is that Meg always knows the right thing to do, to have, to say, even to want. She had once laughed to hear Mary Bundle tell Ned that Sarah Vincent was a witch. If there is a witch on the Cape, Lavinia thinks it must be Meg—a calm, benign witch—a holy witch.

The other children have brought an assortment of objects intended for copying out letters. The usefulness of these things depends on the inventiveness of each family. Several have flat stones and chips of chalk-like rock, Charlie Vincent has the scoop part of a broken shovel to write on, Rose Norris comes without anything and Fanny Bundle has not come at all.

The Three Kings seem to have found the most imaginative substitute for slates. Henry, George and Alfred each arrive with a bird's feather and a tin plate, the bottom covered with a layer of flour. They show Lavinia how they can make lines in the flour with the feather. The only drawback is that each time they blow to obliterate the writing, puffs of flour rise and settle on their faces. As the long morning drags on, Ned's boys discover that flour and spit will make small pellets that are quite useful as weapons.

At her wits end to devise ways of filling the time, which she had calculated to be about three hours but which seems like a month, Lavinia ignores all their antics.

On the second morning there is a slight drizzle so that Lavinia keeps the door shut. There are now only seven scholars, Isaac having decided he is too old and Moses that he is too young, to begin an education. The dimness and decreased numbers make the little assembly even more sorrowful than it had been the previous day. This morning, though, having lain awake for a good part of the night, Lavinia has a plan. To begin the day she makes the children memorize and recite a verse of scripture.

"Remember now thy Creator in the days of thy youth, that the evil days come not nor the years draw nigh when thou shalt say, I have no pleasure in them," is the verse for that morning. Learning it takes the better part of an hour. Before all the children have recited the text there is a persistent tapping on the outside wall.

At first, thinking Ben is at work on some part of his ever expanding house, they pay no attention to the sound. The children have never known, and Lavinia has forgotten, that in more civilized places people do not open doors and walk in. The knocking continues for several minutes before the door opens and Thomas Hutchings steps inside.

The sullen scholars look up expectantly, hoping for release from their confinement. Flustered, Lavinia stands and brushes dust from her skirt, a garment so worn that nothing could improve it.

She is as surprised as the children at the unexpected arrival of Thomas. It is the first time he's come near her since that day on Turr Island, months ago. She has watched all summer, alert for any movement, any glance that might betray some special interest, but there has been nothing. She has started to think he might even be avoiding her.

Reminding herself that, according to Jane and Emma, she's a middle-aged spinster school teacher, she waits, with what she hopes is quiet dignity, for Thomas to speak.

"We'll not need this for the next few months—I—ah—I thought you might have use for it," he said holding out the small slate used to tally landings during the fishing season.

She nods, "Thank you very much."

They stand side by side looking down at the rag-tag youngsters. Charlie Vincent has picked up the Primer and is studying it. The rest sit, faces upturned, mouths hanging open, staring at Thomas as if they had never before seen him.

"Can any of them write?" he asks.

Lavinia feels a twitch of impatience. One of the things that vexes her about the man is the impression he gives of thinking other people are deaf, dumb and all alike. He might as well be talking about a boatload of fish or a herd of goats. Lavinia wonders if he knows the children by name.

"Oh yes. We worked some last winter in Meg's kitchen. Young Char is as good at reading and writing as meself. Patience can read a bit and write out her name. Isaac was doin' real good but now he's off with Ned and I doubt we'll be seein' much of him. Rose and Willie knows most of their letters—so do The Three Kings comes to that... ." Lavinia hears herself nattering and stops.

Alone at night, she has been practising the voice of authority, attempting to duplicate the tone she remembers Mrs. Ellsworth using with the maids. Now she pulls herself up and tries out this voice on Thomas Hutchings.

"Well, you know 'tis only one day since school begun—I really don't think you can expect too much yet, do you?"

She is extraordinarily pleased with this speech. Reviewing each word in her mind, she cannot find a single thing wrong with any of them. She stares straight at him, her pleasure intensified by the shock and surprise she sees his face.

"Oh I don't mean to offer any criticism. I was just thinking, wondering, if there was some way I could help."

He waits for a minute and when she, being dumbfounded, makes no reply says, "Well, you can think about it—about if there's a way to help, I mean. I'll be going now."

He turns stiffly, walks through the door and shuts it. Then he opens it again to stick his head in and say, "You might give them a short lesson about knocking on doors."

His head disappears, the door closes again. Still in her schoolmarm role, Lavinia sniffs. Her knees are shaking. She sits quickly down and ponders the conversation, wondering if it will be followed by months of silence.

Midway through the next morning he comes again.

They have memorized a Bible verse, recited their alphabet and been drilled in six three letter words—cat, fat, hat, mat, rat, sat.

Willie and Rose have both expressed the opinion that they are about to die. "Mudder'll be some put out with you, Vinnie. I heard tell people dies from not movin' around," Willie says reproachfully.

In exasperation she sends the children outside. She is standing in the doorway, watching the wild game of blind-man's bluff, thinking any minute Meg will appear and chase them all back to work, when she sees him coming up the path from the fish store. He circles around the noisy youngsters as if they were savage animals.

Lavinia scrutinizes Thomas Hutchings as he walks towards her, trying to decide what to make of the man. He dresses like other men in the place, wears the same threadbare jackets and pants. But he never looks like them—she wonders why. He is more tidy for one thing, his hair looks combed and his beard is square and always neatly trimmed. He is taller, too, a bit taller than Ned and herself, and more substantial somehow than Frank or the Vincent men. His skin is dark as a Turk's, and the planes of his face are sharply cut. His mouth has a closed, bitter look as if he was forever keeping black secrets.

He has a book under his arm, and as he comes up, opens it, flipping the pages. "I thought the older children might like this story. I enjoyed it when I was a child."

The idea of Thomas Hutchings as a child takes Lavinia's mind quite away from the book. Her imagination gropes to conjure up his childhood: she sees a frail dark-haired boy in a black suit, at a funeral maybe, his mother's funeral? But she is at a loss to put a background to the picture, to imagine a country, a town. She looks down at the book which he holds opened in front of her and sees winged horses, men in armour, turreted castles from which flags fly—Ned's stories—but the words in the book are not English. "But—but the youngsters got to learn English," she says stupidly.

"Oh, I don't mean for them to read this book. I'll read it to them. Just for a short time each day to get them interested in literature. If you like, I'll take the more advanced scholars while you're teaching the little ones. After a bit we can start reading Shakespeare—you have Shakespeare, I think?"

Patience had taken possession of Shakespeare the day after the book arrived. Lavinia has seen her pouring over it, gazing for hours at pen and ink drawings of men in strange clothing and long-necked women with cascading hair. Lavinia herself has not read a word in the heavy book.

"Ah yes," she tells Thomas Hutchings, "we got the Shakespeare one."

"Well then, I can take Charlie and Patience and spend half-an-hour reading from this book and half-an-hour on poetry while you teach the others their letters."

"How easy this all is when you knows what to say!" she thinks as they agree on this arrangement.

For the first few days the presence of Thomas Hutchings makes the children shy. They refuse to say the memory verse or read when he is in the room. Even Rose, the most brazen of the youngsters, will not answer questions in Thomas's presence. "What are we s'pose to call him?" she whispers to Lavinia on his third visit to the classroom.

Lavinia, who has the same problem, cannot think what to tell the child. Adults on the Cape are all called Aunt or Uncle. Only Thomas has not been made an honourary relative. She shoos Rose back to her place without answering the question.

Thomas usually lingers a few minutes after the children leave, and the following day, screwing up her courage, Lavinia asks what he would like the youngsters to call him.

The question seems to baffle him as much as it has her. He thinks about it a minute before asking, "What do they call you?"

"Same as they always called me, Vinnie."

"Then why can't they call me Thomas?"

The suggestion shocks Lavinia. Even the adults, even Josh Vincent who is surely older, seldom call him Thomas. More often they use his full name, or refer to him as the Skipper. But she nods and says, "Thomas." It is the first time she has said his name aloud. It makes her brave. "Were you a teacher before?" she asks.

"If you bring along the Shakespeare, I'll have young Charlie read some of it aloud tomorrow," he says as if she had not asked the question.

The next morning she tells the students to call Thomas Hutchings by his first name. It is a long time before they can manage this, but when they do everyone seems to relax and begin enjoying the foreign book. Its gallant, insane hero reminds Lavinia so much of Ned that she finds herself in knots of apprehension on his behalf. It is hard to concentrate on the spelling she is suppose to teach the younger children during what the students call story time.

Surprisingly, Thomas is a good performer. When he reads to the children his face relaxes, the watchful look leaves his eyes, he smiles. He knows dozens of poems and ballads by heart. Sometimes they are about love and honour, sometimes about war and strange gods. Lavinia has doubts about what Meg and Sarah would think if they could hear the poems. As the weeks go by he tells them about men who hold cities against whole armies, about men who stand all alone on bridges, men who sail to wild, unruled lands and become saints or kings, men who rescue beautiful women, men who fight monsters, stand on burning decks, on mountaintops, on rocks in the middle of the sea, men who shout ringing words out to the gods. Men, always men. Lavinia wonders why.

Still, the poems repeat over and over in her head, she hears them just before sleeping and when she wakes. She begins to know whole verses, then complete poems. She recites them aloud when she is alone. These lines, together with the Bible verses they learn each morning, are the first of hundreds of pieces of literature she will eventually memorize, will cling to in every dark hour of her life.

Thomas continues to linger after his sessions, answering questions for Charlie, and for Lavinia too, about the books he reads from. She never again asks anything about his past, but her curiosity about him becomes so overwhelming that one day, finding Ned alone, she asks him how old he thinks Thomas is.

Ned is vague: about forty, or maybe a bit younger, or a bit older. Lavinia persists, trying to pull Ned's tongue on the subject of his friend. Where is Thomas from? How did he come to be on the Cape? Why does he work for Caleb Gosse? What is the language in his book? Is he well off? How much does Gosse pay him?

Her usually talkative brother is noncommittal. "I don't know where he comes from, girl—I s'pose he's not a lot better off than the rest of us crowd. Far as I can tell, Caleb Gosse is a mean old bugger. Thomas credits what fish he catches to the Vincents in exchange for meals he eats there. I s'pose he gets paid some money, 'cause the only coin seen in this place is what he pays Ben." Ned winks, " 'course nobody sees that 'cause Meg stores it all away for Willie."

With the skill of a practised sea lawyer Ned changes the subject. "What do you think of the chances of young Willie gettin' to be a preacher? Can't see it somehow, our Willie with a collar hind-to-fore. That'll be some day, what?"

He slides into a long story about a minister who was run out of Pond Island for preaching the wrong brand of religion, "...a dangerous occupation if ya ask me. Meg'd do better to make the boy a good carpenter like Ben—tho' I doubts the lad got brains enough for that... ."

When Lavinia persists, asking what he and Thomas talked about in those long conversations they've been having for years, Ned says sharply, "What's all this, Vinnie? I thought you never liked the man. I can still see you that first year we come, scowlin' at him across the table like every mouthful of food was chokin' ya. Changed yer mind, have ya? I notice he's up there with the youngsters every morning—got yer eye on old Thomas, have ya girl?" Ned begins an improvised love ditty.

Cursing herself for having asked Ned anything, Lavinia tells him to hush, "...the youngsters will hear and I'll be tormented out of me mind. I got it hard enough with them now."

But Ned keeps on with his song until she sees that if he is not stopped the whole place will be talking about her and Thomas Hutchings by nightfall.

"I always thought Thomas Hutchings cold as a cod fish and stuck-up along with it—and I still do. If I wanted a man, I tell you, Ned Andrews, 'twon't be one from this place I'd pick!" Lavinia tells him using her practised voice.

Her brother turns suddenly sober. "You'll go a good ways, maid, a good long ways afore you finds the likes of Thomas Hutchings! I don't care where he come from, he's a good man!" Ned says and returns to his work, fitting bows for a pair of snowshoes around a homemade card—a tedious job.

Lavinia watches as he carefully eases the whittled strips down between pegs that will shape them into a bow. She thinks how many strange things they have learned to do since coming to the Cape, wonders if they may have forgotten other things. She, for example, can no longer talk to this brother she once loved so much. She walks away feeling unhappy for the first time in months.

One day that fall, Lavinia happens upon Mary Bundle sitting on the edge of the field doing nothing. Mary is in the early stages of pregnancy. At such times a brief mellowness soothes her striving, but even this cannot account for her sitting in broad daylight occupied with nothing more than contemplating a field of stubble and goats.

It is certainly a pretty sight, Lavinia thinks, a place the children call the marsh meadow. Marsh grass, long and blue-green, provides the only hay grown on the Cape. "Goats in the garden!" "Goats in the meadow!" is the common cry all through the spring and summer, when everyone keeps a look-out over the precious green. This year they have taken in three cuttings of hay from the field and the goats are now free to munch to their hearts' content.

Standing behind Mary, Lavinia becomes aware that the woman is completely absorbed in sorting two piles of small beach stones that lie in her lap, looking back and forth from the goats to the smooth stones.

When Lavinia touches her shoulder, Mary scrambles to her feet. "Lavinia! You could give a person fits, creepin' up on 'em like you does!"

"I didn't creep up, that's your trick, not mine—what in mercy's name are you doin' anyway, playin' jacks?" Lavinia points to the round white stones now scattered in the grass, wondering what could possibly bring such a look of embarrassment to Mary Bundle's face.

Mary sighs, scowls and says accusingly, "After all this time, you think you'd ha' taught me countin'."

Lavinia is mystified, "Countin'? Countin' what?"

"Countin' anything, stones, trees, countin' clouds—countin' goats," Mary flings her hand towards the offending, uncounted objects as she names them.

"All right then, I'll teach you now." Lavinia gathers up the stones. "Sit down, for goodness sake! What is it you wants to count?"

"The goats." Still surly, as if Lavinia is forcing her to do something, Mary sits and nods towards the small herd she and Sarah have lovingly raised. "I can count to ten, and twice ten I can keep in me head, but when I gets past that I can't get it right."

It will be years before Lavinia guesses what this admission costs Mary. Today she just counts the goats and says, "Twenty-three, there are twenty-three goats down there."

"Sweet Lord, girl, I don't want you to count 'em—I wants to count 'em meself!"

In much less than an hour, playing the children's game of chip-chip with stones, Lavinia has taught Mary to count to one hundred and to add and subtract. This, the limit of her own mathematical knowledge, had taken a Weymouth Sunday school teacher weeks to impart.

"Mary, you got the makings of a real scholar!" Lavinia looks in admiration at the woman she thinks of as much older than herself but who is, in fact, the same age. "Maybe I should teach you to read, too."

"Never you mind readin', I got no concerns with old stuff in books. I only wants to figure," Mary says and immediately puts her ability to use. "We got twenty-three goats in the place then, and enough hay for ten or twelve—that means we can slaughter twelve or thirteen during the winter and still have a good lot of milk next summer!"

Delighted with herself, Mary jumps up and begins to leave. Then she stops, turns back to Lavinia. "Thanks, Vinnie, that's the best thing I ever had learned me—sure now I can count good as Thomas Hutchings! You knows with all the fish we made the past summer Skipper Brennan told Sarah we should get some gold?"

Suddenly sober, Mary squints at Lavinia as if counting the specks in her eyes. "I wouldn't trust him was I you, girl. There's something not right, something dark about Thomas Hutchings, mark my words!"

Ned must have repeated their conversation to his wife, Lavinia thinks. Shrewd Mary had not been fooled by her talk about disliking Thomas.

"Every woman in the place is probably watching me like a hawk," she writes in her journal.

The division of responsibility in the schoolroom has not worked out just as Lavinia and Thomas planned.

"What's good comin' to lessons if we got to bide in this corner larnin' old words 'til we's blue in the face with Patience and them over there listenin' to yarns," Rose Norris says, with some justice, Lavinia feels.

The less-advanced students all agree: how can anyone concentrate on cat, mat and rat when six feet away battles rage, demons are chopped up and armies routed from castles. By the second week they are all sitting in one circle, all leaning forward caught up in the story Thomas is reading.

Inexplicably the days, though growing shorter, seem to grow no colder. It is as if eternal summer has arrived on the Cape. Each morning, before he begins reading, Thomas opens the door. Suddenly the room is filled with light, with the smells of outdoors and the sounds, the slap of clothes on the line, the scream of gulls and faint hammering from the neck where the men are working on the first wall of the church.

Meg says the good weather and the abundance of fish is because they have started building a church. To support her theory she recites a Bible verse: "Prove me now herewith, saith the Lord of Hosts, if I will not open you the windows of heaven and pour you out a blessing that there shall not be room enough to receive."

Lavinia, sitting on the dusty floor as Thomas Hutchings' voice fills the schoolroom, thinks Meg may be right, fancies she can see the blessing—a long, narrow ray of sunshine, like pale treacle pouring down on the Cape. They are in the promised land.

Chapter 12

I didn't see Ida Norris that day, years ago when Frank brought her to Cape Random but I remember Mamma telling us how she looked—beautiful as a china doll and saying her words the way proper people do. It's hard now to think of Ida like that. The truth is, until lately we hardly thought about her at all. It was almost as if she had died same as poor Hazel.

For years Meg, Sarah and Annie have taken turns going to the Norris house to change the filthy quilts, wash the mad woman and dress her in clean clothing. Between times Frank and Rose do for her. Annie Vincent, who goes most often to the Norris house, has never been heard to mention Frank Norris' wife. But according to Sarah and Meg, Ida is now completely silent. Her only occupation is stripping wallpaper from all the upstairs rooms. Hour after hour, Ida picks at the flowered patterns with her dirty fingernails, carefully peeling the paper back in long ribbons, leaving it to flutter so that the dusty, unused rooms look as if they are ravelling away.

It must be a strange life for Frank and Rose, Lavinia thinks, like living with a ghost. For the rest of Cape Random, the demented woman is only a grey face glimpsed occasionally in one of the upstairs windows of the Norris house, a name children whisper to frighten each other on summer evenings when they have stayed too long outdoors.

Then one morning Frank Norris pulls on his boots and finds that during the night they have been filled with molasses. The next day he and Rose come in at suppertime to discover two goats barred in the kitchen. The following day Frank's tobacco, his only luxury, is mixed into the flour barrel. The tricks continue; each day Rose whispers a new story of her mother's malevolence into Willie's ear. In time, everyone knows that Ida's sickness has taken a strange turn. It is unsettling, virulent, as if someone long dead had risen and was demanding attention.

Sarah Vincent understands at once that Ida's pranks have something to do with her daughter and Frank. She has known for a long time that the two are lovers, has wept over it secretly, lectured Annie by day and prayed for her by night without speaking of it even to Meg. Taking Ida's acts as a warning from

God that Frank and Annie's adultery must stop, Sarah renews her efforts to persuade Annie of this.

"God is not mocked ... be sure your sins will find you out," she tells her daughter morning and night—with no results.

One evening after supper, desperation drives Sarah to tell Josh her fears. "I don't doubt Ida Norris knows her husband and our Annie been actin' like married people." Although they are alone, Sarah turns deep red and glances around the room.

Josh looks down at his hands, studying each finger, rubbing his thick knuckles, not speaking.

"I tell you, Josh, I'm tarmented out of me mind—I been prayin' and thinkin' about it so long I don't know which way to turn. Still and all, I thinks something got to be done." Sarah sees her husband swallow and in dismay realizes that he is on the verge of tears. "I'm that sorry, Josh—I thought you knowed," she whispers.

Without looking up he shakes his head. Then he stands, takes his cap from behind the door, and goes out.

The next day Sarah confides in Meg, "Heartbroke the man was, heartbroke. I thought sure he knowed—I thought everybody in the place knowed—'tis been plain as the nose on yer face for the longest time. I can't help blamin' meself—I shoulda been able to put an end to it somehow."

The two women are kneeling on the wharf scrubbing rag mats from the Vincent and Andrews houses. Just below the wharf Mary hangs over the side of a dory sloshing other mats in the sea.

"Well girl, I knowed of it, so do Ben," Meg says quietly. "I been wantin' to speak to you about it but I didn't like to say nothin' till you spoke. Still and all I been thinkin' about it and, well... ." Meg hesitates.

She glances down at Mary but her sister-in-law is leaning over the side of Thomas Hutchings' dory, seemingly unconcerned with the conversation taking place just above her head.

"You knows what Reverend told us, 'if we confess our sins He is faithful and just to forgive us our sins and to cleanse us from all unrighteousness'. I thinks we should get all hands together for a special service—for a season of prayer and forgiveness."

Sarah is doubtful. "I don't know, I allow Annie wouldn't even come to such a thing. Besides, who'd do it? 'Tis all right me and you leadin' out in our houses on Sunday, but you needs a preacher for such a thing."

"Reverend Eldridge told us we should confess to one another and pray together for a forgiving spirit and for God's grace. He said only papists need a mortal person to confess to." Meg has had this speech prepared for some time. She speaks softly, careful of her friend's feelings.

"I hates to bring it all out. People'll think we're no better than the crowd up in Cat Harbour. And 'twill be some hard on Josh." Sarah rubs her brush with soap and for several minutes scrubs furiously at a green lamb surrounded by pink roses. "But I s'pose you're right, maid, it got to be done, 'tis a wonderful sin, and the both of them saved, too."

"Annie's always been good-hearted, sure she's up there right now strippin' off quilts. We allowed it's still warm enough to get them dry outdoors," Meg gestures towards the Norris house.

Once the finest on the Cape, it is now grey and run-down. Frank Norris spends as little time as possible in or around the house he built so lovingly. A piece of trim is dangling from one edge of the roof, and the front door has a broken hinge. Lace curtains the women had admired hang in grimy tatters behind dull windows. The fence around the small back yard has fallen over and goats have eaten every bit of green. There are no out-buildings, no hen-house or clothes line, no flowers or bushes by the front step. Even now, in morning sunshine, the house has a cold, shadowed look that makes Meg shiver.

"I told Annie she shouldn't be goin' up there the way things is, but she would take her turn. Said I was just bein' fanciful."

Having talked to Meg, Sarah is already feeling better. "I don't s'pose there's any real harm in the poor soul. After all, three of us been in and out of the house for years."

Meg and Sarah sit back on their heels and study the Norris place.

"I s'pose by rights we should be prayin' for Ida, too—you know, girl, it comes to me betimes we shoulda done more for her over the years," Sarah says thoughtfully.

Mary Bundle snorts and slams the wet mats down on the wharf, spattering all three women with sea water. Mary has always held that Ida is not sick but bone lazy, giving this as the reason she will not take a turn cleaning the Norris house.

"What that one needs is a good kick in the arse. Ye'r all too easy on her, that's the trouble, coddlin' her, doin' housework for her. What odds, I say, if Frank and Annie is havin' a bit of fun? That woman, makin' out she's sick all these years, don't deserve a man like Frank, he'd a been better off too if he'd dragged her out and made her work!"

Although these three spend hours together, most conversation is carried on between Sarah and Meg because Mary doesn't believe in what she calls natterin'. Waste or laziness, however, makes her eloquent: "...if Ida Norris is smart enough to carry on with all this idleness she been up to lately, then she's smart enough to work. What's more I told Frank... ." Mary is interrupted by the sound of glass smashing.

A chamber pot, its contents swirling out across the yard, comes flying through a window of the Norris house and crashes down onto the rocks. At the same instant, the sagging front door is pushed open and Annie stands hesitantly in the dark doorway. She looks wildly around, sees the women and dashes toward them. She is holding one hand to her shoulder, sobbing "Mamma, Mamma, Mamma," like a small child.

A large china wash jug, followed by a bowl of the same pattern, comes hurtling down, barely missing Annie's head. Then, from the broken window, a voice, horrible, scraping, loud, screeches, "Harlot! Whore of Babylon! Jezebel!"

Lavinia and the children, who have been playing rings outside the schoolroom, hear the uproar and race down the bank, scuttling past the Norris house, hands held over their heads. They arrive at the wharf in time to see Annie fall into Sarah's arms.

"Oh Mamma, she hurt me, she took after me with a knife... ." Annie sobs.

Blood drips onto Sarah as she reaches up to hold her tall daughter, patting her back and making warm clucking noises.

Mary pulls Annie away from her mother and unbuttons the neck of her dress. "Tisn't deep—only a scratch by the looks of it. For Lord's sake, stop snivelling, girl," she says, but not unkindly. Then, pushing Annie back towards Sarah, she turns on the ring of awe-struck children. "What's you lot gawkin' at?" she asks, and when no answer comes, "Cat got yer tongues, have she?"

"It was her, wasn't it?" Rose Norris looks afraid. The child jabs a finger in the direction of her house, silent now, the broken window black and empty.

"Course it was her. Stund bugger, throwin' good piss pots outta windows!" Mary is disgusted. She has long coveted the china set.

"Your mother's sick, Rose. Mary and me, we're goin' up now to see how she is." Meg looks at Mary, thinking that small as she is, Mary will be able for the mad woman.

Knowing her daughter is not mortally wounded, Sarah's henlike sounds have been replaced by a flood of words. "I told ya my girl—time and time again I warned ya! Evil begets evil, the Lord will not have his commandments broke nor his words mocked." Without interrupting herself, she beckons to Lavinia, and between them, they lead Annie towards the Vincent house.

Meg takes a few steps away from the wharf, then, thinking better of it, turns back to the children. "I wants no talk of this. No jokin', no tellin' yarns. Not one word, 'tisn't a matter for youngsters to concern themselves with. Mind now, not a peep, not even between yerselves. Ye hears me, don't ye?"

None of the children know the meaning of the words they have heard, but Ida's ear-piercing curses echo in their heads like the voice of doom. Chidden, they nod and keep on nodding as, in a terrible whisper, Mary adds her own threats to Meg's. "If ye don't mind what Meg tells ye, I'll have the boogie man cut yer tongues out same as if ye were cod fish." She looks from face to face. "What's more, get to work cleanin' them mats or there'll be no dinner for ye this day."

The children do not move but stand there, still nodding, as Meg and Mary walk up the lane and into the awful house.

"All the way down to the house Sarah kept on muttering Bible verses, some of them I never heard before. I wonder how it is that she and Meg, who can't read a word between them, manages to learn so much of the Bible by heart," Lavinia writes that night.

"One she kept repeating over and over was 'Lust bringeth forth sin and sin bringeth forth death and eternal damnation', and 'Lasciviousness is an unruly evil and full of deadly poison but the fruit of righteousness is peace and joy'. There was more but them are the only two I remember, and by the time we had Annie's shoulder cleaned and bound up I was doing it too. Only my verses were more about rewards and heaven because we hadn't learned any verses about lust in class. Taking turns we were, Sarah and me, laying a burden on poor Annie and she just kept on bawling like she would never have done of it."

Swept up in the spirit of the hour, Lavinia finds herself kneeling in the Vincent kitchen, joining Sarah in prayer, pleading with Annie to lay aside lust and all filthiness, to receive forgiveness, to resist temptation, to accept the crown of life. She is herself half-hypnotized by the words.

After what seems like hours on the matless, splintery floor, Annie admits her sin. Her round, usually cheerful face transformed with sadness, she begs God's forgiveness and promises her mother she will have nothing more to do with Frank Norris. "Tho' I loves him like you wouldn't believe, Mamma."

The young woman buries her wet face in her mother's shoulder. The two are still kneeling, crying together, when Lavinia leaves the house.

Talk of Annie and Frank's dalliance, of Ida's curses, of the attack on Annie, may be hushed about firesides late at night or whispered of in bed between husband and wife, but it never becomes the subject of talk around the Cape, and certainly never spread to Sarah's family on Pinchards Island or to Josh's people in Pond Island. It is doubtful whether Alex Brennan, or even Reverend Eldridge, hear of it. It is a secret, like many others, kept on the Cape.

As Meg tells Lavinia, "The Lord knows, he's forgiven them, Sarah and Josh have forgiven them, so I don't see 'tis anyone else's business—we don't want this place made a sample of all along the Cape Shore."

When Meg and Mary return from the Norris house they say only that Ida has gone to bed and is sleeping like a newborn. Ida's bizarre tricks stop that day. She returns to silence and to peeling paper from the walls. Years later, when she dies, the younger people on the Cape have all but forgotten her existence.

Annie Vincent is not seen around the place for a week. Then she reappears and begins working by herself at unusual jobs that no one has the heart to tell her are inappropriate for a young woman. The following summer she will put on her father's overalls and oilskins and become a shareman with her brother. She will fish with the men, dress like them and acquire the reputation of being a fish hunter—one of the uncanny people who have the power to sense the presence of fish and lure them out of hiding.

As far as anyone can see—and several, including Lavinia, watch closely—Annie Vincent and Frank Norris never go near each other in all this time. The day after Ida Norris is buried, Annie, by then a sturdy thirty-eight, will burn her oil skins, don her only dress, previously reserved for Sunday service, march over to Frank Norris' door and propose to him.

Such things are certainly not on Lavinia's mind as she gets stiffly up from her knees and leaves the Vincent kitchen. She is reflecting on the scripture she

156

and Sarah have reamed off, all those commandments about impure thoughts and immodest acts, admonishing herself to guard against Thomas Hutchings—strange instructions since he has never made the slightest gesture towards her.

She is unaware of her own future, or of Annie's. Unaware that Thomas Hutchings is at this moment standing in the middle of her empty school room wondering where teacher and scholars have gone and, much against his will, staring at the bed where she sleeps.

Heedless Lavinia! In a mood of sombre but pious enjoyment, she walks thoughtfully back to the wharf where she spends the afternoon scouring mats and hanging them to dry on the flakes.

In retrospect Lavinia will conclude that the day she prayed with Sarah and Annie ended the long summer of pure happiness. After that day, despite the continuing sunshine, despite the still ripening berries, despite goats and children still cavorting outdoors, doubts and suspicions began.

The next morning Thomas Hutchings does not come for his reading period. Lavinia sits on the doorstep, as she has each day, waiting for him and watching the youngsters at their mid-morning games. Still thinking about the events of the previous day, she does not realize how long the children had been outside until she notices the sun has moved beyond where she sits and is falling on the far corner of the house.

It is well past the hour when he usually comes up the path towards her. She sits waiting, realizing that all her time now is arranged around this part of the day. Early morning is spent looking forward to the hour when Thomas will read. When he leaves, the present drops away, and the rest of the day is spent remembering everything he has said, recalling each time he looked in her direction, analyzing each gesture, until time rolls up to night and she can lie in bed thinking of the next day when he will come again. And all of this is happening beneath her skin; behind the Lavinia who walks and talks, teaches spelling, eats, sleeps, writes in her journal.

She sits on the step ruminating on these amazing things, hearing, as if they were far off, the high hollow voices of the youngsters and watching the shadows crawl across the grass towards her.

It takes a long time for Lavinia to concede that Thomas is not coming, and to call the children back into the room. Sitting them in the usual circle, she opens the Shakespeare book at random and begins to read to them herself. The words are meaningless. She keeps glancing towards the door and losing her place on the page. Charlie Vincent takes the book and starts to read. Lavinia paces the room. The youngsters, their eyes full of distress, follow her every move. She glowers, tells them crossly to pay attention to Charlie, then goes to sit behind the desk, holding herself still, trying to calm the distraught Lavinia who lives under her skin.

That the absence of one person should cause her such grief jolts her. "Why, ever since that day on Turr Island I been livin' in a world of fancies, imagining things that are no more real than Ned's old foolishness."

Nailed onto the wall beside the desk is a map of Europe and the New World, a rough outline drawn by Thomas on the brown paper that the books had been wrapped in. Gazing at it, Lavinia remembers her resolve to find maps of her own, adult maps.

"Instead, I been mesmerizin' myself with daydreams. Conjuring up visions of me and Thomas Hutchings, of us livin' together, havin' a house with glass windows, with cups and saucers, a garden, clocks that tick—children. No roads, no sign posts, no pathways or harbours, nothing real." She slowly works her way through the maze of what she's dreamed to the reality of what is.

Then, for all this time some part of her has remained hopeful and listening, she hears him coming. The reading stops and in the silence every head turns toward the door.

He walks in without his ritual knock. For the first time since she has known him, Thomas Hutchings seems confused, even frightened. He leans back against the door and without speaking looks around the room, like someone who has just woken from a deep sleep.

"Does Fanny Bundle ever come here?"

The question is so unexpected, so at odds with everything Lavinia has been thinking about, that she doesn't understand it. She gazes around the room as if searching for Fanny.

"Have you seen Fanny this morning, I want to know." His voice is cross, impatient, his eyes seem not to see her or the children.

"She's not been here for a week or more—she only came once or twice first off." Why is he asking about Fanny? Lavinia is surprised he knows Fanny from Rose.

Lavinia has, in fact, inquired of Mary regarding her daughter's absence from lessons. "Don't pay no heed to that one—she's feckless, sees things aren't there and don't see things is there. Like me own mother, Fanny is—behind the door when good sense was handed out. No use her goin' to school, she'll never amount to anything," Mary had said.

Some time has passed and Thomas still leans against the door. Speaking as she would to a small child, Lavinia asks him what is wrong. Inside her somewhere a snake wakes, she can feel the flick of its tail.

She repeats the question but Thomas doesn't answer. She tells the children to go on home but no one moves and she has to hustle them out, pushing Thomas away from the door as if he were a block of wood. She follows the children outside and stands for a moment, fixing the day in her mind, as warm as July it is with not a cloud in the sky. Then she goes back into the dark room and shuts the door behind her.

"There's nothing wrong is there, Thomas?" Even through her worry, Lavinia knows this is the first time she has followed his directions and used his given name. The thought distracts her for an instant but not long enough for her to miss the look of bewilderment that clouds his face.

"Wrong? Wrong?" he repeats the word as if he had never heard it before.

"How can anyone tell if a thing is wrong?" he asks, and answers himself (or that is what she guesses) with words in a foreign tongue.

"He's gone mad!" Lavinia thinks. "Something has happened. He's lost his mind like the people Sarah talks about who go crazy, whose hair turn white overnight from seeing some terrible thing."

"Lavinia, I think maybe we should talk about something." He pauses as if trying to decide how to tell her, how much to tell her.

"Yes?" she says. "Yes, Thomas, what is it?"

Then Meg comes in through the door from the house. "You're lettin' them youngsters off altogether too early, Vinnie!" Her voice dies when she sees the two facing each other near the door.

Thomas looks towards Meg. He straightens, his face closes over, becomes guarded, alert. Before Lavinia's astonished eyes he is instantly the old Thomas, confident and stand-offish.

"I expect that was my fault, Meg. I wanted to let Lavinia know I was going over to Pond Island tomorrow if this weather holds. I'd like to pick up extra barrels for the fish we're catching and thought I might be able to get the nails Ben needs for the church."

"Goin' to Pond Island this time of year!"

Immediately distracted with the novelty of someone leaving the Cape so late in the fall, Meg begins to review what they might have that can be traded with the Pond Island people. She walks with Thomas into her kitchen, leaving Lavinia standing in the empty dark room, wondering what he had been about to tell her.

"I must be simple-minded, or like one of them people can't tell different colours, else I'd know what he was going to say. There's not a woman in the place who'd be standin' here not able to tell if a man got any feeling for them or not!"

Fighting tears, Lavinia goes to sit on her bed, pulls out her journal and turning to a clean page, writes: *Things I know for sure about T.H.* Below the heading she writes:

1. *He was not born in this country.*
2. *He works for Caleb Gosse.*
3. *No one knows anything about him, not Ned, or Alex Brennan, or Josh.*
4. *He's terrible upset about something to do with Fanny.*
5. *He can hide the way he feels, change his own face when he likes.*

She studies what she has written, and adds:

6. *Mary Bundle says he's not to be trusted.*

The list tells her nothing.

"Can there be something between Thomas and Fanny, something like what happened between Frank and Annie Vincent?" Lavinia can hardly credit such a thing. Fanny is only a child, fourteen or barely fifteen and, as Mary says, feckless.

Lavinia sits on the bed, thinking. She begins two more schoolgirlish lists, one opposite the other. One is of the times she's seen Fanny and Thomas together, very few—and one of the times when they have both been missing. Angry scratches obliterate all three lists but they can still be read with patience and a good light.

For others on the Cape, the season of mellow contentment extends well into December. Enough wood for two winters has been stacked beside houses and in sheds, and two dozen barrels of herring have been salted down. All the uprights for the church are in place. When Thomas returns from Pond Island with nails, everyone turns out, and in three days they have one wall boarded up. It is only then, a week before Christmas, that the ground freezes, becoming dry and hard like brittle taffy that crumbles pleasantly when the children jump on it. Work on the church stops.

"Time to batten her down," they tell each other. They pull up boats, repair the doors of vegetable cellars and pile boughs around the houses.

Thomas continues arriving at the school each morning to read, but his old formality has returned. Despite the growing coldness of the classroom, despite her resolve to renounce daydreams, Lavinia delays moving the students to Meg's kitchen, knowing that he will then stop coming.

The children are finally learning something. The Three Kings can now write their names, Henry Benjamin Andrews, George Frederick Andrews and Alfred Thomas Andrews, an accomplishment that gives them and Lavinia much satisfaction. Their baby brother Moses can repeat the entire alphabet and does so constantly, until Mary threatens to sew his mouth shut. Patience reads well, and Charlie Vincent has advanced far beyond Lavinia's teaching. Willie and Rose are still working their way laboriously through the primer. Fanny has not been seen in the classroom for weeks.

Christmas, formerly thought of as an extra Sabbath day, is celebrated differently this year. In addition to the usual worship service, Meg suggests that the scholars have a concert. The children are happy to show off what they have learned, and on the appointed night jump up one by one to bellow out memory verses. Patience, however, recites a long, long poem about Venus which shocks Meg, causing her to have a quiet word with Lavinia after the concert.

For most of them it is the best Christmas they can remember, one without the foreboding they have felt other years. Emma and Jane are spoken of often. People wonder how they are making out in St. John's, tell each other that the girls are missing a good Christmas. Frank and Annie seem reconciled to their separation and Peter Vincent seems more settled. The young man has started work on a house, although he has no prospects of marriage as far as anyone can tell. The men are all home, and there is a good supply of food laid by.

Only Lavinia is miserable. At Ned's house for a feast of fish and brewis on Christmas Eve, she cannot keep from watching Thomas Hutchings. Following every move he makes, she sees that he, in turn, is watching Fanny.

Fanny, in her usual haze, seems unaware of Thomas' scrutiny, or of his existence for that matter. Somewhere among the half-frozen bushes she has found a tiny rose and pinned it into her hair. Dressed in her rainbow coloured rags, she wafts from person to person, bent on her new pastime of reading fortunes. Where she has come by this idea no one knows. Lavinia watches the girl circle the room picking up hands, studying palms. Charlie dodges out of her reach, Willie and Rose giggle and pull their hands away. She moves on to Isaac Andrews, picks up his hand and drops it after only a glance but Patience submits and listens enthralled to the long and complicated future Fanny predicts for her. When Fanny reaches Peter Vincent, Lavinia is surprised to see the usually sullen young man smile and hold his hand out. With their heads together, his almost white and hers dark as jet, they study Peter's palm.

"You will live with a beautiful princess in that tower you're buildin', you'll have lots of sons and grow to be a crabby old man with a long beard," Fanny tells him, her impish face full of laughter.

Thomas is sitting next to Peter, but before Fanny can reach for his hand, Sarah swoops down. "Stop that foolishness this minute, you pure gives me the shivers. Mary, can't you make that girl stop?"

Mary ignores the request and Sarah reinforces her objections. "I had a second cousin used to tell fortunes with cards when she was a girl your age—one night she seen the devil himself in the cards. She was strange forever after."

Seeing a smirk on her son's face she turns on him. "Get that silly grin off your face, Peter Vincent. Make no mistake, tellin' the future is devil's work—the Bible says we know not the day nor the hour."

Lavinia has a mind to ask Sarah why she is forever foretelling the future if it's a sin, but Ned has already started off on a story about a sailor he knew who had second sight and thereby became enormously wealthy.

The story continues, the sailor is transformed into a pirate, then a prince; Josh dozes and small children fall asleep in their mothers' arms; the fire turns to red embers and Mary announces this is the last pot of tea she'll brew this night. Sometime well into the story-telling, Lavinia notes that both Thomas and Fanny have vanished.

It is already Christmas morning when the story ends. People stand stiffly, pull on coats, wrap scarves about their heads and stumble out into the clear, crisp air. There is still no sign of Thomas or Fanny.

When they have all gone, Lavinia lies in bed and, despite the holy season of goodwill, gives herself up to terrible imaginings of Thomas and Fanny rolling together on his bed in the fish store.

With the new year, the feeling of apprehension that only Lavinia has felt spreads like a fog to cover them all. The bare hills, the skeleton trees, the frozen grass rattling like long needles in the sand, the absence of any colour under the unnaturally white sky, all give the sensation of a season caught in time. The desolate landscape makes everyone edgy. Couples bicker over inconsequential things, Ben begins to worry that they've made a mistake in the location of the church, and Mary picks a fight with Thomas over letting Peter, who has disappeared into the woods on one of his extended forays, take the gun.

"'Twas all bad enough with only that old thing, now we got nothin'! Ya stund bugger, can't ya see we're defenceless as babies if somethin' happens!" she tells him right to his face.

Sarah's gloomy prophecies grow so numerous that even Meg begins avoiding her, the men drag their boats further and further up onto the beach to thwart her predictions of disaster, and Mary mutters incantations against the evil eye. The children recall their former ominous imaginings and refuse to go alone to the pond for water or venture out into their own yards for wood after dark. They drive the women to distraction by being constantly under foot.

The classroom becomes so cold that Lavinia is forced to move the school into Meg's kitchen. As expected, this ends Thomas's visits: he tells Pash and Charlie to come down to his store for lessons. Left with the slower students, Lavinia's voice grows more shrill each day and the children grow more resentful.

"The times are out of joint," Lavinia hears Charlie Vincent say, and writes out the words in her book. It is years before she discovers they are not his own.

Then one morning in mid-January, Josh Vincent, jacketless and unshaven, comes to the Andrews' door before breakfast. "There's something the matter with Sarah," he tells Meg urgently.

Watching her sister-in-law hurry out the door after Josh, Lavinia knows that what they have been expecting has come.

Within days, one-third of the people on the Cape are deathly ill. In the haphazard selection of victims, only the Norris family has been passed over, in each of the other houses someone lies moaning or unconscious. The cause of the illness is a mystery. People awake too weak to get out of bed, and within hours are seized by terrible vomiting, diarrhea, fever, pain, before finally slipping into a coma.

By the fourth day, Sarah Vincent is near death. Annie cares for her mother, working around Josh who sits by the bed holding his wife's hand. Whenever they can spare a minute from their own families, Meg or Mary come to give Annie a chance to rest. At the end of her patience, Mary chases Josh out of the room, ordering him to get a meal for himself and for Charlie, who has been hovering outside his mother's door like a lost soul. In less than half-an-hour, though, the man is back holding Sarah's hand, his eyes fixed on her still face.

In Meg's and Ben's house, Patience and Willie are both ill, and for the first time Meg gives equal attention to both, murmuring prayers over her children as she rushes from bed to bed. Everyone who can walk is recruited to bring water, chop wood, spoon soup into the mouths of the sick, to wash bodies and quilts. When Lizzie and Joe Vincent become too ill to tend to their three children, Lavinia is dispatched by Mary to take care of the family.

Mary Bundle is the busiest person on the Cape. It is she who gives orders, barking them out in the fewest words possible. In addition to caring for Ned, Moses and Isaac who are all ill, she stalks from house to house, swabbing throats, boiling spruce boughs and herbs in great kettles, rubbing ointment on chests, muttering curses or charms to herself, talking to herself, asking herself what to do. She misses Sarah grievously, wishes she could consult with the older woman. What will help? Has she forgotten something, some root or herb, some incantation? Her face grows grey and pinched, her nose seems to lengthen and cast a shadow over her small, pointed chin. She looks like a real witch as she rushes about with steaming pots and bags, but her potions avail no more than Meg's prayers.

Keeping the sick clean is a momentous problem. Endless buckets of water have to be lugged from the pond and heated before bodies and bedding can be washed. Buckets of vomit and excretum must be disposed of. Thomas and Frank dig a pit into which the terrible waste is thrown and covered with layers of lime, sand and gravel. Boys are assigned to hauling wood and keeping the fires going day and night. Smoke and heat, Mary thinks, might kill vapours carrying the sickness. Ben, with the doubtful help of Rose and Fanny, becomes responsible for cooking pots of soup and broth to feed both the sick and the well. The few children untouched by the illness are chased outside where they stand near doors, too frightened to play or even to move away from the house where their parents, brothers or sisters are fighting with death.

In the turmoil, two nights pass without anyone remembering to give Lavinia a respite from nursing Joe and Lizzie. On the third day, distraught with weariness and anxiety, she hears Peter Vincent stacking firewood in the back porch, drags him into the house and pushes him to the chair beside the bed where Joe and Lizzie lie.

"You bide there and watch 'em, I been afraid to close my eyes these two nights for fear they'd die on me." The only sign of life in the husband and wife is the low rasping that comes with each breath.

"Watch them youngsters, too," Lavinia points to the cot where the twins lie and tells Peter that young Mattie is bedded down by the fire in the next room.

"If they seems worse call Mary or Meg, I got to get some sleep," she stumbles out and up the path to her own cold room where she falls on the bed and sleeps until dark.

When Lavinia wakes she washes her face, takes a jug of Ben's soup and hurries back to Jo's and Lizzie's house. Peter is still sitting where she left him, neither he nor the two in the bed seem to have moved. The twins, however, are screaming hungrily and she sends Peter in search of goat's milk.

There is a terrible stench in the sick room. She wedges the door ajar, braces herself and begins to strip quilts from the bed. When the two patients are clean and apparently comfortable, she spoon-feeds the babies with the mixture of milk, tea and sugar sent down by Meg.

Only then does she remember Mattie. The child still lies quietly in the bundle of coats by the fire. Lavinia bends forward, touches her cheek and knows instantly that the little girl is dead. Lavinia, her hand cupping the pretty face still brown from summer, is too tired to weep. Dry-eyed she kneels there, grieving for all the things that can never be, gathering courage to tell Ben, Meg and Josh (Sarah, she thinks, will never need telling) of their granddaughter's death. She is sure that had she stayed in the house the child would not have died.

"I would have kept you alive, I would have kept you alive somehow," Lavinia, still young enough to believe such a thing, tells the dead child.

Other deaths follow. Ned and Mary's youngest child, Moses, the pet of the place since he could walk, turns blue and chokes to death in his mother's arms as she paces the floor. Then, just as Sarah seems to rally, Josh Vincent comes down with the plague. He is dead within a day.

When Lavinia washes the emaciated bodies of Lizzie and Joe, when she feeds and changes the twins, who seem immune from the illness, she is sick with fear that they will all die. She imagines four silent houses, empty except for dead bodies that freeze and lie like wood all winter. She has heard of such things happening in this country, of men like Alex Brennan sailing into a place in the spring to find only bodies—or bones if animals get into the houses.

She feels hot and chilled by turns. Her stomach heaves, she cannot eat and is sure she has caught the sickness. The soft roundness newly come to her face dissolves, and her summer beauty vanishes. She marvels at the vain fancies that filled her head just weeks ago, forces her mind to concentrate on the hateful tasks that occupy her hands and tells herself she has finally become an adult.

"If time should last," a phrase of Sarah's that comes often to Lavinia's mind these days, "if time should last I'll learn to guard against dreams. I'll become like Mary Bundle," she swears.

With so much to be done for the living, little time can be spared for the dead. Josh and Mattie are buried without ceremony, with no more than a hasty prayer. Ned recovers enough to sit up. He spends all day beside Isaac, who seems to be wasting away. The boy is almost transparent—even Mary is afraid to wash him.

Then a week passes without a death, and another week without any new sickness. Willie and Sarah are both able to get out of their beds. They sit, propped like thin scarecrows, in chairs beside their fires.

One morning, just at dawn, the place is awakened by bitter screeches. Patience has regained consciousness and is screaming that she cannot see, that everything is black. Her father and mother, Lavinia, and Mary who has rushed in from next door, gather around her bed trying to console the hysterical girl.

But Patience will not be comforted. She sits all day, her eyes wide, gazing vacantly around the room, searching for some speck of light, and the awful wailing goes on and on. Late that night, when it is clear that no one will sleep unless the sound ends, Mary marches in and commands the girl to shut up.

"Our eardrums are fair worn out with your caterwauling. Ned and Isaac out next door got to sleep." Seeing that her words have not had the slightest effect, Mary raises her hand and gives Patience a hard slap across the face.

The screams stop as if someone had slammed down a window. Blessed quiet. Then Mary, speaking softly, begins to smooth green salve on the girl's eyelids.

"There now, there now, there now, this will do you all the good in the world. 'Tis roots of them white water lilies that grows on the pond, remember them, Patience? Mind how they looks in summertime lyin' like white tallow on the water... ." Mary keeps talking as she binds a piece of cloth like a blindfold around the girl's face. When she is finished, Patience, exhausted by the day's terror, falls back on her pillow and is asleep before Mary goes through the door.

Although there are no more deaths, it is a long time before the pestilence burns itself out. Lizzie, Joe and Meg's Willie recover slowly. Ned seems better almost at once, but in Isaac the sickness lingers. The young man now looks older than his father, his hair has fallen out, his eyes are sunken and ringed with dark circles, his limbs so wasted that he shuffles about, clinging to tables and chairs.

Ned holds the boy up and makes him walk outside, taking a set number of circles around the house each day. Ned slashes a cut with his knife into a plank at the back of the house every time they pass. He makes the notches deep, giving Isaac time to rest before insisting that they walk around the double Andrews house a few more times each day. The blackened line of marks in the wood will always remind Lavinia of the plague. Each time she sees them she will shiver, remembering Ned tenderly holding his son up as they shuffle slowly, painfully, around and around the house.

They grow accustomed to Patience's weeping each morning when she wakes and finds herself still blind. Like the rattle of goats' hoofs on the path or the slamming of outhouse doors, it becomes a sound that marks the beginning of day on the Cape.

There is still no snow, but the weather turns bitter. Cold seeps in through every crack and crevice and they realize how much the snow, for all they cursed it, had insulated the houses. Frank, Ben and Thomas drag evergreen trees out of the woods and stack them around the outside walls. The women hang quilts inside doors and put layers of clothing on the beds. For all that, the piles of firewood they had thought would last through two winters begin to shrink alarmingly.

Communal chores stop. No one stirs, the place is quiet as a graveyard with each family pulled inside itself, nursing grief, trying to make sense out of what has befallen. Meg does not have the heart for Sabbath services and without them time dissolves into a blur of bone weary dullness.

Rather than share a bed with Patience, Lavinia continues to sleep in the unheated classroom. She heats rocks in the fire, then wraps them in bits of old clothing to take into bed. Sometimes, just before sleep, she thinks she has died and been buried, that the unnaturally quiet days are only a dream she is having in her grave. She has no sense of relief that the sickness has passed, is sure something more is hovering over them.

In her journal Lavinia writes a chant she has heard Sarah Vincent say:

Never one without a two, cold and hunger deeds to rue/Never two without a three, death and sorrow come to thee.

Chapter 13

"The heart of man is deceitful above all things and desperately wicked, who can know it?"—If the good Lord can't figure out men's hearts then I shouldn't expect to either.

After the sickness, Thomas Hutchings withdrew from the community. He no longer gave Charlie and Patience lessons, stopped eating his midday meal at the Vincents' house. Despite the bitter cold he began taking long, inexplicable walks alone, never turning up at Ned's fireside where, during other winters, he had spent almost every evening.

"At least the man could have kept on teaching Charlie and Patience like he said he would," Lavinia writes. She cannot make sense of Thomas's actions and feels betrayed every time she thinks of him, which, despite her good intentions, is often.

Not at home with the older women, she tries to make friends with Lizzie, but her niece, preoccupied with husband, babies and grief over her daughter's death, has no time for Lavinia. She wishes with all her heart she could return to being accepted among the children, a thing now mysteriously impossible. Reconciling herself to the lonely role of teacher, she grimly assembles the scholars again.

She lists them in her journal in the order they are seated around Meg's table: William Andrews, Rose Norris, George Andrews, Henry Andrews, Alfred Andrews, Charles Vincent. Every morning she puts a small tick beside the name of each child in attendance. She does not bother to write in Fanny Bundle's name.

The real classroom, annexed to the house and without heat, becomes unbearably cold and Lavinia is forced to sleep in Ben's house, sharing a bed with Patience. The blind girl's terrified weeping has stopped, but she refuses to join Lavinia's class and spends her time sitting on the sofa. Sometimes she seems not to move from the spot for days, eating there and, at night, pulling a blanket over herself and sleeping there.

One night when they are alone in the kitchen, Lavinia looks up to see Patience with the Shakespeare book open on her lap and for a joyful moment thinks that Meg's prayers have been answered. She goes to sit beside her niece:

the girl is staring at the book, her face so strained that the small bones on each side of her forehead press against the skin.

"Patience, what is it? What are you doing?"

The girl, who hasn't felt Lavinia's presence, gives a little gasp. "I'm tryin' to see the pictures," she says as if confessing something shameful.

"And—and, can you?"

"Oh Vinnie, you knows I can't! I liked them pictures so well I thought if I really tried hard enough I'd see them—but I can't, I can't!" she begins to cry bitterly.

The heavy book is about to fall. Lavinia catches it and sees that, strangely, there is a picture on the page Patience has been staring at. Then, because she can think of no way to quiet the weeping, she says, "Here, I'll show you the picture."

Pulling one of the girl's hands from her wet face and holding the index finger to the page, Lavinia begins to trace the ink strokes. "Right here in the middle ya sees this little black feller, dressed only in leaves. Patience—I wonder how he keeps them together? He's kind of leaning over a woman, a queen I s'pose. She looks shockin' uncomfortable with her head on a rock and her hair, great long curls, streelin' right down to the ground. For all that, she's sleepin' peaceful as a babe, one hand fallin' across the grass with the palm up—and there's this frog or toad or some such creature sitting right in her hand. Hard to make head nor tail of what's goin' on, to tell the truth."

Patience has stopped crying. She listens, entranced by Lavinia's description of the picture. "What else is there? There's more'n that there, Vinnie."

"Well," Lavinia leans closer to the page. "Yes, all 'round there's this queer lookin' woods and ya can see faces in between the leaves. Wonderful ugly faces they are, all lookin' down at the black boy and the queen." She hesitates, remembering the face she and Fanny have seen in the woods but Patience urges her on.

"There's this border around the big picture and in each corner of the border is a little picture," and Lavinia traces the small drawings, one of fairies, one the head of a horse, one a boy dressed elaborately with ruffles around his neck and wrists, the fourth a gloved hand holding a skull. She describes each detail, the kind of gauzy material in the boy's frill, the wild, rolling eye of the horse, the letter incised into the glove.

The picture gives Lavinia a strange eerie feeling that is not completely unpleasant. She understands Patience's fascination and tries to convey to her niece how evil the faces in the trees are, how menacing is the light that falls on the sleeping woman.

The exercise has taken an hour or more and has completely absorbed both Lavinia and Patience.

"Do the rest, Vinnie, there's two more pictures, one at the beginning of each part—do t'other two," the girl pleads.

"No, we'll save them for another time. I tell you what, Patience, if you sits with us at class tomorrow then we'll look at pictures for a spell each night."

So they begin. Each night they discover something they have not seen before. Lavinia finds the odd pastime as satisfying as Patience does. Tracing along the black lines gives her a sense that other experiences, other places, other lives, exist outside the triangle of sand and rock she lives on.

One night Charlie Vincent wanders into the kitchen when they are poring over the book. He listens to Lavinia's description, then holds out his hand. "Why don't we three read something? Patience and me did the Hamlet play with Mr. Hutchings, how about hearin' one of them others?" He turns the pages, reading off titles until Patience chooses *A Winter's Tale*.

After that, Charlie comes each night to read aloud. Before long they are joined by Fanny, who slips in from next door without a sound. She doesn't come near the three on the sofa, but sits in the warmest corner with her back against the chimney stones. She listens to each word, then leaves, silently as she came.

Lavinia thinks Fanny has lost her looks. The girl's brown skin, that had glowed like gold that day beside the pond, has faded to a sallow yellow. With her turned-down mouth and bits of moulting finery she reminds Lavinia of a sick bird the children once found on the beach.

When she asks if there is something wrong with Fanny, Meg sniffs and says, "Nothing a good scrub and a bit of chastisin' wouldn't cure."

One night Ned comes to borrow some tool from Ben and, like a fish on a line, is drawn across the room to the sofa.

"Some bloody good yarns in there, Char," he says when the boy closes the book. "I never knowed books had stuff like that in them. Sure, when you takes a run on them words 'tis like glidin' in past the shoals on a fine day."

He leaps onto a chair, declaiming, "We split, we split! Farewell my wife and children, farewell brother, we split, we split, we split!"

Ignoring Mary, who has rushed in from next door, and Meg, who is ordering him to get his hob-nailed boots off her chair, Ned recites the lines three more times, his eyes wide with horror and his fingers raking through his matt of red hair. Then, "Them's Jeezely grand words!" he says and jumps down from the chair.

After that Ned, too, becomes part of the audience and for an hour each night they are lost, all of them: Charlie, hunched over the big book with Patience and Lavinia beside him on the couch; Ned sitting astride a chair directly in front, his chin resting on the chairback and his face level with the boy's; even Fanny, huddled by the fire, thin arms wrapped around her knees, is part of the magic. Lavinia marvels that words are enough to make them forget, even briefly, everything that has happened.

"Now there's a good bit, Young Char—run past her again," Ned commands two or three times each night and soon has an eclectic collection of lines memorized. From these, he selects, seemingly at random, ringing words to shout at intervals during the day.

"A horse! A horse! My kingdom for a horse!" he sometimes bellows at dawn or, when he is not feeling so cheerful, "I am a feather for each wind that blows!"

"Cry havoc and let slip the dogs of war!" he shouts when Mary chides him, or "Once more, once more unto the breech my friends," as he trundles pale Isaac around and around the house.

Ned quotes Shakespeare in much the same way Meg and Sarah do the Bible. Like them, he is not above changing words or combining two unrelated lines to make a point or improve upon the original.

Lavinia derives great pleasure from Ned's rhetoric—no matter that the words are fearful, and sometimes meaningless. Whenever she hears him shout them her heart lifts. "Nothing," she thinks, "will ever get the better of Ned." The resentment she has felt against her brother for years is gone.

Charlie's reading and Ned's soliloquies help lighten Patience's blackness too. She begins to take an interest in Lavinia's lessons and lets Meg teach her to knit, card wool and make bread. Soon the girl's blindness becomes unremarkable, she learns to get about in both Andrews houses and, by summer, ventures outdoors. Eventually she will walk around the Cape, skirting rocks and climbing over flakes so quickly that a stranger would never guess she was blind.

Snow finally comes with a howling gale that rages all night. By dawn, six-foot drifts have piled against windows and doors, roofs are covered, and snow clouds cling to the trees they have stacked around walls, giving the houses oddly grotesque shapes. They barely have time to dig out their doors, clear a path to the goats and shovel out the wood pile when another storm, bad as the first, pounds down. Storm follows storm as north-east gales sweep around the unprotected point of the Cape, buffeting great waves that freeze layer upon layer, encasing rocks, flakes, wharf and boats in a glistening crust of ice.

During one of the brief lulls between storms, Ben finds that the church walls erected in the fall have flattened under the weight of snow. He returns to the house downcast. "'Twas only foolishness thinkin' the likes of we could build a church by ourselves. That be work for them knows what they's about—for master carpenters," he tells Meg sadly.

The winter seems as endless as the summer that preceded it, but eventually there are signs of spring: drifting ice, the receding line of wet as snow packed against the houses melts a little each day, nets being mended, renewed talk of fishing.

"I'm tormented 'bout Sarah and them—how they'll keep body and soul together now Josh is gone," Meg told Ben and Lavinia one evening as they used the last of the daylight to spread out newly barked nets.

"You worries over every single little thing, Meg." Lavinia tossed an armload of blackened net over the garden fence and draped it carefully between posts. "After all there's still two grown men in the Vincent family."

"Joe got his own family now, besides he can't fish alone and we all knows what Peter's like!" Seeing that Lavinia has already dismissed the Vincent's, Meg looks to her husband.

"I knows one thing, Young Joe'll need some good hand in that boat with him to bring in the catches he got with poor Josh." Ben shook his head, "Too bad Peter's not steady."

"That is as near as Ben will ever come to speaking harshly of anyone," Lavinia writes that night, then adds, "All the same, Meg and Ben are right, every one of us depends on the fish and there's only Ned and Isaac, Joe, Frank and Thomas Hutchings to go on the water this summer—five men with twenty-four mouths to feed!"

Two days later Sarah announces that her Annie is going to fish with Joe.

"Annie! A woman fishin'!" Even for her friend's sake Meg cannot hide her disapproval.

Sarah looks old, the skin on her face and neck sags and her hands, always so capable, shake as she pulls a mat hook through the brin. She has been slow to accept that her husband is really gone. After her illness she had sat for weeks by the fire, looking up whenever the door opened, expecting to see Josh walk in, as he always had, carrying a bird, a fish, or a yaffle of wood.

Poor Annie, already worn out with nursing her parents, had to tell her mother continually that Josh was dead. Each time the terrible news seemed new. Each time, Sarah would weep, demand details of how he died, of his burial, then, just hours later, tell Annie, " 'Tis almost dark, go out on the bridge and see if there's any sign of your father."

Ned's idea to hold a special Sunday service, a kind of delayed funeral at which Josh is praised and prayed for, seems to have pacified Sarah. Although she never becomes reconciled to Josh's death (in her later years she will begin holding long conversations with him), at least she no longer torments Annie with questions about his absence.

As she justifies her daughter's strange decision Sarah's old vitality seems rekindled. "I was pure speechless meself first off. Hardly knowed what to say—a woman goin' on the water!" she tells Meg.

"Did Peter make a fuss?" Meg asked. She has never trusted Sarah's second son, not since the day he chopped off his brother's finger.

"Certainly 'tis Peter's place, in the boat with Joe, so I was expectin' him to put a stop to such talk—but he didn't. Don't care what Annie does far as I could see. Talks about stayin' on in St. John's this year when he gets in from the ice. Says that way he'll have a bit of real money. I s'pose 'tis a sin to wish the poor lad away, but I just knowed Peter and Joe'd be forever at each other if they was fishin' out of the same boat. So looks like our Annie will be a shareman this year," Sarah paused and heaved one of her great sighs, "I s'pose, maid, we can't be forever tellin' em what to do."

Nevertheless when Charlie had told his mother that he too wanted to go to the ice this year, Sarah's reaction was quite different. "Your poor father vowed none of ye would go swilin' ever again!" she said.

Unlike his brothers, Charlie, who was so thin, has grown solid, almost stout. He looks more like Sarah than any of her other children. Although she does not cosset him as Meg does Willie, Sarah has always felt closer to him than to her older boys, or even to Annie.

"Uncle Ned and Uncle Frank's both goin'," the boy tells his mother. "They 'lows they can get me a berth now I'm fourteen—besides Joe and Peter went when they was fourteen—and they's still goin'."

"Be that as it may, I can't gainsay Joe, him a married man, and the devil hisself couldn't stop Peter once he takes something in his head—but you I can tell, and you I will tell—while I got breath in me body you're not goin' out to the ice."

Recounting all this, Sarah gave her friend a doubtful look. "You s'pose I done right, Meg? Sure just looking at Char standin' there with his bottom lip stuck out made me think he was only joshin'—just feelin' like he had to, ya know. Still and all 'twas no need really ta be sharp as I was to him, but I knowed he'd want me to take it serious like."

"I'm glad 'tis all settled," Meg says but cannot resist adding, " 'twill be some strange, though, seein' a woman out in a boat."

Listening to the women talk, Lavinia senses a tentative tone in all their planning: as if they are not sure spring will come. Not even the arrival of seals, or Ned's shout of, "We few, we gallant few, we band of brothers!" as he jumps from pan to pan can bring back the exuberant confidence of other years. There is something fearful in the way the men follow Ned, stepping timidly onto the ice, probing at floating pans as if they might bite the gaffs. Unreasonably she finds herself wishing for the return of their flamboyant disregard for danger.

Only Frank Norris and Young Joe go to the ice that year. Peter has vanished and Ned, despite their need for money, decides he must stay home with Isaac. Surprisingly, he has Mary's support in this. "Ned's not right better hisself yet, and what's the use of money if ya loses yer health," she says, pointing out that next year both Ned and Isaac can go.

In her account of the events of that spring, Lavinia tries to pinpoint the date when Ned first mentioned the great bear. She decides it must have been in the last part of March although there was still a foot of snow on the ground.

White, Ned says the bear is, and big as a horse—a meaningless comparison to those who have never seen a horse. Still, from Ned's description they can all imagine the huge furry beast. The creature becomes the talk of the place, yet only Ned sees it. He begins telling stories about the bear, how it has come on the ice floes, drifting down through the black sea past Naskaupi, past Cartwright, Comfort Bight, Cape Charles, Belle Isle, on down to Griquet and St. Julien, then out around the Horse Islands down to Deadmans Point, past North Bill and the Middle Bill. By this time Ned had spent two seasons on the Labrador and delighted in reaming off the names.

He likes to think about his bear, standing upright as a sea captain on an ice pan, sailing down past all the bays, past the tall steep cliffs, past the silent, snow covered woods, on down until he comes to the Cape. "Oh brave new world!" the shaggy brute said as he clambered off his ice ship and swam ashore.

Ned insists the bear is real. "There are more things in this world than you and I have dreamed of, Vinnie," he tells her when she challenges its existence.

"I doubt there are more things than you've dreamed of, Ned Andrews, your head's so full of foolishness that you'd mesmerize the good Lord himself. If you'd been there givin' Him advice on creation day I 'low the world would be filled with outlandish beasts, winged and tailed and two-headed and coloured like flowers!"

She and Ned have become friends again and they laugh, delighted to think of bright winged creatures flying over Cape Random. Only Ned can take her mind off the suspicions that preoccupy her, and she resolves never to fall out with him again.

"I always did fancy flying horses—never could understand why the Almighty didn't create a flying horse," Ned says thoughtfully. "Wouldn't it be a wonderful thing! We could sit on its back and fly up to Pond Island if we had a mind. Right over the hills, look down and see the Cape, a shockin' fine sight that'd be, Vinnie!"

Watching him, Lavinia remembers what Ben had said about Ned believing his stories when he is telling them. Ned can see the flying horse, and himself perched on its back, prancing through storm clouds high above the Cape.

She gives him a poke in the ribs, just as she used to when they were children. "Make sure you puts your wool drawers on, Ned, when your flying horse come for ya!" she says, and he promises soberly that he will.

Three days after the men leave for the ice, Thomas Hutchings comes into Meg's and Ben's house for the first time in weeks. It is afternoon, the scholars have gone, but Lavinia and Willie sit at the table doing the extra lessons Meg insists upon for her son. At the other end of the table Ben is using Willie's slate to scratch out a new plan for the church. Every few minutes he interrupts the lesson to ask Lavinia or Willie to work out a sum.

Hearing Thomas's tap on the door, Lavinia flinches as if she had been hit. He walks in and without even a glance in her direction sits down by Ben. They begin talking about a repair job Thomas wants done on the wharf.

"This is how Patience feels each morning when she wakes and remembers she's blind," Lavinia thinks, "not angry anymore but sad—sad and weary and old."

Speaking carefully to keep the quiver out of her voice she tells Willie to finish the sums she's marked out. She pulls the old knitted shawl around her head, thinking to take a walk down to the landwash but outside the day is so cold that she goes in next door. She can wait in Ned's place until she hears Thomas leave.

No one is about except Mary and Isaac. Mary, again big with child, is bent over a wooden tub scrubbing socks and mitts. Isaac sits by the fire, whittling a boat from a small piece of plank. Mary tells her that Ned and The Three Kings are down on the beach digging out the boat: "Ned expects she'll be stove in with all that ice and snow we had," she says, and lapses into her usual silence.

"Let's go down and watch, Vinnie, I'm that sick of bein' stuck in the house, and Pap'll be some pleased to see me outdoors on me own." Isaac puts the little boat on the shelf over the fire and stands back to admire it.

He is still pale, but Ned's regime of exercise has brought results. The boy can now walk on his own and is getting stronger each day. His red hair and high spirits are coming back and his face no longer looks like a skull.

"I been wantin' to talk to you about somethin'—to ask ya something... ." he hesitates and glances at his step-mother.

"Well young Isaac, what was it ye was so anxious to talk about?" Lavinia asks when they are outside.

He swallows and she can see his adam's apple move in his throat. "Don't say nothin' about this to Pa or Mary, I don't want em to know yet but I'm thinkin' about—about," he gulps again and plunges on, "about askin' Rose Norris to marry me."

It takes Lavinia several seconds to recover enough to say anything. "Go on, boy, Rose is just a youngster, and a real little Tartar she is, too!"

"I don't mean we got ta get married right away—not 'til I gets started on a house—Uncle Ben'd show me, and with all hands helpin' we'd have her closed in good and tight by the time Rose is fifteen. Then we can get married."

Lavinia is sure that Mary will not like the idea of Rose as a daughter-in-law but it seems useless to say so. Remembering how determinedly Ned had courted both his wives, she wonders if Isaac has inherited his father's romantic impulses. It seems likely for he proceeds to draw a picture of Rose that Lavinia cannot recognize.

"You just thinks she's scatterbrained 'cause she tags around after Char and Willie. Char only knows book stuff and Willie's foolish as an odd sock. When she's away from them two, Rose is sensible as you or me," Isaac gives his aunt a wide grin, "and you knows how sensible that is!" Despite his thin face and stubble hair he looks very like Ned.

It is a grey day. Much of the snow has gone but the paths are still covered in hard packed ice. They walk slowly, Isaac explaining how he plans to woo his love. His assets seem pitiful, whittled boats and flowers, and the lure of his father's stories, in exchange for Willie's company and Meg's cooking.

"In the fall I'll start on the house. Look at Peter, he been working on that queer place of his for two year and haven't even got his eye on a girl."

Long before they reach the beach they can hear cracks like gunshots as Ned and the boys beat ice from the boat. Isaac is still talking about his plans but, having decided that her nephew will be as persistent a lover as his father, Lavinia is no longer listening.

First Joe and Lizzie, now Isaac and Rose, eventually they will all marry, or go away like Jane and Emma. And what will become of me? Her thoughts return to Thomas, to his grim face, to the coldness she could feel when he came into the room.

"Strange, how you can lose something you never owned. If I was more like Ned and Isaac I'd have gone after Thomas when he was coming into the school—let him know how I felt. Maybe that would be even worse—could anything be worse that this suspicion that him and Fanny are together?" "Together" is the word she uses when she thinks of Thomas and Fanny, her mind veers away from examining what this means.

"Have you seen Fanny about?" she asks.

"Fanny?" Interrupted in mid-sentence, Isaac gives Lavinia a searching look, "I don't know why people is all the time tryin' to keep track of that one. Talk about scatterbrained! Ya don't know what scatterbrained is 'til ya lived in the same house as Fanny—not even her mudder knows what she's up to half the time. Why?"

She ignores the question and Isaac returns to his dream, "...if I gets on sealin' next spring I should be able ta make enough to buy nails and tarpaper."

Lavinia is about to ask when he will mention these plans to Rose but she never puts the question.

A strange, inhuman noise rises from the beach below. Part scream, part choking moan, the sound swims in the grey haze, a terrible mixture of desperation, fear and sadness. Then silence. Lavinia and Isaac stop dead for a moment, then, without a word begin to race along the narrow, slippery crevice to the sea. Isaac pushes past Lavinia, not even turning when she falls, scrambles up and rushes after him.

They come around the corner below the fish store and see, well down the beach, a sight so terrible that they cannot at first make any sense of it. A dirty white animal rears up on its hind legs, towering over and half-hiding the man it is attacking. The two are locked in a silent, deadly embrace, Ned clinging with all his strength to the beast's great paw, trying to force its claws back from his face.

Yards away, Henry, George and Alfred stand, dark shapes, still as the humps of ice all around. Everything is black and white and grey. In the frozen tableau Lavinia sees her most dreaded nightmare.

Then the animal brings its free paw down in a gashing arc. A spurt of dark red gushes from Ned's shoulder. He falls backwards, wrapping one arm around his head.

"It's killing Ned, it's killin' him!" Lavinia thinks she is screaming—in fact, her words are not even a whisper. Two of the boys are running towards her. Isaac is stumbling down the beach to his father, shouting over his shoulder, "Get the gun—get the gun—quick, get the gun!"

Lavinia falters. Should she follow Isaac? Go to snatch Henry who seems transfixed with terror—or run for help? George and Alfred scurry towards her, making little whimpering noises, fear radiating from them.

Suddenly, all Lavinia can think is that she must reach Thomas. She turns, grabbing her skirt in both hands she races towards Ben's house, bursts through the door, shrieking, "Somethin's down there killin' Ned! Quick, quick Thomas, somethin's tearin' Ned apart!"

Ben and Thomas race past her while she's still speaking. She turns and collides with Mary, who has charged out of her door, carrying an axe. George and Alfred cling to their mother, but Mary pushes her slobbering sons away and, despite the awkwardness of pregnancy, is well ahead of Lavinia as they race back towards the beach. They see Thomas grab a fish prong when he passes out of sight around the corner of the store.

"The landwash wasn't grey and white any longer but red. Red everywhere, like someone had trampled partridgeberry jam into the snow, red and purple and pink—and in the middle the two of them lying. Ned face up, with one arm half torn away, and Isaac to one side, curled down into a heap with the animal still clawing at him and growling like a dog with a piece of meat," Lavinia wrote.

Mary rushes forward past both Thomas and Ben and, still running, drives the axe deep into the broad, shaggy back of the huge bear.

"Mary! Come back!" Thomas shouts as the bear, the axe still embedded in his back, turns, lurching towards Mary, who slips and falls.

Thomas moves forward and rams the pitchfork into the animal's chest. The bear hovers over Mary, who has half-risen and is screaming curses into its awful face. For a second, woman and bear seem to stare at each other—then the creature shakes its big head, hesitates, turns and lumbers off with astonishing speed. Leaving red tracks in the snow it climbs the bank and disappears.

Mary gets to her feet and turns in fury on Thomas, "Where's the gun, you God-damn fucker?"

Ignoring her he goes to Ned and picks him up as if he were a child. With Mary supporting the mangled arm, Thomas carries his friend up towards the fish store.

Ben and Lavinia gently roll Isaac over. The boy's chest is torn open, bones gleam through flesh and blood. Darkness swims up before Lavinia. She holds onto one of the frozen rocks and closes her eyes. She doesn't faint, and when the blackness fades, sees that Ben has picked up a handful of snow and is trying to wipe blood from his nephew's face.

"He's dead, Vinnie." Ben turns, gauging her condition. "I'll stay here, you go find Meg, she's out feedin' the goats. Bring down a bit of canvas—and tell them youngsters to get right back in the house," he points at George, Alfred, Willie and Rose who stand in a tight line halfway down the beach.

Lavinia does not respond. She is trying to turn time backward, willing it back. Just an hour, just half-an-hour, it seems a small enough thing to ask of God.

"Go on up and get Meg, girl," Ben says softly. He pulls her hand away from Isaac's cold face. "Go find Meg, and make them children go in the house."

Then she remembers Henry. "Young Henry was here—he was here the first time... ." She stands, searching amid the mounds of rafted ice. "He's dead, it's killed Henry, too!" She runs from spot to spot. There are a hundred places where a child's body could have fallen.

Ben seizes her, points her in the direction of the house and says loudly, "Go on up to Meg—and tell them crowd to come and look around for Henry," he nods at the children, who have not moved.

By the time Lavinia returns with her sister-in-law they have found Henry. The boy is safe. Crouched behind a slab of ice, he cannot be persuaded to move. Meg pries his fingers away from the ice, gathers him in her arms and, herding the other children before her, goes back to the house without once looking at the mangled body of her nephew.

Ben and Lavinia ease Isaac onto the canvas. Ben weeps silently and Lavinia realizes that her own face is wet with tears and snot, her body soaked in sweat, her hands and clothing red with the bloody snow.

"We'll take him up to our place, Vinnie, they won't be movin' Ned from the store so we'd best not take the poor youngster there."

Only then does it occur to Lavinia that Ned might be still alive. Slowly they carry Isaac, surprisingly light he is, up to the house. On the way they pass Meg, carrying kettles of water. "The young ones is all barred in Mary's place, keep an eye on 'em Vinnie," she says and hurries on towards the fish store.

They lay the canvas-wrapped body out on Meg's table. Ben mutters something about starting to work on a casket and leaves Lavinia and Patience alone with Isaac's body. Patience is frantic to know what has happened down on the beach but Lavinia, incoherent with shock and grief, cannot tell her. And so, weeping, they wash Isaac, bind up the worst wounds and dress him in clean shirt and pants.

"I was beside myself thinking about all the waste—waste of all the care we took over him when he was a little boy, waste of the time Ned put into getting him well and strong again, waste of Isaac's own fine plans for him and Rose. Better he'd died in bed during the winter than to end up savaged like this," Lavinia wrote in her journal.

Near dark, Thomas comes to tell them that Ned is still alive and seems no worse. He warns Patience and Lavinia not to venture out during the night: the animal is still around somewhere. He moves as if to leave, then, thinking better of it, pauses to study the silent young women, sitting one on each side of Isaac's body. "How long have you two been here like this?"

They do not answer and he says, "I just saw Annie go in next door with a pot of something. Why don't you both go over there and eat? I'll stay here." He sinks down on the sofa, closes his eyes and leans his head against the wall.

From the doorway Lavinia looks back at Thomas. During the winter he has lost weight and his clothing, still smeared with Ned's blood, hangs loosely. All his haughty confidence is gone, and he sags as if overcome with despair. With his eyes closed, his face looks just as dead as Isaac's.

Compassion, sadness and longing sweep over Lavinia. She makes a step towards him. Then, realizing what she is doing, she pulls back and follows Patience outside.

"You go on next door, Patience, I wants to go down and see how Ned is," she tells the girl.

In the fish store her brother lies spread-eagled on the big splitting table. He is unconscious. A lantern dangles from one beam; below it Sarah and Mary work frantically to staunch the blood that gurgles up from the torn chest each time Ned breathes. As Lavinia watches, Meg comes from a dark corner, her hands covered in cobwebs. She spreads the cobweb like a grey net over the gaping wound, covering everything with scorched cloth. Sarah immediately packs moss above the cloth. Mary is changing the strips of sheet they have bound around Ned's arm and shoulder.

It is clear that the women have been doing the same things over and over for hours. The floor is strewn with blood-soaked moss and rags that Lavinia gathers and drops in a pile behind the door.

She can think of nothing more to do, and stands back, watching as they warm blankets, remove sodden dressings and press on new ones. They take turns rubbing Ned's icy feet and legs and spooning some warm mixture between his lips. They work in silence. Once, Sarah tells Mary she should go up to the house and lie down for a spell, but falls silent before Mary's look of blazing disdain.

Mary has not uttered one word since her furious curses at Thomas Hutchings. Her power is all concentrated on Ned, on keeping him alive, although it is clear to the other women that this is impossible.

Watching her move back and forth beneath the lantern, Lavinia wonders that her sister-in-law is not chanting incantations, lighting candles, calling up demons to make deals for Ned's life. And it comes to her that Mary, somewhere in the dark recesses of her heathen soul, is doing all these things: willing her husband to keep on breathing, willing the blood to stop seeping out of him, willing him to live. Lavinia thinks of the baby inside that tightly wound body—how can it get air?

Near dawn Ned starts to moan softly, then to mutter. He tries to sit up and the women have to hold him down. Then he opens his eyes and sees Mary leaning over him.

"I thought I seen Isaac comin'. Where's Isaac, is he hurt bad?" he speaks quite clearly.

Mary shakes her head, she even smiles, a wide loving smile Lavinia has never before seen. "Isaac is fine, him and Ben are up at the house with the young ones. Ned—Ned are ya hurtin'?" Then her face crumples and she begins to weep soundlessly.

"Na, girl, don't go carryin' on." He tries to reach up with his good arm to touch her face. "Ah Mary, you're one lovely woman," he says and is dead, with Mary leaning over him, screaming: "Breathe, breathe!"

When he doesn't obey, she pulls him up from the pillow. "Don't you dare die, don't you dare die on me, Ned Andrews!"

But he is dead and past pleasing even Mary. She sees this, drops his head and rushes outside where they can hear her screeching blasphemy at the sky.

For two days and two nights she roams the Cape, pacing the ice-strewn beach like some grotesque black bird, striding over bog and brush. Unmindful of mud and melting snow or of the wind that whips her torn skirt and wild hair, she roams from one end of the place to the other, seeming to see no one, hear nothing.

Meg and Sarah take turns following her, pleading with her to remember the baby she is carrying, to think of her boys. It is just as if they have not spoken. She rages on in search of something, or someone, on which to vent her spite. Finally, half afraid of her strange mutterings, the women withdraw and leave her alone.

"I allow if she come upon that bear she'd kill it with her bare hands," Sarah tells Annie and Lavinia.

Sometime on the third day, drooping with fatigue, her curses reduced to hoarse croaking, but still in a rage, Mary comes out onto the neck near the fallen walls of the church and sees Fanny. The girl appears to be in one of her trances, gazing inland toward the hills. Mary's red-rimmed eyes focus for the first time in days, as she studies her daughter for several long minutes. Then, without speaking, but with her back suddenly straight, she turns away and walks quietly back to her own house.

Mary's grief, at least the outward manifestation of it, is over. From that day onwards she never again speaks of Ned's death or the manner of it.

Finding her house empty, Mary pulls off her torn and filthy clothing. She washes herself, puts on clean clothes, and goes into the back room where she and Ned slept. Using a heavy knife, she pries up a floor board and lifts out a bundle that is grey with dust; the same cloth-wrapped package she had carried when she came down from the *Tern* almost fourteen years before; smaller now, the orange long gone, the kettle and flint sitting by the fire in the next room, and the purple brooch—still her own as far as Mary is concerned—in Sarah's possession these many years.

Inside the bundle are three gold coins and the two shell combs she had worn on her wedding day. She puts the combs aside but picks up the coins, studying each piece, turning the money over and over in her hand. Then she spits on the puffy-faced king, rubs the worn surfaces with her apron and returns the coins to the rag which she reknots and stuffs back beneath the floor.

Mary Bundle rams the shell combs into her hair and goes next door, where Patience and Lavinia are sitting on the sofa holding an open book between them.

Silent as a cat, Mary crosses the room and stands looking down at Lavinia. She asks no questions—about her husband or step-son, about their funeral; asks nothing about her children, who has cared for them during the time she stalked the Cape, or why the houses are so strangely empty. She just stands there with terrible scorn on her face.

Mary looks old. Lavinia has never seen anyone grow old so quickly. The hair that had sprung out like black wire is streaked with white, pulled taut, braided, knotted and pinned at the back, it seems to stretch the weathered skin tightly over her small skull so that her face looks sharper than ever. Her nose and chin jut out like the brown lumps that grow on tree trunks. Beneath the tiny head her pregnant body seems huge.

Lavinia starts to explain that Ned and Isaac are this minute being buried out on the point but Mary forestalls her. "Do you know about Fanny?" she asks in a grating whisper, as if it hurts her to speak.

Lavinia expects the fierce crone standing so close to dash the book from their laps. But she only she stands there, arms folded, regarding them through narrowed eyes.

"You're so bloody smart, Lavinia Andrews, with your books and your writin' and your watchin'—sure you must know about Fanny—know she's havin' a baby!"

A needle of ice stabs down through Lavinia: so sharp, so cold that Patience, sitting beside her, feels it and shivers.

The woman in the book is walking, arms outstretched, as if she too were blind. She is walking towards a stone staircase that curves up into darkness. Lavinia has no need to look down, no need to take her eyes from Mary's face, the picture seeps up through her fingertips. What terrible thing is hidden at the top of the stairs? The picture and Mary's words meld—Fanny is carrying a child. She has known all along—somewhere in the blackness of her mind she's known—and known that the child belongs to Thomas Hutchings.

Mary grows impatient with the prolonged silence. "You knows it, don't you Lavinia Andrews? You knows everything goes on in this place, knows whose it is, too, I'll be bound," she says softly.

Lavinia nods. The ice has made her neck stiff, her jaw can hardly move, but she says "Thomas." Just that and no more. Beside her, Patience sucks in her breath and Lavinia turns to see disbelief in the blind eyes.

"Ah!" Mary makes a small sound, a sound of such satisfaction, of pleasure, even, that Lavinia closes her eyes. She hears the door shut behind Mary.

She and Patience sit on, not moving, not speaking until one of the twins begins to cry, then Lavinia crosses the room and brings the child to Patience. She wants to leave the house—but where can she go? Nothing will ease her misery, not the sea, not solitude, not time. She stays there beside the blind girl.

When Meg and Lizzie return from the funeral they have news of Mary's reappearance, had seen her as they came back from the point. She had been lying in wait for Thomas Hutchings.

"Mary grabbed ahold the poor man, dragged him body and bones into the store. Didn't have that crazy look about her but she acted some queer for all that—just marched Thomas Hutchings off without a word," Lizzie told Patience and Lavinia, seeming not to notice how strangely quiet they were.

"Still railin' on about him lettin' Peter have the gun I daresay. I s'pose 'tis a good sign, bein' mad—more like herself." Meg almost smiles as she ties a brin apron around her waist.

Lavinia and Patience do not mention their encounter with Mary.

The people on the Cape will never discover what took place between Mary and Thomas Hutchings that day. But before the week is out they are confounded to learn from Mary that Thomas has agreed to marry her daughter. The news bewilders them, Fanny seems little more than a child and is, in fact, more than a quarter of a century younger than Thomas—the man they have always had such respect for.

On the Sunday Mary has ordained that the wedding will take place, they wake to pelting rain. When they gather at Meg's and Ben's house for morning service, pans and buckets have to be placed in strategic spots to catch leaks. Despite Meg's best efforts, the room is oppressive, dank and dark. The door must be kept closed to hold in what little heat is given off from the sulky fire and all the sour smells of winter seem revived by the dampness.

Seated on chairs, stools and upturned tubs, they listen sadly to Meg's short homily, mumble prayers and only mouth the hymns they sang so joyfully a year before.

The worship ended, Meg announces that they must stay to bear witness to the marriage service. The Vincent families had been moving towards the door but return to their places and are barely seated when Fanny and Thomas come in. They are accompanied by Mary, who has never before been seen at Sunday service.

Knowing what is to come, Lavinia has stayed seated on a low stool near the chimney. She does not look up, but stares at the fire, where occasional blobs of soot, dislodged by the downpour, fall into the ashes and send puffs of black smoke into the room.

Thomas and Fanny go to the front and tonelessly repeat vows composed by Meg and read out by Charlie Vincent. Thomas's face is like stone and Fanny goes through the bizarre ceremony as though it were a wearisome procedure of no interest to her. After the words have been spoken there is a prolonged silence, a shuffling of feet.

Meg, who has ever been a defender of Thomas, is hurt and shocked by Fanny's pregnancy. It is she, together with Mary, who has insisted that the ceremony must be held at once rather than waiting for the arrival of some minister. She does not relieve the awkward silence with polite congratulations or offers of tea. After a few minutes, the Vincents leave with little more than a nod from Sarah in the direction of the bride and groom.

As the door closes behind them, Mary walks up to Thomas and in a businesslike tone says, "That's it, then—two of you can move right in next door—you can take our room. I'll make do by the fire 'til Ben gets 'round to buildin' on a place for me to sleep."

She waits for some response, and getting none, continues, as if it were any day. "Tomorrow, Thomas, we should heave the boat over. The boys'll give a hand settin' her to right 'fore the season starts."

She is about to outline her plans for the summer but Thomas, a flash of anger momentarily wiping the blank look from his face, cuts her off. "For Ned's sake I'll help you and the boys all I can. I would have done that anyway—without this—this... ." He gestures helplessly, refusing to call what has just taken place a wedding.

Lavinia, edging backwards to the door, pauses to listen. For an instant their eyes meet and she sees cold accusation in his—as if he knows she has been party to his downfall.

"...I thank you, but Fanny and I will live where I've always lived. In the store. And don't think, Mary Bundle, that you've gotten someone to be at your beck and call."

His voice is so grim, so final, that Mary steps back several paces. She doesn't say another word. He looks around at the silent faces, accusing them all, dismissing them all. Then, picking up Fanny's limp hand, he leads her like a child across the room and through the door.

"They looked like people in dreams, the kind you only half remember, not part of the rest of us standing around," Lavinia wrote that night, taking what little comfort she could from the fact that Thomas and Fanny were not sleeping on the other side of the wall from her.

Chapter 14

*Last night, after everyone was asleep, I went down to the landwash and sat with my
back against the big rock. A dark and lonely place this Cape is on moonless nights! I
dozed off and woke with the sea hissing around my feet—thinking for the minute it was
still that first day; that Mamma and Ned and the rest of them were all back on the wharf
begging for a place to sleep, that this book lay beside me on the sand, still empty apart
from Ellsworths' shipping records. Then I remembered. It came to me then, how easy it
would be to walk out, to let the sea close over me and keep on walking. Maybe I could
find that underwater path leading to Turr Island.*

By day, Lavinia manages to seem calm, quiet, and more serious than she has
ever been. Attributing this sobriety to grief over Ned, Meg tries to distract her
with praise for her teaching, and promises of a new book when Alex Brennan
comes back.

No one can know that at night, alone in the lean-to school room, Lavinia
is beside herself with misery. She writes in her journal for hours—then scratches
out whole pages. She reads what she had written the previous summer and
crosses out all the lines that refer to Thomas Hutchings. During long, wakeful
nights she develops the habit of rubbing the palm of her hand back and forth
along a plank that edges her bunk. The plank becomes smooth and her skin
breaks and bleeds but she continues because the repetitive movement soothes
her to sleep. A welt she will carry to her grave forms across the palm of her left
hand.

She goes to great lengths to avoid seeing Thomas or Fanny but she cannot
avoid overhearing talk of them. There is something so strange about the couple
that everyone in the place watches for a clue to the peculiar relationship.

After the ceremony, Fanny's belly seems to bulge overnight. It looks as if
she and her mother will deliver at the same time. However, Mary's baby comes
first. It is a girl, wan and scrawny but brought into the world with Mary's usual
efficiency.

Having given birth, Mary puts the child aside with such disinterest that
it would surely have perished had Meg not passed it like a kitten to Patience.

The blind girl spends hours coddling the poor thing, dripping warmed goat's milk mixed with water between its blue lips.

Spring is well advanced when Frank Norris and Young Joe return home from sealing. They are stunned to hear of Ned's and Isaac's deaths and of Thomas's and Fanny's marriage. The men are weary and disheartened, their boat had been trapped in ice for weeks and most of the seals were gone before they got into the fat. When the ship's owner had taken his share there was three pounds left for each sealer. Peter Vincent had stayed in Harbour Grace, where he hoped to get berth on a schooner going to Labrador for the summer.

The snow, which had come so late, eventually vanishes, even in the dark cool places beneath the trees. The first faint brush of green, like a memory of leaves, appears on the birch and alder, and the Cape people begin to watch for the arrival of a ship.

Since their encounter at the wedding ceremony, Mary has ignored Thomas Hutchings. She, like the others, is preoccupied with getting boats and gear repaired—a big job this year because of damage caused by the terrible winter gales.

"If Annie Vincent can go on the water, so can I. Henry is old enough to be out in boat, all he needs is someone to keep him at it!" Mary, who has always managed to hide her fear and hatred of the water, tells Meg and Ben.

She drives herself and her sons mercilessly. Giving Henry, Alfred and George no rest, she harps at them from morning 'til night to mend nets, bark rope, dig over the garden, repair fences, roll oakum, cut wood. As soon as the boys leave off one job she directs them to another.

Lavinia clings to the routine of lessons, sets goals for the children to work through before the fishing season comes, and braces herself for a battle with Mary over her sons' schooling.

"I thought you had more sense, Mary Bundle," she accosts her sister-in-law one day after the Andrews boys have missed class three mornings in a row. "Didn't you yourself get after me when you wanted to learn to count?"

"Oh countin's all right, 'tis a good thing for a fisherman to be able to tell if he's been cheated. I'll not say a word against countin'. Still and all, countin' got nuttin' to do with all that foolishness you gets on with them youngsters. Look how strange Char Vincent's gettin'—don't know his arse from his elbow—I don't think Sarah should stand for it! Anyways 'tis time lessons was stopped for the summer."

Dreading the summer, Lavinia argues that lessons should continue until the fish come in. Still, on most mornings only three scholars, Rose Norris, Willie Andrews and Charlie Vincent, turn up for lessons, and her argument with Mary continues each time they meet.

"You must want them to grow up ignorant as the rest of us people on this shore?" Lavinia spits out one day. She stands head and shoulders over her sister-in-law but is no match for Mary.

"Learnin' to fish is more important that learnin' to read old books—and it'll be a friggin' sight more important by the middle of next winter. You can't eat learnin'!" Mary turns her back and marches off.

The two finally come to an arrangement that pleases Mary more than it does Lavinia. Henry, George and Alfred will take turns attending lessons. Mary promises to let one of them come to class each morning. As she says, "You only got three books, for Lord's sake—they must be learned out, doin' the same stuff over and over."

In her preoccupation with work, Mary seems to have completely forgotten the baby girl. She looks blank when Meg asks what the child should be called.

"For sweet mercy's sake, Mary, don't you remember you had a baby? Can't you take some thought for the child?"

By this time Patience has the child day and night and is even taking it to bed with her, but, as Meg says, "we can't keep on forever callin' the poor little scrap 'baby'. Didn't you and poor Ned have one girl's name picked out?"

"Tessa," Mary says with a sour smile, "I'll call the baby Tessa."

So, without ceremony or explanation, Mary's last child is named Tessa and becomes from birth more Patience's daughter than Mary's. The blind girl sits for hours in her mother's kitchen, or, as the weather grows warm, in the garden and on the beach, with Tessa in her arms talking and cooing to the infant. That spring, Patience is the only adult on the Cape ever seen smiling. Years later Tessa Andrews will be heard to remark that she was the only thing her mother had ever been known to give away.

Under Thomas's direction, Ben partitions off a makeshift bedroom in the fish store. Meg whispers to Patience and Lavinia that Fanny sleeps there alone.

"It's hard to see how Meg would know such a thing. Despite all, she wants to keep hold of the idea Thomas Hutchings is some kind of saint," Lavinia writes.

Fanny seems to live as she always has, avoiding all work and disappearing for hours at a time. Since Sarah's recovery, Thomas is again eating dinner with the Vincents, and Fanny now accompanies him. It is the only time they are ever seen together.

"I seen some queer ducks joined up in me time but them two takes the cake!" Sarah confides one day in Meg's kitchen. "Fanny and Thomas...." Rolling a piece of wool between her fingers, Sarah tries to work out how to continue. "Fanny and Thomas—'tis like they're together but apart—like one don't see t'other. Thomas Hutchings never was much of a talker. Still, we was all comfortable with him, especially Josh—Josh set great store by Thomas. 'Tis different now. Truth is, if 'twasn't we needs the flour and beef he gives us I'd just as soon they both stayed away."

Meg, who has begun to regret her part in arranging the strange marriage, stands up for Thomas: "There's more to this than we knows, more than any of us knows—'cept perhaps Mary Bundle. Something's gone all wrong, girl—things is all changed—all different!"

"I hopes Reverend Eldridge'll get here soon. I'd be more easy in me mind if Thomas and Fanny was to stand up in front of him afore ... afore the baby's born," Sarah whispers the last words, glancing at Lavinia who has been working nearby.

The talk, as always, turns to Fanny. "I'll not be a bit surprised but the poor little mortal turns into another Ida Norris," Meg says.

The air of distraction Fanny has had since infancy now surrounds her like a fog that no one seems inclined to grope through. Despite her huge belly, growing bigger as the rest of her wastes away, the girl spends hours alone in the woods just as she's always done.

"I don't know how she's carried it so long—if 'twas a Vincent she made fast to, I'd say she was havin' twins," Sarah sighs, adding darkly, "I doubts she'll ever deliver a live child, and who knows, that might be all for the best."

This endless talk of Fanny and Thomas drives Lavinia to distraction. She begins seeking out work she can do by herself; spends more and more time pouring over books. Besides Patience, the one person whose company she can endure is Charlie. He is now far better than her at ciphering and reading and by rights should be the teacher next winter.

Next winter! The very thought dismays Lavinia. She misses Ned cruelly. "I could have stood anything if only I'd had Ned for company!" she thinks, wishing again that she had gone to St. John's with Emma and Jane.

Then the *Charlotte Gosse* arrives and the first person ashore is Jane. The girl comes tripping down the plank looking proud and pretty, wearing a bonnet that according to Lavinia "is made out of a bird's nest with the bird, a small eider duck by the look of it, still sitting in the middle of the nest. I suppose it was stuffed. It has little beady eyes that looked down at Jane's nose."

Jane was followed by a husband who met with more approval than her hat. "She's after marrying Dolph Way, one of the hands on the Gosse ships. He been here a dozen times, though nobody can ever remember hearing him say a word, but he seems nice enough for all that. I know one thing, between Jane and Mary the poor man got some row to hoe."

Dolph is a rosy-cheeked young man with the round, guileless face of a five-year-old. He blushes as he follows his new bride down from the vessel, clearly wishing he were helping his shipmates unload instead of making this grand entrance.

Mary welcomes her step-daughter with a touch on the shoulder, more warmth that anyone has ever before seen her give the girl. Jane preens, pulling a feather down around her cheek she examines the crowd on the wharf, expecting her father to jump out from behind someone.

"Where's Pop?" she asks. Then, realizing there is not one smile on the faces circled around, panic creeps into her voice. "Where's Pop—and Isaac, where's Isaac and young Moses?"

Dolph stands behind Jane, holding her luggage, a wooden keg tied with rope, and one of the two small chests Ben had made for his daughter and niece when they left for St. John's. Dolph hesitates, unsure of how to respond to his wife's alarm. He puts the box down and moves to stand beside her.

Mary pushes Meg forward. "You tell her!" she says harshly. "And you," she gestures to Dolph, "follow me up to the house and I'll show you where to stow that stuff."

Watching the young man trot dutifully off, Lavinia thinks that Mary has found the kind of son-in-law she wants. From the corner of her eye she can see Thomas Hutchings at the edge of the crowd talking quietly with Alex Brennan.

There is a respectful silence while Meg tells Jane about the deaths of her father and brother, about the sickness and Moses's dying, about Mattie and Josh Vincent.

"I'm sorry, maid, that you had to come home to this. 'Tis been a hard old winter for us all." Meg puts her arm around her weeping niece.

After a few minutes, the buzz of conversation begins again. The noise grows louder as sailors, shouting to one another, swing ropes out over the wharf, lower boxes and rattle barrels down from the ship.

Only Sarah Vincent notices Peter come over the hill. She watches her son stop, stare at the *Charlotte Gosse* then start down the path at a quick trot. Peter has not been seen since leaving for the ice, but his erratic arrivals and departures have become so commonplace that no one remarks on them. When he joins the crowd on the wharf, a few people nod, Joe comments on the brace of grey ducks Peter carries on his shoulder, and his mother tut-tuts over the condition of the young man's clothing and the wildness of his beard. She pats his arm almost absently, and, still watching the unloading, begins to tell him about Ned's and Isaac's deaths, about the marriage of Thomas and Fanny.

Suddenly, to Sarah's gaping amazement, her son pulls away from her, flings down the ducks and runs towards Thomas, bellowing, "You old goat—I knowed it. I knowed last summer you had your eyes on her—and more'n eyes by the looks of it!"

All talk stops. A bag of flour swings unheeded over their heads as the seamen, wide-eyed, watch Peter push Alex Brennan to one side and leap at Thomas, grabbing his neck as if determined to strangle the older man. Purple with fury, he shouts abuse and digs his thumbs into Thomas's throat. Thomas makes no effort to defend himself, or even to push the enraged man away.

"I think Thomas would have stood there and let himself be murdered if the men hadn't dragged Peter off," Lavinia wrote.

Held on one side by Alex and on the other by his brother Joe, Peter continues to rant, calling Thomas the devil's whelp, a Turk, seducer and whore-master until Sarah walks over and gives her son a hard slap across the mouth.

"Take him down to the house, and tie 'im up if ye got to," she tells Alex and Joe. She is weeping from shock and shame at the things Peter has said—and in front of strangers!

"I'm that sorry, Thomas, I'd not have this happen for all the world. I'm pure mortified and I asks your pardon," she says with dignity before turning away to walk behind the men who are dragging Peter towards the Vincent house.

In the awful silence that follows, everyone looks at Thomas Hutchings. He stands there, head slightly bowed and one hand held over his eyes as men do when they pray.

Mary, who along with Dolph had returned to the wharf in time to hear the last of Peter's outburst, gives Thomas a cold look and snaps, "Right enough!" Then, turning to her new son-in-law, "I'll be some glad for your help, Dolph—'tis little I gets from the other one," she begins outlining her plans for expanding the house.

People go back to the work of unloading, and conversations begin again. Lavinia watches Thomas turn and walk away. Fanny stays seated on an upturned dory, her face wearing a look of blank bemusement.

When the *Charlotte Gosse* sails the following day Dolph Way is not aboard. He has carried his belongings ashore and, with his new wife, settled into the room where Mary and Ned once slept. Mary has persuaded the Skipper to take eleven-year-old Henry as Dolph's replacement for this trip up the Labrador coast.

"A summer on the water'll do ya a world of good—make a man out of ya," she tells her oldest son.

Henry has inherited his mother's dread of the sea and disappears at the last minute, but she routs him out from under the flake and delivers him aboard the vessel.

Everything seems very quiet after the *Charlotte Gosse* sails. There is no sign of Peter Vincent. Sarah doesn't mention his name but his sister tells Meg and Lavinia that he has gone back in the woods. "Accordin' to him he'll never set foot on the Cape again but I daresay he'll be flick enough to come home once the weather gets cold," Annie said calmly.

Dolph fits into life on the Cape as if he had been born there. Indeed they discover that he was born not fifty miles away in Turk's Head, and that his mother is distantly related to Sarah Vincent. Sarah is so taken with Jane's husband that she has been heard asking if he has a brother Annie's age.

Dolph's arrival solves the problem of who will fish from Ned's dory. The young man soon has the boat scraped, caulked and tarred—in better shape than Ned had ever managed to keep it.

They hear very little from Jane about her stay in St. John's until the day when the women, all working at soap-making, begin to quiz her about how she met Dolph. It appears they had gotten together on the trip in to St. John's. Jane never had looked for work but went to live with his Aunt Cass above a tiny shop on one of the town's back streets. Dolph sailed off almost immediately, on a Gosse ship going to Barbados with a load of salt bulk. Jane helped in the shop, barely venturing out except to go to prayer meeting with Dolph's aunt. They had married as soon as his ship came back.

Meg and Sarah, Lavinia, Annie, Lizzie and Mary, hauling bucket after bucket of water from the pond in order to steep lye from the ashes they've saved for months, are put out with Jane's colourless answers to their questions. Soap making is hard, hot work, with fires going inside the house and in the yard where wash pots of dripped lye and rendered oil have to be watched and stirred until the mixture thickens. They had thought to lighten the day with some good yarns from St. John's but Jane has none of her father's talent for story-telling.

"I s'pose you could say if ya laid eyes on me daughter at all?" Meg asks her niece dryly.

"First off, Emma used to come down to Aunt Cass's regular on her afternoon off, but after a spell she just stopped comin' altogether. Last time she had this one Rowena Crocker with her."

They can tell from Jane's voice that she had not liked Rowena Crocker but when pressed by Meg, she can not tell them why. "She were a townie—thought she knowed it all," Jane said.

The day before they got married she and Dolph had gone to the place where Emma worked. "'Twas one of them big houses in back by the mill. We didn't know no better so we went right up and pounded on the front door—I s'pose I would have walked right in if Thomas Hutchings hadn't taught us all to knock," Jane smiled at Lavinia and went back to stirring seal oil.

"Well girl, go on! What happened then?" Sarah asks.

"We was sent around back and Emma come out to talk to us for a few minutes—said she couldn't come and see us married. Told us we was some foolish to be comin' back home. She likes bein' in St. John's, said there was always somethin' goin' on—not like here. Then she went off and got something for me to bring home to her mudder."

Jane suddenly looks guilty, "Oh my land! Aunt Meg I'm that sorry, I forgot everything about it!"

She runs into the house and returns with a package. "I hopes 'tis one of them fancy lamps like I seen in town," she says, and passes it to Meg.

"'Tisn't big enough to be a lamp, besides I doubt Emma would have sense to send anything that useful," Sarah says bluntly. She has never liked Meg's middle daughter and had passed many an hour worrying that the brazen hussy had set her cap for Peter.

"Go to hell in a handbasket, two of you would," Sarah had railed at Peter one day after discovering him and Emma lallygaggin' around the house he was building up on the hill. But Peter had only laughed, told her she had no worries. She knew now, of course, it had been Fanny he'd been building the house for all along.

Sarah sighs loudly. "It's certainly too bad how things turns out. A pity Peter and Patience couldn't get together—even blind, Patience is more dependable and twice as good a worker as Emma."

Meg, taking her time unwrapping the package, ignores this insult to her absent daughter. She carefully flattens out the brown paper and folds it, then rolls the piece of string up on her fingers before opening the oblong wooden box and lifting out the most beautiful thing any of them has ever seen—a fan made of ivory and cream lace.

Meg opens the fan and lays it on the flat plank where the soap pans are set out.

The ivory of the fan has been cut so they can hardly tell where it ends and the lace begins. The wide part is made of silk on which a picture has been painted, a garden scene with a tree that has a swing hanging from it. Roses climb up the swing ropes and meet at the top. On the swing, surrounded by the roses, sits a woman, a girl really, wearing a pink dress that billows up. Beneath the dress they can see layers and layers of white and blue petticoats. From the petticoats tiny feet, clad in pink slippers, dangle. Froths of lace puff in gathers around the girl's elbows and just above the rosy tops of her breasts. The marvellous dress is gathered in at the waist with a wide blue sash. In the girl's hair, a mass of yellow curls, blue ribbons and flowers are entwined.

All the women, even Mary, stand staring down at the fan for what seems like eternity, held spellbound by the woman on the swing.

"Does she cry, go to the outhouse, does she bleed, eat, does she love someone?" Lavinia wonders. The woman bears no resemblance to anyone she has ever seen. Not even Mrs. Ellsworth, sitting on her plush chair and counting her belongings, had been half so splendid.

It is a long time before the women notice a blue-coated youth lounging in the grass below the feet of the fan lady, his back to the audience, seeming to gaze adoringly up into the pink and cream face.

"I wish he'd turn around so's we could see what he looks like," Lizzie says wistfully.

As she speaks, the women hear a gulping sound and a tear splashes on one of the little hands wrapped around the golden rope. They look up, shocked, to see tears streaming down Meg's face. Aghast at her own weakness, she brushs her wet cheeks with the back of one hand and dabs at the fan with the corner of her apron. Then, very carefully, she folds the lovely thing up and lays it back in the narrow box. There is a sigh as the thin wooden cover slides into place.

"Stund as me arse your Emma is," Mary mutters, then, giving Meg a quick, half-shamed look, adds, "never mind, girl, she'll have more sense by the time she's twice married."

Meg takes the box to the house and places it on the mantle, lining it up with the small china cow whose insides contain the store of coins for Willie's education. She reminds herself of how lucky she is to have a husband and four children alive, and apart from Patience's blindness, all well. Walking back to the pots of fat, she asks God to forgive her sin of envy.

That night Lavinia lies in bed, thinking about the woman on the fan and is consumed with a sense of loss and longing stronger even than that which she feels for Thomas. Do such women exist on earth? Is there really a country where women loll in swings with adoring men at their feet? Lavinia yearns for such a place as fallen angels must yearn for heaven.

She is thirty-two. She does not own a single pretty thing; has never heard another human being say he, or she, loved her; cannot remember a day when she did not have to work. She thinks about her life and the lives of the other women on the Cape and resolves she will leave in the fall. Like Emma, she will go away to St. John's, or perhaps back to England. The idea fills her with such bleak despair that she cries herself to sleep.

When the caplin scull comes, school is forgotten. The smell of caplin, smoking, drying, rotting, permeates the air. Everyone is frantic to get the last jobs done before the cod strike in.

By now Fanny is so ungainly that the women wince to see her moving around the place. "Puts me in mind of seals when they comes up on land, the way the poor creature flounders around—I wish she'd wear proper clothes and I wish she'd get on with havin' the baby," Meg says peevishly.

But Fanny's baby doesn't come. Neither do the cod, just caplin, that roll up on the beach in silver waves.

There is a pause, an hiatus in time, beyond spring but not yet summer. Lavinia will later try to recall what happened between the day of the soap-making and the day the Indian came. She will not remember, nor will the journal help her. The period will remain forever blank.

In his *Brief History of Methodism on Cape Random*, (in which neither Meg Andrews nor Sarah Vincent is mentioned) the Reverend Enoch Atkinson writes: "Despite many stories of encounters with the native people, I have been able to substantiate only one occasion on which parishioners were attacked by the Red Indians who frequented that shore.

"A small band of Indians, led by a savage of impressive stature and fierceness, came one spring upon a group of women and children catching caplin on the beach. The men attempted to carry off a mother and her baby but were driven off by the heroic action of a young man named Peter Vincent who fortuitously returned from the woods at that moment."

Another account of the same event is contained in a reference made by Charlie Vincent in his interview with the St. John's press at the time of his return from India. Asked why he had become a missionary, he was reported to have said: "As a boy I witnessed a savage attacking one of the women in our little village and attempting to drag her away. That day God placed a burden on me and I resolved to take his word to the heathen."

This may be true. Certainly after the appearance of the Indian, no one on the Cape ever again felt innocent, and, although the event became more garbled with each telling, it was the day by which all future happenings would be dated.

Lavinia kept a detailed account of what happened, almost as if she knew the extraordinary occurrence would be the subject of lasting speculation.

"Ben, along with Joe Vincent and Frank Norris, was in by the neck working on the church, trying to get the walls back up. Thomas Hutchings and young Willie was out in boat somewhere. Peter, after the fuss he'd made that day on the wharf, took off with the gun and hadn't been seen since. Annie Vincent and Dolph Way were clearing out vegetable cellars.

"The rest of us was down on the landwash. All hands dipping in caplin, stringing them on sticks to dry and taking buckets of them up to dig in the gardens—apart from Patience, who was sitting by the big rock with Lizzie's twins and Mary's new baby. The weather was so civil we decided, just for fun, to eat our dinner on the beach. Young Char lit a fire and started roasting caplin. They smelled wonderful.

"I mind hearing someone laugh. It was the first time I heard the sound in months. It's a wonder how things like food cooking and sunshine matter even after all that happened this winter. But they do. And the thought that they do was making me feel better. I was thinking that despite all, despite me being alone and Ned being gone, despite all that happens to people like us—caplin still come in every spring, and cod, and summer comes. Right at that moment it seemed to me that such things should be enough—more than enough to make people content.

"We were all busy, paying no heed to the hills behind us—it's the sea we watch. Except for Sarah—she's always on the lookout for Peter. Still, the Red Indian was right down by us on the beach before even Sarah saw him."

——— ——— ———

The Indian is not ten yards away, striding towards the place where Patience sits with Mary's infant in her arms and Lizzie's babies asleep on the quilt beside her.

"Blessed Heavenly Father!" Sarah says in a hoarse whisper. They all hear the fear and everything stops.

The Indian has a loose, jerky walk, a limp really, for all that he is quiet and quick. He crosses the sand like he knows where to put each step. Like he owns the place. He is tall, taller than any human they've seen and seems even taller because of his high headdress, made from some kind of deer head with antlers. His skin is dark red. "Rust coloured" is how Lavinia later describes it. In one hand he carries a long rod. Most frightening of all, the dogs, who bark even when a gull lights on the beach, pad silently along beside the man.

"Never two without three," Mary Bundle says. She reaches out to grab Fanny, who has started to run forward, towards Patience and the babies. "Stay here, not even a wild man will hurt a blind girl."

Patience senses that something terrible is happening and begins to fumble around for the babies, calling out, "What is it, what's wrong?"

Rose Norris starts to scream, "Go away! Go away! Go away!" over and over.

One of the babies begins to cry.

The Indian looks neither to left nor right. He passes within a few inches of Patience's quilt and keeps on coming, straight towards Mary and Fanny, who seems almost to be waiting for him. There is no sign of fear on the girl's face, not even when the man is almost up to her. Lavinia is sure that Fanny even steps forward.

Mary grabs a stick from the fire. She waves it under the Indian's chin at the instant he reaches out and pulls Fanny towards him. The burning stick glances off Fanny's hand. She gasps but doesn't pull away from the man.

Then, with everyone watching, the two turn and begin to walk quickly back towards the low hills that overhang the beach.

In a bizarre way the girl and man seem well matched—Fanny, squat and awkward in her coloured rags, and the giant Indian with the head of a deer could have walked out of one of Ned's wild stories. They do not run but move with ceremony as though a parade of similar creatures might be walking behind them.

For a second everyone hesitates. They would probably have let the strange couple escape had Peter not appeared at the top of the bank and leapt down onto the beach. He carries the gun and falls immediately to one knee, priming the old weapon. He has the gun raised, could easily shoot the Indian but for the cluster of women and children crowding directly behind.

Fanny and the Indian do not pause but keep on walking towards the bank. Towards Peter who, realizing he cannot use the gun, flings it aside and races at them, screaming something no one can make out.

The sound jerks the women out of the trance. Mary, still holding the glowing stick, begins to chase after the Indian. She and Peter reach their prey at the same moment. Peter grabs the man, pulling him forward as Mary stabs at him from behind with the hot brand, at the same time reaching for Fanny. She loses her balance, but manages to pull Fanny backwards so that they fall together to the sand.

Peter and the man are fighting for the rod the Indian carries. The stranger is taller and stronger than Peter but he is distracted by trying to pull Fanny to her feet. As the men jerk the iron rod back and forth between them, Lavinia recognizes it as the tool they had all used for countless jobs, the same rod Thomas had found tangled in his net years before.

Peter gets control of the piece of iron and swinging it with all his might, catches the Indian across his face, just below the eyes. The Indian staggers but stays on his feet and turns back towards the women. Fanny, now half-lying on the sand, lets out a loud wail, one word that she repeats over and over: "Toma, Toma, Toma...."

Though blood covers his face, the man sees her, takes a step towards her. But Peter swings the rod again and hits him again, this time across the legs. For a second the Indian stands still. Lavinia thinks he is about to fall. Instead, he turns and half-stumbling, half-running, makes his way along the beach, up the bank and out of sight.

Peter glances back at the women, then, without even pausing to pick up the gun, but with the rod still in his hand, he races after the Indian. Behind them on the beach, Fanny's wailing becomes a kind of dirge.

All these things have taken just minutes—hardly time for anyone to know what is happening. Mary Bundle takes a few steps as if to follow Peter, then remembering Fanny, she stops, goes back and stands looking down at her distraught daughter.

The girl pays her mother no heed. She sits curled around her burnt hand, making the same pitiful sound. Mary fills a bucket from the sea, brings it back and plunges the hand into the icy water. Fanny's keening subsides to low moans. Only then does Lavinia realize that most of the noise has been coming from Rose Norris who has been standing, rooted to one spot, emitting little bursts of sound, "Like a lost loon," Sarah says later.

Thomas Hutchings arrives, ramming his boat up on the sand. He clamours ashore, followed by Willie who looks sick with fear. No one pays them the slightest attention. Lizzie tries to pacify the twins while Meg kneels beside Patience, patting her daughter's hand and cooing to the baby, Tessa. Charlie is gathering up the scattered bread, caplin and wood. Jane, who had been standing with George and Alfred, giggles senselessly as she uses the hem of her dress to wipe the boys' noses and her own.

"What's wrong? Is anyone hurt? What is it?" Thomas asks of Lavinia, who is trying, without success, to silence Rose. When no one answers he repeats the question. He pushes past Mary to Sarah who is kneeling in the sand beside his wife. "Is the child coming? We could hear Rose three miles out—for God's sake, Sarah! Is the baby coming?"

"Thomas—thank the good Lord it's you! I don't know, she won't stop bawlin'—maybe it is the baby...."

Realizing suddenly that this might be the cause of the pitiful mewing sound Fanny is making, Sarah leans forward, running her hands over the girl's bloated body and gasps, "Mary, Mary, she's going' to have the baby right this minute!"

Mary has been standing by her daughter, studying the girl coldly. She contemplates Fanny's body, then looks at the half-mile of empty beach between them and the fish store.

Sarah says, "Quick!"

Mary runs over and jerks the quilt from beneath Patience. With the help of Thomas they ease the weeping girl onto it. As Lavinia and Jane hover, helpless, a gush of pink water floods across Fanny's dirty, bare legs.

"Jumpin' dyin'," one of the boys says reverently and Lavinia is suddenly aware of the pop-eyed children. She tries to herd them back from the circle surrounding Fanny. Charlie retreats at once but George, Alfred and Rose, her screams having been stopped by wonder, refuse to budge until Thomas turns and barks at them to be off.

As they walk away, Mary calls to Jane, instructing her to bring down a sheet, string, a knife, "...and a kettle of hot water and soap, and that bag of stuff got the red rag tied around it—the one hung by the back door—and be quick about it!"

Jane hurries away. Lavinia and the children follow slowly. They are not halfway down the long crescent of sand when they hear a triumphant shout from Sarah and almost at once the thin, gull-like cry of a newborn. There is no sound from Fanny.

Lavinia and the children stop and turn to look back at the tight knot of figures far down the barren beach. Thomas Hutchings is kneeling beside the circle of women. As they watch, Meg stands and turns back-on. They see a flutter of black and white as she hoists her skirt and pulls off her petticoat. Thomas passes the baby to her: she wraps it up and begins walking towards them.

Everything seems to be happening slowly, the way fish move around under water, Lavinia thinks. Even the waves rolling up the long arch of shore look tired, without energy, as if all the violence of a few minutes ago has drained the world of movement, even of colour. It takes a long, long time for Meg to reach the place where they are standing.

She is about to pass by but Lavinia puts out her hand. "What's happened? Is the baby all right—is Fanny all right?"

Meg stops. She looks down at the wrinkled, red face surrounded by white flannel.

"The baby seems good enough—'tis a boy—but Fanny's in a bad way. It wouldn't be amiss if you said a prayer for her, you and Char—you too, Rose."

Meg starts to walk on, then turns and comes back, her usually serene face troubled. "I allow, Vinnie, between us we done some wicked things these last few weeks," she says and goes on up towards the house.

The younger boys trail after Meg, but Rose and Charlie stay with Lavinia. They sit in the soft dune to watch and wait. Hours pass without a word between them. Lavinia is unaware of the two beside her or of Jane who comes and goes with quilts and buckets of water.

Thinking harder than she ever has in her life, Lavinia Andrews sits in the sand trying to fit together bits of the terrible puzzle, sorting truth from lies, allocating blame. But each question leads to another, and another. Why did Thomas marry Fanny? Did he love her? Who is the father of Fanny's child? Has she, sensible Lavinia, done the very thing she so often accused Ned of, twisting her own imaginings until what is false seems true?

Lavinia will never know the answers to some of her questions; years will pass before she finds the answers to others. But in those hours spent watching from far off as Fanny dies, Lavinia decides that Meg is right, they have been part of something wicked. She tells herself they are all to blame, with their speculation, their endless talk—tells herself Mary Bundle is most to blame. But she is not convinced. Again and again she returns to her own act of betrayal, her naming of Thomas on the day Ned was buried.

The golden day has gone, twilight and grey shadows shiver across the sand before the people around Fanny stand. Thomas Hutchings folds the quilt over his wife's face, picks her up and walks slowly towards Lavinia. Mary and Sarah trail behind. As the procession comes close, the three sitting in the sand get to their feet. Lavinia knows they should turn away, not look, but she must look, must wait, must watch. Must see his face.

Yet, when the silent cortege files past, it is not Thomas, his face blank as stone, that Lavinia is thinking of, but Fanny. Fanny, lying dead in his arms. Lavinia weeps, remembering the elf child who sat on the rock beside the pond on a day that now seems lifetimes ago. Beautiful and brown, Fanny had been that day, with drops of water sparkling in her hair and in her ragged net wings as she chattered happily of being a princess.

The procession passes and the watchers follow behind. Lavinia wants to run ahead, to turn and face him across Fanny's body, to plead for forgiveness. But would that, too, be conceit, or even jealousy for Fanny who is being held so tenderly?

Instead she hustles Char and Rose up the path and into the classroom, where, by sheer force of will, she holds them, repeating all the Bible verses they have learned, "...for a thousand years in thy sight are but as yesterday when it is past, and as a watch in the night ... in the morning it flourisheth, and groweth up, in the evening it is cut down and withereth ... for all our days are passed away in thy wrath, we spend our years as a tale that is told ... before the mountains were brought forth, or ever thou hadst formed the earth and the world, even from everlasting to everlasting, thou art God...."

The same words over and over, on and on, around and around until they have no end and no beginning, until hunger gives the children courage to creep away, leaving her alone with only words as protection: "For a thousand years in thy sight are but as yesterday when it is past, we spend our years as a tale that is told... ."

All night, alone in the pitch blackness, she whispers Bible verses. They mean nothing, make no sense, yet they soothe her, take the edge off her despair.

When the room begins to lighten, she takes out her journal and writes what she believes to be a truthful account of the day. It will, she thinks, be the last entry in the book.

Part Two

Thomas Hutchings

Chapter 15

"Things come around, my son, wait on the Lord, give the Lord a little time."

How often did Father Francis repeat these words to me—but I forgot them, ignored his good counsel and again I am holding a body that would run and breathe, and smile and see the sky but for my interference.

Fanny is dead. Once more I have walked down a beach with death in my arms, now I remember Father Francis—things come around.

During my years on Cape Random I have kept careful records, not only the accounting of Caleb Gosse's affairs, of the salt, nails, tools, flour, molasses, advanced in exchange for fish; I have also noted the winds and tides, measured the slow, imperceptible receding of the shoreline, kept the yearly cycle of melting, freezing and melting again, written down all dates—births, deaths, the arrivals of ships, of seals, when the grey geese fly over, when we see rainbows, storms, fog, hail—all these things and a thousand others I have writ down. A precise and accurate record I have. All the facts and none of the truth. Tonight, for the first time, I am trying to write down the truth about Thomas Hutchings. Even the name is a lie.

Where, though, does the truth start? Walking up the beach with Fanny in my arms? Or on that other beach in Ireland, carrying another body? Or back to my childhood in a country I scarcely remember?

I was born in Spain in the year 1796. My childhood memories are as disconnected as slivers of glass fallen from the windows of ruined cathedrals, fragments of colour, sound and smell: birds' wings flashing against a brown hillside, water splashing and the pounding of cloth against rocks, the feel of sun on stone walls, the clean smell of my father's workshop, shavings and wood smoke, the house smells of baking bread, of warm dust, of chickens and children enclosed within safe walls. Safety. Yet, even as I recall these things, these bright shards, I know they are not the truth, but the shiny varnish I have spread over the reality of my childhood.

To find the truth I should begin with my father, Michael Angus Commins who came to Spain from Ireland in search of Thomas, an uncle and his only living relative. My father was eight or nine and alone, his parents, a younger sister and three brothers having starved to death after being driven off a plot of land the family had farmed for generations. Somewhere between Ireland and the seaport of Vigo, my father's fortunes took a turn for the better. An Irish priest, on his way to the shrine at Santiago de Campostela, befriended the half-starved child. Before continuing his journey, the priest, whose name was Hutchings, arranged that my father be indentured to a cooper in the village of Abino.

By the time I was born, thirty-five years later, my father was well established in the place. He had married the cooper's only daughter, a plain girl who became a handsome woman, a fact my father maintained he had foreseen from the first. My mother had stayed at home to care for her parents long after her nine brothers had made lives for themselves in other occupations. I was their youngest child, the second son in a family with six girls. By the time of my birth, my father owned the cooperage and was, by the standards of Abino, a prosperous man.

Michael Angus Commins was a small man, shorter than my mother by a head. When they argued, as they often did, my father said nothing. He danced around her, clapping his hands, tormenting her so that she had to keep turning to see him, infuriating her all the more. In all other circumstances, with his customers, his neighbours, his brothers-in-law, even with his children, my father—who never mastered the strange dialect of the area, a mixture of Spanish and Portuguese—was a quiet man listening to everyone with grave thoughtfulness. He had one great hatred—it encompassed all things English—and two loves: my mother and the Catholic Church of Ireland. The Catholic Church of Spain, he felt, was given overmuch to festivals, to processions, dancing and the ringing of bells. He longed for the dour comfort of a more serious faith.

I was baptised Manuel in honour of our priest, and Thomas after the uncle my father had never found, and dedicated to the church from birth—no—before birth. My father, as he often told me, had promised on the holy relic buried beneath the altar of our village church that if he was given a second son the boy would become a priest. This promise, along with the story of good Father Hutchings, who had not only saved his life but led him to my mother's house, was told often at night before the family said the rosary and went to bed. When I was still so young that I could barely understand the words, my father would hold me on his knee and tell me that someday I was to go back to Ireland, an educated man, a prince of the church.

"Father Thomas Commins, Father Thomas Commins—or maybe, maybe even Bishop Commins," he would whisper in my ear.

My parents' house, the same house in which my mother had grown up, was on the edge of Abino. It was small and low, built into the side of the hill with a tiny courtyard where dogs, cats, children and chickens scrabbled together. It seemed to me there was always bickering there, between the children and animals or between my mother and my sisters, who fussed endlessly over the most trivial of daily rituals. I hated the constant fretting, considering it the product of small, female minds. Thinking on it now I wonder how even a child could have missed the thread of love and pleasure that ran beneath all their exchanges.

By the time I was old enough to walk, my brother Philip had been working in the cooperage with my father for several years. I longed to be with them and sometimes wandered down to the ramshackle shed where they spent their days making barrels and small casks. But my father disliked seeing me there and would often take the tools out of my hands. I never learned how to shape the hoops around the ringtable, to make pegs or even to pull the drawknife easily through the clean wood, peeling off long smooth curls the way Philip could. My father and brother worked in silence, each seeming to know when the other needed a tool, when to drop the hoops over the staves, how far to turn the capstan that drew the staves in. I loved watching, especially at the end when my father would toss burning shavings inside the barrel, spin it around on its side, then flick it over so that the fire went out. It was done in an instant, like magic, the flash of flame, the quick spin, then the barrel set upright no longer white inside but brown, smelling of seared wood.

The only time I remember feeling part of that closeness was in the long summer evenings when my mother and sisters cleared away the evening meal. My brother, father and I would sit in the newly quiet courtyard, on a bench my father had built against the wall. I think (or do I imagine?) that the air was softly scented with some flower that does not grow here. Often we sat in silence with our backs against the warm stones, listening to the murmur of voices and the muted clatter of crockery from inside, to the low clucking sounds of hens on their roosts and the soft cooing pigeons made as they settled away for the night under the eaves of the house.

Sometimes on these evenings my father would tell my brother and me about Ireland, the beautiful misty country that he said had been trampled half to death by the English; all the rights of the people taken away so they could not so much as own a horse or a house, or keep religious schools to train their own priests. Because of this, he told me, I would have to go to one of the big cities of Spain to study before I could go back to Ireland to serve the church. Listening to his plans, I felt part of the family that, at other times, seemed to circle me protectively while still excluding me.

At the age of seven, I was sent to Father Don Manuel, who, in addition to many other duties, was tutor to a dozen or so boys considered by birth or by some slight show of intelligence to be worthy of his attention. The old priest was revered and loved and the thought that I might someday attain such high office gave me certain status among my sisters, younger cousins and my countless aunts, who treated me with a mixture of indulgence, curiosity and awe as if I had been chosen for sainthood.

Poor Father Manuel was a holy man but stern with his pupils. With great effort he managed to drum some Latin and a small erratically chosen amount of canon law into the heads of the boys who came to him for instruction. I went gladly down the road for lessons, happy to escape the noisy women's world of house and yard, pleased to be pointed out as our village scholar. I thought at the time that I had a great love of learning—what I loved was the opportunity to show off for older boys who usually chased me away from their games.

When it came time for me to be sent to a seminary, the priest and my father decided that I should go not to one of the great cities of Spain but to Lisbon. This was in part because Father Manuel had some slim acquaintance with the Bishop of that diocese but mostly, I think, because I could travel free as far as Oporto with a wagoner who came every September to buy my father's barrels. Arrangements for my admission into the seminary at Corpo Santo took more than a year and most of the small savings my parents and grandparents had managed to hoard in two generations.

I was very happy as I climbed aboard the long-cart, piled high with barrels and pulled by four donkeys with a fifth tied on at the rear—delighted to be getting away from the embarrassment of tears and loving good-byes I had received. Not only my mother and sisters but, it seemed, every woman in Abino had pulled me into the musty blackness of her bosom that morning. Not even trying to look sad, I waved gleefully as the creaking cart pulled slowly away and dust rose in pink clouds around my family, standing in the roadway dressed for the occasion in Sunday black. I was fourteen. I am sorry now that I left so coldly. I hope that word of my disgrace never reached them.

In the seminary it took a very short time for me to discover that my father's dream was unlikely to be realized. Despite my reading of all Father Manuel's books and despite his careful drill in Latin, I had not heard of any of the great thinkers of the day, had no knowledge of mathematics, of astronomy, or philosophy, and even less of theology. Many of the seminarians at Corpo Santo were the younger sons of noble houses whose families had for generations owned libraries, entertained churchmen, been courtiers and diplomats. Although it sometimes happened that the son of an artisan or small land owner might, by sheer brilliance or great effort, surmount his poor beginnings and rise to a position of influence within the church, I knew from the first that I lacked both the cleverness and the will to be one of these. This knowledge did not sadden or even surprise me. Maybe I had suspected it all along.

What I had not suspected was that both Spain and Portugal were oversupplied with clerics. Great numbers of priests, friars and monks wandered the streets of Lisbon. In the markets where novices were sent to purchase food for the kitchens and around cathedrals where we sometimes acted as altar servers, there seemed to be as many clerics as there were lay people. The church's influence was seen everywhere, not just in monasteries like ours, but in hospitals, universities and alms houses. Priests also administered great tracts of farmland owned by the church outside the city, and were active in the markets, mills, storehouses and other church-owned businesses. They were employed privately as chaplains to serve the spiritual needs of wealthy households and used by the state in a variety of ways. Despite this, not all the holy men were occupied. Hundreds of unattached priests seemed to drift from church to church, making me think how useful their services would have been to poor Father Manuel.

My own humble prospects did not disturb the happiness of these years. The dim tranquillity of the white-washed corridors, the low sounds of voices in chapel, of chanting, of bells, of regular prayers, the hours of contemplation and study—even the walls—higher and cooler than those around my parents' house, gave me a sense, not of confinement, but of freedom. For the first time I had space that was uncluttered by emotions. I had peace, silence, order, and these, I decided, were the essentials of real freedom. Even the work, at first to buy market vegetables and later to keep the accounts for the storerooms and kitchen, seemed to have a precision far removed from the drama surrounding the preparation of food at home. I loved the library where I read for hours, and my own small room that contained nothing but a bed, a chair and a washstand. I began to think I would stay there forever—like other Dominicans at Corpo Santo, spend my lifetime translating texts, researching church law or studying some obscure point of theology.

Instead, after four years, I was told to leave Corpo Santo and go to St. Patrick's College in County Kildore to continue my studies. These directions came from outside. I guessed that my father had somehow heard of the newly founded seminary in Ireland and gotten word via Father Don Manuel to the Bishop. I left without having distinguished myself in any way, but sadly, for I had been happy there. This time the only person to say goodbye was Father Pedro, the cellarer who valued my ability to keep an accurate accounting of the supplies we were responsible for. He rebuked me for using some heretofore unsuspected influence to be transferred out from under his authority.

Thus, without any sense of mission or feeling of homecoming, I crossed the Irish Sea and went directly to the seminary at Maynooth, which was very different from the one in Lisbon.

Begun by a group of priests who had escaped the French Revolution, St. Patrick's College was struggling to establish itself in the stony ground of Ireland. I found the place colder, the work harder, the hours of prayer longer and the rule enforced more rigidly than it had been in Portugal. But the peace was still there, and I grew accustomed to the new order. I spent what time I could in the library, much poorer than the one I was used to, improved the English I had, learned to speak some French and discovered, to my pleasure, that I could use a plane and hammer almost as well as my brother.

I was ordained a year and a half after arriving in Ireland. I was barely twenty. During my years in seminary I had formed no friendships, seen no visions, received no gifts of the spirit, but I had learned, I thought, to submit to authority and had replaced the nervous impatience of my childhood with a kind of tranquillity. At Maynooth I saw little of the Irish poor and, despite my father's passion, felt no kinship with them or with their cause. I lay prostrate to receive the blessing of the Bishop of Dublin and the following day left the cool silence of my room for the steam pudding house of Father Francis Ewen. I was to be his assistant in the small town of Borriswater, not a hundred miles from where my father had been born.

It had been implied to me before leaving the seminary that I would find my superior an easygoing man, more lax than a priest should be in such times. This was indeed true. Father Francis was kindly, rotund, short of memory and willing to forgive both rich and poor within the greatest latitude permitted by mother church.

In all things secular the priest was ruled by Mrs. Griffins, his housekeeper, who seemed to know every soul, not only in Borriswater, but also in the larger town of Durnford, and to have constant communication with most of them.

Neither in Mrs. Griffins' house, in Father Francis' church, nor in the countryside could I find the peace I had left behind. Nowhere was there a niche I could retire to, no place of repose. For months I drifted, doing small, unnecessary jobs around the church and translating an old parchment I found behind the crypt. A more demanding man would surely have complained of me to the Bishop, but Father Francis did not appear to notice that I had no special duties or responsibilities.

As my self-absorption lifted, I began to see the land and people my father had so often spoken of. Large estates around Borriswater and Durnford were owned by English landlords who let out bits of land in exchange for a share of the harvest—harvests that became smaller and smaller each year. The lovely open countryside with its rolling fields and miles of woodland was reserved for riding, hunting and for feeding the prize cattle owned by the English. Only a small amount of overworked land was under cultivation.

The people were as overworked as the land: women, too frail to bear the babies they carried each year; children, too weak to survive the mildest infections; all too toil-worn from bending over the stony ground to give a thought to the cause of their poverty. Beyond the age of nine or ten, rotten teeth, scurvy and bent backs were considered the normal condition. Men and women of my parents' age looked ancient.

I could not remember such things in Abino. I wondered if I could simply not have seen what was around me in Spain, or if the Spanish climate and the Spanish character did not show poverty so starkly as it appeared in the damp hovels around our parish. Very different from the people I'd grown up with, these Irish on their cheerless little patches were quiet, eternally downcast, always expecting the worst, suspicious and sullen, yet strangely eager to please outsiders like myself.

Within a year of my arrival, although I could not enter their stinking huts without my stomach heaving, although I did not know one person well enough to call by a first name and could not for the life of me have held a five minute conversation with any of them, I considered myself an authority on the condition of the Irish poor. Almost three years passed before I discovered there were others in the parish who had thought longer and deeper on the subject than I.

It was a lovely midsummer's day, at the funeral of Sally Whitty and her infant. Lying there in the same coffin, the mother and baby resembled old carvings of the Madonna and Child I'd seen in niches of churches in Spain: pale and sorrowful, the bones of their faces and hands pushing out against the skin. The sight sickened me. I walked out into the graveyard as Father Francis said the final prayers over the mahogany box that had a slip bottom and was used for all our funerals.

As I left the church, I was suddenly overtaken by rage—my father's rage—like a boil that had broken in my mouth. I could taste the poison running down my throat, feel the sickness as it hit my stomach.

Trying to control my anger, I stopped near the graveside behind two old men, one of whom was muttering a mournful liturgy that had become familiar to me, supplying small details of the lives, and deaths, of people lying in the plots round about—what they had been known for, how they had died, who they had left behind—"Hits harder, somehow, to see them go in summertime," he concluded.

"She'd not have died, nor the babe either, if we'd managed to hold onto more of last year's crop. 'Tis been a bad year altogether, four deaths since Christmas," the other man, whom I saw was Toby Carroll, Sally's father, said.

The man who had spoken first looked down into the grave and said quietly, "Maybe it's time we started payin' attention to what Mick Tracey's been tellin' us these five years."

Then Toby Carroll saw me, sucked in his cheeks and shook his head, "'Tis a mystery—a great mystery, don't you think so yourself, Father?"

I nodded and resolved to find out what I could about Mike Tracey. But after months of careful prying I learned almost nothing.

Mike was what the Irish call an old soul. His face was so darkened by dirt and sun that his features were hidden, and all the cracks filled in. I could not tell if he was thirty, sixty, or even ninety. He lived, miraculously it seemed, outside the town in a sod hut built up against a cave. No one was able to tell me how Mike existed, and one day, in exasperation, I asked Father Francis if the man was fed by ravens like the saints.

"Not so far as I know—although I suppose it's possible," the priest said, as if considering the idea that ravens might indeed be bringing bread and fish to Mike in his hut out by the bog.

Sometimes I suspected Father Francis of joking with me, but I could never be sure. He asked me what business I could have with Mike Tracey and I, quite openly, told him I suspected Mike to be involved in some movement to help farmers keep more of their crop.

For the first time since coming to Borriswater I saw displeasure on Father Francis's face. It was a priest's job, he told me, to look after the souls of men and not their bellies. "Don't meddle in what you don't understand, my son. Take care of their spiritual comfort and let God do the rest."

But I had already begun to suspect that physical comfort was just as important as spiritual comfort and continued to watch Mike Tracey. After some months I concluded the man was a poacher and probably a thief, and a very successful one, too.

Then, one night on the back road, when returning from administering extreme unction to Old Hegerty (something that happened on a regular basis, the man having made a lifetime job of dying) I met Mike walking happily along as if it were midday. We nodded to each other and he commented that I was a wise man to be about on such a night.

"People don't have the first notion what they miss layin' abed on a grand night like this," he said, waving his hand at the road that had turned silver in the moonlight, at the velvet fields and the moon-filled valley below.

I agreed. Staring pointedly at the bag hanging fat and full on his shoulder, I asked what he was doing on the back road.

"Ah Father, I don't ask what sorrowful mysteries you got in that little box you're carrying under your arm and you mustn't ask what secrets are in my bag—but never you mind, before the night is out I'll bring as much comfort to poor Liam as you yourself did."

I allowed he might be right and we began talking. Before long we were sitting on a rock by the side of the road, taking turns drinking from a container Mike fetched up out of his bag. After we'd been there for some time I made as if to go, muttering something about Mrs. Griffins being worried.

Mike snorted at this fiction. "Ever hear of the Land League, Father?"

"No," I said and sat down again. Other places, less backward than Borriswater, already had Land Leagues, he told me, "...and they'll be the salvation of Ireland, for until the people who put their hands on the ground get some benefit from it, there'll never be a decent life in this benighted country."

We talked for hours, or rather Mike talked. He summarized for me the history of Ireland, a country, he said, that had been civilized when the English were still bowing down to trees and painting themselves blue, "...but they had to make us out to be barbarians no better than animals as an excuse for treatin' us like they did."

He took me, step by step, through events that led up to my father and his neighbours being dispossessed of the land they had worked for centuries. His telling was much different from the emotional accounts I'd heard from my father.

Mike Tracey was no raging revolutionary. He spoke quietly, he'd thought about these things a long time, worked out the steps that had resulted in Ireland's condition and the steps that must be taken to undo the damage. He was probably not much older than I but, I know now, much wiser. He saw the enormity of his plan to form a land league in Borriswater, whereas I saw it as an easy step, one that would surely be acceptable to everyone.

I was immensely pleased with myself that night, sitting there on the rock, drinking stolen whiskey, feeling accepted, talking to Mike Tracey (whom, God help me, I thought of as "one of the people") the way I'd dreamed of some day talking to my father. Delighted to have Ireland's problems, and the solutions to them, set before me in a reasonable way. Proud that I'd contrived to gain such a man's confidence—even more proud when I realized through my befuddlement, that he was asking me not just to be part of the Land League but to be a leader in getting it organized. I feel hot shame now when I think of that pride. Had we not met on that night, had I not so eagerly taken over Mike's cause, he might have gotten what he wanted—in his own time—in God's time.

We met regularly after that. He introduced me to other men, to Jake Lucas, the tallest man in Borriswater, to the brothers Brian and Kevin Reilly, to young Matt Carroll, who despite his reputation had a good head on his shoulders.

We met in the little room at the back of the altar on nights when I knew Father Francis to be in Durnford saying Mass at Holy Heart Convent. It took us a full winter to make maps of all the property around Borriswater. We marked in every plot, each yard, barn, chicken coop and hovel, drew up lists of tenants, counted their children, the old people and wives they had to support. We calculated what the harvest of each little holding had been for the past three years, deducted the portion that went to the landowner. And there, for anyone to see, was proof that no matter how hard they worked, the tenants could not make enough to keep body and soul together. Finally we wrote carefully worded letters to London estate offices requesting meetings with the representatives of the largest estates.

Eventually, of course, Mrs. Griffins discovered us and told Father Francis. The priest forbade us use of the church for such a purpose.

Then he called me into his study for a conversation that was probably more painful for him than for me. Somewhere in my training, Father Francis told me gravely, I must have come in contact with certain dangerous ideas that in recent years had seeped into the teachings of seminaries. He was, of course, referring to the French priests at Maynooth for whom he had deep distrust.

"It is not part of God's plan that his servants be the sowers of discontent. The church has just come through terrible times in this country, times that even now would not be over but for the intercession of powerful Catholics in England. Mind yourself, Thomas, you cannot know what you're tampering with. It would not take a lot to bring black ruin down on us all," he warned.

But by then it was too late for such advice.

Less than a fortnight later, word came that four of the landowners we had written were travelling together to the races in Kerry and would break their journey at Westerland, Lord Edmund's estate midway between Durnford Head and Borriswater. The stopover would not be a long one. They were expected to arrive late in the day, have supper and leave next morning for Kerry.

The details were well known since Bloss, the overseer at Westerland had set a dozen women to work cleaning the house, airing bedding and polishing the silver and china which had not been used for years. Mrs. Griffin's own nephew Tomsey, the farrier, had been told to be on hand to check the gentlemen's horses. He was to be sent for as soon as the men arrived at the big house.

Since our letters had never been acknowledged, much less answered, this seemed a God-given opportunity to present the estate owners with our request, and I urged this action on our little group. Only Mike Tracey objected. It would be better for us to approach these great men separately, he said, to give them some time to mull our proposals over before they got together. All that, I argued, might take years at the rate we were going, and the others seemed to agree.

By then I had great confidence in our cause, was sure the landlords were simply ignorant of what was happening and would make changes once they saw the inventory and heard our ideas. I must not have listened well to my father's stories.

So, two hours after watching Tomsey set off for Westerland, seven of us, armed with the papers on which we had recorded the plight of the countryside, walked quietly up the tree-lined driveway to Sir Edmund's house. We came less boldly than we would have liked; for all our talk, we were intimidated by the grey bulk of the house outlined against the darkening sky.

Mike Tracey, although he'd been against our coming, walked up front with me. I carried my breviary in my hand and in my head some foolish idea that after we had explained the situation, we would talk and maybe I could have a prayer before we went on our way. I had even marked a page I thought appropriate.

We hesitated below the steps leading up to the huge front door, and a man we had never seen before came out and asked what our business was. I, who should have spoken, said nothing. Mike glanced at me and in a voice that held just the right touch of deference said, "We come about the horses, sir, we was asked to see his lordship about the horses."

The young man, who must have been a servant brought over from London, looked confused. After studying us for a minute, he gestured Mike and me forward.

"You two follow me. The rest of you stay there. Sir Edmund and his guests are relaxing, they'll not want all of you tramping in."

He sounded quite pleasant, but we had agreed to stay together so when Mike and I moved forward the others followed, pushing past the man and into the hall. Inside we were dazzled by brightness—a dozen lamps shone on polished floors, red hangings and mirrors. From behind two rosewood doors to our left came the sound of laughter and the smell of cigar smoke. Ashamed of my backwardness on the steps, I took a deep breath, put my hand on the brass mounting and swung the doors apart.

In front of us, ten men in evening dress sat around a circular table holding cards in their hands, every face turned towards us. Each face registered the same haughty annoyance. Near the back of the room two servants, one on either end of a sideboard, froze like gargoyles in the act of pouring drinks.

We did not move into the room but stood in the doorway, three abreast, Mike on one side of me and big Jake Lucas on the other. As we stared I saw annoyance change to caution, then to alarm. For the first time I felt a shiver of fear, a premonition of what was about to happen.

I stepped forward, thinking to say, "No—just listen!" but I'm not sure I spoke—maybe I said nothing. I saw the servant nearest the fireplace reach behind and pull on a plush cord that hung against the wall. After that, everything seemed to happen at once. Even if I were in a court of law, I could not swear surely what thing followed the other.

I heard feet running down the hall, and the man behind jostled me further into the room. Before anyone had a chance to speak, I heard a thud and spun around to see Matt Carroll brought down with a club swung by the man who had met us on the steps. A cut glass decanter splintered at our feet and liquor splashed across the floor when one of the servants hurled the bottle he'd been pouring from. Bloss the overseer had come into the room from another door and was rushing towards us with a fire iron in his hand. Mike was hand wrestling with a bearded man and in the hallway someone was fighting with the man who'd hit Matt.

Beside me Jake raised his arm, to protect himself I think, then one of the men in evening dress reached inside his coat and pulled out something that looked like a toy. He held it straight out in front of Jake's face and fired. There was an explosion of flesh and blood, and using all the force I could, I hit the man across the throat with the edge of my breviary. He dropped like a stone, pitching his head forward on top of Jake.

By then twenty men must have been fighting inside the room. Servants and cardplayers swung canes and broken bottles. Two of our men were doing as much harm as they could with chairs. Someone hit me a glancing blow on the head and I thought for a moment I would go down. I think I heard another gunshot. I grabbed Mike's arm and shouted that we must get out before we were all killed. Mike gestured and yelled and, with the two holding chairs in front, we backed to the door, over the two bodies, pushed out into the hall and slammed the brass bolt into place. We picked young Matt up between us and made it out into the darkness as the doors behind us splintered. By the time we reached the shadows of the trees, men were already running down the steps swearing and calling to one another to get lights, to bring horses.

Dragging Matt, we half-ran, half-crawled across the woods and thicket towards a gorge that separated Westerland from the shoreline. We would have been caught then, but those following were strangers, while Mike, who led us, knew every hill and hollow, every rock and brook for miles around.

Within an hour we had doubled back inland and were huddled in temporary safety beneath the ruined wall of an old round tower. It had begun to rain hard, and we sat in silence against the ancient, moss-covered stones, trying to catch our breath, slowly becoming aware of our cuts and pains and of what had befallen us.

"We're done for," Brian Reilly whispered and fell into a spasm of coughing that he tried to muffle by holding his hand over his mouth until the hacking turned into sobs. Brian's brother Kevin was unaccounted for. Thinking about what might have become of him, we sat there without a word of comfort, listening through the rain and Brian's crying for the sound of horses or dogs.

Apart from our wounds, we were in a terrible state of shock. We all knew that Jake Lucas was dead and thought Kevin probably was, too. We'd seen the Englishman who met us at the door lying in the hallway not far from Matt—had he been dead? And what of the man I'd hit? I reached into my pocket and touched my prayer book, wondering if I could have killed a man with it. We had probably left four dead bodies behind. None of us, not even Mike, had considered that anything so terrible could happen. We had no plan for getting away, had not considered the need for one.

Matt was still unconscious. We took turns holding him, wiping blood and rain from his face. After a while, Mike whispered that he was going to take a look around. He was gone more than two hours and returned with bad news. He'd walked three miles up river to the nearest farm and gotten close enough to see there were constables and a wagon already waiting there.

By the time Mike came back, Matt had died in my arms. When I told the others, Mike said it would be best to bury the boy right there beneath the rocks that had once been part of a holy place. While it was still dark he wanted us to start out across the bog so we could get over into the Killduns before dawn. There were places in the hills, Mike said, where we could hide for months, maybe years.

Mike and I argued then. I wanted us all to go back and ask for whatever mercy we could get. Brian was still coughing and spitting blood and one of Dan's hands was mashed to a pulp. I didn't think we would have much chance in the hills.

In the end we split up. The others all went with Mike. Carrying Matt's body, I slowly made my way down through the wood and up the narrow shoreline around to the back of the church. It was still dark when I came out on the pebbled beach. I hid Matt's body underneath a boat, and ran crouching up through the church yard and into the church. Inside I found Father Francis praying, without even a candle lit.

Hours before, boys had knocked on his door to tell him what was happening. Men, women and children were being hauled out of their beds and questioned. Two men, having acted belligerent, had been beaten and taken off, to be locked up in town, and every hut for miles around was being torn apart. When light came, they would search along the river and up the beach.

The bailiff had come too. He had searched the church and warned the priest of the consequences of harbouring any of the men involved in the night's affair. He had my name and Mike Tracey's. Murder had been done, he told Father Francis and swore he'd have the name of every man who had a part in it before sun-up.

"Tragedy always follows when we put the desires of mankind above the glory of God, my son. It was their souls you were sent here to minister to," Father Francis said. "But I expect you've thought about that already tonight. We'll have to get you away and do our best to save the others—but first let me hear your confession."

He knelt and I knelt beside him, little knowing how long it would be before I would again see the inside of a church or receive absolution.

By sunrise, through the quiet efforts of Father Francis and Mrs. Griffins, I was miles out to sea in a fishing curragh waiting for the ship that was to take me to another life. Before putting me into the safekeeping of the fisherman, Father Francis had not spared my feelings.

"You have started something evil, Thomas. There will be more killings, more hangings and beatings and probably not a few starving because of last night's work. Wherever you are going, and I will never know where that is, I ask you to change your name along with your ways. The church has a long arm but so also do her enemies. It would cause me and the church grief if you were to be brought to London, charged with the murder of an English landowner."

He kissed my cheek. "Good-bye, Thomas, God protect you. Learn patience, my son, learn to wait on the Lord."

Before I climbed into the little boat, he put a package wrapped in oiled cloth into my hands. He stood on the rocks, watching, for as long as I could see him.

I have thought of him often. I think about him tonight and about what he had to face when he turned and went back to his church. How many men did he have to bury, how many could he hide, how many save? How many wives and children was he able to protect from the vengeance of the land owners? What questions did he have to answer from London, from Maynooth, from Spain?

Chapter 16

I can remember my feelings, or lack of feelings, that morning as I sat in the fishing boat just outside Durnford Head. I did not feel fear, sorrow, shame or relief, only a terrible numbness. Faces, as if lit by a moving candle, appeared and receded: the sorrowful face of Father Francis as we parted, the scornful faces around the card table, the dead face of young Matt Carroll with rain washing the blood away, the shocked faces of men now hiding back in the mist-covered hills, the suddenly blank face of the man I'd felled. All meaningless images that seemed unrelated to the past or the future, or to myself slouched in the curragh beside a silent man who baited his lines and waited. I did not even wonder what we waited for.

It was a clear morning, I remember. The storm had blown itself out, and when the sun came up, the sea glimmered rosy pink. Within the bay, under the protection of the hills, only a slow ripple, like soft breathing on the water, indicated the tides and currents moving below us.

I slid to the bottom of the gently rocking boat and fell asleep. I was wakened by the rough jerk of the boatman pulling me to my feet and pushing me towards a basket-like chair that dangled in front of my face. The bowl-shaped boat tilted dangerously as I climbed into the basket and was hoisted up the side of a vessel that must have come out of the harbour behind us. The curragh owner, who had not uttered a sound throughout our time together, rowed quickly away without a farewell look or gesture.

It did not even jar my apathy that the man who helped me out of the basket spoke in Spanish. I asked no questions of him, nor of the burly seaman who hurried me below. I assumed, without really thinking about it, that I was aboard one of the trading vessels that often took shelter in Durnford Harbour on their way to the Spanish possessions in the New World. Where I was going did not matter. I went below and slept.

The day had gone and it was again dark before I woke and went in search of the captain. Captain Lorca was a surprisingly young and well-spoken man. When I asked what my position on his vessel was, how I was to earn my passage, he told me that my way had been paid.

"You can enjoy the trip—it will take three to five weeks, depending upon what winds we encounter." He paused. "Maybe sometimes you will say mass for us."

I shook my head, "I am not a priest."

Only then did shame come, shame that I had led the men into such danger, shame that I had betrayed the church, shame that Father Francis had paid for my escape from poor resources that might have helped feed wives and children of the men to whom I'd brought downfall. The burden of guilt dropped on me and started days of such remorse that I thought of ending my life. It was not fear, I think, nor even the teachings of the church, that kept me from such action but the terrible tiredness that made any decision seem impossible. On many days I did not rise from my bunk, not even to eat or wash.

In my first exchange with Captain Lorca I identified myself as Thomas Hutchings, taking, for reasons I have never understood, the name of the priest who had befriended my father when he fled from Ireland.

After our talk, I hardly spoke to the captain or to any of the seamen who manned the vessel. Isolated by my black brooding, I was completely unaware of life aboard the ship and took no interest in the happiness or trepidation of the men who slept and ate in the same room with me.

I now know that each vessel has a different atmosphere, an ambience that comes not just from the age and condition of the ship itself, but also from the character of the captain and first officers, from the success or failure of past voyages, the length of service and personality of the hands, from the moods of wind and sea through which she has passed and is passing. It is a strange, undefinable thing, very like the balances within a family.

Although I was not aware of it, I had been fortunate to have gotten passage on *The Seven Sisters* rather than on one of the half-rotted luggers that plied this route. She must have been one of the best run merchant ships afloat, well maintained and with a record of five successful crossings under the same officers and with much the same crew. Every man aboard had confidence in the captain, a fair, well-educated man, far removed from many sea captains, who are often brutal and autocratic.

But if Captain Lorca was the mind of the ship, then the navigator, Signor Boito, was her heart. The Italian had been with the ship since the day of her launching and was one of those men sailors say can smell their way across the Atlantic. Such men were considered wizards. Each had his own strange instruments, his notebook and charts containing his lifetime experience and the experience he had managed to coax or steal from others. Temperamental and jealous of their knowledge, these old time navigators were handled with care by both captain and crew. It was common for a vessel to be hove to for days, waiting for time, until the navigator judged moon, stars and tides to be in accord for sailing.

Captain Lorca maintained a nice balance between his own modern ways and the old fashioned methods of his first officer. But Signor Boito had complete authority in all things related to navigation. *The Seven Sisters* had the captain's records and a ship's compass, but even known currents can carry a ship hundreds of leagues off course, and compass needles have a habit of wandering. In such circumstances the men and the captain put their faith in the old Italian to bring the ship back on course.

Wrapped in my cloud of guilt and self-pity, I was not aware of any of this. Did not know that Signor Boito had collapsed and lay in his berth, not knowing if it was day or night. Late in that week, I sensed that the men sleeping in the bunks around me were sharp with each other, more surly and less talkative than they had been. The man who played the pipe was silent, and there was none of the banter I'd heard during our first nights at sea.

One morning before light, a sailor appeared beside my bunk and told me curtly that the captain had ordered I be roused, washed, fed and brought to his cabin. It was well over an hour before I could present myself, and then I was so weak that I needed someone to help me climb to the forecastle.

Without explanation, Captain Lorca began to interrogate me as to my knowledge of mathematics and astronomy. Discovering I knew a little of both subjects he informed me that, in future, I would report to him at each bell to help set our course.

Every day after that, the two of us spent hours making calculations. We took readings with a chip log and sandglass, checked the compass, and at night made lunar observations, taking note of the positions of the stars. Between such duties, I poured over Signor Boito's notes, which were written in a crabbed Italian style and faded with time. I began eating, stopped sleeping and spent hours pacing the deck watching for seaweed, sniffing the air, trying to catch the old man's magic.

The hands did not return to their former cheerful confidence, but neither did they sink into despair or fighting among themselves as is so often the case on poorly-run ships. Even when the navigator died and was buried at sea (with his astrolabe clasped in his arms, for neither the captain nor I could make sense of it), the sailors continued about their duties, apparently feeling we were making for our destination which, it transpired, was St. John's in Newfound-land where our cargo of port wine and rope would be traded for codfish and seal oil.

When St. John's harbour came into sight, the feeling of gloom began to drop down on me again. To distract myself, I went below and opened the package Father Francis had given me. It contained a change of clothing—something I was much in need of—and two books: one, the readings of Saint Augustine, the other a Spanish novel by Cervantes that I had been reading on the day I led the men to confront the estate owners. Grateful for Father Francis's last kindness to me, I washed, shaved and changed into the respectable clothing before going up on deck to watch as we slipped between the towering cliffs that guard St. John's.

I barely had time to register the beauty of the hills, threaded by little rivers that splashed down to the sea, when the air was torn apart by a blast that echoed and re-echoed between the cliffs. Something plunged into the water in front of our bow. To my amazement, this did not in the least alarm our hands, who laughed and waved at a rock outcropping high above our masts.

Looking closely, I could see four cannons mounted atop a platform built into a crevice of the hill. The guns pointed directly down at us. The sailors threw mock salutes as they hauled sail and put an anchor over the side. Within minutes a British naval sloop of war came towards us from the town, signalling, quite unnecessarily, that we heave to.

Apparently this boarding party had been expected. Our captain sent one of the men to fetch me to his cabin, where I found him pouring good brandy into glasses arranged on a silver tray.

"Have a drink, Thomas—and stand by—you're about to learn how business is conducted by the English."

I had no opportunity to ask questions, for he turned immediately to greet three well-dressed gentlemen accompanied by a British naval officer who entered his cabin without so much as a tap on the door.

"An uncivil welcome gentlemen, to shoot at old friends. What happened to the chain?" Captain Lorca slipped smoothly into English, smiling as he passed a drink to each man.

"As you will recall, captain, the chain was a cumbersome arrangement and didn't work too well. We find the cannon suits our needs better." The tallest of the four, a giant who looked as though the stiff collar and silk cravat were choking him, emptied his glass and reached for another.

After a few such exchanges, the men entered into serious bargaining. In much less than an hour they owned the entire cargo. The man named Caleb Gosse took all our rope. The port wine we carried was divided three ways between Gosse, Willie Johnson—a Scotsman—and the big man whose name was George Stripling. In return, the captain, clearly not unskilled at this sort of thing, arranged to buy various amounts of salt cod (at the time the weights meant nothing to me) and several dozen casks of seal and whale oil. After heated discussion Captain Lorca conceded that the fish and oil was slightly more valuable than the line and port, telling them he would bring the outstanding amount in bullion to their places of business the following day.

In the course of the negotiations, I gathered that being stopped at Chain Rock was a long-established practice devised by the foremost merchants of St. John's in collusion with the Navy—it gave them first option on all incoming goods. At the end of the bargaining, all swore with the greatest good will that they had been outwitted, finished off the brandy and went above deck where we watched three barrels of port carefully hoisted aboard the naval vessel. The smaller ship immediately pulled away, leaving the three Englishmen to direct us to their premises.

Captain Lorca, having already told the men of the problems we'd had on the voyage out, enquired about the prospects of finding a new navigator for the return journey. I hardly heard the conversation, my attention being focused on St. John's harbour, which is the kind of berth sailors dream of. We came up a long valley into a basin that was filled with vessels of every kind: tiny shallops, a fifty-gun man-of-war, frigates, whalers, brigantines, huge sailing ships with strange rigging and dozens of fishing schooners.

As *The Seven Sisters* manoeuvred her way between the forest of masts I heard Captain Lorca say, "...you'll have to ask Thomas that, he's not part of my cargo you know."

I pulled my attention around to discover that all three merchants were vying as to who would be first to offer me employment.

"Don't be hasty to accept offers from these good gentlemen, Thomas, you've already seen what rogues they are. There's a shortage of men who can read, write and cypher in this place. You'll have a dozen propositions—some of them legal—by tomorrow," the captain smiled pleasantly as he gave me this warning.

As the ship edged towards wharves that clawed out into the water like rotting fingers, I half-listened to the descriptions of positions the merchants had in mind for me.

Suddenly I could smell St. John's, an appalling mixture of rancid oil, human waste and fish guts rotting in the stagnant water beneath the wharves, all overlaid with smoke and the stink of people living crowded together.

The town, which had appeared so pleasantly situated from a distance, presented quite a different aspect when viewed close up. Behind the respectable stone and brick business premises that lined the harbour, I could see ramshackle shanties and mud-clogged lanes crowded with animals and people.

The look of the place, combined with the stench, exuded a sense of evil. If I tarried here I would fall into despair, crawl into one of the hovels and die. The premonition was ominous and so vivid that I turned and immediately accepted employment from the man who was speaking as the ship touched the wharf.

The man was Caleb Gosse. He was offering a position in some remote part of the country, far from St. John's, at a place he called Cape Random. Eyeing me as if I were a horse at market, he told me I looked a healthy young man who'd be able for a good day's labour.

This was true—apart from the low-mindedness, I was fit. Pacing the deck night and day had given me back my strength and I was probably in better physical shape that I had been since entering the seminary. I owned two books, my breviary, the clothes I was standing in, and what seemed to me to be a large sum of money—wages Captain Lorca had insisted upon paying. Telling myself that life had dealt more kindly with me than I deserved, I concentrated on what the man Gosse was saying.

"...after a year or so you'll have a bit saved to buy a good piece of waterfront property—you won't find it here, though." He waved his hand at the ramshackle wharves.

Willie Johnson snorted, "He's right about that, you'll get no land along here. These days you'd have to go way up to Riverhead to find even a garden for sale. Still and all lad, don't leave town if you want to get rich. Every man jack of us made fortunes here—legal ones too, despite what the captain thinks. You're better off comin' into my office than lettin' this old skinflint send you to some God-forsaken outharbour where you'll never see a civilized creature, and years from now still have nothing but the clothes on your back."

Caleb Gosse didn't even glance at the Scot, but eyed me shrewdly, guessing, I think, that I was running from something and more likely to accept a job in an out-of-the-way place.

Caleb Gosse was—still is, I suppose—a fat pig of a man. A few strains of straight pale hair, plastered across his bald head had come unstuck and fell forward over his round, pink face. Less carefully dressed than the other two, his jacket looked slightly green, and the collar of his shirt was dirty and frayed. At first glance he appeared to be a jolly soul, but upon observation I saw that his smiles were just quick grimaces slipped in at random to disarm his listener. He was pleased, though, that I had accepted his offer, and began telling me about his station at the place he simply called The Cape.

"Had two green hands ashore there all summer makin' fish. Once they're picked up, the place will be empty again—empty most of the year—that's what worries me. I'm sure Red Indians are stealin' me blind, takin' salt and gear, and likely to burn the wharf and store down, come winter. They're harmless, of course," he added hastily with one of his strange, perfunctory smiles.

"A bit simple from all I hear, like most savages. There'll be no harm in your winterin' over and stayin' to oversee things in the summer months too. Not a lot of work to it, but I'll give you wages or share—you'll be better off takin' a share...."

Mr. Johnson snorted again, but Caleb Gosse paid him no heed. "I got a ship leavin' noon tomorrow to pick up the men and what fish is still down there." Without waiting for further acceptance from me, he marched off the ship, barking orders at the ragged boys who were helping unload his rope.

"I've traded in some strange corners of the world but never found a more greedy or dishonest lot than St. John's merchants," Captain Lorca told me next morning before I left the ship.

"Surely," I said, "some of them are honest."

"I suppose one in twenty might be half-way honest, but most would rob their own mothers—and with the British Navy acting for them as judge and executioner you've got to watch where you put your foot. I've known of more than one man went ashore in this place and was never heard from again!"

Caleb Gosse, the captain said, was considered unprincipled and unpredictable even by local standards. "He's perfectly capable of abandoning a man to starve in some little cove if his services are no longer needed—take your wages in coin, lad, rather than in some promised share of profit. Gosse shares nothing. Don't rely on him for anything!" He studied my face, "I don't know what you've done, Thomas, but I calculate it couldn't be anything too bad. Why don't you sail back to Spain with us—or even to Portugal? We'll discharge a good part of our oil at Oporto. I could put you ashore there without anyone being the wiser."

Unexpectedly, I felt homesick. For the first time, I longed to return to Spain, to the cooperage, the low stone house, to my mother and sisters. But I remembered Father Francis' warnings. Though only an unimportant priest in a small Irish parish, word of my mad plan and its consequences would now have travelled from church to church, between seminaries, convents and cloisters across Europe faster than any sailing ship. I shook my head, thanked the captain and, without setting foot on land, jumped from ship to ship until I came to the Gosse vessel that brought me to the place called Cape Random.

Before leaving me on the Cape, Gosse's men helped me reinforce the walls and tar the roof of the store which was the only shelter in the place. The store was just a large, partitionless room intended for the storage of salt, lines, nets and fishing gear. A bunk had been built against one wall. Next to it was a fireplace made of mortar and good brick.

Drying wood was stacked around three walls, and against the other were my supplies: barrels of potatoes and turnip, a pile of dried fish, a cask of pickled beef, a flour barrel. The walls of the store were hung with a hundred things: flint, block and tackle, snare lines, a dozen unfamiliar tools along with two hammers, hatchet and saw, rope, bags of nails, knives and odd bits of sail cloth. There were tubs of lard, a jar of oil, a box of tea, a basket of candles, oars, two suits of oil clothes, cooking pots, a length of chain and brin bags filled with birds' feathers. I arranged and rearranged everything several times and restacked the wood to form an enclosure around the fire where I could sleep and eat.

Leaning behind the door of the store was an unwieldy muzzle-loading rifle. Before he left, Alex Brennan, the *Tern*'s captain, took me down on the beach for a lesson in loading, priming and firing the ancient piece. I thought it unlikely I would have occasion to use the gun, and when I expressed this view the captain seemed to agree.

"They do say Indians all move inland in winter. Anyway I doubt they'd bother you—Ralph and Ab never saw no savages and they was here all summer."

I asked if he'd ever seen any Indians.

"The one time I ever set eyes on 'em was years ago out on the Funks. I was a green lad workin' for Perkins in Fogo. We was drivin' birds aboard, the ones they calls penguins in these parts, when we saw two savages paddlin' up in their hide boats. They looked harmless enough to me, but the captain had the men fire on them and even laughed when the poor brutes drowned."

If there were no Indians around the Cape, then why, I asked, had Caleb Gosse hired me?

Alex shrugged, "Who knows—the man has his own reasons. Some think he's strange in the head but I been workin' for him these twelve year and I tell you if I was strange like him I'd be a rich man. You'll see no Red Indians but you might see white ones—or you might need the old piece for some animal comin' out of the woods during the winter."

He gave me a long, quizzical look, then asked if I had any idea where I was. When I told him I didn't (for we had entered a dozen little coves to collect fish, had tacked back and forth against the wind so many times on the trip down the coast, that I knew only that we were well north of St. John's) he took a stick and drew a rough map of the island of Newfound Land in the wet sand.

"We're right here," he said and put a stone on the part jutting farthest out into the ocean, "and St. John's is about here."

He straightened up and pointed to a tall outcropping of rock behind the Cape: "There's your lookout—if you go past that, on through the bog and barrens and wood and over the hills, keepin' to the coast and goin' due south, you'll come to the nearest place where there's people—that'd be Pond Island, I expect. Tho I don't know how you'd get there unless you're able to walk up on the ice."

I nodded, not understanding what he meant, and took a cursory look at the map before a wave rolled in and washed it away. I had to restrain myself from asking what part of Ireland he'd come from.

"Remember, if you wants to find other people in this place, keep to the coast, if you goes inland you're lost for sure," he said. It was clear he disliked leaving me here and was not sure I understood how completely alone I would be once he sailed out of the bay.

He could not have guessed, and I should be shamed to write, that I was in a state of exhilaration for days after the *Tern* sailed out of sight.

It was fall, the time of year when everything on the Cape seems steeped in a dye that makes all colours deeper, clearer. In the mornings when I came out of the store, I would stand tasting the air, clean and cut through with salt; drinking in the circle of my world from blue sky down to dark green hills, to the bright bushes along the pale beach, on down to the frill of white edging the blue sea that blended back into the sky.

I cannot call what I felt happiness, it was something more brittle, like the false confidence that comes between sobriety and drunkenness when all doubt appears petty, all dreams possible.

The days did not seem long. I chopped more wood and began, with great care, to repair a little boat I'd dragged out from under the store. I had begged paper and ink powder from Captain Lorca, and at first kept a log recording the weather, the tides high and low, and which direction the wind was blowing from. I must have spent hours that autumn watching the sea, trying to catch the instant the tide turned. I kept count of days in the book but had no means whereby to count the hours. Still, I had no need to count hours, I rose with the sun and when it went down, I slept.

When the days shortened, I began to read after supper by the light of the most primitive of lamps—a wick in a bowl of oil. Each night I read from one of the books Father Francis had tied up with my clothing, allowing myself only two or three pages each night. Then I would read my book of prayers and, when my eyes became tired, said the rosary. I slept, without longings, without regrets, without worries about the day that was coming.

At first I found the snow pleasing. The stillness and simplicity of a world covered in white reminded me of the corridors of the seminary. I had found my cloister and it suited me well. I prayed and meditated, and thought I was becoming a better man.

I think my apprehension began when I saw the sea freezing over. Then the snow piled into drifts against the door and around the walls of the shed. By December, the days were never light. I lived in a world filled constantly with the sounds of ice and wind, always aware of the noise, sure the store would be pulled up by its roots and flung out to sea by the force of the frozen waves crashing up beneath it. At night I only half slept, by day I was only half awake.

Without being aware of it, I was spending more and more time lying in my bunk, until one morning I awoke convinced—I know not how—that I had missed a complete day. The idea frightened me. I could sleep myself to death in that dim twilight—in the spring, Alex Brennan would find me rotted away in my bed. I became preoccupied with time, tried to devise ways to measure its passage: the lengthening of an icicle outside the six-inch square of window, the burning of a wet stick stuck end-ways into the fire, the drip of oil down a piece of string. It dismayed me to doze and wake, not able to tell how long I had slept, but I was not a man of science, and none of my methods proved satisfactory.

I tried to occupy myself, dividing the day up into tasks. I set myself to writing down latin verbs and the bits of canon law Father Don Manuel had taught me. I recited poetry, made drawings of the stars and tried to name them. I paced back and forth the length of the shed, discovering that walking from end to end took me thirty-two steps and from side-to-side, fourteen.

I began to carve a crucifix, which occupied me for some time until I saw what an unlovely thing it was, and burnt it. Then I set myself to building a desk, which proved a most successful way of passing the days. The desk, though rough, was a useful object which I possessed for years.

Much of the time I spent gazing into the fire, recalling the past. I tried to call up the faces of my sisters, my brother, my parents, of the boy who had chased me home from mass when I was six, of the old woman who went from door to door selling bundles of sticks. I worked my way through my life, remembering each face until I came to the faces of the people in Borriswater and forced myself, at last, to think of each of them. I prayed for them—I still pray for them—even now, when I cannot pray for myself.

So January and February passed, and I knew it must be March, although the ground was still covered in snow and the sea in ice. The ice began to break apart, and Alex Brennan didn't come. I became alarmed. What if Captain Lorca's warning had come true? Might Caleb Gosse have found a more profitable place and left me here to starve? I tried to recall the map Alex Brennan had drawn in the sand, but all I could see was the white stone sitting on a spot representing the Cape.

Like the old navigators, I began looking for signs, deciding one day to pack what remained of the food and start for the nearest community, the name of which I could not remember; deciding the next day to wait. I would go as soon as I saw moss appear from under the snow, when the flour in the barrel was almost gone, when the moon was full, when the first buds came out, or when a certain star reached the highest point above the lookout hill.

Then the Vincents came.

Chapter 17

I was on the wharf, watching slob ice drift away from shore, wondering if this was the omen I'd been looking for, the signal that I should leave the Cape, when I saw something coming towards me. A little boat, so low in the water that at first I thought it a piece of wreckage or some dead sea animal. When I realized what it was, I felt such a lifting of my spirits that I knew I did not ever again want to live completely apart from mankind.

Like a family of floating gypsies, the Vincents were, like Noah without his animals. Their boat was loaded to the gunwales with children, barrels, tools, blankets, buckets, pots, pans, a huge carpenter's chest, a roll of roofing paper, a keg of nails and a wire coop containing a rooster and three hens.

Although both Josh and his oldest son were pulling hard on the oars, the craft made slow progress, sometimes disappearing completely in the swell. As I waited on the wharf, smiling foolishly, I had time to study the boat's occupants: the two at the oars were obviously father and son, although the boy looked healthier, more substantial than the man could ever have.

Josh Vincent's skin was rough and blackened from years on the water, but his faded blue eyes, pale beard and hair gave the impression of fragility, and his body seemed lost beneath a jacket and heavy breeks. His two sons have the same fair hair, long thin noses and pale eyes, but because their voices are loud and their movements full of energy, they seem to resemble their squat, heavy-boned mother. The girl Annie, their oldest child, was thin then, and fair like her father but already taller than her mother by a head. When they came alongside, the man shipped his oars and stood. I could see him swallow before he spoke.

"We'um Vincents, from up Pond Island. I'm Josh Vincent and this is me wife Sarah, she's one of the Gills from Pinchards Island. Vincents been fishin' outta Pond Island for fifty year or more but...." He stopped, seeming to have forgotten what he was about to say.

"'Tis gettin' crowded," the woman said. She gave her husband a nod, and after a minute, he began speaking again.

"Tha's right—hard to get a good fishin' room, so we're thinkin' to find a spot here for me—and for Young Joe and Peter, too, when they starts on their own."

I decided that the man was a good-natured simpleton who had turned in to the first place showing any sign of occupation. He probably planned to sponge off whoever lived here. I remembered Alex Brennan's remark about white Indians.

Still, I could not help but be delighted to hear a human voice, and I found Josh Vincent's voice especially appealing. It had a soft child-like quality that made you lean forward to catch every word.

"But Mr. Vincent, this place is exposed to the sea with no harbour, hardly any flat land, and what there is belongs to Caleb Gosse. I've been told the only real wood is well inland—you'd take days dragging it out to build anything." I tried to speak with some authority, having, I felt, a good knowledge of the area from my long walks the previous fall.

"Very true, sir, very true. 'Tis a vicious spot sometimes," the agreeable voice said, "but see out past them sunkers? Shoals comes around in a big circle, best fishin' grounds in Bonavist'—man and boy, I fished most of 'em and I tell'ee this be the best place on the coast." The man waved his hand towards the ocean as if I could see underwater.

"Father and me come ashore here thousands of times, long before Caleb Gosse was heard tell of," he continued without inflection. "And there's a fresh water pond back there and good berry pickin' grounds, a place up top the hill you could make a garden, had you a mind. We'll cruise what wood we needs down along the coast. Me and Sarah been talkin' it over this past year. We woulda' come before now but 'tis a bit mournful bein' alone in a place. This winter, when word come someone was livin' here, we figured time'd come for us to move. This cape is as good a place as any man's likely to find on God's earth, sir, and if you're agreeable, we plans to 'bide."

It was the longest speech I would ever hear from Josh Vincent. When I came to know him, I realized he must have spent every minute of the trip from Pond Island composing it. But I knew before he even finished speaking that his soft voice and child-like manner were deceiving. No matter what Caleb Gosse's agent said, this man had made up his mind to live on the Cape. His request came from an innate sense of politeness, not from any doubt about his right to settle wherever he wanted to along this coast.

I looked down at him and marvelled: here at last was a peasant not held in bondage to the land!

The Vincents waited, regarding me calmly from the clutter of their household goods: the man, impassive; his wife chewing her lip nervously, her eyes full of doubt but her broad face ready to break into a smile if I said yes; the three sober children, two boys and a girl, as expressionless as their father.

Such a force they were, standing there in their little boat, waiting for my answer. To think a man could take his life and pack it up like that, all of it, wife, children, chickens, job, and carry it to where he wanted to go, set it down and spread it out around him like a blanket! For the first time in my life I felt real awe—and real envy. The feeling was so strong, so pervasive, that I took a step backward from the edge of the wharf to hide what must be showing on my face.

I gestured to them to come ashore. Did I smile? I don't think so—another thing to regret. The woman nodded and gave me a broad smile before turning to her family.

"All hands heave to. I wants this stowed away before rain starts."

Within minutes, their belongings were piled on the wharf and I heard myself telling them to bring the stuff up to the store, "You'll have to sleep there until you have other shelter." The words were out before I thought, and immediately I wondered how long I could stand such an arrangement.

Within the week, Josh Vincent's brothers arrived. They brought his fishing gear in one boat and towed a dory loaded with lime, bricks, tar and tools. They left again the same day, taking Josh and Young Joe, and were back two days later, dragging long timbers behind three boats stacked with dried lumber.

Will and Ezra stayed a month. I had never seen people work the way the Vincents did. Within days, they had a house studded, the rough walls up, and were mortaring the chimney. The back half of the house was set atop a flat rock. The three children and Sarah, who was well along in pregnancy, carried rocks and built a wall around the open sides and along the front under the beams as the men planked over the floor and roof. They made doors and cut a single window over which they stretched some kind of animal gut, then put up shutters both inside and out while the children went around caulking the seams.

The roof was covered with sheathing paper which the men tarred and battened down at the peak with a line of sods. The three brothers were small men. They looked as if a good wind could blow them away, yet when I worked alongside them, I fell behind.

They didn't know what to make of me, and little wonder. Beyond telling them that I represented Caleb Gosse, I offered no information, and, although they must have been curious about my past, they asked no questions. In fact it was some time before they began to talk to one another in front of me and to make shy jokes about my rough carpentry.

Sarah Vincent was less constrained, and before long, I passed what was left of my food supplies over to her and began eating most of my meals with the family. Even so, they all continued to call me "Mr. Hutchings."

By the time Will and Ezra went back to Pond Island, the Vincents had a solid two-room house with a loft above. They were well settled away in June, when, with an amazing absence of fuss, Sarah gave birth to her fourth child, another boy. His name, she told me, was Charles. With the entire Vincent family watching, I wrote his name in my log book, noting that this was the first child ever born on Cape Random.

When the *Tern* came, Alex Brennan unloaded my supplies and a small mountain of coarse salt without commenting on the new house. He already knew Josh Vincent and it was obvious that the two liked and trusted each other. They talked to me about fish and boats as if I had as much knowledge as they.

I found this a very satisfying experience, and in time came to understand most of what they were saying.

Alex called the *Tern* a "schooner boat." He told me she had a forty-two-foot keel and twelve-foot beam. She carried mainsail, foresail and jib with another square sail to go before the wind.

"She floated like a cork when we got her ten year ago, but she's waterlogged now—slow. Soon as Caleb Gosse sees a chance, I allow he'll be rid of her to some poor bugger up north or some black in them hot places he sends fish to. But she'll see us through another season or two, won't you, old love." He gave the boat a pat as I've seen men do with horses.

Alex was continuing up the coast where his crew would fish with hooks and nets until they had between two and three hundred quintals aboard. Then they would bring the fish back to the Cape.

"Seein' as how you got Josh and his crowd here, I don't need to leave as many hands behind to make fish," he said, and I nodded wisely.

I learned that my employer owned four vessels like the *Tern*. They fished all summer, dropping fish off at stations along the coast and picking it up in the fall to be taken, cured and stacked, into St. John's. In peace time, half the world, according to Alex Brennan, lived off Newfound Land fish, and wartime was even more profitable since armies on both sides were fed on it.

The wage Caleb Gosse paid me was not large, but I doubt I earned even that during the first spring and summer I spent on the Cape. Just as I'd watched the birds and animals the year before, I now watched the Vincents. Sometimes I would observe them from close-up, looking over Josh's shoulder as he gutted fish, mended nets, brought down sea birds, or baited his hooks. I tried to duplicate his skill, but was far more ignorant about these things than any of his children. Even the girl Annie could scull a boat and make fish.

Sometimes I climbed the hill and watched. From up there, I could see that we were making paths on the Cape: Josh from the flakes to his house when he went back and forth for cups of tea between jobs, Sarah to her hens. I could even see the path I was making between the store and the Vincents' house. From my lookout, I could observe the small gestures I missed when people were nearby, noticed that when Josh and Sarah passed each other she would reach out sometimes to give him a playful push; saw Annie sitting on the doorstep with the new baby in her arms, brushing her lips across his fair hair. Once I watched Josh and Young Joe sit for two hours shaping out a pair of oars with not a word passing between them. It reminded me of how Philip and my father used to work.

I had never before found people interesting but I was spellbound by the Vincents—and it seemed they were by me—I would often look up from some job, one I was probably doing with painful awkwardness, to find one of the children, Young Joe or Peter, or Annie with the baby on her hip, studying me with solemn interest.

This quiet order disappeared when the Andrews family arrived. It was late fall. Alex Brennan had made his last trip for the season, dropped off our winter supplies and picked up Gosse's men along with the fish we'd cured.

"Well that's it—time to batten her down," Sarah said when the *Tern* disappeared over the horizon.

And we did, using the last civil days to pick berries, cut wood and catch a few more fish. Josh shot two big grey geese which Sarah cooked with spices and stored in crocks against the winter.

Snow had already started to fly when a French captain, foolishly and perhaps illegally, put the Andrews ashore on the Cape. From the first I thought them an odd collection of people: the overly friendly old woman with a merry face, who dressed in widows' weeds; her sons, one red-headed and laughing, one dun-coloured and silent; their wives, a poor creature near death and an imposing woman called Meg, who was as ignorant as the rest but looked like a queen. They had a motley crowd of children, every age, from a boy who could barely walk to a great loping girl with orange hair, who glowered at me each time we met, as if I were somehow to blame for her plight.

There were twelve of them in all. I was forced put to share my accommodation with them and, as it turned out, my food, too, since they had been improvident enough to come without any—an omission that almost cost us our lives.

I cannot explain even now why their arrival disturbed me so much. It was more than their coming without food, without tools and without skills (Ben Andrews could hardly stand on the wharf without getting seasick, and Ned's clumsiness was so complete that it sometimes seemed deliberate). It could not have been that their arrival posed any threat to my authority.

Could my pride have been so great that I thought to create a perfect world on this forlorn bit of sand and rock? I could swear I had no such idea. I have learned though, that in some dark centre of us all, there are terrible ambitions we only catch sight of in our nightmares. Maybe the Andrews family, in their glib disarray, did bring to an end some hidden dream I had of a pristine and orderly community, of a world populated by clean, hard-working souls like the Vincents. People I considered safe, responsible, worthy.

The Andrews certainly brought an end to my solitude. That winter I remembered again what it was like to live close to others, pressed together until every word spoken seems aimed at someone's discomfort. I found myself reliving my childhood sorrow of talk and laughter flowing over and around me without me ever being part of it. Long after the Andrews family had been accepted by the Vincents, long after they considered themselves part of the Cape, I still felt them to be intruders and wished them back to whatever wretched place they had fled from.

During these first years on the Cape, black moods descended on me when I thought of my abandoned vocation, of my parents who had impoverished themselves for my sake, about Borriswater and the people I'd left. Whenever this happened, I used to take myself to a place I'd found in the hills behind the beach, a scooped-out hollow surrounded by tall grass, where I felt completely alone. Sometimes I would pray, sometimes gaze out over the endless sea until my mind was empty.

But these seasons of remorse came further and further apart and so did the time I spent in prayer and meditation, until in the end my conscience stopped troubling me. I no longer counted how many days, months, years had passed since I had received the blessed sacraments, celebrated Holy Mass or made my own confession. I remembered these things briefly whenever Meg Andrews pressed me into service as a pastor.

We worked like peasants. I began to understand why peasants think of little but work, food and sleep. I slept well, as only men with clear consciences are said to sleep.

Except when I dreamed.

During these first years I felt no attraction to any of the women on the Cape. They were like my sisters, like my mother or the village women who came to our house in my childhood. As unrelated to the women in my dreams as hens are to seagulls. But after Ned Andrews married Mary Bundle, my dreams changed. The women in them became one woman, a woman with Mary Bundle's face.

Ned, the red-headed Andrews son, was our minstrel and raconteur. If I could be said to have had a friend in my life, it was Ned. We had nothing in common. The man could neither read nor write, had never gone willingly into a church, made no distinctions between angels and fairies, fiends and ghosts—all of which peopled the stories he told. He was vain and often thoughtless, sometimes lazy and completely without the morose sense of original sin that seemed to haunt other members of his family. I have many times heard his sister-in-law Meg scolding him for idleness or for what she called "holding the truth careless," which he most certainly did.

But he loved people, and his imagination was broad as the ocean around the Cape. His mind was amazing. Ned could encompass a new thought, grasp it, examine it, twist and turn it and hold it up to the light until you saw what a wonderful shining thing it was.

I came upon him one day on his knees in the woods, staring at a spider's web hung with raindrops. It was a pure miracle, he said. He saw the world as a place filled with miracles and considered anything possible. I have heard him discuss the likelihood of sailing to the moon as seriously as if he were talking about taking a skiff out past the sunkers.

Ned was the heart of the place. He balanced out something in us all, especially in me; made me see the joke of things I would take too seriously, made me less likely to fall into traps of my own design. If he were alive, I would not this night be out on the ocean sailing away from the Cape.

Mary Bundle was certainly not like the seagull women of my dreams, or like any other bird. She was much too silent, more like a field mouse perhaps—little and brown and quiet—except when she was crossed. A field mouse who creeps into your house, and before you know it, has a nest of babies tucked away under your rafters.

What misfortune washed her up on the Cape I never discovered, nor cared to. When she first arrived, I thought her plain, dim-witted even. She had an odd way of appearing out of nowhere and standing about in corners, silent, but seeming to expect something. After Ned married her, I began to sit by their fire each night, listening to him but watching her, and found myself for the first time desiring a living woman—my friend's wife.

Mary changed after she married Ned, lost her half-starved, suspicious look, grew graceful and confident. The sharpness of her face and body rounded and she would speak up and laugh at Ned's jokes. She was sometimes so lewd that I wondered if she knew I lay awake at night wishing her in my bed. During those months I was so tormented by desire for Mary that I was unable to sleep. Often I would climb the hill and look out over the Cape. It was a beautiful spot on a moonlit night—the quiet houses, the long empty beach, the shimmering sea.

It was on these nights that I became convinced there were others besides ourselves on the Cape. I noticed rustlings and stirrings in the grass and bushes around the hollow and at first assumed that my presence disturbed small animals and birds nesting in the place. Then, one night, suddenly and positively, I knew that the eyes watching me were not those of a bird or animal.

I sat for an endless time, still as the rocks, my eyes focused on the dark mass of bushes outlined against the moonlight. I was not afraid. I knew that whoever crouched there watching had foregone countless opportunities to do me harm. Moreover, I felt no threat, no impression of menace or evil.

I went back to the same spot for several nights but saw nothing, although I sensed that someone was still nearby. I did not mention my suspicions until many weeks later when we were in back, cutting wood for the winter. I asked the men if they'd seen any sign of Indians, but none had.

Josh Vincent told us his father often spoke of the Indians and remembered when the savages were regular visitors to this shore. Apparently they travelled out from the interior each spring to kill seals and make arrowheads out of the flint hereabouts. Josh's father had known a man from Trinity Bay who said someone up there owned a Red Indian. He'd captured the Indian about seventeen years before when he shot an Indian woman running away with the child in her arms.

"I never seen one meself," Josh said, "and I doubts there's any left. I wish we would see one, Skipper Brennan tells me there's some crowd in St. John's offerin' good money to anyone bringing them a live Indian." Josh, one of the kindest men I ever met, did not consider Indians as human. "Accordin' to me Pap, they're dirty, stinkin' things, what would steal the eyes right out of your head," he said.

When I told them I thought I'd seen someone up on the hill (I did not say I'd only sensed someone, thinking they would dismiss such fancies), Josh said it'd more likely be some poor escaped servant, some man who'd signed his soul away to get over to this country and ended up living like a slave and getting deeper into debt each year.

"Sometimes they runs away—takes off. I can't say I blames 'em—they're treated barbarous. Sometimes the navy finds 'em and brings 'em back, bemore times I expects they dies, poor brutes."

He said that once such a man, half-starved and raving, stumbled into Fox Harbour. He was taken in by a family there and hidden. When this seemed unnecessary, he'd mixed in with the community and eventually married a Vincent.

"As good a man as you're ever likely to meet, but I doubt even Hannah could tell you what his real name is," Josh said.

I wonder how many of us there are in this country who go by names we were given at birth. From Ned's stories and songs you'd think the entire island was peopled by dashing pirates, the younger sons of noble houses and princesses, but I doubt any of these exist in real life—and if they did, who would know? In all my years on the Cape, not one soul ever asked me about my past—and I asked no one about theirs.

During our sixth or seventh year on the Cape, I saw the Indian whom I suspected had been watching me.

The women had been digging potatoes and had built a huge fire to burn weeds and brush, and also for heat because there was a touch of frost in the air. When the men came back from the woods at dusk, the fire was still high. I volunteered to sit by until it died, and the others went on down to their suppers. I knew Sarah would save supper for me, and I was happy, after a day hacking down trees, to sit alone watching the flames and smoking my pipe.

There is great satisfaction in gathering things in, stowing them under a roof, in preparation for winter. I remember feeling very content sitting there thinking about the potatoes, cabbage, fish and wood we now had safe in vegetable cellars, back yards and lofts.

Then, behind me in the line of scrawny trees I heard something fall, a sound like the body of a large animal, splintering small twigs as it hit the ground. I heard a low, quite human, moan. Only one, but I knew where it had come from and ran towards the spot just at the edge of the trees. I was thinking one of the children had fallen, a thing that happened with alarming frequency but which, so far, had resulted in no serious injury.

But it was not a child. The person who lay on the ground was a man—a man like none I'd ever seen. Even lying as he was, on his side with one leg pulled up under his chin, I could see that he was taller than most men. I thought him young, but people have told me such things are hard to judge. He was beardless and almost naked, wearing only a kind of short leather skirt. A fur skin and bag lay on the ground beside him. He looked dark, very dark, but this may have been dirt, or the red mud I later learned Indians rub into their skin. His teeth had clamped so sharply down over his lip that a trickle of blood was running down his chin.

When he saw me, he tried to stand but could not. He turned his head away and vomited, then said something that was unmistakably a curse—on himself for his carelessness, I suspected.

228

After that, he seemed resigned to whatever fate had in store for him. He helped as best he could when I dragged him over the rough ground to the fire, where I could see the gleam of bone breaking through the skin of his leg just below the knee.

I said, although I knew he would not understand me, "I'll go get someone to help—down there." I pointed towards the houses below and stood up.

I knew that Sarah Vincent and Mary Bundle with their ointment and herbs could help the man better than I. But he would not let me go, his big hand reached out and wrapped around my ankle like a clamp. He spit out some words through his teeth and shook his head.

I had no idea how to set a bone, but indicated to him that this was what I would do. I searched around for reasonably smooth sticks, took off my shirt, sweat stained and dirty as it was, and ripped it into strips. The Indian watched each move. I think he would have stood, despite the pain, and stopped me if I'd started towards the path.

I knelt there for a good long time looking at his leg, at the torn flesh, the little strands of sinew, at the bone that looked unlike anything I had imagined being inside a human body. It was like a shell, clean and white looking. Finally I eased the fur under his leg and straightened it out. Slowly, with shaking hands, I began to push the bones back into place, trying to fit the edges together as best I could.

I had seen Mary Bundle sew up cuts with thread and needle and wished I had at least these. I tried to tell him I needed such things, and water too, to wash the blood and dirt away. But he grunted some sound at me, pointed at his leg and jabbed at my chest with his finger. His face was glistening with sweat, and I'm sure mine was, too, as I bent over him, nudging the splinters of bone together.

It took a long time, but he didn't make a sound. When it was all done, bandaged around with my heavy work shirt, supported by the sticks and then bandaged again, it looked from the outside a neat enough job, although it was large as a tree trunk. I touched his foot, which was sticking out of the ungainly arrangement, and found it to be still warm. I knew this was a good sign. The blood was still flowing down through the broken leg and there was some chance the Indian would walk again. But not, I thought, for many months.

I tried once more to tell him he must be taken down to the houses. I wondered afterwards why I was so sure he was alone, that he had no one of his own kind to turn to. When it was clear he wanted to be left there, I made him as comfortable as possible, thinking he would change his mind by morning and come down to the houses with me. I brought his skin bag and a crock of drinking water the women kept in their tool chest over to him by the fire. Then, looking around for anything that might be of use to him, saw the long iron rod we used to pry up rocks and for a dozen other tasks. I picked the rod up and passed it to him, thinking this would show that I intended to do him no harm during the night. He seemed to understand, nodded and lay back on his fur quilt. When I left him he was running his hand up and down the piece of iron, holding it close to his face and staring at it as if he'd never seen such an object. Before I turned away he looked at me and said something. I nodded, knowing I was agreeing not to betray him.

At dawn I came back to the garden. The fire was a pile of white ash and the Indian was gone. The only sign that he had ever been there was the empty water jar set down against the tool box. I swear he had even brushed over the earth to erase the imprint of his body. I walked back through the woods—really just a ring of trees—and came to the marsh on the other side without seeing any trace of him. I walked on across the marsh, through the long grass and back across the neck, looking, but not really expecting to see the Indian. I knew a man who had managed to keep silent while I manipulated skin and broken bone would not have fainted until he was out of sight of the Cape.

It was not until the next day, when Sarah asked if I'd seen the iron rod, that I realized he must have taken it as a walking stick. For some reason knowing that he had it gave me pleasure, or at least comfort. That winter when the snow howled down on the Cape I often though of him, a solitary figure walking through the black and white interior, and hoped he'd made it back to his own people.

Chapter 18

How can a person wake one morning and see a completely different world from the one he saw yesterday? As if the eyes he is looking through are not the eyes he closed the night before. Trees and rocks stand in the same places but appear unfamiliar, shadows fall differently, people are not the same, their looks and gestures strangely altered, even the sea and air has been transformed—but to none of these changes can you give a name. They are nothing, they are the sum of a thousand things, they are everything.

I remember in the seminary there was a saying: "Husbands and priests go mad at forty." Maybe, then, it is something that happens to all men, old age laying its cold fingers on our necks.

It was one of these sudden springs we sometimes have when the wind veers south-westward and overnight, winter vanishes. The day before, I had turned over my dory and started scraping her down. That morning I should have gotten on with the job of caulking new oakum into places where the planks had split and warped. It was work I enjoyed. I like the sharp smell of oakum, the rusty colour and the way, with care, it can be packed into cracks so that after the boat is tarred she will be as sound as the day she was built. But when I looked at my dory that morning, disfigured by years of tar, old and beyond redemption, I wondered why I hadn't long ago gotten Ben to build me a new one. I left her and wandered down to the landwash where two boatloads of women and children were setting out for Turr Island to gather birds' eggs.

Two or three other men were there, watching with quiet amusement the efforts of the women and young boys to manoeuvre the overloaded dories away from the beach. As they pulled off, Moses, Ned's youngest, wailed and started into the water after his mother. The child, who had been standing directly in front of me, was no more that two feet tall. Before we knew it, he was up to his neck in water. I plowed out after him, the cold sending needle-like pains up my legs, and grabbed the straps of his overalls. Then, instead of returning to the beach as I'd intended, I kept on walking and rolled ungracefully into the nearest boat.

This surprised the occupants of the boat as much as it did me. They stopped rowing and offered to turn around, but I told them to keep on and passed Mary her badly frightened son. She took the child, shook him like a cat shaking a kitten and called him "a stunned little bugger." She was the only woman on the Cape who used such language.

By then Ned and Mary had four sons. Ned coaxed, teased and petted his wife, but Mary, except for a brief mellowing at the beginning of each pregnancy, never changed. I had long since recovered from my infatuation for the tense, earthy woman; had almost forgotten it. I may even then have begun to dislike her: she certainly had no time for me, never missed an opportunity to suggest I might be cheating the Vincent and Andrews families of their fair credit for the summer's catch. Still, she retained the power to embarrass me, and often did with pointed references to my celibacy and to the rollicking sexual life she and Ned enjoyed.

Safely in the boat, Moses smiled happily at his mother's curses, pulled her shawl across his face and curled into her arms. I tugged off my water-filled boots and leaned back in the stern of the boat, hoping the sun would dry me.

Had I changed even then? It seems to me I had, that the people in the boat looked different. They seemed coarser, louder, more ragged than they had the day before, yet infinitely more human, more vulnerable. I noticed that pink scalp showed through Sarah's greying hair, that on Meg's madonna-like face, small lines were creeping down from nose to mouth. The children, some of them already barefoot, all looked underfed. On the seat facing me, Lavinia Andrews and Charlie Vincent were pulling on the oars with all their strength. The wrists sticking out from the unravelled sleeves of his sweater were thin as twigs, but his hands, wrapped firmly around the oars were capable as a man's, and his face beamed with pride as he shouted to the other boat and pulled ahead.

Everyone, except me, was in high spirits at the prospect of a day without work. Even Mary chuckled at something Sarah was whispering in her ear, and the young ones squirmed with excitement. It takes so little, such happiness. I found myself wondering why God doesn't let it happen more often.

Just before I fell asleep, my eyes rested on Lavinia Andrews. She was sitting a little above me, between me and the sun, so that sunshine bounced off her orange hair and dappled her already freckled face. I stared at her face: I had never before seen how remarkable it was. She caught me staring, and I closed my eyes but the picture imprinted behind my lids was of her nipples pushing against the thin cotton blouse as she pulled on the oars.

I slept until the boat jolted aground, jerking me out of a dream in which Lavinia Andrews, her blazing hair falling forward, had been leaning over me, quite naked.

All day I followed the others, climbing from ledge to ledge, stealing eggs from frantic birds that screeched and dived at us, coming so close we could see their red eyes. That was the day we found the two men, both, I judged, younger than I, dead from cold and starvation and half-eaten by the birds. They are buried now in our graveyard here on the Cape, without names for the wooden markers that Ben Andrews made and into which I cut only RIP and the year of their deaths.

After we discovered the bodies, I climbed to the top of the island and found Lavinia alone, sitting as if she were weeping with her head down on her knees. Ned said once that his sister and Mary were the same age, but looking at her there I thought he must have been mistaken. Mary was a woman, just seven or eight years younger than me and already showing signs of age, while this girl sitting on the grass looked little more than a child. Her hair had fallen forward to expose the back of her neck. It took all my will to keep from reaching forward to touch the soft curve.

I sat down a few feet away, searching for something we might talk about but not really wanting to talk. My mind was like the sea on a day when the water is so clear you can see schools of fish swimming above and below each other, see on down to the moving waves of seaweed and bright stones on the ocean floor. I was thinking of so many things, feeling so many things—and they all seemed clearer and yet more complex than anything I had ever thought or felt before. Why had I never seen her before? Spoken to her before? I thought, how lovely her copper coloured hair would look spread on the green moss; imagined how it would be to lie naked in the moss with the birds swooping through the sky over us and the sea rolling out all around us; saw the wonder of life. The wonder that we were here at all, sitting together on the crown of Turr Island, thinking of the dead men in the cave down below, of how short a time we have to enjoy the earth before we are under it, of all the men and women who had gone to their graves without ever having done such a simple thing as make love on moss in the sunshine.

These things crowded into my head as naturally as prayers once had. I had no time to consider why they came or where they might lead before the women and children came clamouring noisily over the ridge of the hill demanding tea, molasses bread and gory details about the dead men.

During the summer that followed the trip to Turr Island, I lived in a haze of desire. I have read that the Greeks believed that if a man missed some stage of his life, he must go back and relive it in his old age: thus explaining why old men become childlike and crones sometimes act like coy virgins. It may be true—certainly through that summer and fall I became the lovesick school boy I had never been in my youth.

I saw Lavinia Andrews everywhere. Before, weeks or months would have passed without my noticing the existence of the girl; now she was in front of my eyes constantly. I do not mean that she put herself in my path or singled me out, quite the contrary—she often disappeared for hours at a time, which almost drove me mad. She seemed to be able to slip out of a room or vanish from the flakes without being seen. I wanted to know where she was each minute, even when I could not see her, I wanted to picture her in someone's kitchen, spreading fish, or walking along the beach.

I followed her, spied on her, arranged my work so that we would be in the same places, so that I could spend hours in the school room or working beside her on the flakes. I often saw her writing in a big ledger she kept in her sack. In my longing to know what she was thinking, I even considered stealing the book. She had no talent for needlework or baking, or for most household jobs, but she worked as hard as the other women on the stagehead, splitting fish, gutting and salting it. Mary never accused Lavinia, as she did others, of being lazy. She spent a good part of her time with the youngsters and could make peace among squabbling children just by looking at them. The young ones came to her with their troubles. Mary's daughter Fanny in particular confided in Lavinia, running to her each time she was chastised by her mother.

It seems incredible, but during the long summer I spent tied to Lavinia Andrews by an invisible thread, not once did anyone notice the state I was in. I worked side-by-side with the other men, side-by-side with her sometimes. She gave off a special aroma, quite unlike the other women who smelled of bread, milk, sweat and fish. Lavinia exuded a scent like apples or burning rosewood, a soft tang like the fragrance caught inside the pink swirls of small sea shells. I mended nets, hauled fish, repaired the store, recorded our catches—did all of my usual work and no one, not even Meg Andrews, who was sometimes able to read my thoughts, noticed that I was out of my mind. I had established my reputation for dour aloofness and reasonableness and, as I have observed often, once people decide you are inclined to be one way, you can act quite differently without anyone noticing.

Have I dwelt overlong on my feelings of that summer? Maybe I am trying to delay recording what must follow—but it was the longest, most lovely summer I have ever known. I spent hours, especially at dusk and in the early dawn, walking. I did this not only when I thought to catch a glimpse of Lavinia, but even when I knew she was safely in bed. At such times I could indulge myself in fantasies of what might be—and sometimes, yes, think carnal thoughts about the girl who was innocent of any knowledge of my obsession with her.

I hate to write of the other thing that happened late that summer. The thing that ended what might have been, the thing that started what is.

I suspected the Andrews family must have been involved in play acting or with some carnival or travelling fair in England. Ned certainly had something of the actor in him. Moreover, they brought (thinking I know not what about the place they were coming to) a great barrel of silk, satin, gold cord and glitter, old costumes of net and velvet. On the Cape nothing is wasted and most of these bizarre belongings have been used somehow. The net became curtains, the velvet pieced into bed coverings, the bits of fur and plush sewn onto coats and hats and the odd scraps of cloth long ago used for patches or hooked into mats. All that remained, tatters of dirty lace and thin ribbons of silk, had been confiscated by Mary's daughter Fanny and concocted into a costume that would, as I once heard Sarah say, frighten the birds away. Indeed that is just what the child looked like, a thin scarecrow with picket legs and arms all draped in frayed ribbon and bits of feathers and flowers that floated in each breeze.

During my years on the Cape, although I spent many hours sitting beside Ned's and Mary's fire, I seldom saw Fanny. She and her mother were always at odds with each other and the girl would duck out of any room Mary entered. She seemed to get along better with Ned, who was only her stepfather. I often heard him teasing her and had seen them dancing around the room together when he was in one of his exuberant moods. In many ways, Ned's relationship with the youngsters was like his sister's. The children seemed to think that both Ned and Lavinia occupied some middle world between adulthood and childhood.

One morning in early fall—really an extension of that long summer—when I was walking in the dunes behind the beach, I met Ned. Such encounters usually resulted in my turning around and walking back to his house, where I would have a second breakfast before starting on the day's work. This morning, however, Ned barely saw me. Looking startled and, I thought later, guilty, he passed by with only a nod. Such a thing had never before happened. I walked on, wondering what could have come over the man.

When I got to the hollow hill which had once been mine but which the children considered their secret spot, I climbed to the top, parted the rose bushes that tangled around its rim and stood looking down into the scooped out bowl.

Below me, kneeling in a swirl of colour, was a beautiful, naked woman. Her hair was pitch black and her skin a soft fawn that seemed to glow in the clear light of morning. From above I could not see her face but the top of her head, her perfect breasts, and lovely legs. She was giggling, a low, clucking sound that reminded me of the doves in Spain, and running her fingers through her tangled hair.

She seemed the essence of my most sensual imaginings, of all my nighttime dreams and daytime fantasies. So like the exotic beings that occupied my secret world: women who became birds, women with long necks and wings, women who flew. I waited, expecting the creature below to unfold coloured wings and vanish.

Then she stood, picked up the bits of clothing and began to dress herself. Assuming, so quickly that I almost called her name, the shape of Fanny Bundle.

When I saw who it was, I pulled back, left without making a sound in the soft sand. I was sure Fanny and Ned had been together, could almost see their energetic coupling in the hollow, the gyrations of arms and legs, the tangle in bright cloth.

Sick and confused, with no idea of what I should do, I walked for hours before turning back towards the Cape. Although Meg had once considered me the spiritual leader of the place, in recent times she had relieved me of this role. The Cape was now safely within the fold of Methodism and this, I finally concluded, absolved me of responsibility.

In the days and nights that followed, I tried to forget what I had seen, but the thought of Ned and Fanny was continually before me. Their sin stained everything I did. I avoided Ned, stopped going to his house and stopped reading to the children in the school room. I tried to stop thinking about Lavinia.

Yet I could not banish the feeling that it was my duty to do something about Ned's adultery. No matter that he was not Catholic, no matter that I was a disgraced priest—I could not escape the terrible fact that he and Fanny were committing a mortal sin, a sin not only against chastity but against Mary, who was the wife of one and the mother of the other. With those thoughts came the realization that Ned and Mary were truly married in the eyes of the church, and that I, who had performed the sacrament, carried some responsibility for bringing him to contrition.

The euphoria of the summer vanished completely. I began to read St. Augustine again and say my prayers each night. I was shamed to see how far I'd fallen from my vows.

"Servants of the Lord must not consort with women, for of all the sins a priest can commit, the most severely punished on earth is lust. It has been the downfall of angels, the cause of the deluge and the source of fire and brimstone that destroyed Sodom and Gomorrah," I read, thanking God I had not broken my vow of celibacy in deed. I asked forgiveness for having broken it in my thoughts.

The distaste I had felt in the beginning for the Andrews family returned and I avoided being in their company as much as possible. I resolved that when spring came I would leave the Cape. I would find a Catholic community where, if I could not be a priest, I could at least live within the comfort and solace of the Church.

To my eternal sorrow, I did not have the courage, either as a priest or as a friend, to confront Ned, to point out the danger he was in, to try and bring him to a state of grace. And that was my sin, a greater one perhaps than his.

The terrible sickness that came did not surprise me. It had grown like a malignant plant, out of the miasma of evil that had fallen on the Cape. I do not mean that I welcomed the sickness, that I did not pray for it to be taken from us, that I did not suffer to see others suffering—only that it seemed part of the sin and gloom that surrounded me.

I felt more alone that winter than I ever had before, more alone than ever I had felt during my first solitary winter on the Cape. I worked along with the others at the grim tasks, cleaned the filth, buried the bodies, poured lime over them and, like the others, grieved, especially for Josh Vincent whose knowledge and kindness had saved all of us many times.

Once during that terrible season, I did come near asking Ned to take thought for his immortal soul. Passing the Andrews house one day, I came unexpectedly upon him, leading his son Isaac around the yard. Thin as skeletons they both were, with ash grey faces. The boy held onto his father and they limped with painful slowness around the house, looking like spectres risen from the dead. A wave of compassion swept over me. I took a few steps towards Ned, who was so intent on keeping Isaac moving and holding him upright that he did not see me. I turned away, but the scene bothered me: could the same man who harboured such evil show such compassion?

Even in my isolated state, word of the white bear reached me. Charlie Vincent, who had become something of a scholar and sometimes brought questions to me, told me that Ned had seen an animal the size of a small horse coming in off the ice. I paid no attention to the story and told him he shouldn't either.

A few days later, I went up to Ben Andrews's house thinking to have him replace some supports under the wharf. Lavinia was sitting at the table as I came in but she immediately got up and, skirting around me as if I carried the plague, went through the door.

Ben gave me a puzzled look, "Thomas, I expects 'tis none of my business—but is there bad blood 'tweenst you and Vinnie? And Ned too—'tis a good long spell since I seen you in his place."

I just shook my head, and we began listing what we would need to repair the wharf. Minutes later the door burst open, and Lavinia came in, screaming that Ned was being killed by the white bear.

And what did I do? Nothing! I stopped, watched as the beast tore at the two bodies, stood and let a woman run past me. I left Mary Bundle to try and drive the beast off.

I'll never forget it, never stop dreaming, will see again and again that dirty white animal rear up against the sky, see the bodies bleeding in the snow, see myself frozen in time, waiting, hoping I would wake.

And so Ned died. Died in a state of sin and Mary a widow, left with a houseful of children and carrying another—and with her daughter Fanny carrying a child—a child Mary said was mine.

I discovered this right after Ned's and Isaac's funeral when Mary cornered me—came stalking into the store, looking as if she would gladly kill me. Mary is not a subtle woman, and her anger is frightening, but when she has achieved what she wants, she reverts to silence and good sense. As Meg has often said, Mary has no side doors.

"I never trusted you, Thomas Hutchings, you with your swarmy ways, comin' pretendin' you was Ned's friend—you're like all the rest of your kind—friendly when it suits ya. Where was you the last few months? Where was you when Ned needed ya, and where was that God-damned gun I told you should be kept here? Stupid and a coward too, bejesus, that's what you are! 'Tis your fault Ned's dead—and don't you ever forget it! I knows I won't!" She spit this much at me before she had even closed the door, then leaning against it, she accused me of raping Fanny, of fathering a child on the girl.

I could see Mary's mouth move but the words no longer registered on my shocked mind. Dressed in black and half hidden in the shadows of the fishing room, her face shone out, sharp and pale with hate. She looked like one of the wraiths come from hell and I did not need to hear her words to know my doom.

Fanny, she said, had told Lavinia all about my lecherous ways and Lavinia had told her: "...and I'm here to tell you! You got to pay—you got to be responsible for this child, Thomas Hutchings—and for Fanny too, God knows I can't, I got enough to contend with!"

So, I thought, God does have a sense of humour. It was something I had often wondered about.

I must have smiled, because Mary's mouth stopped moving, her hand came up, and she hit me across the face with all her might.

"...laugh, would ya—we'll see who'll laugh. There be no bastards brought home on my floor, Thomas Hutchings—you'll marry the girl and that real quick!"

"Yes," I said. It was all so easy, so clear, so simple, almost as if it had been divinely ordained. And I was so tired.

I married Fanny. We lived together in the store for five weeks. We lived as a father and daughter might if they did not know each other well. I never touched her, and we hardly exchanged a word.

I wondered why she had named me as the father of her child, but I never asked. She spent her time as she always had, roaming about the beach and back in the woods and bog. I think she was happy to be out from under her mother's control. I would like to think she was happy during the last weeks of her life.

I carried Fanny's body up to her mother's house. It seemed the right thing to do. Meg had already cleared the table and spread a white sheet over it. The room was full of women: Mary herself and Annie Vincent and her mother, Ned's daughter Jane and Patience, who sat with someone's baby in her arms, gazing into nothingness as she rocked the child and hummed. Her humming was the only sound in the room when I put Fanny's body down on the table, turned and walked out. Lavinia was not there.

I had not seen the Indian, but from Meg's and Sarah's description of him I guessed he was the man whose leg I had splinted up. Sarah said Peter had been in a rage and had chased after him like a mad man.

"He never even picked up the gun he'd thrown down—still I allow he'll make away with the savage if he catches him," Sarah told me, with a quick look, hoping, I think, that I would voice approval for such action, but I said nothing.

As I walked away from Mary Bundle's house, it was getting on towards dark. Not even in the dead of winter had I seen the place so still, not a living thing was in sight, neither animal nor child, nor the birds that usually circle the Cape at dusk. I was sure that by now Peter had tracked down the wounded man. They would have fought, and one of them would be lying dead in sand or bog somewhere behind the Cape.

I walked down the wet beach where the incoming tide was sweeping away all signs of what had happened that day. Up in the dunes I saw footsteps and blood, and later, a place where the Indian had fallen and lost the horned headdress. I picked it up and carried it, following a trail that I could tell was leading to the old hiding place in the hill.

He was there. Sprawled face-down across the smoke blackened stones, blood clotting in the sand around his head, the long iron rod I had once given him lying across his broken skull.

I stood on the rim of the crater, searching the dark hills, the dunes around me and the long crescent of beach below. Nothing moved but the sea. I cupped my hand to my mouth and called out Peter Vincent's name. There was no sound, no movement. I didn't call again.

I went down into the pit and touched the Indian, although I knew he was dead. I rolled him over but could not bring myself to close his eyes, startling blue they were, staring up at the darkening sky.

My hands were covered with blood, sticky and still faintly warm. I picked up the rod and walked all the way back down to the water where I washed it and my hands.

I found Dolph Way helping Ben in the shed, and asked them to come up to the hill with me. We wrapped the Indian in a blanket I'd taken from my bed and carried him back down the hill. The Indian had been big; thin, but hard and well muscled. He made a heavy load even for three men. We took his body to the shed and put him down on strips of lumber laid between two of Ben's sawhorses. I placed the strange headdress on his chest the way I'd seen done with bishops and cardinals.

A night and a day passed, and no one set eyes on Peter Vincent. Late last night I went up to the house he'd started to build, thinking he might be sleeping there. It is a roofless house with staring empty holes in the walls. I remember his anger the day he came home and found I had married Fanny. He must have been building this house for her.

Like his father and older brother, Peter is a master woodsman. He could live off the land for months without coming near a community. Unlike the rest of his family, he has always been quick-tempered and solitary. Now he has committed the first murder on the Cape. I suspect it will become one of the secrets we are so good at keeping.

Last night Meg Andrews, Ben's wife, came to see me, knocking on the door of the fish store for the first time since I've known her. Meg has always stood up for me and, despite the many times I have denied it, has never quite relinquished the hope that I might be a minister of some acceptable Protestant faith.

Meg is a strong woman, as strong in her way as Mary Bundle, but less direct than Mary and less self-centred. Meg, although she does not know it, has set herself to civilize this place. Through her encouragement the school was started, and under her direction the church will eventually be built. It is Meg who says she will make a preacher, the highest calling she can conceive of, out of her son Willie.

Somewhere in Meg's ancestry is the blood of old kings and queens. She looks completely unlike other women on the Cape who seem always to dress in bits of clothing snatched hastily off a nail. Meg's skirts fall neatly, her face is always clean, her hair always coiled around her head in a thick roll. She looks like one of the tall women who hold up the corners of buildings: goddesses who cup the sun and moon in their hands.

I let her in and waited as she stood, palms pressed together over her clean apron like a child preparing a recitation. "I think we should have a word of prayer, Thomas."

We both knelt then on the floor of my store, on the dirty boards that have rarely been scrubbed or swept, and Meg Andrews prayed for me and for herself and asked forgiveness for any wrong she had done me. Then she prayed for Fanny, for the Indian and for Peter, asking God to keep him safe.

When we stood, she looked more at ease. She had gotten her bearings. "I hope, Thomas, you will find it in your heart to forgive us," she said, and then, "Thomas, what will become of the baby?"

It must have taken a full minute before the question had any meaning for me. The baby. There was a baby, of course, something had been born down there on the beach. I'd seen Meg wrap it in white cloth and carry it away. I had not thought about it since.

"We think—I do anyway, that the Indian fathered the child—still, it's Mary's grandson," she said.

I did not, could not, speak. Still trying to hold onto the idea that a living child existed, a child I had thought to be Ned's, I could not grasp what she was saying about the Indian.

Fanny's child fathered by the Indian? All the blame I'd laid on Ned, all my bitterness towards him, all founded on nothing? Was it possible? Or, and the thought came to me clear as crystal, founded on my own lustful reflection? This I could not face, could not think about. I still cannot.

"I'm leaving the Cape. I expect a Gosse vessel within the fortnight and I'll be going then," I said.

Meg nodded, "Mary said most likely you'd go—you know, Thomas, Mary's a strange one, even stranger since Ned died. She's not even caring for that little girl she had herself. Our Pash has it all the time, day and night. This new baby—it can't be left with Mary."

She waited for me to speak before going on. "The baby will carry your name, you knows that, Thomas." There was no inflection in her voice, she was simply stating a fact—the child would be considered my son, would be called Hutchings.

We settled the matter before she left. With the help of her blind daughter, Meg will care for Fanny's child. I took all the coins Caleb Gosse had paid me over the years and, holding back barely enough for my passage to St. John's, passed Meg the rest. She took the money, knotted it into a handkerchief and tucked it in her apron pocket.

"I'll do me best for the youngster. Thomas—there's something else, something Mary wants me to ask you...."

"When has Mary Bundle needed someone to speak for her?" I was suddenly weary of them all, even Meg. I wanted done with them, longed to go back, or forward, to some orderly, simpler, life.

Meg was smiling, "I know—but even Mary's gall's got limits—well, what she wants—what she wants is your job. The job Caleb Gosse pays you for."

"But Mary can't read or write." I did not say, "and she's a woman," I knew Mary Bundle was capable as any man, although Caleb Gosse might not think so.

"She says she can reckon. Vinnie's been teachin' her and can help her if she gets stuck. Mary says, why should Caleb Gosse know you're left the Cape? He never comes here, anyway. Thomas, I don't ask that you deceive the man, just not let him know you're goin'. He'd be gettin' a good worker in Mary, and you knows she got a lot of mouths to feed."

Reluctantly, I agreed not to tell Caleb Gosse of my leaving. I even promised to ask Alex Brennan not to mention the matter.

So I left the Cape without ceremony. Without saying goodbye to anyone except Meg Andrews, without telling my employer, without exchanging one word with Lavinia Andrews, I left without looking at the face of the child that will be called my son.

We were well out past the sunkers, I was leaning against the rail, gazing back at the place I had poured more than fifteen years of my life into. A wretched enough little place where half a dozen shacks cling helter skelter to the raw rocks—the only sign man had set foot ashore. As I stood there, thinking how paltry were the results of all my worry and labour, Alex Brennan came up and put a package wrapped in brown paper into my hands.

"Here, I been directed to give you this when we got outside the Cape." His voice was gruff, and he turned away without another word.

It was her journal—the book I'd thought of stealing. Sitting here in the galley of a vessel ploughing away from the Cape, I've read everything she's written. How could God have made a man so blind as I've been?

My life on the Cape is over. In a few days I will be in St. John's. I remember nothing of that town except a row of crooked buildings and the stench that filled the harbour. I will find a Catholic church there and make my confession, I will receive absolution, do whatever penance is required of me. I will beg to be taken again into the priesthood. I will return to Ireland and face the consequences of what happened there half a lifetime ago.

Chapter 19

The stench of rancid oil and filth still hung over St. John's harbour, but as Alex Brennan and I walked up the hill to the Catholic chapel, I could identify a profusion of individual smells: the familiar smell of fish, the clean wood of a cabinet maker's workshop, the stink of a tannery, the pleasant aromas from rope lofts and bakeries, a cobbler's shop, the smell of horses and oats and the smell of strong spirits wafting from grog shops that occupied every corner. Although it was barely past noon, these drinking establishments were already crowded. Intoxicated people, both men and women, overflowed onto steps and into the muddy street.

One of the public houses displayed the first likeness of Victoria I had seen, and I stopped to study the picture. The new queen is little more than a child and will doubtless be as weak-minded as her uncles. I asked Alex if he thought it would be a good thing if the British Empire vanished. The canny man talked for ten minutes without giving me an answer.

Despite the squalor of the streets and the poverty of the people, the town exudes a rough energy, teeming with life, throbbing with sound. Handcarts and horse drawn wagons squeaked and rumbled by. All around us there was hammering and sawing, the blaze of forges and the ringing of hammer on anvil, dogs barking and the shouts of street urchins who hawk molasses candy, painted whistles, pin wheels and less savory things.

"Buy now mister or you'll be gypped by the Maggoty Cove crooks," one dirty-faced youngster yelled as he pushed a tray of grubby sweets at me and, when Alex told him to be off, said, "Bugger ye then, ya black papists!"

I asked if there was any friction between the Protestants and Catholics in the town and Alex laughed. "Not usually, though you'll hear a lot of that kind of name calling. It don't come to much unless it's stirred up by merchants lookin' for cheap labour or by the political crowd wantin' to set one lot against the other for their own reasons."

Inside the chapel, a two story wooden building only a little more sturdy than the houses surrounding it, we found a solitary nun laying a fresh cloth on the altar. Alex introduced her as Sister Xaverius, one of the Presentation Sisters who had established a convent in a vacated public house nearby.

"You'll not find a blessed soul here until after dark, Father, they're all in back working on the Bishop's new church." The soft accents of Ireland so dazed me that we were out in the pathway again before I realized she had called me Father.

Looking slightly embarrassed, Alex pointed quickly to the building across the yard and began to explain the layout. "That's the Episcopal Palace where the Bishop and his personal staff live, but he'll be up at the building site, too. On this side, joined to the chapel, Father Fitzgerald lives, he's the man you should see, I expect. He's the one in charge of the day-to-day running of the parish, oversees the priests, things like that. Why don't you come over to my place for a wash and a meal? We can come back later when Father Fitzgerald gets home."

I insisted that Alex go on home to his wife, told him I'd leave my belongings in the porch of the chapel and find my own way up to the construction site. Shocked by the pleasure I'd derived from the sights and sounds of the town, I was afraid that if I stepped aside from the path I had set myself, I would be led into new byways, detours longer even than the one I had just returned from.

Four boys who had followed us up from the road stood near the gate, openly straining to hear each word we spoke. Alex called to one of them and directed him to take me up to the old garrison woodyard where the church was being built.

"I'll come by before I sail, Thomas, and see how you're making out," Alex said. I heard the hesitation before he used my name and shook his hand feeling I was losing my last friend.

Since Alex had told me there were probably eight thousand Catholics in St. John's, I expected to find a reasonably sized church under construction. What I saw when we arrived at the hill was a vast hole in the centre of several acres of churned-up earth, all roughly enclosed with wooden posts, some of which were already falling over. Inside the muddy chasm, hundreds of people worked.

I told the boy I had nothing to give him, but he ran off cheerfully enough to find Father Fitzgerald while I stood gaping, completely absorbed by the sight of so many people and animals working in what seemed to be chaos. Most of them laboured with picks and shovels, but others, men, women and even children, carried buckets and pushed handcarts filled with rocks and dirt, which they dumped into mounds that were rising to form a kind of wall around the gigantic hole.

Some of the digging men stood knee deep in black water, and each swing of their shovels sent a spray of mud over people working nearby. Everyone and everything inside the fenced area was layered with mud. Mud covered faces, hands, clothing, tools and the piles of quarry stone being unloaded block by block from mud-covered wagons pulled by mud-covered horses. On most surfaces the wet ooze had dried to a dull, gritty grey. The scene reminded me of Biblical paintings of slaves building the pyramids—except in such pictures the artists had added sunshine and colour. Here everything was mud-grey.

The only colour came from the flame of a fire built squarely in the middle of the excavation, probably where the altar will one day be. Women tended an iron pot suspended above the fire, ladling something into bowls, tearing hunks of bread from loaves stacked in a bucket, passing the food to men who stood and gulped it down before returning to their work.

I did not realize that I was standing in one of the pathways, where rocks had been laid to keep cartwheels from bogging down in mud, until someone tugged at my elbow and asked sternly if I had no better occupation than blocking the way for those who wanted to work.

I turned to meet the eyes of a man slightly taller than myself, a thin man with a face so long, so narrow and pointed, that he resembled a very wise horse. An ageless face, showing considerable annoyance. Covered from neck to foot in an oilskin greatcoat and as mud-spattered as the other workers, he held a rope that steadied a towering pile of cut stone being pulled by two exhausted animals. A man I could not see was holding the rope on the other side of the wagon and murmuring encouragement to the horses in a language I recognized as Gaelic.

The slowness of my reply did not please the horse-faced man. He commanded me out of the path, "...or better still, here, take this rope. Careful, man! Keep it tight and follow this wagon down to that corner—over there where the long ditch is."

He handed me the rope and turned to walk back to the next wagon, calling over his shoulder to my unseen partner, "Watch it Danny, you've got a green hand on this side. Make sure the blocks are laid down by the line now, don't dump them in a pile."

I worked through the afternoon, helping the men with wagons descend the slippery path between the gateway and the edge of the excavation, easing blocks of granite down in a row beside holes where the footings will go. After several trips back and forth, I began to see some order in what was happening around me, imagining an outline, like the shadow of a great church, in the pattern of grey blocks.

Near dark, workers began to leave the site: men with tools, women carrying baskets of food and babies, calling out to toddlers, grabbing a child, spitting on their aprons and scrubbing mud from grimy faces. Most of the rag-tag crew trooped down the hill to the rickety houses I had seen earlier, but some had more miserable shelter. I watched them crawl into shacks I had thought to be mounds of tar paper, canvas and discarded wood piled outside the fence.

While I hesitated, wondering if I could find my way back to the chapel where I'd left my books and clothing, Father Fitzgerald found me.

"You must be the stranger young Tim said was looking for me." He leaned forward and peered through his spectacles, "I can see by the look of you that you've earned your supper—come on along with us then, we'll talk later."

Father Fitzgerald is stout and past middle-age. He always seems a little out of breath and always has a surprised look, caused in part by his spectacles, which enlarge his eyes making them look like round marbles in his round face, and partly by his astonishment at finding himself, a classical scholar trained to translate medieval manuscripts, on the edge of the world ministering to a parish of illiterate Irish peasants.

As we turned away from the excavation, I saw three men walking slowly around the perimeters of the foundation holes. The horse-faced man I had encountered earlier was in the lead, giving orders, it seemed, to the others, a clerk carrying a roll of drawings, and a priest who was writing in a notebook. I asked Father Fitzgerald who the tall man was.

"That, my son, is Dr. Fleming. Michael Anthony Fleming, Bishop of Carpasia and Vicar of the Roman Catholic Church in this place."

Father Fitzgerald's near-sighted eyes gazed sadly across the huge excavation at his Bishop. "A holy man of great determination and spirit—a Franciscan."

As we followed five younger priests down the hill I prayed that Bishop Fleming would not remember me the next time we met.

No one talked. We were caked with mud and too tired to exchange pleasantries. We reached the chapel yard and Father Fitzgerald said, "Since you are a stranger within our gates I should offer you the use of our tub and the hot water that Mrs. Tobin has doubtless been warming for me—but I am too tired, too old and too selfish to make such a sacrifice."

In the hallway, I could see the priest's face. Where he had wiped the dirt away it was pale as death and his hand, reaching for the railing, shook.

"It is not serious," he assured me, "I am not well suited to the part I am called upon to play, but no doubt with a hot bath and God's help I can do all things—even be an overseer in hell. Go along with Father Dowling, he'll show you an ingenious way to get clean."

When we were finally clean—a process that took some time and consisted of the six of us, one by one, standing under a small brook that had been channelled into a wooden sluice so that it splashed down in a fenced corner of the yard—we ate together at a long table. The refectory was a pleasant room, running the full length of the second storey. It had three windows that looked down over the lower streets and the harbour.

Father Fitzgerald, bathed and dressed in well-cut clerical garb, looked much improved. He introduced me, as I had asked him to, as Thomas Commins. The others did not seem in the least curious. I later learned they had been told by Father Fitzgerald to ask me no questions.

We spoke of the day's work, of words that had been exchanged between the Bishop and Mr. McGrath the architect concerning a change the Bishop wanted made in the plans. Father Fitzgerald mentioned Bishop Fleming's health. The Bishop's sister was concerned, had asked him to help persuade her brother into taking a short holiday at his estate outside of town.

"Persuading our Bishop of anything against his will is not easy," one priest said.

The conversation faltered and we ate in silence until Father Fitzgerald began to tell me about the city which, he said has a floating population: soldiers from the fort, sailors off foreign ships, naval seamen and, during the fishing season, hundreds of fishermen newly come—along with tricksters, cutpurses, fortune seekers and the dissipated younger sons of every country in Europe. All these, the priest said, prey upon the poor, taking every possible advantage of them before vanishing through the 'Narrows', as the harbour entrance is called.

I asked what the history of the Catholic church in St. John's was, and heard a story similar to those Father Francis had told me in Ireland: years of proscription, of imprisonments, whippings, of deportations for holding mass.

"That's all changed now, of course," Father Fitzgerald said. "Largely because of the Bishop's work, we have friends among the town's most influential people, and at least half the twelve thousand souls in St. John's are Catholics with many more in the remote outports."

Thinking I had newly come to the island the others began to tell me of the severity of the climate and the isolation of the outports. I ate in almost complete silence, wondering what they would think of me tomorrow. If, as I hoped, I could re-enter the priesthood, I must tell at least Father Fitzgerald the story of my life.

"I would like to talk with you alone, Father," I said as we rose from the table.

He nodded, saying we must first go to the chapel for vespers.

"I cannot, Father—I must make my confession first," I said. But he told me to come along to prayers, and I followed him down the corridor that joined the residence to the chapel I had seen earlier.

It was dimmer now, more beautiful that it had seemed in raw daylight. Bare beams, lovingly polished, curved over the altar, which was just a table covered with the long linen cloth we had watched the nun smooth in place. Two brass candlesticks threw red shadows on the ebony crucifix hanging on the wall behind the altar.

The familiar scent of incense and candle wax, the terrible symbol of the cross and the nailed man, even the sound of feet shuffling softly up the bare aisles, brought me to an abrupt halt just inside the door. I stood there, trying to control my breathing, unprepared for the wave of joy that left me weak. The other priests moved around me and past me. I eased myself down into the nearest pew, well back against the side wall, shut my eyes and let the old words work their power.

"Pour forth, we beseech Thee, O Lord, Thy grace into our hearts, that we to whom the Incarnation of Christ, Thy Son, was made known by the message of an angel, made by His passion and cross be brought to the glory of His resurrection, through the same Christ Our Lord, Amen."

I sat there long after the service ended, engulfed by peace, comforted, convinced, even before I spoke to Father Fitzgerald, that I had at last come home.

Despite my resolve, I have written nothing in this book since the night of my arrival. An account of the tedious processing of my case through the various tribunals of ecclesiastical bureaucracy in Quebec, onto what I pray will be its way to the Roman Curia, would make dull reading. I had thought, though, to keep an unofficial record of the building of Dr. Fleming's cathedral and have not found time even for that, despite each day seeing a hundred things that should be written down.

By nature I am a clerk. It is the job I do best and Dr. Fleming, not slow to spot any talent that can be turned to good use in the building of his cathedral (others may refer to it as a church), has set me to checking supplies when they arrive from ships or from the warehouses of merchants. Should the count be under the number charged, I am to go directly to the firm's business office and ensure that we receive full measure, and, if possible, extra for the trouble this shortage has caused. If the count is over I am to make note of it and see that special prayers are said for the soul of our benefactor.

On the construction site, only the overseers, skilled artisans and those tradesmen who cannot be cajoled into volunteering their goods and services are paid. The poor work in exchange for their midday meal—a measure of the high regard in which they all hold the Bishop.

Their lack of regard for Father Fitzgerald, who, if it were given to him to decide, would sell every stone, nail and brick to feed and shelter them, is also remarkable. They laugh at the priest's misery and behind his back call him "feather fingers" because he shudders each time his hands touch dirt.

Bishop Fleming is a gentleman, too. As Father Dowling, the English priest who acts as his secretary, says, "You'd have no doubt about it if you could hear him discussing wine at Government House."

Yet when the Bishop works, he gets as dirty as any ditch digger, and revels in it. He relishes the shouting men, the sound of tools being used, delights in supervising the laying of courses, the coming and going of wagons, the raising of scaffolding. Bishop Fleming knows every one of the workers by name, and who their fathers were, which is more than half of them know themselves. He knows which county, even which parish in Ireland they are from, can recite the names of their relatives and remembers to ask after them when his travels take him near their birthplace. For these traits the people forgive him anything, even roast pig, wine and candlelight dinners with Governor Harvey.

Work at the site, the political intrigue, the local newspapers that Father Dowling brings to us, the noise and clamour of the town, where roads are being built in every direction, and the frequent arrival of ships with news of England, Portugal, Italy, America and Quebec, give me the feeling that I am at the centre of a maelstrom—living a life so far removed from the Cape that it hardly seems to be in the same country.

It requires great effort now to think of them back there catching fish, doing all the summer work—eating, sleeping, walking about living in a world so small that it would almost fit into the great hole we are making for the foundations of the church. My wasted years on Cape Random are fading from memory. Slowly, I am making my way back to the certainty of faith I knew before I led men to their deaths down that tree-lined avenue in Ireland.

——— ——— ———

There has been no time to write. The Bishop says he could put a thousand good men to work on his cathedral and not have a man to spare. Since he does not have a thousand good men and must perforce make do with us, he drives us mercilessly. We cannot sit on a rock, stop to contemplate the scaffolding or gaze out at the harbour but he is there, offering a level, a saw, rope, shovel or, for me, the suggestion that I count something to make sure we have not been gypped.

I am in no frame of mind to write after such a day's work. So, through last winter and this summer, Lavinia's journal has lain on a shelf above my cot in the attic dormitory where we sleep amid barrels of apples and potatoes, until today, when I met the girl Emma.

When I saw her on the lower path I thought, at first, I was looking at Lavinia—a terribly gaunt, ragged Lavinia, dirty and unkempt, carrying a pail in one hand and dragging a starved-looking child with the other. Such sights are common in St. John's, where widows go from shop to tavern begging scrub jobs in exchange for food. But this woman had Lavinia's long confident strides, and her hair, though darker than I remembered, glowed red in the last flecks of daylight. My stomach tightened as if I'd been dropped into ice. I called out, but she paid no heed, and I stood, watching as she walked away through the dirt and confusion of the street. Then I ran after her.

She stopped and turned to face me, jerking the child around with her. She knew me at once. "Mr. Hutchings—what you doin' in town?"

As soon as she spoke, I recognized her: Emma, Meg's and Ben's daughter who had left the Cape with Jane to find work in St. John's. Jane married and came back but I could not recall anyone, even Meg, saying what had become of Emma.

She was well along in pregnancy, and her rising stomach pulled her skirt up in front exposing grey-blue legs and dirty feet. The boy, too, was barefoot, although it is fall and the muddy streets are already beginning to freeze.

Having stopped her, I could think of nothing to say. We stood eyeing each other as animals sometimes do, until, rather stupidly, I asked how she'd been. Then I realized that both she and the child were shivering. Before she could answer, but not before I'd seen a flash of derision cross her face, I took her arm and turned into the nearest grog shop, an establishment of unsavoury reputation called The Black Dog.

The place was almost empty. We sat down at a long plank table occupied at the other end by a sailor, sleeping like a baby with his head on the table and his arms dangling over the sides. Once seated, Emma looked embarrassed and began raking her fingers through her matted hair.

I do not wear what they call here the Roman collar, but there is, I think, a clerical air about me, "the smell of incense and port," Father Dowling calls it. When the owner, who is said to deal in goods stolen from ships and warehouses, came over he eyed me up and down. "Well Em, proper odd fish you hauled in this time!"

She ignored the man, and I asked if it was possible to have some food. He allowed that the woman out back was cooking a stew, disappeared and returned with three steaming bowls that would have done credit to the Bishop's table.

"How's Mam and me Pap—and how's Lizzie? I knowed her little girl was took, and Isaac and Uncle Ned too, when ye had that sickness. But I heard nothin' now for months."

The girl seemed to have gotten a garbled account of events on the Cape. I wonder who could have told her. She sat warming her hands on the bowl of stew but the boy had lifted his and was slurping great mouthfuls. Emma snatched the bowl from him, slammed it down on the table, picked up a pewter spoon and poked it at the child. "Here, ya little brute, eat like a 'uman, can't ya!"

The boy, who must have been about three, kicked her under the table and the two got into a scuffle as if they were both children. It was hard to believe that Meg Andrews is the mother and grandmother of such street urchins. When the distraction was over, I had still not decided what to tell the girl.

I pointed to her untouched stew and we ate in silence while I tried to organize my thoughts. Clearly she did not know I had left the Cape and seemed not to realize how Ned had died. Did she know anything of Fanny's death or of what had proceeded it?

"Your parents were well when I left, that was some time ago now. You knew about Patience, I suppose, I don't think her eyesight will ever come back, but she keeps busy. She seems to have adopted Mary's last baby."

And the other baby? Who adopted him, I wondered. Suddenly all the people left behind came to life in my memory, faces, hands, gestures. The hills and houses, the sea, the stones on the shore, people—people I had not thought about for sixteen months crowded into my mind as clearly as if they were in the room with us.

"How is Jane doin' with her new husband?" I heard Emma's voice and was aware that she was looking at me with great curiosity, wondering perhaps, at my long silence.

"Jane is well, or was well—Dolph seems to fit in—he works hard and that suits Mary Bundle. They are, were, living with Mary."

"What are you doin' then, here in town?"

It was the question she had begun with. I told her I lived in St. John's now, that I'd left the Cape for good, that I worked for the church. That was what I said, "for the church." I remembered how her mother had always insisted I was a clergyman, how she'd compelled me to baptise the baby who would have been Emma's brother.

I tried to divert her attention by asking if she ever saw Alex Brennan.

"No—no we don't have much to do with respectable people down where I lives," she smiled and I saw her mother's cheek bones and lovely mouth. She might be pretty but for the dirt and emaciation.

She finished her stew and sat studying the spoon, turning it this way and that, as if she'd never seen its like before. Then, without looking at me she said, "I'm married to Peter Vincent now—but he don't go down home no more."

"So!" I could say nothing else.

I thought of the Indian with his head bashed in, recalled the story of how Peter had chopped his brother's hand and how he'd turned savage on the day he found me married to Fanny. I looked at the girl across from me and wondered what her life must be like with Peter Vincent.

"Aye, so!" she mocked me and slid the spoon into the pocket of her skirt. "Of course 'tis little I sees of 'im. He always was one to disappear. Not steady and not likely to change, Peter is. Still—he turns up wintertime." She gazed around the empty tavern as if expecting him to rise from the floor.

After another long silence she jumped up, pulling the dozing boy to his feet. "I'll be seein' ya, Father," she smiled saucily at the title, "or maybe I won't—if you sees Captain Brennan, ask him to tell Mam I'm doin' fine, tell her I'll be down to see her when me ship comes in."

She snatched up her bucket and swung through the door while I was paying the owner. When I got into the street there wasn't a sign of her.

With darkness the fog had rolled back in. I walked through it up the hill, listening to the fog horns and muffled whistles of ships in the Narrows and thinking about Emma, remembering that her mother had been a good friend, perhaps my only friend apart from Ned.

The girl was obviously in need, and I wondered if I could get work for her, cleaning for Father Fitzgerald or helping the Sisters in the charity school. It's not likely. Every day brings a stream of our own people looking for such jobs. Still, I should have found out where she lives. St. John's is not a big town but, as she said, you only meet your own kind—and not all of them. I have seen Alex Brennan only once since the day I landed.

——— ——— ———

It is spring again, and the Bishop has returned from what his secretary Father Dowling calls "begging in high places." In addition to promises of large donations, the Bishop has brought with him a new superintendent from Cork and two master-masons to oversee the stone cutting.

The cavernous hole is again filled with noise and confusion, just as it was when I came to St. John's. The corner pillars are now in place. Scaffolding and the great wooden hoist can be seen outlined against the sky from every part of town. On summer evenings before dark, townspeople walk out to look, marvelling at the size of the building growing out of the heap of rubble and dirt. Catholics are very proud of it. Others seem divided, one group maintaining that the Bishop is mad to erect such a huge church so far away from the middle of town, the rest that it's a disgrace for Catholics to be putting up such a building when the Church of England is still meeting in the decrepit garrison chapel.

Such talk has brought on a flurry of building that has, indirectly, made our job all the more expensive. The cost of renting horses, for example, has doubled. Sent to make inquiries as to why this was so, I discovered that a certain Timothy Drew, hearing of plans to build a House of Assembly as well as an Anglican cathedral, set himself this winter to purchase every nag and cart he could come by. After considerable bickering with an employee of Mr. Drew's. I made the cartage arrangements at a price I considered outrageous.

I never saw the man Drew until he came one day to talk with the Bishop. Short, with unhealthy yellow skin, Mr. Drew dresses impeccably, takes snuff from an elegant jewelled box, and constantly consults a large gold watch attached to a chain draped across his round middle. Father Dowling says the man has for years operated a very successful business dealing in damaged and second hand merchandise, and that he has recently married a well-to-do widow and is now expanding his interests into other areas.

Every day we became more concerned with the condition of wagons hired from Mr. Drew and with the fact that he sends only one man to drive the wagon and to keep the precariously piled loads steady at the same time. This is almost impossible when climbing up the hills and even worse coming down the steep slope into the excavation. Before long both Father Fitzgerald and Father Dowling were coming to me with stories of overturned carts and injuries to men and animals.

When I approached the Bishop suggesting that I should make Drew's agent send two men with each load, he ordered me to do nothing of the kind: "The man has given us a good price and we certainly cannot pay for the additional man. Send one of our own people to help steady the loads once they come into our own ground—or do it yourself. I seem to recall you were good at it," he said with no trace of a smile.

The next time Father Dowling complained to me about the carts, I repeated what the Bishop's instructions.

He swore an unpriestlike oath. "That's because Drew's wife has promised a stained glass window for the church, and we might not get it if we annoy her husband."

The young priest looked around at the slowly rising walls, at the huge piles of stone that lay everywhere: "Have you ever heard of stone sickness,

Thomas? I fear our Bishop has caught the disease," he shook his head and said softly, "and we are like to die of it."

Father Dowling may be right but it is the Bishop himself who is most likely to die. The man is up there at the first glint of dawn, standing alone, waiting impatiently for the rest of us to arrive. He spends all day striding around amid the dirt and noise, picking his way between the jumble of handwinches, treadwheels and ropes, crawling under scaffolds, pacing out the foundations. One could grow tired just watching him.

His sister, fearing he will starve himself to death, has taken to visiting the site each day around noon. She brings a basket and follows him, passing pieces of bread, cheese and cups of tea to the Bishop. Sometimes he eats absent-mindedly, other times he passes the food back to her, telling her quite rudely to go home to her husband.

As summer progressed, I began to see another reason why we were having more and more accidents.

Our people have begun making a celebration of each pillar raised. They tie branches of evergreen to columns and get merry around the fire on days when a cap stone has been eased into position.

At first Bishop Fleming accepted these ceremonies with good grace, but when it became apparent that the men, and women too, were lacing their tea with rum, he began lecturing them on the evils of drink. Then, as he predicted, someone was killed. A young man stumbled and fell from a spider-walk smashing down across a pile of granite.

The Bishop discovered that a crock of liquor had been passed around in a dim corner underneath the scaffold. He went into a rage, smashed the bottle and swore he would excommunicate the next person who brought a drop of strong drink inside the cathedral fence.

I expected the site to be empty the next morning. Instead, more people turned up for work than the day before. I have become convinced that most people live all their lives waiting for some great cause, for some leader who can command their confidence, give their lives purpose. In Bishop Fleming they have found such a man. I wonder if he will continue to hold them when his cathedral is finished—if it ever is finished.

Chapter 20

Several times during the winter I have gone back to the Black Dog where I talked to Emma Andrews—Emma Vincent now, according to her, though I cannot imagine Peter making promises before any minister—but I have not seen her. The tavern keeper tells me she's not been seen for months although she came regularly to scrub his place last year. I left three shillings, asking that he give them to her if she comes in. I doubt the man's trustworthiness but it is the only thing I can do to ease my conscience.

It is December, but work on the cathedral will not stop this winter as it did last year when the Bishop was away. Under his direction part of the east transept has been enclosed with rough lumber and canvas to make a large workshop with a pit in the centre where we can keep a fire going all winter.

As the work progresses, we are more and more in need of skilled craftsmen. Because of this, the Bishop has convinced a mason and two of the stonecutters to stay behind this winter and teach some of our people their trades. Since these men are members of families who have worked on cathedrals in England and Ireland for generations, belong to secret societies and have probably sworn not to pass their skills to outsiders, it has taken all the Bishop's powers of persuasion to get them to agree with his plan. Still, they insisted upon the right to choose their own apprentices and to limit the number to three apiece.

"Sure this place is the back of beyond—you'll not be takin' work away from us in Dublin," the mason justified himself to his mates as I fixed the amount they should be paid for the winter months.

Determined to get as much as possible for the money he must pay to keep tradesmen here, the Bishop directed me to take notes; to list each tool used and write down as much of the lessons as I possibly could.

On the first day, I stood openly holding pen and paper as a cutter showed his students how to recognize the invisible line along which a stone is likely to break. Seeing what I was about, he became very angry and threatened to leave. Like most tradesmen, however, he could not resist demonstrating his skill to an interested audience and kept on talking when I put my writing away. Since then I just watch and try to remember enough to make notes at night.

A few of our people turn up each day, but we are hard pressed to find work they can do in winter. We usually set them to sorting rubble, sanding cut limestone and tending the fire.

St. John's becomes a silent, frozen place in wintertime. Streets and footpaths fill with snow, men return from the woods talking about packs of roving dogs, or perhaps wolves. There are no ships in the harbour, the fishery is over and roadwork ended. The wealthy go to England or to their estates in the West Indies, taking with them all talk of politics, of new buildings, all social occasions and all discussion of things that happen outside this island. Activity, planning, almost life itself, is held in abeyance awaiting spring. The only occupation for the poor is to stay alive until they are needed again.

Our work room is dark. On windy days the canvas walls billow and snap like sails, and on cold days everything is covered with rime from our frozen breath. Still, the people come to the excavation because here there is some heat and usually a bowl of food.

Father Fitzgerald says that one hundred and fifty-three families, most of them with five or more children, now live in the warren of shanties surrounding the cathedral. In the grey labyrinth, tiny houses lean against one another so that a woman in one doorway can reach out and pass something to a neighbour in the next doorway. Almost none of these shanties have proper chimneys, and what passes for a pathway between houses is a gutter through which sewage flows.

Father Fitzgerald has long maintained that conditions inside these one room hovels lead our people into all manner of evil, and since the arrival of bitterly cold weather the fear of fire has added to his other worries. The poor man goes around each day warning the women that an overturned pan of hot coals or a stray spark could set the entire town ablaze.

Sometimes I see Alex Brennan and his wife at Mass. I have not met her, but she has the look of a lady, a pretty woman whose head barely comes to her husband's shoulder. Mother Bernadette tells me that Mrs. Brennan leaves packages of food at the convent door and is one of the women who can be depended upon to help when there is a sick child or a death in one of our families.

I have grown accustomed to the distant nod Alex gives me, as if we were men who had met briefly once and did not like each other. I was surprised therefore, when, after Mass this morning, I saw him leave his wife chatting with Father O'Connor and come to the front of the chapel where I was locking the cupboard.

He asked how I'd been, I told him I was well and asked after his welfare. With these rituals over, he seemed at a loss for something to say, then as if remembering why he had sought me out, asked, "Have you had any contact with Caleb Gosse since coming here?"

I said I had not, "...naturally I've heard his name mentioned—and we even have some dealings with his firm—he must be one of the biggest merchants in town. But I've managed to avoid going to his office, and I don't think he is a Catholic."

Alex began to laugh, then remembering where he was, clapped his hand over his mouth: "No, no he's not Catholic—in fact, he's one of them who'd like to have us all deported back to Ireland."

"Yet he employs you."

"Ah yes, he never lets his heart rule his head. Catholic or no, good men like me are hard to come by. He knows I don't cheat him. So, you've not heard the news of his firm, then?"

I shook my head and felt the tightening of muscles I have come to associate with thoughts of the Cape.

Alex saw my alarm. "Oh I don't s'pose it could affect you—Gosse is gone—packed up his gold and gone. He's already sold his big place outside town, rumour has it the government's bought it for a fortune. The Gosse waterfront premises and his holdings in other parts—even his vessels—are all up for sale."

"Where has he gone?" I did not care, it was just the first thing I thought to say.

"Back to Devon, I understand, they say he's got a mansion there. He was gettin' on, you know. Gettin' queerer every year too. That son of his got no interest in Newfound Land, spends his time on his father's estate in Bermuda."

"What about the Cape?"

"Someone else will take over the store I s'pose, and the place in Pond Island, too—along with the right to collect fish all along the coast if they're fast enough gettin' to the right person. We'll have to wait and see how the new man runs things—maybe he'll want to change the agreement he had with you—with Mary Bundle now, I guess. Anyway, we'll see."

He waited with his head cocked to one side, rubbing his hand across his fuzzy cheeks and watching me as if expecting something more. When I didn't speak, he said, "Well, well that's it then! I'll be gettin' along. No doubt the wife's half froze."

"Have you see Meg's girl Emma about?" I asked as he moved away.

Apparently it was not the question he'd anticipated, he looked mystified and I had to remind him who Emma was.

"No," he said, "she and the other young one, Jane was it? Come to see us a few times after the wife found places for them but I don't think she's been in for two year—probably not since Jane went back to the Cape. Fact is, I'm not even sure I'd know the girl."

He looked at me thoughtfully, nodded good-bye and walked down the aisle and out into the cold sunlight where I could see his wife waiting. I had not asked about the people on the Cape, I had not asked about Lavinia Andrews—I could not.

Alex and his wife would go home to their narrow, neat house. I know the house, one of the more solid ones that line the road just below the convent. There would be a fire, and food cooking. They would sit across from each other and eat, talk perhaps. He would tell her he'd spoken to me, maybe recall for her things that had happened on the Cape. They would chat about the coming spring, who he would be working for now, when he might sail. Maybe she would knit, and they would talk about what she could plant next summer in the sloping garden behind the house. The vividness, the details, (I could see a china shoe on the mantelpiece, the grey cat lying on a hooked mat) of the imagined scene frightened me.

I'd never had such an experience before. I was still there, holding the iron key to the vestment cupboard in my hand when Father O'Connor came in, locked the chapel door and, seeing me, asked if I was not going to take dinner this day. I told him that I did not feel well and came up to this empty loft room where we sleep.

This room is like the hold in a large boat, bunks are built around the walls and a long study table down the middle. It is a room I have lived in for almost two years. The room I might live in for the rest of my life, since Father Fitzgerald hopes I will stay here if the church accepts me back into the priesthood. It is an empty, cold room. It smells of male bodies, bare wood, of the turnip and white beans that are stored out under the eaves. It smells of loneliness.

——— ——— ———

Months have passed since I last wrote in this book. Now that I know my fate, I will complete this last entry in Lavinia's journal.

The day on which I received the news from Rome was warm, so warm we had rolled back the canvas to let the sun dry the mould that has grown in corners of the workroom. Everyone was cheerful. The sunshine pouring in on us seemed like a benediction. The Bishop said it was time for the mason and stonecutters to leave off teaching apprentices and get back to their own work. He asked me to give him all the notes and diagrams I have made on their lessons. Bishop Fleming's new secretary, Father Ryan, will copy them neatly into a workbook for the apprentices. We are well pleased with the progress local men have made but the Bishop plans to test them before putting them on half-pay under the master mason.

At the end of the day, I took my notes to Father Ryan at the Bishop's residence. The secretary said that His Grace would like to see me and led me to the Bishop's private quarters for my long-awaited interview.

The Bishop did not keep me on tenterhooks. He told me at once that word had come from Rome via the seminary in Maynooth that there was no impediment preventing me from resuming the duties of priest. The only restriction placed upon me was that I must not return to Ireland. Apart from that, my future rested in the hands of Bishop Fleming.

He looked up and smiled—he had never smiled at me before: "Now, Thomas—Father Commins—what will you do now?"

"Surely, Father, that will be for you to decide."

"Yes, but what would you wish, if you could choose?"

I knew that some day I would want to return to Spain, perhaps join a cloistered order. But now, what did I want to do now?

"I think," I said, "I think I would like to stay here until your church is finished."

"My church?" The smile vanished, "Not my church, Father Commins!"

I had touched a raw nerve. Only two days earlier there had been another accident—the one we'd been dreading. A cart loaded with granite blocks had slipped, careened downhill and overturned on top of two men. When the rock was removed one man seemed to be still breathing. Thinking to save him, Father Dowling had taken him to the town hospital—a place of such horrible repute that the man's wife had tried to pull her dying husband off the cart.

Later that day, tired and angry, Father Dowling had returned to the construction site and quarrelled openly with the Bishop. According to reports, he'd demanded to know why such huge amounts of money were being spent on a church in a place where people had to die unattended and in filth. He had accused the Bishop of fostering his own advancement and feeding his own pride at the expense of the poor, then he'd walked away. The young priest had not been seen since. There is speculation that he may have taken passage on some ship bound for England.

Remembering this, I wished that I'd chosen my words more carefully. "I am sorry, Father. Of course I should have said 'our church'," I apologized.

"But do you believe that, or do you, like Father Dowling, think the church we are building is for me?"

Although I had often pondered on this, I was not prepared for the question. "I don't know," I said, "I suppose it's for the poor—for all the people of the parish—who is it for, Father?" I was amazed at the boldness of my whispered question.

"The poor, ah yes, the poor. The poor that you and Father Fitzgerald—and Father Dowling too—pine over, weep for—are repelled by."

I started to deny this, but he shook his head. He brought his folded fingertips to his lips, as I'd often seen him do in the pulpit when thinking through a point of doctrine.

"The church," he said, loudly this time, "is her own greatest responsibility. Our duty is to serve her first above and beyond all earthly things. Do you think, my son, that by spending all we have to feed the poor, to care for the sick, and at the same time worshipping our God in hovels, we will serve the church, or the poor, or the sick? Read your church history. Look around you in this place where we have had priests for almost a hundred years—good men, some of them—but poor and ignorant. Just as those they served were poor and ignorant. And what have we gained, what headway have we made in those hundred years for mother church? We have been ridiculed, despised, driven out, not given leave to practice our faith even in the most necessary ways—that is how well the meek and humble serve the church!"

He was thundering now. I wondered why Father Ryan in the adjoining room did not come running.

"No, my son, the first duty of the Lord's servants is to raise churches that will stand as testimonies for all time and all people that the Lord is great and powerful and that His people are not to be despised. Such churches are the court of God and the gateway to heaven."

He was not talking to me, no longer saw me standing uneasily in front of his desk. He stood up and walked over to the window looking down on the harbour.

"Just look at this place! Here we are, a pivot between two worlds, sitting on the very edge of a huge bowl filled with food," he gestured towards the sea, "and right beside us are the Americas. The world will come to our doorstep—must come to our doorstep—to trade and to buy. A hundred years from now, when St. John's is one of the new world's great cities, our cathedral will bear witness to the devotion of our people, to the endurance of our Catholic faith! For generations to come no one will be able to deny us the right to worship, the right to trade, the right to hold public office, to become judges, merchants, governors—whatever we will! Don't ever doubt that the church we are building will do more for the poor and sick than all the charity houses, all the hospitals and asylums we could ever raise up!"

There was a long silence. Though not convinced, I struggled to form a reply, to give him an honest apology for the things he knew I had been thinking.

But he spoke first. "I apologize, Father Commins. I have had two days in which to prepare the answer I should have given Father Dowling, and you, I fear, have borne the brunt of my preparation."

He returned to his desk, picked up the letter again and reread it, an act of kindness, I think, to give me an opportunity to regain my composure.

"Your ordination to the priesthood, insofar as the Church is concerned, has not been interrupted. You have remained a priest, there is therefore no need to repeat your vows. However," the Bishop looked at me across the spire of his folded fingertips, "should you wish it, we can hold a service of reconsecration."

I nodded, "I would wish it." The confirmation that I had been a priest throughout all these years on the Cape was disquieting.

"I think we will wait until after Easter." Bishop Fleming turned the pages of his ecclesiastical calendar. "We always hold special services imploring heavenly blessings on our earthly work during Rogation days—we will hold your service on one of those days—it seems an appropriate time."

He gave me his blessing and dismissed me without saying anything more. I walked across the yard and went into the chapel to give thanks. The doubts that had filled my mind for months vanished. For that night I was at peace.

The next morning one of the sisters, returning from the stores with food, told me that the tavern keeper across from the forge wanted to see me. She looked at me thoughtfully, curious no doubt about what business I had with this trader in stolen goods.

As soon as possible, I hurried down the hill to the Black Dog. The owner recognized me at once. "Em come in and asked after you. Said you was to meet her down at the waterfront when the *Godspeed* comes in—said there are people on her you'd want to see."

When I asked what vessel the *Godspeed* was and how I would find her he looked astonished.

"The *Godspeed*, man! The *Godspeed*! Why she's one of the best ships ever sailed in the Narrows, don't ye fellers up there in yer little round beanies and red shawls know nuthin'? She's a barque, one of Gilberts'—first back from the ice last spring, brought in a bumper load, too. I hear tell Gilberts got back what they paid for her outta' that one trip."

When I asked when she might be in he was more vague. "Oh any day, any day. Belike she'll be first in, tho' they say 'tis a hard year at the front and I doubt she'll do so well as last time. Still and all, I got a few bob ridin' on her."

He wiped a sour looking cloth across a mug and filled it with black rum. "That'll be a shillin'," he said pushing the mug across the counter.

The price was outrageous, and from the smell of it, I knew I would not be able to drink the rum, but I paid him, understanding it to be part of our bargain.

"I'll send a boy up for you when she's inside the Narrows—that's if I can find one who's not afraid of bein' turned into a billy goat." He roared with laughter at this sally and waved happily to me as I left.

From the time the sister brought me the tavern keeper's message until I went into the chapel that night, I did not think once about my renewed priesthood. How unfaithful the mind and heart of man is! No wonder the Lord loses patience with us. I asked forgiveness and did penance. Yet in the following weeks I spent much time watching the Narrows and looking for the boy who would tell me the *Godspeed* had come in.

Since coming to St. John's, I have avoided the waterfront, going there only when I had business, but in recent weeks I took to walking among the wharves whenever I could get away. As the evenings lengthened, I was surprised to find that the place is the gathering spot for most of the townspeople.

After supper each night, the coves are crowded. The well-to-do sit in carriages and overlook the gaudy scene, while those on foot go from cove to cove visiting every wharf along the lower path. At the end of each wharf they congregate, gazing out the Narrows, counting the masts of ships that are sometimes packed so tight a person could walk across the harbour jumping from deck to deck. There are barquentines and brigantines, ships on the way to Greenland taking on water, ships being fitted for a season on the Labrador, Yankee traders and vessels flying the flags of a dozen European nations.

Townspeople crowding the wharves and seamen hanging over the rails of their ships all seem part of a performance that includes the whores, beggars and an old woman who sits in the same place every night telling fortunes. There are foreign sailors who kick a ball, jumping from ship to ship between tangles of ratlines hung with their outlandish wash; baymen in search of a season's berth; soldiers from the fort and men from the Queen's navy; merchants, with ladies who hold their skirts up and tiptoe over the slime; Spanish sailors selling strange green and red wines and Dutchmen bartering cloth and spice of a kind seldom seen in local stores.

And the sounds—a hub-bub loud as Babel! Calls of a man with roasted caplin for sale, a sailor playing a tin whistle and boys selling puppies. People jabbering in French, Spanish and Portuguese; discussing news and gossip from London, Madrid, Lisbon and Paris as well as from nearer ports—Halifax, Quebec, Boston. Businessmen dickering over the price of fish still swimming in the sea, talk from the fort and the town, loud arguments about politics, speculation on what the seal hunt will bring, tales of winter happenings in a hundred coves and outports, all filling the spring evenings with a kind of heady excitement that is almost visible.

I wondered why Father Dowling had not introduced me to this educational experience, or if he had known of it. Nowhere in the crowd have I seen a priest or cleric; maybe the coves are considered too great a temptation for the pure of heart. Maybe they are.

The false spring vanished, the air was cold again this morning when the boy, looking around as if he were in an enemy camp, touched my arm and told me the *Godspeed* was coming through the Narrows. I left my work without telling anyone my errand and hurried down the hills towards the harbour, wondering who would be on the ship. Probably Frank Norris and Joe Vincent, they had been to the seal hunt several times before, or maybe even Charlie. The youngest Vincent boy would be old enough—or Willie—although I could not imagine Meg letting her darling son go to the ice.

I had not asked directions of the boy, but part-way down the hill realized that I was walking with a crowd. When we reached the cove, if seemed that half of St. John's was already there.

Even inside the harbour, a strong sea was running and the *Godspeed* came in slowly, rising and falling as she cut through the waves. I circled around the crowd, trying to see Emma, and eventually found her leaning against a pier, on top of which her boy sat. She had a baby in her arms and waved to me over the heads of the people around her. She looked more cheerful. As I came up, she smiled and pointed to her shoes and those of the boy.

"Thanks for the money, Mr. Hutchings. You know who's aboard *Godspeed*?" Her cheeks were pink with excitement and she didn't wait for an answer.

"My Peter and his brother Joe are both on her! She's s'posed to be lucky, got a bumper load last year. Frank Norris was s'posed to be on her, too, but he had to take a berth on a different vessel—I don't know which one. Peter'll get more money bein' first in—first lot always gets a better price for the pelts and the flippers, Peter says. He and me's goin' to build a house out back of the barrens—out there we can just take a bit of land. Peter says he's going to find work ashore from now on..."

Emma chattered on, she seemed to have overcome the shyness or resentment that had kept her so quiet at our first meeting. I, though, had not gotten over my shyness of her. Her bold manner and loud St. John's voice, so different from the voices of her parents, made her seem a complete stranger.

When she ran out of things to say, I asked what the baby's name was. Before she could tell me, a kind of rumble passed through the people pressed around us and everyone began talking at once. Since neither Emma nor I knew what had happened, I had to ask an old fellow nearby.

"Look, see? She's signallin'," he pointed towards the ship, still well out in the channel but coming around broadside so we could see a message being run up. There was dead silence on the wharf and someone behind began slowly reading the signal flags: "Four dead men aboard, two lost, one injured. Bumper load."

As the message was read, the vessel came abreast of where we were standing. Instead of turning in, she continued up the channel. As soon as the crowd realized this, they began running back to the street. I picked the boy up, and we hurried along the road after them. The crowd kept pace with the vessel, which we could see through gaps in the buildings until she turned into Rankin's Cove.

The brightness had drained out of Emma's face. "One of them dead will be Peter. If there was trouble, he'll have been in middle of it."

It was useless for me to try and reassure her. I was sure she was right.

When we reached Rankin's Cove, the wharf had been roped off with soldiers from the garrison ringed around to keep people back. The *Godspeed* was still tying up, but they had already lowered a canvas stretcher over the side. The doctor's carriage came past us and the soldiers made an opening to let him onto the wharf. Before they could close ranks, the crowd rushed past the cordon and streamed out to the edge of the pier directly below the ship.

Emma and I were pushed along until we, too, were staring up at the faces of the crew. They looked down from the ship, waving sometimes if they saw a friend or family member on the dock but most of them staring out, grim and unsmiling. These were men from out of town. They had days of walking ahead before they would see their families. Emma and I stretched our necks back, examining each face but there was no sign of either Peter or Joe.

People at the back of the crowd saw it before us. We heard the creak of the capstan, noticed the men above turn towards something being lifted up from the ship's hold. Then the derrick swung out, and dangling over our heads was something that looked like a huge hacked piece of coal, tied around with rope. I heard a woman scream. It may have been Emma. At the same instant I realized that the thing being lowered towards us was the black frozen bodies of two men—men standing, hunched together, their arms wrapped around each other.

Slowly, slowly the grotesque shape dropped down until it hovered in front of us, swaying slightly. And we stood, like statues ourselves, staring into the frozen faces of Peter and Joe Vincent. I did not even think to keep the child in my arms from the sight of his father's dead, black face.

Someone came up, caught the ropes and pushed us aside to make way for a longcart. The man guided the grotesque thing onto the wagon, someone spread a sail over it and the cart moved away to make room for another.

It was Emma, her teeth chattering from shock, who had the presence of mind to ask the driver where he was taking the bodies.

"Where we always takes 'em—up to the widow's, the bottom of Lime Kiln Lane." He might have been talking about a load of firewood.

Emma began to follow the wagon, but I held her back. She stopped and stood quietly, holding the baby, waiting to be given instructions. I looked around, hoping against hope for a familiar face, searching, I think, for someone to tell me what to do next.

What would I have given then for a miracle, for Mary Bundle or Meg Andrews. For one of the women who always removed the things we could not bear to see, who took them away to wash, to soothe, to cover with useless salve and, when all else failed, to wrap in fanciful cut-out shrouds before calling the men to perform the necessary rituals. How I wished for these women who could make the unendurable minutes pass.

We stood uncertainly, Emma and I, at the edge of the crowd. No one else had moved. There was more to see, other bodies to be unloaded from the frozen hold, seals to be lowered onto the wharf, flippers to be bartered for. The wagon carrying Joe and Peter had disappeared. I closed my eyes and prayed for wisdom. When I opened them Emma was still there, stone-faced, waiting.

There were several carriages in the street and one of them, I saw, was driven by a baker from whom I sometimes bought bread. I pulled Emma towards him, and asked if he would be kind enough to take us up to the convent in the building where the Rising Sun public house used to be.

He knew the place and dropped us at the convent door, declining the coin I offered. But when I knocked, and Sister Bernhard came to the door, Emma refused to enter. She pointed at the nun and began to howl. Sister reached for her, but the girl pulled away and ran with her baby back down the path. She would probably have taken off except for the boy who stood in the doorway, clinging to my hand and sobbing as loudly as his mother. I pushed him into the hall and ran after Emma, so exasperated by her behaviour that I was tempted to slap her. Instead I grabbed her free arm and pulled her roughly back up the path. It took all my strength to bundle her through the door.

The very ordinariness of the inside, which, though cleaned and waxed, still retains something of the air of a grog shop, must have comforted the stupid girl. She sat down quickly on the nearest bench, put her head down against the baby, and began to weep quietly. Two other sisters appeared, one with a cup of warm milk for the boy. He sat close to his mother, drinking the milk and staring at the black robed nuns as if they were strange birds who might any minute peck his eyes out.

I told the sisters what had happened, explaining that I would have to go back and find out what arrangements were to be made. While I talked, Sister Bernhard kept patting Emma's back and making comforting sounds. As I left, she was leading the girl down the hallway, telling her, "Ye'll have to lie down for a spell, poor child—before the soul flies right out of ya."

I stood in the road outside the convent, taking great breaths of the chilly air, surprised to see it was still morning. It would be hours before the *Godspeed* had all her cargo discharged. Then maybe, I could talk to her captain. I needed time to think. To do this, I am ashamed to record, I went not to the chapel but to the Black Dog where I sat and grieved for the Vincent boys.

I kept thinking of the very first time I'd seen them, all those years ago looking up at me from their father's overloaded boat. Now they are dead, and Josh too. Half the family gone.

I decided Joe and Peter would have to be taken back to the Cape no matter what. Sarah Vincent could not bear to have her sons buried in this far off place.

"Who should I see about getting the money due to sealers on the *Godspeed*?" I asked the tavern owner.

"You'd best go down to Gilberts' premises. I doubt you'll see old man Gilbert, but his bookkeeper'll be able to settle things up," he said.

I had another drink and told him what had happened to Emma's husband.

He became quite friendly. "Tell Em to come in and see me—the missis needs help in the kitchen betimes and I can always use a hand." He nodded around the nearly empty tavern.

"Emma and her children won't be staying in St. John's. She'll go back to her own people—and her husband's people, down on the Cape," I said, not knowing I had decided this until I heard the words.

Of course Emma must go back to where Meg and Sarah could take care of her. How could we send the dead back without the living? Peter's son (if the boy was Peter's son) and the baby, and Emma too, would be far better off on the Cape.

After making this decision, my spirits improved. I asked what each of the men might expect for their five weeks sealing.

"What they expects or what they gets? Them's two different things from what I figger."

The tavern owner carefully filled two glasses with black rum before he continued: "When they goes out they expects fifty or a hundred pounds but in all the years I been here I never hear tell of one gettin' more'n thirty pounds—and that were a crowd made two trips in the old *Elgin*. Most I sees gets ten or fifteen pounds."

I suggested that was not much for the men if, as he'd told me, the *Godspeed*'s owners had paid for the ship with one trip to the ice.

"Well, the companies owns the hunt, see. They owns the vessels and provisions them, hires the captain and so forth. So when the trip's over they divvies up what they expects to get for fur and oil—one third between the men, one third to cover the firm's expenses and one third profit. Leastways that's what they says—though from what I hears tell they gets twice, sometimes three times what they expects when they finally sells the skins and oil. Funny in'it how the men always gets less than what they expects and the owners more?"

He would have gladly discussed this phenomenon with me until the cows came home, but I told him good-bye and set off for Gilberts' office. If I could manage to get even fifty pounds, it would be a help to Emma—and to Lizzie. I had almost forgotten that Joe, too, had a wife and children back on the Cape.

They would be watching for the men down there now. Expecting each day to see them come walking across the neck, or climbing off a boat if they had been lucky enough. The youngsters would be thinking about the sticky candy the men always brought, the women wondering if there would be extra tea, cloth, a pair of knitting needles or a spool of coloured silk in the men's sacks.

The head bookkeeper at Gilberts', a haughty young man, asked on whose authority I was to be given the dead men's share. When I told him on the authority of their wives, he eyed me up and down. "I've never known a Vincent to be Papist, do you have authorization in writing?"

I stared him down until he grudgingly told me that the final count of pelts had not been made. "Of course, we have no idea right now what their quality might be. Moreover, you know what this year's market for fur and oil is." He turned the pages of a big ledger that lay open on the counter between us. "We've made what we feel to be a fair estimate and are giving each man seventeen pounds."

At this point a much older man, who had been sitting at a desk placed as though to guard a big safe in the corner, caught the bookkeeper's eye and silently beckoned him over. They held a whispered conversation, and the bookkeeper returned to the counter.

"I am sorry, sir, but I have to tell you there will be no share for the Vincent men." He closed the ledger firmly, expecting me to leave at once, but I demanded an explanation.

"These men died the first week out." His voice was peevish, as if they had contrived their deaths to annoy him. "Captain Abbot has informed Mr. Gilbert that on the second day in the fat they did not return to the ship. They were not found until two days later. The Captain says it was their own carelessness that led to their deaths." The man tapped his long fingers on the cover of the ledger.

I asked if the same was true of the other men whose bodies had been brought in on the *Godspeed* that day. He assured me that it was. "We at Gilberts' pride ourselves on treating our men fairly and in a Christian way."

Had I not consumed two glasses of rum at the Black Dog, I might not have been so persistent. As it was, I tried to look immovable and asked to speak to the man at the corner desk. Another whispered conference ensued before the guardian of the safe rose majestically and came towards me. He was tall with snow white hair and beard, dressed in dark serge and gleaming linen. He might have stepped out of a bank in one of the great capitals of the world.

"Sir, I am owner of the firm—I understand you will not take Mr. Robinson's word in this matter."

"How can men die hunting seals for you and not get even a pound for their families?"

He carefully opened the ledger, extracted a paper that was folded between its pages and ran his finger down a list.

"I will tell you how, Sir. Here, here are the names, Peter Vincent, Joseph Vincent, each signed with a X." I imagined a sneer in his voice as if the value of men who could not write was hardly worth bickering over.

"You see, each of the Vincent men was outfitted by this firm. They came with no knives, no rope or gaffs and only one of them had a gun. Therefore crop deduction took up ten percentile of their share."

He, too, closed the ledger, resting his hands on the covers as I've seen priests do at the conclusion of a service. "Were I to be precisely correct, sir, your friends would owe me three pounds four and six."

Before I knew it, I was halfway over the counter with my hands reaching for his throat. He called out, the bookkeeper and another man appeared, grabbed my arms and without ceremony pushed me through the door.

I landed on my knees in the mud of the road. As I got up, the bookkeeper, not having lost an ounce of dignity, informed me that if I dared show my face on Gilberts' premises again, they would send for the constable. "Indeed we should have done so already but for the regard Mr. Gilbert has for your Bishop and the embarrassment the arrest of one of his priests might cause." He went inside, closing the door quietly.

I stood there and tried to clear my head. I was glad I had not been permitted to hit the old man, but ashamed that I had not managed to get any money for Emma and Lizzie. Emma might have done better if she'd come herself, I thought.

I had intended to go from Gilberts' to the morgue, but seeing the house where Alex Brennan lived, decided to find out if he might be sailing for the Cape within the next few days. But when his wife answered the door, she told me the captain had left for the north-east coast a fortnight ago with the *Charlotte Gosse*. She saw how disconcerted I was by this news and asked if she could help.

"I hear that the new owner is taking the *Seahorse* down the coast sometime this week," she said, when I told her what I needed.

Alex's wife knew a good deal about comings and goings along the waterfront. I learned from her that the new owner of the Gosse business was Timothy Drew. Having hired horses and carts from his firm, I knew where the Drew premises were and went there directly. I arranged to have Emma, the children and the bodies aboard the *Seahorse* by sailing time the next day. I told Drew's clerk I would return later with passage money.

The morgue was located in a neat two-storey house owned by a Mrs. Coyle. It seems the woman has some arrangement with authorities to care for the unidentified and unclaimed dead who must be laid out before being taken to the potters' field up near the fort. An agreeable woman whose demeanour gave no indication of her grim occupation, Mrs. Coyle asked me to be seated in her front parlour. She inquired if I wanted to see the poor souls who, she said matter-of-factly, were thawing out in the basement. When I assured her I did not, she excused herself a moment and returned holding a small package wrapped in a clean linen handkerchief. She unfolded the handkerchief and placed two sculping knives, a clay pipe, Joe's tin mouth organ and a pocket knife on the lace covered table beside me. I recognised the knife as having once belonged to Josh Vincent. He had shown me how to do a hundred things with that knife: smooth a paddle, clean fish, cut twine. Looking at it, I came close to weeping.

There was another object in the handkerchief: a smooth white beach stone marbled with flecks of pink and grey-blue. It had a natural hole made by the sea through which a frayed leather cord was threaded. I had last seen the stone around Fanny's neck. She had worn it for years, it was her amulet, her good luck charm. I could swear it had been on her neck when I laid her body down in her mother's kitchen. I wondered when Peter Vincent had taken it. I put the little stone in my pocket, carefully rolled the cloth around the other objects and pocketed them as well.

"Could you arrange to have the bodies put in plain boxes and taken down to the *Seahorse* tomorrow morning?"

The woman nodded and followed me to the door, as though I'd come to tea. When I was about to leave she asked, rather reluctantly I think, how she would be paid for the boxes and rent of the cart.

"I'll come by in the morning—on the way down to the boat," I told her. She nodded pleasantly and wished me good night.

It was getting dark. As I walked back towards the upper path, I passed Gilberts'. A light was still burning at the back of the office. I climbed the two steps in front and looked through the tiny glass window. One lamp burned, beside it the bookkeeper sat alone, pen in hand, hunched over the ledger I had seen that afternoon. I found myself thinking it would not be difficult to force the door, to hold Josh Vincent's knife to the man's throat and make him open the safe. I could hide the money in the boxes with the bodies, not tell Emma until the ship was ready to sail.

What justice to use Josh's knife in such a way—how satisfying to send some of Mr. Gilbert's gold back to the Cape!

The idea was so exhilarating that I could not bear to let it go. It was madness, and I gave myself up to it; stood staring in at the man, thinking what pleasure it would be to hit him again and again, imagining what the money could do for women and children on the Cape.

Wet snow was falling, but I was sweating. I could hear my own breathing. With huge effort I pulled myself back from the window, stumbled down the steps and ran up the hill.

I went straight into the chapel, knelt and asked first for calm, then for forgiveness. I was still shaking—aghast at my violent thoughts and how close I had come to murder, to repeating the deed I had come so far to escape. I stayed there a long time, praying for myself, then for Emma and her children, for the souls of Peter and Joe, for all the people on the Cape. I prayed to be shown some way to pay for Emma's passage and the passage of the bodies back to Cape Random. Then I knelt just thinking about money—knowing I would have to go to Father Fitzgerald and ask for money—something I had been dreading all day.

I was so tired that I dozed off with my head resting against the pew in front of me. When I woke it seemed like the middle of the night but I found Father Fitzgerald still in his study. I told him the events of the day, omitting both my visit to the Black Dog and of standing outside Gilberts' office contemplating robbery.

He counted out the amount I needed and even pressed extra coins into my hand: "Send some of the candy you spoke of, for the children," he said. When I murmured something about paying the parish back someday he shook his head.

"I hardly see how you will, Father Thomas, I understand you will be staying on with us, and I certainly don't intend to give you money to pay us back." He smiled and told me to get some sleep: "Come to prayers tomorrow after work, in the meantime go with God—and don't concern yourself about the money."

The next morning I called at the convent and discovered that Emma and her children had not spent the night there. She had insisted upon going back to her own house, a one-room lean-to built in an alley behind the forge, that I took almost an hour to find.

She came to the door fearfully. She had been crying and from the dismal room behind her I could hear the baby wail. I stood in the doorway explaining what I'd arranged and told her to gather up her things quickly and come with me.

"You comin' with us?" she asked.

When I told her that I was staying in St. John's, the old surly look came across her face. I expected her to refuse to come but she disappeared inside, and in a minute was back, passing me a gunny sack containing her belongings. Then, without a word, holding the baby on her hip and with the boy streeling along at her coattail, she followed me. She looked so woebegone that I decided to take her around the corner to the Black Dog for a cup of hot tea and some nourishment before we went down to the harbour.

While Emma and the boy sipped tea and ate bread and cheese, I told her what had happened the day before. I was surprised at how calmly she accepted the merchant's word that there was no money coming to Peter.

"That's it then, innit? No more than I'd expect." She spooned some of the tea into the baby's mouth, it gagged, then stopped crying and began to swallow.

We went to Drew's office where I paid for their passage before going on to Mrs. Coyle's house. The woman looked fresh and pretty, she wore a bright yellow dress and her hair was arranged as elaborately as the day before. She greeted us both by name and I discovered that Emma had come during the night to see her husband's body.

The woman said the boxes had already gone down to the *Seahorse* and that I had no need to pay her, "A messenger came from Gilberts' early this morning. It was addressed to me." She pulled a note from her pocket and passed it to over.

"Dear Madam," I read, "It has come to our attention that Peter Vincent's sealing gun was left with the captain on the *Godspeed*. Taking this into consideration and deducting the cost of outfitting the said Peter Vincent and his brother, I am forwarding herewith the balance of two pounds six to you for services rendered.

"I should be obliged if you will be so kind as to pass this information along to the Roman gentleman who seems to be attending to their affairs. I wish him to know that our firm operates under the highest principles. Not a penny owing the Vincent men has been withheld, indeed, if anything, we have been overly generous." The note was signed by R. J. Robinson, head bookkeeper.

My first impulse was to pay Mrs. Coyle, go to Gilberts' office and get the gun back. I had no doubt that it was Caleb Gosse's old muzzle loader that Peter always took when he left home. But common sense told me that the money would be more use to Emma and Lizzie than the gun. Without her noticing, I tucked it, together with the money Father Fitzgerald had given me into Emma's sack.

Before we left the doorstep Mrs. Coyle passed a shawl of some kind to Emma. "I remembered after you left last night that I'd knitted this years ago—here, it's for the baby—and this is for the little boy." She gave me a paper bag. "It's for when he gets on the boat."

We reached the cove just as the last barrels were being hoisted aboard the *Seahorse*. She is a larger, sleeker looking vessel than the *Charlotte Gosse* and I wondered if she could get into the Cape. The captain, a man I'd never seen before, told me sharply that Emma should have been aboard an hour since. The bodies, he said, were stored in the fore hatch and tied down, although he was not expecting weather.

When I asked where Emma and the children were to sleep, he answered gruffly that they would have to make do with a bunk in the hands' quarters since the owner and his wife had the only cabin on the vessel. I gathered from the way he said this that the man's ill humour was caused not by our lateness but by the prospect of having his new employer looking over his shoulder during the voyage. He had a distracted air. As he talked, he looked not at us, but beyond our shoulders to where sailors were hauling in the lines and making fast the deck cargo.

It was just as well that he did not study us too closely. We were an odd looking group, Emma, even more slatternly than usual, holding the baby wrapped in a lovely wool shawl of pale cream, a bedraggled-looking boy and a man everyone seemed able to recognize as a Catholic priest.

I'd set Emma's sack down but was still holding the bag of candy Mrs. Coyle had passed me. I also carried Lavinia Andrews' journal, rewrapped with the same paper in which it had been given to me two years before.

I had thought about it a long time and had finally decided to return the book to the Cape. I was shamed imagining what Lavinia would think of me when she read the pages I had added, but she deserved some explanation of the things I did that last year on the Cape. I would entrust the book to Emma at the last minute, ask her to pass it along to Lavinia. In the meantime I waited, enjoying the feel of the square package under my arm.

I was no longer displeased with myself. All things considered I'd not handled the situation too badly, I decided. I studied the skyline, where the scaffolding of our cathedral rose above the town like the rigging of a huge ship.

I heard Emma give a small moan and turned to look at the girl. She seemed very nervous, her skin was damp and had a greenish cast. I asked if I could help her and the children get below, but she said no, she would stay topside until they got out into open sea. I wondered if she, like her father, was afflicted with seasickness. If so, she would have a hard few days of it at sea with two small children.

I was thinking this, when she suddenly pushed the baby into my arms and ran towards the rail. I thought she was ill, but she pointed to a man standing on the wharf below, and called back over her shoulder that he was Dan Hamlyn, "...he owes me ten shillin's for cleanin' his shop—I'll get it from the old tightwad!"

Before I could speak, she was down the gangplank and running towards the man. The boy began to whimper and I, awkwardly holding the baby and the journal, tried to pat his head. "There now, she'll be back in a minute."

Even as I said this I realized that Emma was carrying her sack and that she had run right past the man. Before she disappeared into the cove she looked back and screamed something I could not hear. She was crying.

The town began to glide past. The man on the pier raised his hat and waved to someone in the bow. I stood with a baby in my arms and a small boy sobbing into the leg of my trousers. I stood there until the scaffolding of the cathedral dissolved in mist, until the gentle shudder of the ship became the familiar roll and pitch, until the wind snapped at the canvas, until the *Seahorse* swung around and plowed out between the towering cliffs.

In the centre of all the sound and movement, I stood suspended in an island of quiet—seeing more clearly than I had ever seen, or may ever see again, that all creatures—the child in my arms, the boy beside me, the men scurrying around me, the ship, the waves under the ship and the fish under the waves—moved in great swirling patterns which God alone understands and over which He alone has control.